THE WOMAN OF
LA MANCHA

THE WOMAN OF
LA MANCHA

by

Karen Mann

Karen Mann (signature)

For Jennifer,
Wishing you the
very best of luck with
your own writing,
Karen
5/24/14

❧

FLEUR-DE-LIS PRESS
LOUISVILLE, KENTUCKY

Printed in the United States of America
First Edition

This is a work of fiction. Names, characters, locations, and incidents are a creation
of the author's and are fictitious. Any resemblance to actual persons, places, or
occurrences is coincidental.

Library of Congress Cataloging-in-Publication Data
Mann, Karen
The Woman of La Mancha
I. Title
Library of Congress Control Number: 2014936575

ISBN: 978-0-9652520-4-1

Cover art: an oil painting by AJ Reinhart
Cover and book design by Jonathan Weinert
Printing by Thomson-Shore of Michigan

Fleur-de-Lis Press of The Louisville Review
Spalding University
851 S. Fourth St.
Louisville, KY 40203
502-873-4398
louisvillereview@spalding.edu

. . . for no one can possibly foresee or even imagine
the way the world turns . . .

—Don Quixote, *The Ingenious Hidalgo*
Don Quixote de la Mancha

TABLE OF CONTENTS

It turns out, according to some people, that not too far from where he lived there was a very pretty peasant girl, with whom he was supposed, once upon a time, to have been in love, although (as the story goes) she never knew it nor did he ever say a word to her. Her name was Aldonza Lorenzo, and he thought it a fine idea to bestow on her the title of Mistress of His Thoughts. Hunting for a name as good as the one he'd given himself, a name that would be appropriate for that princess and noble lady, he decided to call her Dulcinea del Toboso, since Toboso was where she came from. To him, it seemed a singularly musical name, rare, full of meaning, like all the others he'd assigned to himself and everything that belonged to him.

—*Don Quixote*, Volume 1, Chapter 1

" . . . As for the love letter, you can use this signature: 'Yours until death, the Knight of the Sad Face.' And if it comes in someone else's handwriting that won't matter . . . Both my love and hers have always been platonic, never involving anything more than a modest glance. Even that, indeed, has been so infrequent that, in the dozen years I have loved her still more than the light of these eyes of mine, which the earth will eventually swallow up, I can honestly swear that I've barely seen her four times, and it may very well be that on none of those four occasions was she ever aware that I was watching her, so chastely and privately has she been raised by both her father, Lorenzo Corchuelo, and her mother, Aldonza Nogales."

"Oh, ho!" said Sancho. "Then the lady Dulcinea del Toboso is Lorenzo Corchuelo's daughter, otherwise known as Aldonza Lorenzo?"

"That she is," said Don Quixote, "and she's worthy to be mistress of the entire universe."

—Conversation between Don Quixote and Sancho Panza
Don Quixote, Volume 1, Chapter 25

"And so, to sum it all up, I perceive everything I say as absolutely true, and deficient in nothing whatever, and paint it all in my mind exactly as I want it to be. . . ."

—Don Quixote
Don Quixote, Volume 1, Chapter 25

In memory of Terry Lester
for his vision, his encouragement, his friendship

In honor of all Spalding MFAers
for their support and kindness

PROLOGUE

HRISTOPHER," MY MOTHER whispered in the dim light of morning of February 14, in the year 1572. "She is born."

I sat up in bed. "What will they call her?"

"Luscinda."

"To me, she will be Cinda."

My mother patted my head and pulled up my covers, as if she thought I would go back to sleep. But I was six then, and there was a new baby, and I knew, though did not understand, she and I were betrothed, and it was important news for our families. King Philip had agreed to it.

Three days later, I stood with my two brothers and her two brothers—the five of us like a hand, me the tallest, with Estevan the thumb and shortest; Fernando, the little finger; and my brothers, nearly as tall as I on either side of me.

Before us was the sleeping baby, held by her duchess mother, Doña Isabella. The baby had dark, dark hair, a good bit of it. Her mouth puckered rhythmically in her sleep. I held out my hand towards her and let it hover there. My hand would engulf hers were I to pick it up.

In my pocket was the gift my mother and father had given me to give Cinda. I handed the pouch to Doña Isabella. "For her, my Cinda." I liked knowing that I would be important to this baby and she would be important to me. She was the first girl in either of our families, the families of neighboring duchies in Andalusia in the south of Spain.

Out of the pouch came the tiny silver bells, tinkling their way toward Cinda. They were on a knotted cord ready to tie to her wrist. My mother leaned over and tied the bracelet so Doña Isabella did not have to jiggle the new baby. Cinda would wear them every day until she was two.

"Boys, do you want to hold her?" Doña Isabella asked softly in her mellow voice, her auburn hair wisped around her face.

Fashioning a wave from our finger-like arrangement, our heads nodded in unison, and "yes" popped from some of our mouths.

My mother lined us up on a bench like stair steps and cradled her arms so we would mimic her, ready for the baby. Starting with Estevan, only two, Doña Isabella held the baby in his arms for a long moment and just so with each successive boy. She never let go of the baby, never trusted those toddling boys solo with her baby.

As she paused at each station of open-jawed boy, she announced each of their names. "Luscinda, this is Estevan . . . Fernando . . . Miguel . . . Juan." They only stared, as if mute, at the sleeping baby.

Now it was my turn. I held out my cradled arms ready for the weight of the warm bundle, so wanting to hold her on my own, not with aid as the others had, and then I was. Doña Isabella stood up, her arms at her side, slightly flexed.

Staring at her round baby face, I pulled Cinda close and willed her to open her eyes. And she did! Blinking them. Blue. Now she moved and stretched, and I saw Doña Isabella shift as if ready to take the baby, but I held on and watched.

She waved her arm, the tiny silver bells pinging like crystal.

"Cinda." I said, not softly, but in a normal voice. She turned her head and looked at me. Her bells tinkled, and she opened her mouth and cooed, a little baby coo, her first song to me.

I came every day to see her, if only for a moment, even after the other boys grew bored. I wanted to be near, and her sturdy baby arm waved and chimed the bells: our futures tied together like the ends of the bracelet.

∽◯◯

Eleven years later, she went missing. I thought my eyes would melt from the heat of my tears, the heat of my anger. Oh! and the fear! I cursed our Holy Mother Mary for not keeping my betrothed safe then fell to my knees, begging Mary to protect a bewildered girl, gone from her home, with safety and shelter. Surely the blessed Virgin was used to imperfect and changeable men and could forgive my initial rancorous outbursts.

Within the hour, I was on Beleza, my sturdy horse, pounding the rutted road from Alcala to Madrid, feeling assured I would find my missing Cinda.

CHAPTER 1

in which her memory is jounced out

AWOKE WITH STRAW in my mouth. I had been dreaming, dreaming that black storks were pricking me with talons and beaks. Or was it devils sticking me in my legs, arms, neck, and face? But awake, I saw it was only the straw and the jostling cart.

My body had a lightness about it that was unfamiliar. Everything was unfamiliar. The jouncing of the cart during the miles it had traveled had quite simply, it seems to me in writing about it years later, bounced my memories right out. At the time, I could not have described it; I would not have had the words. My past was wiped clean, like a new babe who has no existence but the moment of birth. I did not know that it was not my normal state because I did not know anything or much of anything.

My mind began to work. First rustling in my head, then down my body searching for information. *Fear* was not what I found, but *curiosity*.

I was in a *cart* filled with straw, and when I turned around, I discovered a red-haired *man*, the driver, his shoulders curved as he slouched on the *seat*. It was rather *dark*, but I could see the *sun* coming up.

In between foggy impressions, these sparse words jumped into my head. Like walking through pudding, my thoughts were sluggish, and every word and the concept of everything did not float immediately into my brain. I picked up my arm and saw my . . . *hand*, and when I wriggled my fingers, it took me a moment to remember *fingers*.

My cloak was *soft*. It was black fur, lined with white velvet, and flowed around me. I felt lumps under my skirt. Lifting it, I found a bag and unhooked it. It was bountifully embroidered with *flowers*. In it I found two hair *combs*, inlaid with rubies; a *shell*; and some *rocks*. The rocks were nut-sized and different colors—one pink, one gray-white, one milky green, and one red. I set these items in my lap.

The cart rolled in an uneven rhythm, and in front of the cart moved the gray haunches of an ox. The man driving the cart hummed aimlessly in a deep, gravelly voice.

I took a locket from my neck and, in it, found two miniatures. A man and a boy of about twelve. I touched the rough painted surface over the man's face. He was dark-haired, dark-eyed, and handsome with a high forehead and a hooked nose, a noble beak. The boy had silver gray eyes and a dimple in his chin. He appeared gentle and good-humored.

I did not know who they were, nor did it seem as if I should. With my fingernail I flicked the miniatures out of the locket. One of them, the boy's, had T-o-p-h-e-r written on the back. I pressed the picture backward in the locket and stared at the word. Nothing came to me. I returned the other picture to the locket, also backward. I closed the locket and saw T-i-n-t-o-r-e-t-t-o etched on the back. Another word I didn't recognize. I put the locket and the other objects in the bag.

When I hooked it under my skirt, I discovered pockets,* where I found a handkerchief, soft and white and edged in a scalloped and delicate lace. A worn wooden thimble, which I put on my finger—though I did not *know* that was the right place for it. A shiny oval of metal—a mirror—smaller than my palm. As it moved, it caught the morning sun, spilling streams of light across the straw. Instantly I turned over the mirror and dropped it. My palms grew warm, and my breath caught in my throat: I put the mirror away.

I found two biscuits wrapped in a plain cloth. I ate them. They crumbled in my mouth and became pasty. I wished I had a *drink.*

The last item from the pockets was a *rosary* made of carved blue beads. The rosary, unlike my dream, did not tell of demons, but of mysteries, of which I had some inexpressible sense. I replaced the rosary and other things in the pockets, and I pulled my cloak and hood completely around me and lay back in the cart, sheltered from the dewy morning chill and light. I slept.

The cart stopped. Nearby a man yelped, his cry joined by another's. Though at the time I did not understand their startled country words, I heard, many times, the story of what was said.

"What is this!" Lorenzo thundered in his rumbly voice.

"Who is it?" Sancho sang out.

"Is it dead?" Lorenzo asked.

I peered through a slit in my hood—two men were staring at me; the red-haired man was tall, and the other one was short and rather stout. To them, I was a long black-furred lump on the straw—seemingly a body, but at first it was not clear if I were animal or demon. Their eyes, round like a fish's, were dark in fear-blanched

---

* Pockets were separate from the garment on a sort of belt that tied around the waist.

faces. Each man had one hand poised in the air, as if to touch me, but something stopped them from reaching out.

Slowly I sat up, presenting a moving black shape—my head still covered—quite a grim figure, unexpected and unknown. As if connected, the men slapped their arms to their sides and jumped back.

I pulled the hood from my head. The cart, no longer on the open road, sat in front of a store. I looked at the still-as-statue men.

In a moment, Lorenzo clapped his calloused hand to his mouth. "God in heaven! What have we here?" His bushy eyebrows rose high on his forehead.

"A girl," Sancho, the shorter one, said matter-of-factly. He had dark hair and a short beard.

"Sancho Panza!" Lorenzo cried in his rumbling voice. "I can see that! But who is she?" Though his red hair was thinning on top, he had a full red beard.

"Where did she come from?" Sancho asked. His voice rich and musical.

Lorenzo rubbed his broad, flat nose and shrugged. His skin was freckled, weathered, scorched from the sun. "*She* wasn't there when I unloaded in Madrid," Lorenzo said flatly. He took a deep breath and said, "Aldonza will not believe this!"

"Where else did you stop?" Sancho asked.

"Once on the road near Sondia and also in Magdelona. Quick stops for Aldonza."

"She climbed in . . . somewhere."

Cautiously Sancho fingered the soft chele* trim of my cloak. His smile was simple and sweet. The men seemed good-hearted.

Lorenzo touched my hand.

I smiled at him. I saw there was a scar on his temple. It was deep and curved to just below his right eye.

"When did you get in the cart?" Lorenzo said. "Aldonza will ask me."

The words were familiar, yet not. I said nothing.

"Are you a mute then? Oh, what will Aldonza say!"

"Can you talk?" Sancho was eager now to find some answers.

"What *will* Aldonza think?" Lorenzo scratched his head. "Did you crawl in when I stopped? What is your name?" He stared at my mouth.

I did not understand the question, but I mouthed the word he kept repeating: "Al-don-za." The slightest sound came from my lips, as if I did not know how to push air through my dry throat to make full sounds. "Al-don-za." The word seemed a bit familiar. I was sure I had heard it. It was pretty, I thought.

"Aldonza!" he exclaimed. "But that's my wife's own name."

Name! Was Aldonza my name?

---

* Chele comes from a marten's throat.

"Do you think that's it?" Sancho asked excitedly.

"And a pretty child you are," Lorenzo declared staunchly. "Like my Aldonza."

Child! A child was a young person. Why would a child be alone in a cart with a man she did not know? Where would the child have come from? And why would she be here?

Vaguely I knew *I* was the *child.* My head hurt.

Lorenzo motioned me to come to him; his eyes were kind and soft. Unafraid, I rolled over the straw, and he helped me from the cart. I was as tall as his shoulder, a bit taller than Sancho.

Lorenzo clumsily brushed straw from my cloak. He smelled of fresh air and evergreen. Patting my arm, he said, "Aldonza will know what to do."

I did not know what to do.

Sancho said, "I will go to the churches and tell the priests. They may hear of a missing girl."

"We don't know how long she's been missing," Lorenzo mused.

"No," Sancho agreed. "Perhaps a priest will already know of her."

Through the window I saw a man staring at me. He retreated to the side as if to watch in secret. He was tall and thin and had a gray *pickdevant.* * A plain young woman with straight brown hair came up to him. He turned to her and held up his hand in which he carried two books. Together they walked away from the window.

Lorenzo entered the shop; he nearly ran into the old man, who was the *hidalgo*† Alonso Quesano, who would later become Don Quixote with Sancho as his squire.

The shopkeeper (Ricardo González, a man short of stature but long on decency) helped Lorenzo with boxes and bags of goods. As the shopkeeper glanced at me, he said, "I have not seen her in Toboso. I will keep my ears open."

Toboso was in La Mancha. *Why did I know that?*

Lorenzo loaded the cart. A bag of nails clattered noisily as it flattened away from him. A gray cloud rose from a bag of flour as it settled in the cart. When Lorenzo found a brown tapestry satchel, he gave it to me, as though it was mine, but I did not recognize it. When I opened it, the odor of *chocolate* and *cherries* came to me. On top were an ivory comb and brush, bejeweled with blue topaz and garnets. I set them aside and looked at the other contents. A full black velvet dress, another soft and yellow, items embroidered and white, some beaded and some lacy. I closed the bag, but I put the ivory comb and brush in my pocket.

When Lorenzo finished loading the supplies, he got back in the cart, but Sancho did not return, and Lorenzo motioned that I was to sit in the seat beside him. I pointed to him, for I had not yet heard his name, and he said, "Lorenzo."

---

* Similar to a goatee
† Gentlemen of the lowest rank of nobility

I smiled.

He motioned to me and said, "Aldonza."

I pointed to me and then to him.

He laughed and said, "Hello, Aldonza Lorenzo."

He named me, and I did not have to speak, and I did not—for more than a year.

He snapped the reins at the ox, unsettling a patch of flies that had settled on its back. The cart rolled through a countryside that seemed strange, though I was not sure what it should look like—more hills? Perhaps orchards. I wanted more green, though it was late autumn and the trees had lost most of their leaves. The narrow road was dry and had deep ruts that Lorenzo carefully guided the ox around. In the distance we saw herds of sheep grazing on flatlands. Lorenzo talked, but his voice was only the rhythmical sound of kindness, not words I yet comprehended.

Taking some bread out of a bag, he tore off a piece for me. It was dry and hard, though the texture was good. I ripped off small pieces and moistened each in my mouth until I could chew it. The flavor was strange—a bread of spelt and millet, I found out later.

My eyes ate up everything there was to see. We passed a few small, thatched-roofed houses. If people were outside in their yard or a field, they sometimes hailed us. Lorenzo waved but never slowed the ox.

Now in the distance I could see two big hills, which broke the evenness of the pattern of little farm after little farm. While passing through a village with both a green and a small mud church, Lorenzo said, "Parado," and waved his hand at the little town: some houses, a few little shops, and a store, much smaller than Señor González's in Toboso. The road now ran beside a pleasant stream that we were following back toward its source in the hills. Water tumbled over the rocks, and in places a fish or two swam lazily, the midmorning sun glinting off their backs.

Soon after we passed through the village, the road went up a little rise, blocking our view of everything but the hills, which were quite close now. The stream was still below us on the right, but as we crested the rise, the water flowed under the road. Now in front of us, nestled at the foot of the two hills, was Lorenzo's farm. Above the thatched-roofed home and a few small outbuildings, including a creek-stone windmill, the two hills rose like breasts (pardon my metaphor, but it's true!), as if put there in the flat country to nurture this peasant family.

Lorenzo's farm had a bit of everything—a few goats, sheep, pigs, a couple of cows, a mule, and the ox that pulled the cart. He grew grains—now harvested—and there was a large garden that had the remnants of a summer full of vegetables and rich-colored flowers. The stream we had been following flowed from the two hills, pooled at the foot into a neat pond near the house, and provided water for the garden and bathing.

Two white ducks stood, slow and gawking, in the wide welcoming pathway that led to the door of the house. Along the path were the year's leftovers of flowing roses, some still in bloom. As if we were expected, the door stood open. Smoke wavered from the chimney. Clothes, hanging from a line, snapped in a brisk breeze, and a black dog, rather scruffy, with patches of gray, ran to greet us.

"Lobo," Lorenzo said to me, pointing to the dog. "Lo-bo."

I nodded and smiled. Lorenzo seemed pleased. I liked this man, and I liked that I had pleased him. As he stopped the cart outside the front door of the little house, the dog and the dusty ox touched noses. Lorenzo helped me from the cart. Before we could begin down the path, four people burst through the open doorway. One of them, Carlota, I soon discovered, nearly tripped and fell into her sister—Fredrica. Carlota was my height, though she seemed smaller as she was narrow and gangly with a long neck.

The other two women were Meta, the oldest daughter, and Aldonza, who smiled easily and was small-boned, though tall. Her hair was dark and pulled back into a small tan cap.

They were talking and talking and talking. Most of the words were a mystery. Aldonza held her hand, a graceful hand with long and welcoming fingers, at the top of my head, showing I was the same height as Carlota, who was thirteen. Fredrica was nearly as tall; she was twelve. Because I was exactly Carlota's height, I was pronounced thirteen; though in looking back, I was eleven and younger than both of them.

Carlota looked at me with openness. Fredrica glanced at me from the corner of her eyes, and if she saw me looking at her, she looked at the ground.

Lorenzo told them he believed I was mute. "She's not said a word," he declared. "She mouthed her name: It's Aldonza."

"No!" the original Aldonza cried, her hand, fingers outspread, touched her chest. "I have never known another Aldonza!" She sounded pleased.

My cheeks hurt from smiling, but I knew not what else to do. Sometimes I nodded. The clamor of our homecoming—my appearance quite unexpected—was confusing, yet merry.

Aldonza touched my blue silk dress. Carlota gently touched my hair, which she held up, and I noticed it was wavy and black, nearly to my waist. Fredrica, who had straight and lustrous russet hair, was interested in my blue satin hair ribbons, which I willingly gave to her. I was just as fascinated with Meta's hair. It was intricately plaited; the braids, I soon learned, tamed a mass of disobedient curls.

Lorenzo showed them the tapestry traveling bag, and the articles of clothing—shifts, dresses, and nightclothes—were touched and *ahh-ed* over. Carefully putting everything back in the bag, Aldonza carried it. She kept the satchel in her room, and we did not use these things from my former life except from time to time to make use of the fabric.

I walked along the path to the house between Aldonza and Carlota, who cheerfully held my hand, and as we, one by one, stepped over the threshold of the house, this family melded into a new shape: six instead of five.

The main room of the house was large with space for cooking, eating, and working. In the front corner were stools for sitting, a spinning wheel, a butter churn, and reed baskets holding various handiwork. In the center was a table which was used for all manner of tasks and for eating.

To the left side of the large room was an alcove—Meta's small room—separated from the main room by a curtain. Aldonza and Lorenzo's room, in front of Meta's, also opened off the main room. A ladder led to a low-ceilinged loft above Meta's room, where I would share a straw tick with Carlota and Fredrica and Carlota's cat, Piccolo.

A strange upright fixture on the back wall near a basin caught my eye. I went to it. Lorenzo came and moved the handle. Water whooshed out! It was a pump—in the house! I would soon discover Lorenzo was an innovator of sorts and handy in many ways. Their outside well was operated by the windmill, which doubled as a small mill.

Lorenzo motioned for me to wash my face and hands. Aldonza handed me a coarse towel. After I finished, Lorenzo washed.

Also on the back wall was the fireplace in which a fire blazed under a cookpot, which emitted a tantalizing odor—not because the fare was exotic, merely a rabbit stew, but because I was quite hungry! So was Lorenzo, and shortly we were all sitting at the table with a helping of stew in front of us, served in a bread bowl.

Before we ate, Lorenzo led the family in a prayer, which I recognized and thought along with them. I knew the appropriate gestures to make. I saw Aldonza nod to Lorenzo as if this assured them I was from a Christian family.

As we ate, I studied these people who would soon no longer be strangers to me. I already loved the kind and mild-mannered, red-haired Lorenzo and the gentle and confident Aldonza. With a swoop of her long fingers, she had added a stool to the table for me and pulled me to it to sit. I sat beside the already familiar Lorenzo, who was on the end, with Meta on the other side of me. Carlota was across the table. She scarcely ate her stew and did most of the talking in her thin, breathy voice. She had grayish circles beneath her round dark eyes, and her cheeks were hollow. With each breath she took came a little wheeze, and often her breath seemed to catch in her nose with a little click, which caused her hand to fly to her mouth, perhaps in hopes of easing her breathing.

During the meal, the black cat Piccolo with an irregular white patch on its neck jumped to Carlota's lap. She let it drink from her cup. Only Meta seemed bothered by this. "Momma!" she yelled and pointed. But neither Aldonza, nor Lorenzo, responded, and shortly the little cat jumped from Carlota's lap, and under the table it began to rub against my legs. When I put my hand down to pet it, I felt its tiny rough tongue against my finger.

Her braids bouncing around her shoulders, Meta still complained about "Piccolo." Meta was a hardy, wholesome girl. She was clear-skinned with her mother's straight nose.

Fredrica rose to get more stew from the pot. She moved with grace and had a strong, supple body. She was comely, though her nose was unfortunate—a bit too long, slightly crooked. Her eyes were black and narrow, but her long lashes, just as black, gave them a beguiling look which helped hide their shiftiness. Still, she did not meet my eyes, though I thought she was curious about me. When she smiled, dimples bloomed in her cheeks, but I sensed from the beginning her fetching smile could mislead one to think she was convivial and easygoing. Her voice, when she spoke, was inviting. Even with Fredrica's beauty, I knew I would like Carlota better.

Within a day or two of my arrival I understood most of what was said. I found silence easy; I made no attempt to talk. I learned that if I did not know something, I was eventually told. Now I know that I was healing from my life that was and resting in the peace of this farm family, where there seemed—at least in the beginning—little time for betrayal and secrets.

The first few days on the farm were strange not only because I was in a new place, but also because I was a stranger to myself. Everyone called me Donza.

When I saw my reflection in the old mirror, which hung in Aldonza and Lorenzo's room, I was startled, for I had not given a thought to my looks. Dimples greeted me, and I had wide blue eyes rimmed with thick dark lashes. Laughing, I saw I had perfect teeth, like Aldonza's. My skin was creamy, and it looked as if I had brushed rose petals against my cheeks. My lips were full; I traced the line around them with my finger: heart-shaped. Wavy dark hair framed my face. I saw that I was pretty, but at that time it was merely information—I did not yet know the power of beauty.

The words that had come so slowly when I awakened in the cart began to tumble back to me in a jumble from which I could barely make sense. I would look at an object, a door, maybe, and I would have to sort through a string of words before I could settle on what it was called—*puerta, deur, porta, door, la porte*. As I listened to my new family talk, the words settled into their words. The cacophony in my mind stopped, and I embraced this life.

When the sun glinted through our little loft window in the morning, I was ready to see what new things the day held. Rising from our mattress on the floor, I quickly dressed in the dowlas blouse and burragon* skirt provided by Aldonza and descended to the large room ready for a new day.

Quite early on my first Saturday morning, I was sitting in the corner mending a tear in one of Fredrica's skirts. (It had not taken long for me to find ways to help in my new family—and to use the thimble I had found in my pocket.) Aldonza was making quince jam.

A woman came to the door and with an energetic step entered the house.

"Ana!" Aldonza cried happily. "Come in!" Wiping her hands on her apron, she went to greet her friend.

"Greetings!" the woman said. "I've come to see if I can get some fenugreek and peppermint. Maybe some blessed thistle?" This last was a question. Aldonza had shown me her collection of herbs, which she gave out as medicines and cures to help with this or that complaint from constipation to chilblains, heart palpitations to headaches.

Ana spied me. "And who is this?" Her words were measured, her voice soothing. I smiled at her.

She was a tiny, vibrant woman. Her dark hair, which was bundled in a cap, had a single white streak at her temple and forehead. Another time she told me the streak had appeared overnight after she been caught, but unharmed, in a stampede on the *meseta.*†

I was told Ana Alonso was a midwife and often came to get herbs which helped in pregnancy and childbirth. Aldonza explained to Ana how I happened to be there and that I could not speak. She brought out the tapestry satchel and showed Ana the contents. With her delicate hands, Ana timidly fingered the embroidered nightgown and a yellow brocade skirt.

"But what of her family?" Ana asked. "Would they be noble?" She now held the bodice to the yellow skirt. It was trimmed with flat shiny beads. "I have never seen such fine things."

"Nor I," Aldonza said. "Noble or maybe merchants," she ventured. "Or tax collectors."

Ana grimaced.

Carlota came in from hanging clothes on the line and said, "She's a . . . mysterious princess. Her family was cruel, and she . . . wants to live with us!" She was out of breath.

---

* Plain and coarse fabric
† A plain for grazing, usually sheep

I smiled and nodded at her sentiments. Then I jumped up to give Carlota my stool. The circles under her eyes were darker than usual. I reminded myself to help her more. She could mend; I could hang the clothes.

Aldonza shook her head. Little wisps of hair that had escaped from her cap curled around her face. "Alas, she cannot tell us."

Ana moved closer to me. "Where are you from?"

I thought for a moment. I lifted my hands and shoulders and shook my head to show I did not know.

"We have asked every question." Aldonza sighed. "At first she did not seem to understand, but now she does." As if to demonstrate, she folded her hands in front of her and said, "Donza, please get Ana a drink."

Eager to do as I was asked, I went to the indoor pump and caught the splashing fresh water in a cup. I handed it to Ana, who took it, and said, "Thank you."

"I think she has no memory," Aldonza said. "Have you heard of that?"

Ana pursed her lips and in a moment, she said, "I knew of a man in Pronto Real who lost his memory for several months."

"And it came back?"

Ana nodded. "Be patient. Your visitor may yet be able to tell you where she belongs."

My heart lurched: I knew I wanted to belong *here*. I remembered no other life.

Aldonza put her hand on my shoulder. "Already she is more than a visitor."

I smiled up at her and then smiled at Ana. I liked the petite, cheerful woman.

"Rosemary," Ana suggested. "It is said to help memory." She laughed, a melodious and rich laugh. "But I don't have to tell you that."

Aldonza patted her arm. "I am always happy to hear your opinions." The women were good friends—each having a skill that helped others.

The two women—one tall and one short—stood and watched me. I was glad when Fredrica brought in a few eggs and their attention went elsewhere. "Hello, Ana," Fredrica said with a cheery, dimpled smile and put the eggs in a basket by the basin.

Ana said, "Julio asked for you to meet him this afternoon." Julio was Ana's son and Fredrica often fished with him.

Fredrica's cheeks grew pink, and she ducked her head, glancing at Ana through long lashes. To Aldonza, she said, "Momma, we will have fish for supper." Fredrica turned to Ana. "And so will your family." Fredrica left the house, humming.

In a moment Lorenzo entered, and Aldonza excused herself to go to her shed for the herbs Ana requested.

"What do you think of our new addition?" Lorenzo asked in his rumbly voice while he patted me on the back. "Here is the way to get one! Already mending and helping out. Not like the ones you bring in the world who spit up and wet their cloths."

Ana laughed. "Yes, much simpler!"

"She's smart too," Carlota said. Her hand went to her mouth and she made that little click in her nose. "She can bake bread and make tarts."

"Apple tarts," Lorenzo said and picked up the platter from the table. "Try one."

Ana took one and bit off a piece. "Mmm." She looked at me. "The crust is tender. How do you know how to do this?"

Aldonza came in with three small fabric bags. "It is a puzzle, isn't it?" She handed the bags to Ana. "A lady wearing fine fur and silk would not know how to bake." She said this with so much conviction that I thought it must be true. Though here was a contradiction: I had velvet and silk, and I *did* know how to bake and cook and mend and sew.

Those first few days I had tried to remember something from before waking up in the cart, but though I felt my brain reaching for information, no memory appeared out of the blankness. Soon I stopped searching as already it seemed to me that there could be no better place on earth than Lorenzo's, where laughter and singing were a part of every day.

But I soon saw a dark side to their family. Lorenzo had asked me to put out hay for the cows. The black dog Lobo came with me to the large shed, wagging his tail alongside me. When he saw Fredrica, he ran off. She was skinning an otter. I walked into the shed. She set down her knife and followed me.

She pushed at my chest with both hands, forcefully enough to knock me down, flat down. She put her foot firmly on my shoulder and pushed my head to the dirt floor. "Don't cross me, pretty girl," she said, her bottomless black eyes looking down her long unfortunate nose, not at my face, but at her foot. "You will be sorry!" She, here in privacy, was telling me her view—quite different, it seemed, from Aldonza's. No trace of Fredrica's dimples now.

Fredrica reached over and picked up a stick from the floor. Leaning over me, she snapped the stick in two. The end flicked against my face and stung my cheek right below my eye. I remembered the knife she had left outside the door next to the entrails of the otter.

Pushing her foot from my shoulder, I rolled over and knocked her off balance; she fell to the floor. Quickly I got up and put my foot on her shoulder and grinned, as if I thought it were a game.

I backed away from her, my arms open, my palms out, and stood there, waiting. She stood, her cheeks red, her russet hair a cloud around her shoulders. She turned and left. A *truce*.

But, no, I was mistaken. She returned with the knife, cocked, ready to fling it, and *pphhfft* it flew by me, not so near, yet not so far, and thunked into an upright beam behind me. The flash of fear I'd felt at the sight of the knife was gone and red anger took its place.

I strode to the knife and tugged it, not easily, from the beam. I walked toward her, unsure at first what I would do. She stood her ground, her fists rising to chest level. When I had nearly reached her, I turned and threw the knife. It followed her previous trajectory to the same beam, to nearly the same spot, and thudded into the wood.

I turned from her and, with the hay-lift fork, began tossing hay outside, over the open wall of the shed. I felt my insides begin to calm as the rhythm of my arms collected my anger and tossed it out with the hay.

She retrieved the knife. "How did you do that!" she cried. "Girls don't."

I stared at her: Was she right? *She* did it. But was it something Carlota and Meta could not do, did not do? I felt uncertainty, confusion. I wanted to belong here, and I knew I wanted to be more like Carlota or Meta than Fredrica.

Fredrica left and I felt relieved. I resolved to avoid her and to be good and helpful so they would all like me—for *here* was all I knew.

∽∝

The priest, Father Jude, for the village of Parado only came every three weeks. On that Sunday, we walked to the village, not quite a mile away, to the little church, a rude, mud building on the village green.

"Halloa!" Sancho Panza, the man who was Lorenzo's companion that first day in the cart, sang out in his rich, musical voice. He told us how he had spread the word about my surprising presence in Lorenzo's cart. Several people came over to hear his story and to see me. Sancho said, "I've already asked in Cuidad Real and the towns between here and there." Having a flair for the dramatic, he paused, then said, "No luck!" But he did not say it sadly, and he added, "I'm going to Sondia next week—I'll ask everyone I see."

I heard Sancho's wife, Teresa, say to Aldonza, "He's hoping there is a reward." Teresa cleared her throat. "Of course he wants to help her." Teresa, a sturdy woman with broad hands, blushed.

Sancho said, "When I was a child, I always heard the adults say anyone who didn't know how to grab good luck, when it came calling, had no business complaining if it passed him by." Sancho patted my arm. "If helping Donza find her family benefits us, then so be it and good for her, too."

Slowly Aldonza said, "I wish you good luck, of course, but what if she's better off here?" Aldonza's eyes glittered with concern and hope. She took my hand. *Could luck be good and bad at the same time?* Nothing—no feeling of eagerness or sorrow—no memory—made me think I should seek my previous life, and I sensed Aldonza agreed.

Other neighbors asked questions and gave opinions. "Take her to the bishop." Another man suggested. "She's a runaway."

"Runaway from whom then?" an old lady asked. Her name was Isadora Princhez; she was a seamstress. "You must tell Father Jude about her."

"Yes," Aldonza said. "Just what we thought to do."

"Or Master Nicolás," another suggested. Master Nicolás was the barber-surgeon of Toboso and the surrounding villages.

"Or Alonso Quesano," said Pedro, Ana's husband. Señor Quesano was an *hidalgo*, but he was not the highest ranking nobleman in the surrounding area. Salvatore Rodriguez of Toboso, baron of Quartos, was the local don. Someone else suggested Lorenzo take me to him.

Father Jude—no one had noticed him approach—overheard our conversation. "Do not bother the baron." His voice was a thin tenor with a sharpness to it. "A missing girl is not worth his time." Glancing at me, he walked on.

Lorenzo walked behind him. "Should we not try to find her family?"

Sighing, the priest turned back. His disdain was worn like his frock. "Where does she say she is from?"

"She cannot speak," Aldonza replied, though Father Jude did not turn to look at her.

"A half-wit," he said. "Her family is probably glad to have the girl gone." He removed a coarse handkerchief from his pocket and wiped his nose. "Send her to the orphanage in Pronto Real. The place for orphans and idiots."

Idiot? My cheeks burned; I wanted to hit him. Instead I looked down and toed the dirt. Aldonza shuddered and Ana, who was nearby, came and put her arm around me.

Lorenzo said, "I would not send a sow there."

Father Jude shrugged and led everyone into the church. Mass began and all talk of my origins ceased. It was not unusual for families to acquire new members—an orphaned cousin, an immigrant looking for a home, a homeless child to help on the farm—so even as I was folded into the family, I was accepted by the neighbors and townspeople.

Never once did I consider that my previous family was relentlessly searching for me. Even King Philip's men . . .

CHAPTER 2

in which the humble knight, Don Christopher, finds a squire

 COULD NOT HELP but wonder if her disappearance were my punishment because I had let thoughts of another—in night dreams—cross my mind. *Oh, dear God, if so, do not punish* her. *Let me, Christopher, be stolen. Return her to us* whole.

When I was twelve and she was six, at an audience with King Philip, he held our hands together and said, "Be true to each other—you will find great happiness."

Later as she and I walked through the gardens, I found a small pink rock on the ground and gave it to her. "To remember the day the king blessed us."

Her blue eyes alight, she took the rock in her small hand and put it in her pocket. She looked up, shading her eyes from the sun, and said, "I heard Papa say to Mama he would 'be true.' And now the king. What does that mean?"

"That we will only love each other and no one else."

Her face puckered in disappointment. "But I love many people. Grandmother Elizabeth, Mama, my new sister Catherine . . ."

"That's a different kind of love," I said. "The king means as husband and wife."

"That seems easy. I will do it."

I laughed, but only for a moment. "It is not always easy, Cinda, but I will be true too."

I will keep that promise now. I will find her.

Four days after I heard of her disappearance, I was exhausted from searching the streets. I went to Our Lady of Sorrows and spoke to the priest there. His only word of comfort was *pray*. But as I turned to go, he suggested I set forth on a pilgrimage to Santiago de Compostela to appeal to God for help through Spain's patron saint St. James.

I determined to do it. In the spirit of a pilgrimage, I would go alone, not even a servant to accompany me. I would arrange for my valet Frondo to meet me at the end of the trip with my charger Beleza. Frondo would object for he was meticulous in his oversight of me, but he would do as I bade him, and I knew he would arrive by the appointed day. But before embarking on the pilgrimage, I took myself to tell Cinda's parents.

Doña Isabella, her auburn hair mussed and her auburn eyes red-rimmed, reclined on a resting couch. "Don Christopher, there is no word." Her normally mellow voice was tight, thin. The baby bracelet that last I saw many years ago on Cinda was on a chain at the duchess's neck

I told her I'd roamed the Madrid streets, asking at every stall and door if anyone had seen her. I'd looked at every woman hoping to see Cinda's ruby combs or Tintoretto locket.

Doña Isabella said, "She walked from the house unseen. We don't know what she was thinking."

"Perhaps she was coming to me," I said. "Only last month at the king's palace when I was knighted, Cinda and I agreed that if she were unsure or confused, she would discuss her thoughts with me—but why not write or send a messenger? "Where is Fernando?" I asked. Fernando was fourteen and the oldest son.

"He takes to his room," the duchess said. "My children are bereft."

I nodded. "But he could help look for her."

"I forbade it. I am too fearful to let any of them leave. It has not even been a year since we lost Catherine." The duchess's face twisted with pain at the memory of the accidental death of her young daughter, only six.

Cinda had adored her younger sister Catherine. Like Cinda, Catherine had been a remarkable child. Not only could she sing, but she could play the harpsichord. She watched Cinda and listened, and then, as if by magic, her delicate hands glided like wings over the keys to make the same music.

Cinda had called Catherine her songbird and had treated her with a special tenderness. Her death, falling from her own bedroom window, was never talked about, as if some mystery surrounded it. The day her body was discovered, I came upon Cinda and Fernando sitting on the steps of the chapel. To her nose, Cinda clutched Catherine's blue blanket. She held it out to me. "Let's not forget her." I held the blanket to my nose and, yes, it smelled of Catherine's favored limes and of hot bread and roses. I saw her in my mind, happy and laughing, wanting me to take her for a ride on my horse, which I had often done.

———

The duchess rose. Tall and regal, even in her sorrow, she paced. As she walked, the chain around her neck wavered, and the bells bounced, tapping and dinging, though sometimes they were muted in her dress. She said, "Alicia cannot be coaxed from bed." She was the sister Cinda always compared to a silent, plain-looking grouse. "I still mourn Catherine," she said. "Our bright star gone, and now Luscinda, my greatest comfort, my oldest daughter, my hope . . ." Her voice, heavy with sorrow, seemed to caress each word.

Don Marco, Cinda's father, had entered the room and took up her sentence: "Our hope for the joining of Solariego and Gasparenza, our two great estates." Cinda's father and my father had wished this union from even before I was born, but today his words seemed out of place and unimportant. "We will find her, Isabella." Don Marco, broad-shouldered and the same height as his wife, put his arm around her and held her to him. The duke's noble blood was evident in every aspect of his body, especially his regal, raptor-like nose. "Christopher, know that the king is doing everything to find her."

I changed the subject rather than say something angry to the grieving parents, who, it seemed, had informed everyone about the disappearance before me. "I am going on a pilgrimage to seek St. James's help."

Doña Isabella was concerned. "Christopher, this does not seem wise. We do not want you to meet with some mishap too." She turned to her husband. "Stop him, Marco."

I pulled myself up tall and straightened my shoulders. "Have no fear, your grace; I am capable of taking care of myself." My voice rang out, echoing in the high-ceilinged room.

"You have no experience to go without servants. How will you eat? Sleep? Who will dress you?" The duchess's eyes widened; her voice was shrill.

"I will take bread and cheese, sleep in the open, simply wear what I wear." I didn't see these considerations as problems. "I will walk. It will but take a week." I looked away from her to hide my impatience at her motherly attitude. Let her worry about her own children. I, at seventeen, was grown up!

Don Marco said, "You'll take weapons, will you not?" His dark hair, cut to his collar, was full and thick, even unruly, but at court, he was said to be the most handsome of the dukes.

I shook my head. "A knife for bread, a pen for my thoughts. I am a pilgrim. No one will take notice." I was six years older than Cinda. I was able to fend for myself, and I did not need their advice.

Before I left, I encountered Fernando. He did not meet my eyes, but he denied that he knew anything of her disappearance. He was three years my junior and, while it would have been normal for me to act as mentor to him, he did not often seek me out. Instead he had enlisted Cinda to help him practice with knife and sword and bow and arrow, a very strange practice—to have the help of a girl.

He was small for his age, and I suspected Fernando's pride kept him from showing his inabilities in front of other boys before he felt he had perfected his moves. Cinda, though younger, had always kept pace with his height and, truth be told, was a good match for him, not because she sought manly pursuits but because she wanted to be good at everything she did and to help her brother.

"She can protect herself," I said, but of course, I knew that if she were pitted against a grown man, her defense would be inadequate. "You have helped in that."

He nodded. He had his father's black hair and eyes.

"We must keep faith with God and believe she is all right," I added.

"You are better at that than I am." He had always had a dark temperament and had trouble choosing good or relying on God's help.

"Do not think that, Fernando. We can all be honorable men."

His brow narrowed, as if he were remembering something unpleasant, and he walked away. I considered he might know something about Cinda's disappearance, but I could not believe he would be so dishonorable as to not tell us.

Even after less than a day, I began to regret my decision to travel alone and without my horse, but I comforted myself with thoughts that St. James would know of my ardent desire to be humble and would help me.

What will happen to me if she is never found? She is my little light! It is in her smile, her eyes, and her chatter. Before I left for the university, she stood before me and said, "I will miss my knight, my very own chivalrous knight."

I wanted to be chivalrous—to honor Honor. But it seemed, and I knew from my recent conversation with King Philip, that the knight as a righter of wrongs or defender of his angelic and virginal lady was a thing of the past.

No, no one any longer campaigned for the glory of God, king, and purity, but only for the glory of the narrow self. And that was how the desecration of chivalry took place: when on the pedestal we put our impatient self and took down our universal soul.

As I walked, I prayed: *Dear God. I renew my vows of knighthood. Honor. Charity. Piety. Chastity. Loyalty.*

ᔕᗒ

On the third day of my pilgrimage I imagined Cinda safe in some peasant's home, like one I saw on the trail with children laughing and playing in the yard. Yet if she were well with a taxpaying family* somewhere, then why not let us know? This silence of hers engendered fear.

Dear God, Let it not be death that keeps her silent.

My resolve was that she *be* alive until I knew she was not.

⁓ ᴓ ↄ

I soon passed into the mountains above El Escorial.† Only weeks ago my family and Cinda's had been at court. I had ventured into the garden, hoping that I might see the *other*, the one who fired my body. The moon was full, and I thought it would be such joy to see *her* then and watch the moonlight on her skin, even knowing I could not touch her or seek an easing of my central ache for her.

Suddenly, Cinda came upon me! And she would not go back. I accepted this as a sign that I was to think of her, though child she be (wife she was to me), and endeavor, rightly so, to keep myself celibate, in thought and deed, until she, long years away it seemed, this bouncy child, could be my wife in duty.

When I had been summoned by the king to guide Cinda in her decision of whether to accept a gift from him, chivalric choices had come to me with ease and words to match.

"Young Solidares," King Philip said. "I wish to give your lady," he touched Cinda's hair, "a gift, and she seems uncertain whether to take it."

"Your majesty." I bowed and waited.

To Cinda, he said, "Show him." She held out a rosary.

I took it and saw that it was of blue amber—quite rare and precious. "Why would you give this to Cinda?"

Our monarch laughed. "Do you question my good intentions?"

I hesitated and took a deep breath. "I wish to always be ready to defend my lady's honor."

"A clever answer," the king said. "And do you defend your lady above your king?"

I stood tall and straight and said, "I defend the Holy Catholic faith, my king, and my lady, in that order. Though they are equally important to me. One lives a whole life hoping one is never forced to choose."

"You are wise, for your youth." The king continued, "I only wish to thank her for her kindnesses to my late wife Anne and my late daughter, María."

I handed Cinda the rosary and said, "When we do a good deed, we cannot know the value of it. Only the beneficiary knows."

---

* Peasant family. The nobility did not pay taxes.
† A royal complex of King Philip II, north of Madrid

The king cleared his throat. "Where do you get the wisdom to know this?"
I did not have an answer.

Pacing the room, he talked to the walls. "What has happened to Honor? Will we find it among the reckless youth, who call the lie* and fight to puff their chests?" He looked angry, then sad. "They die young and do not want to wait for wisdom." He groaned. "They come to me to gain an easy court appointment. Instant wealth is what they want, to win some unknown lottery. And then, when at court, they become fops and swoon in lust, not love." He laughed, a laugh without mirth. "Ah, for knights who are wise men." He looked at me. "I think, young Solidares, from you I get a spark of hope, for I sense you are a truly honorable man."

∽∝

On my pilgrimage, I reached a particularly flat place on the path; I rested there, against a large boulder, and wished to be honorable: to be good and temperate. It was true of my mind; if only my body responded as well to that end.

Here, man! Stop! My thoughts of honor, my current loneliness, gave rise to stiffness.

In marriage, could I remain faithful to her? I have promised to, but was the flesh as weak as our priests believed? Would I fail? I knew many who had. Save for some monks. Therein lay a solution.

Think only pure thoughts. Think on your purpose, your pilgrimage! Do not give in to bawdy thoughts which awake your manly parts!

Last year, for sure, I carried, always before me, books or bags, or any handy thing to hide my wayward interests, over which I had no control, as if this harried part of me had a mind of its own. I often thought of it as my second mind but knew it to be base and not refined.

In fact it lacked discrimination, for while my first mind showed discernment as in choosing the better wine, my second mind rose to follow any turn of skirt or show of breast, winsome smile, or toss of hair.

I came from most noble blood, straight from Noah, and that I had been so honored and thus chosen was a gift from God. But surely my virtue, and thus my honor, came not from my gift of blood but from my actions.

I walked through rain and that evening I built a large fire hoping it would dry my things, else I would be miserable again tomorrow. Warm food, bugless sleep, a horse for tired and blistered feet, a change of clothes. Yes, I missed these. I

---

* Forces a needless duel. The argument goes like this: "I say you insulted me, and you say you didn't. Are you calling me a liar?"

thought—too late—I had never done without or been alone or without servants. Was this what Doña Isabella tried to tell me? I should have listened.

✢

I met a family, parents and two children (one a comely girl about my age), also going to Santiago de Compostela and walked with them a way, which raised my spirits and my hope. They had lost their home and things to flooding. They did not know where to go, so they, too, sought an answer from St. James.

At noon we stopped by a stream and fished for our meal. The mother cooked the fish not quite to my liking, but I'd had nothing hot since Madrid so I ate all my share.

After, when the girl walked into the water to wash a pan, I saw her damp feet and ankles. She bent over and I saw more of her leg. I closed my eyes and found I was thinking of how she would feel in my arms, my fingertips brushing her firm young breast, my lips on hers. Ah, Lust, do you never fold your hand? Must you game with me?

But I prayed for calm and drew a card against my foe and won. Though always in this winning there was regret. I resolved to look away and think not again of her.

Their company was grand. I found them fresh and friendly. It gave me new strength to be on my journey.

✢

On the sixth day I took up with two likeable and good lads, about my age. Juan and Gomez, they called themselves. We walked together for several hours and shared our stories. And their stories were heart wrenching, and I was so sad for their losses.

As it was growing dark and we thought of stopping for the night, Gomez drew my attention to an owl, or so he said, and Juan hit me straight away upon the head with his staff and felled me. I could not rise for dizziness (a twinge of fear also!). I hated their laughter and their telling me I was too fresh to be walking alone along the Way* and unarmed, except for a silly knife—and not even a pilgrim's staff.

"I am the son of Hernando Solidares, duke of Gasparenza," I said, outraged that they would treat me so.

Another blow! "A daft nobleman," they called me.

"But how can you," I cried, from my knees, "disrupt the journey of a pilgrim, who seeks help from God?"

---

* The route for pilgrims to Santiago de Compostela

Nastily, Juan said, "Perhaps he sends fool pilgrims on *our* Way to help us."

"I will pray for you," I said. Which got me several kicks. They made me strip my clothes, and I thought they would beat on me again, so I crouched down and covered my head, but I heard yelling and they ran off.

A young lad found me and helped me to a little cabin, dilapidated from disuse. On a rickety cot, I lay and fell asleep while the lad was talking. I slept through the night. As the sun sauntered across my face the next morning, I found I was lying flat on my back on the cot; my limbs were weighted down with something firm and heavy. I groaned, my mouth so dry I could not speak, and my head so hot and heavy I did not think it would move.

The lad, with wheat-colored hair and dirty fingernails, was sitting near me and jumped to my side. "Oh, good señor, you are awake, I see," he cried. "I thought you nearly dead."

I tried to move.

"Wait! I will remove the blankets!"

Ah, that was it. I was covered with several blankets, and as he told me—for his tongue never stopped—he had given me a cure for aches and bruises.

Claiming he learned it from his mother, he proudly reported: "I took a whelp, the fatter the better, and drowned him in a stream." His hands seemed sacred to his talking, for they moved throughout his dissertation. "Then I pulled his innards out and stuffed the hole with black soap and spittled (here, I knew the lad meant spitted) him until I had much droppings in my bucket." His eyes were green, large, and round.

I had heard enough, I thought, but his intention was that I should know all.

"Then I covered you with the drippings and on top added blankets to keep you warm." He scarce stood still through his explanation and bounced from foot to foot as if his energy were so great, he could not contain it. His stalky hair bobbled on his jouncy head. I soon discovered he had energy enough for three lads. He declared, "It's good to sweat!"

He removed the blankets one by one and said, "I heated sage, for you to breathe." I was glad the place smelled strongly of savory sage for I certainly would not!

He removed the last cover. I gasped as the crisp cold air slapped against my naked greasy skin. Limb by limb I moved, thinking I would be stiff and sore, but— God bless this cure and this vociferous lad's mother—I moved easily.

Sancho (for this was his name) handed me a sheet and said I could bathe in the stream. Though it would be quite cold, I was happy to bathe, no matter the temperature, and rid my skin of this greasy whelp-mess! So with some soap I went to the stream and scraped my body, finding many bruises, some nearly healed cuts, and got off the grease, even from my hair. I filled my mouth several times with water and drank a little at a time. I was weak—from the sweating. Nothing else seemed wrong.

When I returned, a grand fire blazed in the fireplace. I lay before it, exhausted and shivering. Sancho threw a blanket over me and let me sleep. When I awoke, I had some gruel, the roughest stuff I had ever eaten, though handy now. I ate it all and wanted more, but it was gone.

I said, "Tell me how you came to find me."

"I saw those whackers over you." Again his hands punctuated his words. "I ran at them, a-yelling. They grabbed your clothes and things and took off running."

I looked around the cabin and he was right: nothing of mine was there except my writing pouch, for I had been writing every day of my thoughts. I looked at my hand. My family ring, gone, too. I felt my face grow hot as I was confronted with my naiveté.

Sancho ruffled his short hair with his hand a few times before continuing. "I could see they had a gentleman's things," he said. "Are you a gentleman?"

"Yes." I felt shame that this short lad had driven them off, when I had been caught off guard and scarcely defended myself. What had I been thinking when I began this trip? I had never been alone in my whole life. Why had I thought I would be all right?

Sancho said, a bit impatiently, "Are you a-going to tell me your name?"

I took a breath and tried to regain some confidence. "Christopher Solidares, first son of Don Hernandez Solidares, the duke of Gasparenza, near Cordoba in Andalusia."

He looked confounded. "What do I call you?"

I studied that for a moment. "Don Christopher, I suppose." Though I was not sure I deserved the honorific.

He began tidying up from my meager meal. "I don't suppose you are a knight." He didn't wait for an answer. "No, for no knight would be without his speed (steed, he meant) and armor." He rubbed my bowl clean. "Or sword."

I was mute, now, in my humiliation.

"And you would have a squire with you then. To help you in times of duress."

I frowned a bit to hear the word "duress" come from this peasant lad's mouth, since I noticed other slips of tongue. Perhaps he was not what he seemed. "What do you know of knights?"

"My mama," he said, "reads to us of Amadís."

"Your mother reads?" I asked.

He picked up a wineskin and helped himself to it, then offered it to me—the wine tasted strongly of resin and pitch.

"She was raised in a covenant since she was six." (I surmised he meant convent.) "My father delivered eggs. They met." He told this story quite succinctly. "They married. They had twelve children. I, Sancho, am number six." He bowed a funny little bow as if introducing himself, which I guessed he was. "She owns three books," he continued. "Amadís, a psalter, and Reynard the Fox."

"And you like Amadís?"

"I want to be a squire." His eyes shone in the firelight, ardent in his desire. "I want to ride with a knight and polish his armor and follow him into battle. I will cook for him and see that all is right with his horse. I will ride with him into battle and right wrongs and rescue the weak." He scratched his head, then under his arm.

"How old are you, Sancho?" I asked this spiky lad.

"Eleven."

"The right age for a squire," I declared. *Cinda's age.*

He looked pleased.

Impulsively I said, "Then come with me, for I am a knight of King Philip."

"Señor, you make a joke on me," he said. "You are not a knight."

"Yes. I am humiliated at my tender ways," I said. "I was on my way to Santiago de Compostela, walking as a simple pilgrim should, and those two 'whackers,' as you say, befriended me and then unjustly stole my things."

"For shame on them," he cried. "We should find them and show them what a true warrior you are." He pretended to draw a sword and dagger and pounded around the cabin as if sparring to the death.

I laughed. "Sancho! Please!" I grabbed my head. "Your jouncing is too much. I am still weak."

He stopped. "Then you must rest." He sobered quickly and then brightened. "When shall we go?"

"Tomorrow," I said. "Do I need to speak to your parents?"

"No! I will make it right."

My night was uncomfortable with cold and tiny bugs, and I awoke early to take another dunking before he returned.

The birds had quieted from their early morning songs, and the sun was no longer pink in the sky when Sancho entered the cabin. He had with him a pack and two large sticks—a staff for each of us. For me, he brought a worn shirt which was too short and much too wide, and breeches, also short and wide, but he wisely brought a rope to belt them up. He had been unable to find shoes, but he had none either.

For him, he had only a blanket and some odds and ends. He packed the blanket I had slept under. As for food, he brought a few withered oranges, a half loaf of darkest bread, and a hunk of moldy cheese. Also an old and chipped knife.

After seeing what he had, I lost my appetite though made to eat a little, for I needed something. He was delighted with the fare and insisted that I have as much orange as he. I truly hoped we would arrive in Santiago by noon and that Frondo, my valet, a man short on stature and long on loyalty, would be there with Beleza and some money.

I heard a growl outside and reached for the knife.

"It is my pet," he said and went to the door to call it in.

As it came through the door, I jumped on a stool. "That is a wolf."

"Shh," he said. "I don't want him to know." He laughed.

He explained to me he had raised the wolf since it was a pup and trained it to obey. "His name is Sosiego." He put his hand down, palm toward his leg. "Hold your hand so. Let him sniff at you."

I did as I was told.

"Sosiego. Friend," he said firmly. The wolf wagged his tail and sniffed me, then sat and looked at me, his tongue hanging from his mouth. "You can pet him."

Carefully I put my hand out and petted the animal on the head, then behind the ears, as I did the dogs at home. The silly thing flopped on his back, an order for me to rub his stomach. "He does not seem wild," I said, scratching his belly.

"He isn't, but if I tell him, he will attack."

Sancho (my squire! ha!) was anxious to begin. He led the way, often stopping for me to catch up. I still felt weak from my ordeal yet found I was not sore, though soon my feet had a few bruises to match my body. I watched Sosiego carefully but soon grew comfortable with him. He acted like every dog I knew and obeyed Sancho's commands without fail.

Early in the trip he asked, "Why are you on a pill grimace?"

I told him I was on a pilgrimage because of Cinda's disappearance and I looked to St. James for help.

Sancho looked happy, as if he had a grand thought. "Luscinda is the maiden of your *gwest*."

A quest? "What do you mean?" (*Ah, Cinda, your favorite question: I wish you were asking it.*)

"Every knight has a lady who is his love, and with each victory he seeks her approval and admiration," Sancho said with enthusiasm. "And when he has defeated the giant or *ogry*, he sends that *retching* soul to find her and tell her that she is the most beautiful of all women." He stopped and flung himself on his knees as if he stood before the woman. "And you will have the giant say to her, 'Good and kind Luscinda, who owns the heart of Christopher (and all the rest of your name). He sends his undying and devoted love, and I, too, whom he has defeated in fair battle, see that you are the most beautiful woman in all of Spain.'" Sancho bowed his head. "'Your beauty *binds* me; I cannot even look to you.'"

I laughed, but he looked so serious, I turned it into a cough. "Yes." I nodded and then gravely, I added, "We will send everyone we meet to find the fair Luscinda and send her back to me." Why not? For the yawning hole of my uncertain future opened before me; we must find her.

I was limping badly by the time we reached Santiago de Compostela at midday. I found my servant Frondo, as we had arranged, outside the inn. He was alarmed to see me and immediately came to help me walk. He was a tiny man, scarcely reaching my shoulder, and yet he insisted I lean on him as he led us to our rooms.

"Frondo," I said heartily. "Be glad you were not with me." I proceeded to tell him of my misadventure and how Sancho had helped me. "Sancho is most handy with liniment." Frondo eased me to the bed. "And I have need of more."

"I can see that." Frondo turned to Sancho and said, "Thank you for taking care of Don Christopher. I regret that he would not let me accompany him, but you have proved a noble squire." How Frondo knew that was exactly what Sancho wanted to hear, I did not know, but it was not uncommon for him to say the very right thing at the right time.

Sancho beamed and pranced around the room. "We are going on a journey to find the fair Luscinda."

Frondo said, "I wish you good luck." He had always been fond of Cinda. "The sooner, the better, I think." He looked at the floor. "Shall I come too?" I knew he would not relish such a trip where we would be going from hither to yon, never knowing if we would even have a bed. He changed his comment: "I will come too."

"It is not necessary," I said, understanding the nature of his loyalty.

He tried to hide his relief, but I couldn't help but laugh at his expression.

"I will teach this lad how to take care of you," he said enthusiastically.

"First arrange a fresh meal and a bath for me, then see that Sancho too is fed and suitably clothed."

Sancho beamed and happily went with Frondo. His tail wagging, Sosiego accompanied them.

And so I had a hot meal and a bath, and when they returned, handy Sancho rubbed another greasy liniment on my bruised and blistered feet.

Frondo showed me the leather breeches and jerkin, a plain woolen shirt and doublet, they had found for Sancho. Also stockings and boots. "These will keep him warm as you ride through the country."

I nodded. "Go on," I said. "Put them on."

Turning to pick up the new shirt, Sancho quickly doffed his. We saw his back was striped with scars.

"What is this?" I asked, and to have a better look, I quickly stopped his new shirt from lowering. "Who beat you so?"

He pulled away from me and jerked down the shirt. He said defiantly, "My father." He bit his lip and looked away. "Do not send me back!"

I put my hand on his shoulder. "But they have agreed to let you come with me. Why would I send you back?"

"You have endured so much," Frondo said. "You will fare better with Don Christopher."

Looking at the floor, Sancho flushed and mumbled something.

I remembered the little houses I had seen along the Way. One or two rooms, most of mud and thatch, and in his lived a family of fourteen! "Were your parents so cruel?"

"Oh, no!" he cried, "It's not their fault." He put his hand on my arm to show his faith in them. "Sometimes my father wants more from me than I can do." He hung his head. "I try."

"I'm sure you do!" Frondo cried out even before I could.

"Mama doesn't want him to hurt us. I don't think Papa does either." How gallant! This lad's defense of his family! He knew of loyalty. Fervently he said, "It's wrong for people to be treated so."

I agreed and Frondo said, "And you are so young." His brow was furrowed and his eyes were sad.

"I want to be a squire so I can *dally forth* and right wrongs."

I was used to his misspeakings, but I noticed Frondo bit the sides of his cheeks to keep from laughing. My noble manservant!

"We will do what we can," I said and in my heart I wished for Sancho that he could right some wrongs. My father never beat me, but sometimes my brother Tomás, but not like this, not to bring up scars; that was for infidels and criminals.

"Go on," I said. "The breeches."

And he quickly donned the breeches, tucking in the long-tailed shirt, and put on the doublet, leaving the jerkin for later. Then the stockings and boots.

"As a squire should be," I said. "Would you not agree, Frondo?"

Nodding his approval, Frondo gave Sancho an infrequent smile that showed perfect white teeth, a feature I had never noted before.

Yes, I was sure this was a good plan that had been inspired by Sancho's enthusiasm. What better way to seek Cinda than to put hoof to road and seek her wherever Beleza could go? I would sound the alarm of her disappearance with everyone I saw, and perhaps, in time, she would be found.

The three of us spent the afternoon collecting provisions for our journey on which we would "*dally forth,*" as Sancho said, "on our *gwest* for Luscinda." As we walked down the street, Sancho ran and skipped ahead, then waited. He had energy to spare and eagerness to match. Sosiego had quickly taken to Frondo and walked easily by his side. The wolf brought many stares, but no comments, and did not cause any problems.

I began to think of our journey as a continuation of my pilgrimage, or maybe it was the beginning of it. I would start, instead of end, at the holy place, and the pilgrimage would end . . . *finding Cinda must be the end! I must know of her!*

By late afternoon, my feet were like new. "These cures are from an angel, lad," I cried, walking firmly on the street. "Your mama has taught you well." I clapped the lad on the back.

There was one more matter to arrange. "We'll find a horse for you," I said. "And we'll need a pack mule."

Frondo, who always seemed to know what was needed before he was asked, already had us on the road to the farrier's where he had left Beleza and where we found a suitable horse for Sancho and a good pack mule.

"Can I ride Diana now, master?" Sancho was bouncing in place.

I chuckled at his name for the rather rickety mare. I looked at the sun. "Yes, there is time."

Frondo showed him how to ready the horse to ride and then helped Sancho prepare Beleza. Frondo was patient and Sancho was strong and willing. He and I rode side by side through the streets and out of town a mile or more and then returned. I watched him carefully and instructed him. He matched the rhythm of the horse easily. I told him: "You are a good student."

He nodded solemnly.

When we returned from the ride, I found Frondo had ready my finest silk shirt and garments of brown velvet and tall deerskin boots. Now that I had paid the dues of being a pilgrim, that is I had survived the arduous and meager walk, I intended to present my best to St. James.

We left Sosiego with Frondo, and Sancho and I made our way to the cathedral. In the plaza, merchants still had their stalls open to catch the pilgrims on their way to the overnight vigil. The stalls were full of shoes, wine, straps, belts, candles, herbs, food, leather bags, hooks, and shells, the traditional icon of Santiago de Compostela pilgrims. I bought a shell for Sancho. It was strung on a leather cord so he hung it from his neck. (*And where is your shell, Cinda, like this one, I gave you so long ago?*)

The tradition was to stand vigil near the tomb of St. James the first night you arrived. Soon several hundred people were waiting. We all held candles. The cathedral was lit as if it were noon. Some had brought instruments and played music. Zithers and lyres, even flutes, trumpets, and harps. Besides Spanish, I could hear the voices in German, Italian, English, and languages I did not know singing Psalms. I felt ardent devotion for a Lord who could create this adulation in so many people.

I prayed fervently that I would find Cinda, for my future would be determined by her life or her death. By morning, I was confident the answers to the search for Cinda lay in the journey that Sancho had put in my mind.

At the end of the service, we gave the traditional kiss to the back of the head of the statue of St. James and left the cathedral.

We returned to the hotel. I put Sancho in Frondo's care, telling him to instruct Sancho in how to dress a gentleman, help him with his toilet, at meals, to bed, and so forth. "Easy enough," the cheerful Frondo said. I left intending to air out my brain after the vigil.

I found Beleza as eager as I to go for a run, and we ended at the ocean, where it was known as "the end of the earth." I walked the beach, glad I had purchased a new cloak of fur, for it was biting cold. I found a cave out of the wind and slept, awaking in time to see the sunset. I had heard that others, seeing the sun extinguished in the ocean, here, at *Finis Terri* were seized by a "religious terror." But I saw only beauty and remembered when, years ago, Cinda and I stood on the deck of a ship and watched the sun extinguished, just so. It was on the voyage to Venice with our families—the time Tintoretto painted our portraits.

I rode the path back to town, though more slowly now, for it was dark and only stars lit the way. I thought how Cinda would love to see these stars, so clear and sharp above.

At the feast for her baby sister Catherine's baptism, Cinda, then six, tired of spinning and whirling to the music with the children, came to sit with me. She held up her arms. "Do you think birds fly to the stars?" Her eyes were dark in the torchlight.

"I don't know. What do you think stars are like?"

"Why they are like candles, only they have more tallow and wick, so they never burn out. That's the magic of them." She tossed her dark curls.

I hugged her and laughed. "I hope your imagination never runs down."

"It is not a clock, Topher," she said firmly. "It does not need to be wound!"

Upon my return, I discussed my plans with Frondo, making certain arrangements, including replacing my family ring and designating towns where I could expect updates on the search for Cinda.

"The lad will serve you well," Frondo said. "He listened closely then fell asleep." I looked over at the lad. His arm was thrown over his wheat-colored locks, his face fair and childlike. My fierce squire. Ha! But we would see. Would his enthusiasm for a life of chivalry lift the pall of sadness and of wayward thought?

CHAPTER 3

in which Donza settles into life on Lorenzo's farm

N ONLY A few weeks, I was comfortable in muteness and my surroundings. My days at Lorenzo and Aldonza's became routine. For breakfast, we ate cooked porridge, sometimes rice, sometimes *polenta* made with toasted ground barley. For noon and evening meals we had bread and cheese, eggs, fruits and vegetables in season, also fish and meat stews several times a week—Fredrica spent her mornings fishing and hunting (thus her accuracy with a knife, also a bow), so keeping my distance was not difficult.

After breakfast, I ventured out with Lorenzo and learned how to do the chores. After the midday meal, Aldonza and Lorenzo rested. Carlota often too. For as long as I knew her, she tired easily. In the evenings, Lorenzo went to his woodcarving shed to work, and I often accompanied him, while Carlota, Aldonza, and Meta sat by the spinning wheel with thimbles and needles, thread or yarn. Before going to our beds, the family knelt together and prayed. I held my blue-stoned rosary, once remarkable to us all but now as ordinary as dandelions.

Carlota, Fredrica, and I slept as close as a pile of logs on a straw tick in the loft, which was small and low-ceilinged and had one small shuttered window. It was chilly in autumn, and I thought it would be quite cold in winter.

The black cat Piccolo helped with the chill and made me feel welcome. Piccolo was thirteen, like Carlota herself. From the first night, I slept with Fredrica and Carlota, Carlota in the middle. Piccolo curled up between her and me. I loved the little cat's warmth and the weight of its body, like a pliant sack of flour, against my hip. But Piccolo was definitely Carlota's. It was Carlota he followed and Carlota he loved.

One brisk and sunny morning, Aldonza said to me, "Finish your chores and we'll go gather roots." I was eager to go anywhere with this woman, whose name I inadvertently shared and who had welcomed me into her home. Quickly I finished sweeping out the old shavings with the palm broom and spread around fresh ones—slivered chips of juniper and cypress. When I finished, Aldonza picked up four large baskets, stacking them in twos, and handed me a set.

With our baskets, we carried digging tools: a shovel and a long, sharp knife. Aldonza showed me a path directly behind the house that led up the hillside. I had not yet been up into those comforting hills, which oversaw our little farmstead.

In her hesitant voice, Carlota had told me, "In the spring . . . we will go up in the hills. And have fun."

"Yes," said Fredrica, looking at the ground. "Poppa made a big wooden bowl for us to slide down the hill." This information intrigued me, though I could not ask about it. I thought, *when it is warm I will see what it is they are talking about.* They called Lorenzo *Poppa* and Aldonza *Momma.* In my mind I called them those names too.

The sun was still in the east as Aldonza and I began our adventure up the hill and into the woods. From the beginning of our hike, Aldonza told me about the plants. "Here are the lilies of the valley." She pointed to some dark green and pointy leaves. "The flowers are gone now." As we walked on, she said, "I gather a few leaves in May or June. It is a very potent medicine for heart troubles." She looked back at me. "Ernesto Traduccia has heart problems." I knew she was talking about the skinny bald man on the next farm. I could see their house and outbuildings from our house. His son Enriquè was Meta's age and walked with a limp because he was born with a crooked leg.

Aldonza stopped by some ferns and began turning over the leaves. "Here," she said. "Look." She pointed to some tiny growths on the underside. She put down her baskets and took a shovel and began digging. "Don't dig too close." *Scrape* went the shovel in the ground. "Get all the roots." Another slash of the shovel into the dirt. "Don't damage them." And with the third stroke, she pushed down and uprooted a large plant. She picked it up by the green top and shook it. Dirt flew. I jumped back. She laughed, showing her even, white teeth.

"Sorry. I'm not accustomed to anyone coming with me!" she explained. "The girls, long ago, tired of my herb gathering." She looked sad. "None of them wants to learn." She looked away for an instant, then back. "Perhaps you will."

I nodded.

Her honest eyes showed her pleasure.

With her large hands, she split the plant in two, and I helped shake the extra dirt away. She explained how everything needed to be cut with a sharp knife; that tearing the leaves or roots would bruise and damage them. She took the knife and showed me how to chop the root from the plant and how to cut out the rhizome, for that was the part of the fern plant that was needed for the medicine to eliminate worms.

We continued up the hillside, and our baskets became waterfalls of greenery: valerian, again the rhizome, used to calm and help sleep; marshmallow root, used for digestive or breathing problems ("I give this to Carlota," she said), also toothbrushes; and echinacea root used for nearly every kind of illness. ("Though for echinacea," Aldonza paused and wiped her forehead on her sleeve, "the fresh extract is better.")

I, too, was perspiring, and little insects were flying around us. I brushed at them, but they did not seem to bite.

Near the top of the hill, Aldonza stopped by some golden seal. "This is why we came," she began. "I have been watching these plants for three springs and now is the time." She began digging. I spied the tiny yellow rhizome and pointed to it. "Yes," Aldonza said. "That's the part we want." Our baskets were nearly full.

Now at the top of the hill, Aldonza put her hand, now dirty around and under her fingernails, on my arm to stop my progress. "Come, we'll go back now."

I motioned to the other side.

"More of what is on this side," Aldonza replied. "Little farms, small towns, and farther on, a city about like Toboso. We have everything we need on this side."

I was not quite old enough for a statement like this from a parent to make me instantly want to go across the top of the hill and down the other side to see how the places and people were the same or different. And we could not know that the people who were searching for me would choose those small towns and farms to pose their questions about whether anyone had seen a lost dark-haired, blue-eyed girl.

I was that close to discovery and the end of my time with Aldonza and Lorenzo, but only once did I ever venture over the crest of that hill, and I did not discover my origins but other unwelcome information—but hold, I get ahead of my story.

The sun had passed overhead and with our baskets full we went down the hill in the most direct way. Still Aldonza continued to point out plants. "Dandelion. We'll dig some leaves next spring. Makes for good eating. And good wine." Upon reaching the foot of the hills, we took the baskets with the roots and rhizomes to the stream below the pond and washed them in the flowing water. "Who wants dirt in their medicine?" she asked merrily.

It was difficult to clean the dirt from the little hair-like roots. I could see why Carlota, Fredrica, and Meta were not interested in it, but I was determined to learn from my newfound mother and teacher. We spread out the new roots to dry. Later we took them into the herb shed.

She showed me how her herbs were organized and told me often how to use them—and eventually I began to remember. Several months after that first root-gathering walk, a day came when I knew what she was going to say before she said it; still I never tired of listening to her.

One chilly December morning, I was in the sun churning butter when I heard Aldonza call, "Halloa!" I looked up to see Sancho Panza on a mule.

Aldonza walked out to meet him. "How is Teresa?"

"Bright as a toad on a rock," Sancho said. "Any luck in finding where Donza is from?"

Aldonza looked tentative. "We told Xavier Padua the situation, and he has asked around, but we have heard nothing." Padua was the sheriff in Toboso.

Sancho slid off the mule. "I've found nothing myself." His shoulders slumped and his belly seemed to hang lower than usual. "I've been to Sondia and almost to Magdelona, but . . . nothing."

Aldonza relaxed, but then she began wringing her hands. "I hated to see you come, Sancho," she admitted. "What is wrong with me? You are our friend."

Sancho's head came up and his eyebrows raised. "Why didn't you want to see me?"

"Because," Aldonza glanced at me and lowered her voice, but I could still hear, "I want her to stay." Her voice was husky. "I love having her here." She looked at the ground. "She's different than my girls—healthy and quick and interested in my herbs." Her hand went to her heart; her long fingers splayed across her chest. "Oh, I love them all!"

Sancho patted her arm. "I will stop looking," he said, as if his looking were the only way I would ever find my way back.

They stood silently for a moment. Sancho patted the mule's back; Aldonza scratched its nose. Finally Sancho said, "Donza seems at home in your family." He hiked up his pants over his belly. "Even if she is from a noble family."

"We do not know." Aldonza shrugged. "It does feel as if she belongs."

I smiled to myself, glad for her comment.

Sancho stood as straight as he could and said, "I do not agree being born to nobility makes one better. Were I born a nobleman, I'd know how to act, because I've got as much soul as the next man, and maybe even more body." He patted his belly.

Aldonza shared a chuckle with the little man. "Yes, Sancho, you and Lorenzo both have noble souls." She gave him a wide grin.

"We just lack the gold!" Sancho said. "But we know the best sauce in the world is hunger, and because poor people never run out of it, they always enjoy what they eat." He ruffled his dark curls. "My old grannum (rest her soul) was wont to say there are but two families in the world, have-much and have-little." He sighed. "I guess we're likely to stay have-little."

∿∿

Winter came and was mild. The animals had to be looked after, but there was nothing to be done in the fields until spring. Lorenzo turned to his woodcarving, which provided some of the family's meager income. Each year, he carved a large wooden chest that he delivered to wherever the shopkeeper in Toboso, Ricardo González, told him. Usually to Seville or Toledo or Madrid. It was on his last such trip that he ended up with me. The chest he was now making had grapes and vines on the corners and along the edges of each side. In the center, he carved scenes of the stories of Jesus. He laughed and told me in his gravelly voice, "Once a man in Toledo ordered a chest carved with naked women, but Aldonza would not let me make it!"

Over time Lorenzo carefully explained to me about woods and how to tell the good pieces from the bad; he explained how each tool was used. He built each chest or piece of furniture from the beginning, first cutting a tree or trees and letting the wood cure, sometimes as long as two years. He was a master carpenter and woodcarver.

My favorite piece that he made over the years I was with them was a small, sturdily made box with a tight-fitting lid. It was not carved but had beautifully grained wood. Lorenzo fitted it with decorative brass corners. When we delivered it to Señor González, the shopkeeper showed us a brass plate to attach underneath it. "Your work is like art," he said. "You should sign it."

Lorenzo laughed for he could not write, or read. Señor González carefully wrote on the soft metal plate with a narrow and sharpened wooden stick: *Lorenzo Corchuelo.* I picked up a nearby pencil and wrote on a paper "Lorenzo Corchuelo." The men stood open-mouthed—then someone asked Señor González a question and he moved away. I wrote: "Aldonza Lorenzo." I liked how it looked.

Lorenzo frowned. He could not read what I wrote and I could not tell him. I crinkled up the piece of paper and walked away to discard it. Then I waited outside for Lorenzo.

Later I overheard Lorenzo tell Aldonza, "She can write." They were in the herb shed. I was pulling weeds by the door.

"I do not think she knows her history," Aldonza said quietly.

After a silence, he added, "We could find someone to read it. Father Jude?"

Aldonza barked, "He would not think it worth his time."

Lorenzo suggested, "Señor González." I knew the little shopkeeper would help them, if they asked.

Aldonza murmured something I could not hear.

"The sheriff has heard nothing," Lorenzo said. "No bills have been posted about a missing girl."

"As if she is meant to be with us," Aldonza said happily.

"She can read," Lorenzo said.

Aldonza was silent.

"She came from somewhere."

Still, Aldonza did not speak.

I walked away. I could forget how to write; I could forget how to read. Here is where I wanted to be.

In winter we stayed close to the house and spent much time in handiwork: knitting, sewing, and weaving. I discovered I could make a little money helping Isadora Princhez, the seamstress in Parado, and was pleased to help the Corchuelo family coffers in this way.

To rest our eyes from minute stitches, we played cards and dice. Outside we played with whipping tops, balls, or hoops. Fredrica often practiced with her knife by throwing it into a circle she inscribed on a tree. Carlota or Meta would have nothing to do with the knife-target game, and when Fredrica offered me the knife, I hesitated.

"Are you afraid?" she asked. Her smile was mocking; her eyes looked at the knife in her hand. "It's a game." She now smiled in innocence.

At first it was uncomfortable because I remembered the day we had thrown the knife, when I had first come, and it was not a game but some kind of warning I did not quite understand. Holding the knife seemed familiar. I knew it was some talent I had brought with me to this life. I usually bested her, and she did not like it; it made her try harder.

And now I realized it was odd for a girl to have this ability—for once Lorenzo and Aldonza had said of Fredrica that she was, in some ways, like a son, but they were glad for she helped feed the family. I had seen Fredrica dispatch hares on the hillside with one throw of her knife. Had I hunted in my earlier life? I shuddered to think so. I did not want to have Fredrica's ways.

One day when we were tossing knives out behind the house at the foot of the hills, we watched a family of squirrels skitter from one tree to the next. They were empty-mouthed and chattering at each other, as if they were playing tag.

Fredrica looked at me and said, "Can you hit one?" Without waiting for an answer, she threw her knife, and a squirrel fell from a low branch to the ground. "I like killing."

I thought she meant to say, "I like hunting," but maybe not. . . .

With a haughty look, she said, "You do it." A direct challenge!

I wanted to do it; I wanted to show her. I hefted the knife to balance it *just so* in my hand and let it fly. I hit a second squirrel.

Her black eyes narrowed. "Where are you from?" she asked me harshly. "Where did you learn to do that?" Her russet hair was pulled back from her face and shone in the afternoon sun.

I looked at her wide-eyed, hands open and upward, showing innocence, for I had no answer.

"You are from the Devil, I think," she said, but she said it gleefully, not as if she believed it or were afraid of me, but as if she wanted me to be.

I threw my knife on the ground and went back to the house.

Fredrica was a strange weed, reckless and bold, growing among more whole-some flowers—but still I did not want to think of her as dangerous; only unkind, at times.

I shuddered. *Did the Devil teach me to write?* Surely Aldonza would know if I were from the Devil. She was very wise.

꩜

And what of my missing family? For I would think, "Mother," and I would see Aldonza. Sometimes I wondered where I came from, what kind of family I had had, where they lived, if they were alive or dead. In the blankness I recognized a pain about which I did not want to know the source, like a broken bone that was knitting and could not take much pressure.

As time went on, I did not try to press against my past, and when Carlota and Fredrica, or Meta, talked of sometime before I came, I imagined that I was there too and their memories became mine: I was there when, at three, Carlota, wanting a ball of yarn for Piccolo, found Aldonza's knitting and unraveled a week's worth of sweater or when Meta, at seven, fell from a sycamore tree and broke her arm.

Aldonza was my mother and Lorenzo was my father, for didn't I have both their names?

CHAPTER 4

in which Christopher continues the quest with Sancho

Y LITTLE SQUIRE and I were near Madrid. Once there, I had arranged to meet a messenger from my father. Then I would again have a family ring and more money, and I could tell the messenger my plans for further places to meet us, chiefly to let us know whether Cinda had been found.

Our plan was to circle Madrid around and around in ever widening circles through all of Spain. All along we had stopped in every village. At every house we saw, we stopped and questioned any person there. "Have you seen a stranger, a girl?" And I described her. Then we gave her name and home and asked for any information to be sent there or even to the king—for one might forget Don Marco's name and place, but not the king's.

I discouraged Sancho in his embellishments, else he would ask,

> Have you seen angelic Cinda with dimples fair
> in each cheek and lustrous black and curly hair?
> Her eyes are skyward blue and skin like silky marble
> with blush of tamest rose. Her voice, a warble
> of the freshest birds. And, you ask, what is her scent?
> That of lilac and carnation petals bent.
> If you see her, I beseech you do your part:
> Send her to the Knight of the Seeking Heart.

"Speak plainly, Sancho," I said, choking down my laughter—not at his spirit, of course, but at his gangly verse. "For these folks are simple, and we want them to know and remember what we say."

He sighed and then at the next house, he would try to do as I told him, but it was hard for him to hold back his chivalric impulses and, at the least, he said,

"If you see her, you must tell her of my master's undying devotion. He is her lowly subject; she, his lofty mistress." And he always called me the Knight of the Seeking Heart, which I found to be the truth of me.

He had in his mind the way our "gwest" was supposed to be, and I had to remind him—this was it: stopping at house after dull house, mostly cob and mud, often suspicious faces in the windows or folks too busy to hear us out.

The dog-like wolf, Sosiego, stayed near the boy, though at night he sometimes came to me to scratch his belly or behind his ear as I had on our first meeting.

As we cantered along, I told Sancho of the tradition of chivalry, and when I finished, he said, "Begin again." So I would. What better way to spend the in-between time? "Honor, charity, piety, chastity, and loyalty," I told him many times until he could repeat them back. "This is the way we strive to live our lives."

Sancho was tireless. He was awake before and after me. He cooked for us and took care of the horses. He asked me to teach him to use a sword and dagger. Each evening he whittled away at making wooden ones. "Until I can have real ones." He looked at me slyly.

I laughed. "We will see."

꧁꧂

One day we rode by a field and found a man beating a field hand.

Sancho halted and, before I could stop him, cried, "Hold, señor!" He ordered Sosiego to lie down, for the wolf was growling at the man. Then Sancho motioned to me.

"What?" I whispered, leaning close to him.

"Master, you must stop him!" he cried. "You are *forsworn* to protect the weak."

I seldom corrected Sancho's words and, now, I had to focus on the problem at hand. Hesitantly, I walked Beleza over to the man, whose black bushy brows were as one on his forehead, and said, "Kind sir, what is the cause of this altercation?"

The man looked puzzled. "What!" The man lifted his arm to beat the cringing boy. "You lazy, good for nothing! I've had enough!"

"Excuse me," I said uncertainly, "but could you, please, hold off a moment?"

He looked at me. "Make it quick or I'll turn this stick on you!"

I dismounted Beleza, now seeing what must be done. "Perhaps you would be willing to fight with me, rather than the youth."

He swaggered over to me and said, "Maybe I would! Who do you think you are to interfere?" He laughed a nasty laugh. "A knight?"

"Shall we make the wager that if I defeat you, you will leave the boy alone, and if you defeat me . . ." I did not know what to say.

But Sancho did. "We will work for you a day to make up for his laziness."

I looked at him in surprise. Surely this was not the role of a squire.

"Make it until the field is cleared," the man said. "I need it done before snow."

"Done," Sancho said.

Again I looked at him. He threw me a staff which most closely matched the weapon the man had in hand. I caught it, but I said to the man, "Swords, perhaps, would be better."

But the man began his attack without another word.

The next day we—the poor gangly lad, who had a great sense of humor despite the beating; Sancho; and me—cleared the field, and I quite felt I needed another round of whelp's droppings for my bruised and aching muscles.

Because of Sancho, I was in this predicament. I spoke with him firmly and explained that his zeal has much to be admired, but it was not always the cause of the knight to interfere with others' affairs.

"But, master," he said, his eyebrows raised, "would you rather let the man keep on beating?"

I didn't know. Where was the line? I didn't remember reading anywhere the answer to that.

But for Sancho, who knew firsthand of beating, the answer seemed clear.

∽◌∾

By late December, we had been through many villages and had spoken to many people. Yet no sign or word of Luscinda. In one village, I saw my squire again be bold and act more knight than squire. When a young lad of six or so plucked a loaf of bread from a market stall, the merchant quickly chased and caught the hapless boy. Grabbing the bread, the merchant held fast to the boy's arm.

I jumped to stop this and cried, "Good sir, I will gladly pay you for the bread and more, if you will let this boy be gone."

The merchant, a lithe and nimble bald man who had lost his cap in the chase, said, "He is not new to stealing from me, but now I have caught him. I take him to the sheriff."

Fear written on his face, the young boy started to cry.

"Señor," I said. "Maybe this boy's family is in grave need of this bread."

"No matter." The merchant shrugged. "They eat no longer on my bounty."

Sancho said, "You could give him work to earn a loaf or two a week." He looked at the boy. "Does this seem good to you?"

The lad stopped crying, and looking up at the merchant, boldly said, "I can deliver bread or even help you bake."

"I doubt that now." The merchant laughed. "But we will see." He looked at me and said, "Thank you for a way to stop a deed I scarcely wanted to do myself."

I nodded, wondering who was the wise man here. Sancho or me. He had been quick to offer an alternative.

"That was a good solution," I said to him later.

His green eyes were serious. "Money isn't always the answer."

After a while, I said, "Sancho, you take my words to heart."

"I long to learn knightly ways."

"But as you see, days go by and little happens," I said. "This is only our second adventure, and only one has turned out well."

"It doesn't matter," he said, "I can learn from success or failure."

Yes, wise, this lad. *Dear God. May I be open to learning from all quarters.*

We traveled south from there, but we did not avoid snow. Often driving sleet beat against us, and the wind tore through our cloaks of fur. Sometimes we would find an abandoned cabin or camp and stop, but not for long for I was anxious to visit more villages before the weather got too bad.

৩৫

In February, my squire spoke too quickly and got me in a fray. In this little village, after retrieving a message from my father—no news of Cinda—we happened upon three men. They were dragging a struggling woman, who I took to be of mottled reputation, along with them.

She yelled, "Let me go!" Yet the man holding her continued to pull.

Sancho (what was he thinking!) confronted them. "Let this maiden go!"

The man laughed and threw the woman to the ground. To his friends he said, "Did you hear a little bird say something?"

"*Chirp, chirrup,*" another man said, looking around as if for the bird. The woman began crawling away, and the man clamped his foot upon her back. The other two men grabbed Sancho by the arms and dropped him in a water trough.

By now I had dismounted and had sword in one hand, buckler in the other. I was quite angry, for this behavior was crass and unacceptable for gentlemen (of which these were not). The first man drew his knife. I quickly cut his arm half off. I saw the bone and sinew among the blood. (Sancho had learned to sharpen well.) But that left the other two at me together. One had a sword, the other a knife.

Another went down with a happy cut to his leg. I successfully won this battle—by default. The third man ran off, leaving his comrades lying in the street, bleeding and moaning.

The woman was gone, and so we never knew the story of it.

To the two wounded men, Sancho gravely said, "You have been bested by this grandly knight. You are charged to find the fair Luscinda and tell her of his devotion, and when you see her, you are to bow and declare she is the loveliest maiden of all time."

The bleeding men ignored him.

Later I wondered if we were right or wrong to interfere.

"No matter," Sancho said. "Three against one is wrong, and she was quite insistent that she didn't want to be with them."

I could think of a half dozen reasons why the men deserved to have the woman. Perhaps she stole from them. Perhaps she was married to one. . . . But Sancho stood at my chest, his green eyes flashing, and yelled up at me. "They were dragging her, and they threw her to the ground and he stepped on her. That is enough to know who's right."

I shook my head. He was so certain. Of everything.

"She could have said, 'Thank you,'" I grumbled.

Sancho was still exasperated. "It is enough we've done the good deed."

All I could think was, "Who is master here?" *Dear God, Grant me patience.*

∽◯∾

About a month later, we happened upon a sheriff, and when we told him of our search, he looked away and rubbed his neck. He had a large cigar and he puffed on it and finally said, "There was a girl we found yesterday."

It could be she! my heart sang.

"We found her in the woods," he said. He took another puff. "Dead."

I gasped. "But was it she?" I asked. "Dark hair, fair-skinned. Did she have blue eyes?"

"Her eyes were gone." He shook his head. "Animals, I think. Maybe vultures."

I was heartsick but tried to keep my mind on facts and not my feelings.

"Where is the body?" My voice shook. Sancho put his hand on my arm and waited silently for the sheriff to answer.

"Buried," he said, shaking his head. "How would you recognize her?"

My knees gave out. I sat on the ground. I could not bear the thought of Cinda being like the bones of the old kings in the casket room at El Escorial.*

In a moment, I said, "She has a scar," I pointed to my arm, "right here." I took a

---

* El Escorial was built by King Philip II. The king collected the remains of all his ancestors to be housed in one place in a royal mausoleum. The remains were initially housed in a makeshift mausoleum, referred to here as the casket room.

few more breaths to settle down my heart. "Shaped like a shield."

He shrugged.

"But how will we know?" I cried, looking at him. The sun behind his head was blinding.

Sancho, again the one for action, said, "We'll dig her up."

And it was arranged that we would. Two men came, and they and sturdy Sancho began to dig up the grave made only yesterday. Sosiego helped dig too.

I paced impatiently and worried what I would do if it were she. How would I give the news at home? To Don Marco. And Doña Isabella. I remembered the sadness in her eyes, the tears that shadowed them, how the little bells had shivered at her breast, a reminder of Cinda. I wanted to know and yet did not. My inclination was to pray but I didn't know what to pray for, so I settled on, *Dear God, Help me survive either answer.*

Yet if it were she, would it settle my future? How could I live knowing she died alone in a strange wood and wondering how she happened there? Would I be free? Would I feel relief? Or would this haunt me always? I paced until my knees again gave out, and my hands shook as if I were terribly cold.

Unable to wait another minute, I jumped up and grabbed Sancho's shovel and dug and dug until we hit the box. We grabbed the ropes and pulled it up. I made Sancho leave, though he did not want to.

We opened the box. *Dear God!* I must not record how bad it was. This dead, decayed, and decaying body. Still I shudder. But good cheer, it wasn't she. I could see right off, for here was an older woman with rotten teeth. What was the sheriff thinking? Hadn't I said *eleven* (or had I? My poor mind, I have asked so many people).

But soon Dread, my friend now, set in again, and still I do not know of her. Is she moldering in some other grave that I'll never find? *Oh, God in Heaven. Hear my prayer.* How can I live with this vision now wondering if her skin is rotted and torn like that poor anonymous soul's?

CHAPTER 5

in which Donza learns certain lessons

HEN THE WEATHER warmed and the air was springtime fresh, Carlota, Fredrica, Meta, and I went in the pond nearly every evening. After a day of chores, the water was cooling and washed away the dust of the fields and animals. Fredrica, Meta, and I raced each other through the water, while Carlota, not having the stamina for a race, usually stayed near the edge. She would say, "Go," for the beginning and often call the winner, though we, more often than not, argued with her.

Sometimes Aldonza and Lorenzo joined us. Lorenzo's large and hairy body was a contrast to ours. Aldonza's full breasts were a reminder that someday we would become women. Meta, nearly sixteen, already showed the signs.

One night Fredrica noticed a scar on my arm. She poked at it. "How did you do that?"

I could not tell her. I looked where she pointed: a scar shaped like a shield.

Aldonza looked at it with solemn brown eyes. "From a burn, I think." Another mystery of my past to which we did not have the answer, but this time in my mind I sensed the heat from many fires and saw a coal, like a shooting star, arc through the sky, landing on my arm. In the vision, a sleeve whooshed into flame. I shook my head to clear the image—an unbelievable image, accompanied by an odor, unpleasant and unforgettable.

Each evening, after paddling and playing in the water, we sat at the pond's edge in a circle, combing each other's hair, pulling it out and making it smooth, feeling the texture change as it became drier and drier. I think we must have looked like wood nymphs, naked and luminous in the fading light.

And each night, I looked at Meta, Carlota, and Fredrica, and in my head I heard the words, "You are beautiful."

Were these memories—the sound of a gentlewoman's mellow voice and the startling burst of flames—or my imagination?

ॐ ∝

Most afternoons, when Lorenzo and Aldonza were resting, Meta, Fredrica, Carlota (unless she was too tired), and I walked up into the hills. They initiated me into the thrills of sliding down the hill in a large wooden bowl Lorenzo had fashioned. It slid best on mud, so if we were a mess after our sliding time, we stood under the waterfall near the source of the stream and splashed around in the water.

Because after our play we were always hungry, we brought food with us. Once while we were eating and talking, I, idly, pulled from my pocket the little oval mirror that I had with me when I came in Lorenzo's cart. Now the mirror prettily caught the sun and brightened the grass. In a while, the little pile of grass and twigs the polished metal illuminated began to smoke. Fredrica's unfortunate nose noticed the smoke first.

"Look!" she cried and jumped up and blew on it, adding bits of grass and dried chips of bark and sticks and soon we had a fire. Because she begged me and because I had learned the power of the mirror and wanted nothing to do with it, I gave it to Fredrica. She smiled broadly, showing her deceptive dimples, and for the rest of that day she was friendly and sisterly to me.

When she walked behind me later as we went down the hill, I thought I heard her whisper *Idiot*. But as often was the case with Fredrica, I could not be certain.

While I had wanted nothing to do with the mirror, I then thought perhaps I had given it away too casually. Fredrica was not always dimples and sisterly affection.

If I had run away from my first family, if . . . was there someone like Fredrica? The kindness of Aldonza, the strength of Lorenzo, the wholesomeness of Meta, the fragility of Carlota, I thought I recognized, but not the ways of Fredrica.

ॐ ∝

For the time I was at Lorenzo's, Fredrica and I switched back and forth from being allies to foes. I chose to see her as fearless. Given to a sanguine humor and thus an innately optimistic person, I could not imagine evilness as a constant state of being—a deficit in me—and so did not imbue her with it, though I knew she was capable of a maliciousness that most persons were not. Certainly her charming smile and prettiness belied this blemish of her soul and made it invisible to everyone else, even the wise Aldonza.

Some of the tricks she played, on the sly, I thought were amusing, though some went awry. And sometimes I was persuaded to participate. When Meta started keeping company with our neighbor Enrique Traduccia, I thought Fredrica's idea of doctoring their drinks with a particular herb sounded like good entertainment for a slow evening.

I used a bit of coin that I earned from my work for the seamstress, Isadora Princhez, and bought some chocolate, a delicacy for a farm family. I knew because of my helping Aldonza which herb would produce the desired effect on the young couple. I did not know how the herb would make the chocolate drink taste, but I knew the chilies would mask the flavor, for while I liked my chocolate with sugar, cinnamon, and a dash of salt, others preferred the hot spices.

Enrique and Meta were sitting on the porch, watching the sun go down when Fredrica and I offered them the steaming chocolate. Meta seemed grateful. I had a twinge of conscience and wanted to take the cups away before it was too late, but Fredrica pulled me in the house and scolded: "Do not change your mind."

Soon we heard a cry from Enrique. He dropped his cup; the lovely chocolate ran in a puddle on the ground. He was up and on his way to the outhouse. I heard him yelp as he ran. It was not long before Meta sat down her cup, and her braids flying behind her, she ran for the chamber pot. Success!! Fredrica and I had divided the lovers!

In the morning Carlota found Piccolo dead from drinking the remnants of the chocolate—his life fluids literally drained away. *Remorse* resided in my stomach for quite some time.

One afternoon soon after, while we were shelling beans, Aldonza said to me, "The thing to do before taking an action is to consider the consequences." Her sure fingers made quick work of the freshly picked beans. "And if one of those consequences might cause harm, then think again." Her thumb flicked at the shell. *Plink. Plink. Plink.* The beans fell into the bowl.

Wishing to avoid the disappointment in her eyes, I looked at Aldonza's straight and honest nose. I took another handful of stringy beans.

She said, "I have always tried to live my life in moderation." Her pile of hulls was growing. "To keep things in balance—a bit of fun, a bit of work, a bit of love, a bit of prayer, a bit of family, a bit of friends. See, all of these are good within themselves. But too much of any . . . someone might get hurt."

And that was it, a gentle slice of wisdom.

These few words hardly hurt me, and I wished she would have flayed me or made me drink of the stuff for punishment. It would have been better than bearing Carlota's tears or her silent sobs next to me at night or knowing that Piccolo would never warm me again. It was all the more unsettling to realize Fredrica had no remorse—had Aldonza shared her wise words with Fredrica?—and seemed to get pleasure (what was *pleasure* to her?) from Carlota's anguish and Meta's embarrassment.

I tried to set things right, but I could not replace Piccolo, though I tried in the form of another kitten. Still Carlota soon warmed to it, and I encouraged Carlota to sit with the kitten while I did her chores. I often wished Aldonza's herbs were more help to Carlota.

ᔐ ᔕ

When one does something that fills one with remorse, one often wants to escape. The pain of my remorse caused me to wonder about my first family. I thought of the bag with the embroidered flowers on it that I had with me when I first got to Lorenzo's. Perhaps you have thought of it too. You know it held clues to help me remember my past. But I had hidden the bag and had not given a thought to the contents—the colored stones, the shell, the locket, the ruby-set hair combs. But now I thought of retrieving it and taking it to Toboso to see if anyone recognized something to guide me home. But in the end I did not because I loved Aldonza and Lorenzo and did not want to leave them.

When I turned my thoughts toward the past, I could not remember. I felt turmoil and darkness, and rather than thinking I might have run away—and what terrible secret may have made me want to—I preferred imagining my first family was dead. And nothing could have made me return—short of remembering the knight, who did not forget me but travailed heartily to find me.

CHAPTER 6

in which Christopher has a mishap

ROM ABOVE ON a hillside, Sancho and I saw a halted carriage with a wealthy man and woman near it. Two robbers circled the carriage. Two servants were already dead, and the man was wounded and lying on the ground. This time I was certain who was right and who was wrong.

We kicked up our horses and rode as quickly as we could. By the time we got there, one robber had taken off with the woman on his horse. From Beleza's back, I wounded the remaining robber with my sword. I left Sancho and Sosiego to watch the downed robber and took off after the other.

From a distance I saw him pull the woman from his horse and try to push her to the ground. With the most barbaric war whoop I could summon, I charged them, waving my sword. The man gave her one last shove and jumped on his horse and left.

"You have saved me, your grace," the woman said.

"I am glad to be of service, señora."

When we returned to the carriage, I found Sosiego had killed the other robber as the man had attacked Sancho. The robber's throat had been ripped open.

Sancho had found a spider web to stanch the flow of blood from the gentleman's wound. Then Sancho sewed the flaps of the wound together, the man biting on his knife to keep from crying out.

We put the bodies of the servants over our horses and tied them to the back of the carriage and drove the carriage, with the husband and wife in it, to their home. Upon arrival, I stepped from the carriage. My spur caught, and I fell, breaking my leg.

Not a very illustrious ending to this adventure.

Again, my trusty squire took care of everything. He tied together a sled that would be drawn behind Beleza and had me lifted onto it. The couple we aided offered us a small guest house on their property, and that was where we went.

Sancho set my bone. I learned the numbing powers of wine as I drank enough to float a merchant ship and hovered in some netherworld, knowing, but not knowing, what he was doing.

He soaked some linen cloths in egg white and wine and rolled them into bandages. Then having had two servants set me in a chair, Sancho quickly pulled the injured leg straight and felt to be sure the bone was in place. He unrolled the bandages, first around the break and then above it, then below it, and again in the middle.

I have to stay "a-bed," Sancho says, for many weeks.

I asked, "What of our quest now?"

"Still it is good to be alive and wagging your tail. Even with a broken leg," he said jovially. Then added, "And master, it is glory! You have been wounded in battle trying to save a maiden, who was wrongfully used."

I was not convinced by his interpretation of the events.

I was restless as a colt to be out on the trail again. From my window I see two large hills—like two breasts nurturing this little valley in La Mancha. I long to be on the trail again. Precious time was lost. Sancho rode to the next town and sent word to my father at Gasparenza of the accident, asking him to send Frondo to help care for me.

Our host was Francisco Spinozo, a wealthy *hidalgo*, who was often gone on business. His young wife, Miralda, visited and read to us.

ꙅꙅ

One night, a few days into my healing, I awoke to the sound of crying. It was Sancho. I propped myself up in bed, my casted leg quite stiff and awkward.

He shook his head and blurted, "I never thought I'd miss them." His head, with hair all sticking out from sleep, wagged from side to side.

Of his large family, all I knew was of the scars on his back and healing remedies he used. Quite separate things, I thought. "Come here, Sancho." I patted the bed next to me. "You must tell me everything about your family for memories are sometimes better than nothing."

Carefully, so as not to jostle my leg, he sat at the end of the bed. He told of a life that only included two meals a day, where he never had a pair of shoes until now, even in winter. Millet was all they raised and had for bread. For warmth they simply slept together back to back or chin to chin.

I could not help but think of my own life, three full meals, warmth, wheat bread, and so much more than this sturdy lad had ever seen or dreamed of. How far apart our lives were!

He did not tell of the beatings, but he talked of how his father got down on his hands and knees and gave the smallest children horse-rides. As for his mother, she had red hair and smelled of roses all year long, for oil of roses was the base of nearly everything she made to heal. On Sunday, when they had an hour or two of no chores, she would sit with all of them at her feet, each one trying to be the closest, and even his father would listen, while she read to them. She had a zither, and she taught them many Psalms. Not because they went to church, because he never had, but because those were the songs she knew.

When he finished, he said, "Now tell me of your family, master."

But I would not for I wanted that time to be for his memories. I gave great thought to Sancho's disturbing confession that he had never been to church. I have heard this is true of some peasants. Should I educate him of our Lord? I was not inclined to do so. He seemed to have right action very well in hand. The Lord loves the innocents.

ꝏ

A few days later, it was raining, thick as a waterfall, and Miralda did not come to read. Sancho asked me to fill up the day with stories so I told him memories I had never told anyone. Tintoretto's daughter, Marietta, was my first love. My true Beatrice. She did not awaken my second mind; I was yet too young, but she fired my heart and my thoughts; she took away my tongue and all good sense.

In 1578, our families, mine and Cinda's (eleven family members and many more servants), traveled to Venice to have family portraits painted by Tintoretto. From the instant I saw Marietta, I was captivated by her. On the first day, when my family entered the studio to begin our portrait, she greeted us, her painter smock's gathered sleeves covering her arms and flapping with authority at her sides. What attracted me was her confidence—her certainty of her own talent in the shadow of her father's, the ease with which she posed us for the painting, even calming my querulous sister, Luisa.

Marietta's laugh was merry and seemed to come straight from her heart. Her long brown curls shimmied down her back and wispy, tight-curled tendrils framed her face. She and I were the same height, though she was eighteen and I was only twelve, eager and awkward. And when she spoke, her voice soft and throaty, I had to lean toward her, pay attention to hear every word.

Within a few days I was coming to the studio early before my family's sitting time, and staying after, as did Cinda—for in her way, she, too, loved Marietta. Of course Cinda had the same kind of love for me—of adoration, the longing to be near that person, the longing to be seen by that person. Cinda bounced before us and cheered us on, in whatever task was at hand.

Cinda and I learned to oil the pear wood palettes, clean the brushes, even assist with mixing the paints—although we did not grind or add the oils. We handed Marietta the pestle, a bowl, a container of cerulean or moved something that was in her way. We learned the secret of cochineal for red, something that had been discovered by the Spaniards only a few dozen years ago in the New World. Between each painted layer of the portraits, after it was dry, we helped rub the canvases with onion and paint it with linseed oil.

Marietta talked to us of painting, and painting became the most important thing to us during our time in Venice. Marietta explained about *chiaroscuro*, the art of light and shade. An Italian term: *chiaro*, light or clear and *scuro*, dark or obscure. She instructed: "Always see objects as light, lighter, dark, darker. One shade moving into the next." And Cinda seemed to understand, but for me, my charcoal drawings lacked any subtlety and tended to be black and white, without the grays.

Another day Marietta took Cinda, Cinda's older brother Fernando, and me into the city, that is, after Marietta outfitted Cinda in breeches, shirt, and cap!

"What would Mama say!" Fernando exclaimed. I said nothing but thought Cinda looked bonny with her hair pulled back and hidden beneath the cap—her long-lashed blue eyes wide in her cherubic face.

"Where we go today, we go easiest as boys," Marietta said. "I have, all my life, gone out in the city with my father dressed as a boy. Many think I am a son!"

Fernando said no more—I knew he was ready for an adventure. And I would have done anything, gone anywhere with Marietta.

The streets of Venice were among the dirtiest of all cities, a veritable quagmire when it rained or because of high tides, not to mention the rubbish. Pigs roamed the streets and fed on the garbage and wastes of the city. Men and women wore shoes built on platforms to walk in the streets.

"Look!" Fernando said, pointing to a wine stall. "Wine from our vineyards." Yes, there were several casks of Solariego wine and other wines from Andalusia, including our estate Gasparenza, as well.

Now Marietta and I kept Cinda between us, for many people were in the market, and we were jostled along our way. The sea breeze ruffled our sleeves and felt cool and delicious until the freshness of morning faded and the day became moist and warm.

Fernando reached for his handkerchief and was surprised to find it was not there.

"Ah," Marietta said, "be wary of pickpockets." Then she spied a lad of her acquaintance and cried out, "Arrigio! Arrigio!"

The lad was tall, with a hint of a manly shape—probably Marietta's age. He grinned broadly and clapped her on the shoulder, as he would a fellow. "'Retto," he said. "You are out in disguise again!" He laughed, a jolly wide-mouthed laugh. I frowned and grumpily cleared my throat, not saying that I wished he would leave us!

Marietta said, "Fernando's lost a handkerchief."

Merrily, Arrigio said, "This one?" He held up Fernando's pocket handkerchief.

Scowling, Fernando began, "How . . ." but stopped. Arrigio returned it to Fernando's pocket with a grin.

"Are you a thief?" Cinda asked. I squeezed her hand to hush her—I did not like her talking to him.

"Yes, youngster, I am," Arrigio said. "I do not find many who give over the contents of their pockets of their own free will."

How bold this fellow was! I rocked on my heels and looked around the market. I wanted to move on but, of course, dark Fernando was interested. He burst forth with questions. "How do you do it? Where do you live? How do you eat?"

As we walked through the market, Arrigio regaled us with tales of his adventures, even giving us demonstrations of his techniques for thievery. Marietta and Arrigio walked together, and Cinda, as if sensing my disappointment, whispered, "Marietta still likes you."

Sweet child! She knew my feelings!

Arrigio turned to me and said, "You must be careful of your possessions here."

I felt for my knife and found it gone. Arrigio produced it. He showed us how to carry our knives in our boots so as not to have them pickpocketed. "The carriers of knives, like the strings of women's purses, can be easily cut." He moved behind Fernando to demonstrate.

How could my divine Marietta be friends with a thief?

∽∾

Outside, the mud was like a viscous stream and Sancho would not leave and no one would come, we were sure.

Sancho ordered, "Tell me more of Marietta and Cinda."

And I did. Cinda and I, with our fathers, and Marietta went to see the garden at the Villa Baciare Meraviglio of the Afferrare Capriccio family, some twenty miles from Venice. Though my father had been to the villa, Don Marco had not, and because he had a keen interest in architecture, he was eager to see this marvelous structural feat.

In the carriage Cinda and I sat across from Marietta. I had never taken much notice of women's clothing, but I noticed every detail about Marietta, the way her soft yellow silk dress conformed to her young woman's curves, how, though we were the same height, her hands and feet were smaller and more elegant. Her dark curls framed her handsome face—dark eyes, a glossy heart-shaped mouth, and blushed cheeks.

To pass the time she played hand-clapping games with Cinda, and though I had never played, not even with my delightful sprite Cinda, I joined in and found such joy in the touch of Marietta's hand that I wanted the game to continue—world without end! My feelings for her were such a surprise, such a rush of warmth and heart fluttering and moist hands and hot neck, that I could not and did not try to understand them.

Cinda squirmed in her seat, and I sensed she knew I liked Marietta too much— but I did not care! Cinda was six—for heaven's sakes—I had always been good and kind to her and, for once, couldn't I enjoy the company of a grown woman?

At the Villa, our host suggested Marietta escort Cinda and me through the gardens, as she had been there before. She took each of us by a hand.

We walked by a carpet of flowers—purple, leafless cyclamen; bell-shaped gentian; white and blue ladies' delight; and rock soapwort. The breeze carried a cornucopia of smells to our noses! My heart was full, my mind flowery with words of love I wanted to share with Marietta.

When Cinda walked ahead of us, I said, "Beautiful lady, you are more lovely than any of these flowers, and I will never see a flower, but that it will remind me of you." I put my hand to my chest. "I feel as if I am floating through this garden." Shyly I looked down and happened on her bosom, from which my eyes flew! I stammered, "I-I am floating on your sweetness. I think I-I-I love you!"

Marietta stopped and looked me steadily in the eye. "Don Christopher," she said—her throaty voice vibrating each syllable, "I am deeply honored by your attention. But I cannot return it, even if I wanted to. You are betrothed to Cinda, and while you may think today she is but a child, in time she is going to be a woman. You will see she will be even more beautiful than I, and she is more worthy of you, a duke's son, than I, a painter's daughter."

I wanted to protest but she stopped me by putting her hand on my arm. "Let's find Cinda," she said gaily, "for today we are a trio of friends."

I was no longer Christopher, the lover, but Christopher, the twelve-year-old. My chest narrowed, my legs became mushy, my heart ached, but I knew the wisdom of her speech, and I instantly wanted to make it right with Cinda.

We found Cinda in front of two identical fountains, each set in a curved ten-foot alcove of a rocky hillside. A steady stream of rushing water rose from the basin bowls to the ceiling of its rounded nook.

"They are the same," Cinda cried. "Twins."

Shaking her head, Marietta said, "They are different. Can you discover why?"

I looked at Cinda and smiled. "I thought they were the same, too."

The marble basins were carved identically down to the squirrels, which sat on their brims. We walked closer; the rush of spurting water filled our ears. Finally I put my hand in one fountain and then the other. I lifted Cinda and had her feel the gushing water also.

She said, "In one, the water hits the top of my hand, and in the other, the water hits the palm." The water in one was like a hanging stalactite and in the other, an ascending stalagmite. She smiled at me. We had discovered the secret together.

Cinda laughed and said, "Here *up* and *down* look the same." She shook her dark curls, her head bobbing in wonder. "Opposites."

Marietta said, "Confusing, isn't it? As if good and evil could look the same."

Cinda asked, "Like Arrigio. He steals, but he is your friend, so he must be good too."

Marietta looked thoughtful. "Like *chiaroscuro*. Shades of light and shades of dark."

"People are both." Cinda nodded, as if she'd known this fact all her life. While I tended to think Arrigio was a bad one—surely he did not have to steal.

Back at the Villa, we sat on a patio, which was a garden all its own of bright green plants with parrots, blue birds, and toucans among the trees. We were served fruit—a variety of melons, pears, papaya, and grapes—in colorful porcelain bowls and platters of cheeses and breads. While we sat, we drank pomegranate juice and watched the birds. Growing on a trellis near the middle of the patio was a sweet honeysuckle, and I walked close to see the tiny hummingbirds, hovering in the air like an idea that was not quite clear.

Marietta came to see us the morning we left Venice. She was wearing her bright yellow dress. To Cinda she said, "I have a gift for you." Her voice trembled, as if she were sad. She opened her hand and in it was a locket. Opening it, she showed it contained two miniature paintings, one of Don Marco and one of me!

Cinda gasped. "They are perfect, Marietta."

Marietta closed the locket and showed us the back on which was etched the master painter's name, Tintoretto. Marietta placed the chain around Cinda's neck.

Sancho had fallen asleep, but I stayed awake awhile longer thinking of Marietta

60

and wondering if she'd ever gotten to sign any paintings as her own in her father's studio.*

In time Frondo, my loyal valet, arrived from Gasparenza to help Sancho care for me.

My first question to Frondo was, "Is there any news of Cinda?"

He solemnly shook his head. "And it is nearly eight months now, and she has turned a year older." Frondo was always fond of Cinda; it was like him to have marked her birthday.

With Frondo's help, I gave Sancho a sword. His hair bouncing, the lad thrashed around the room. "Now I will be the best squire in all the land!" His green eyes sparkled. He went outside to fight invisible giants and ogres.

Frondo sat with me, and though he was usually a quiet man, he talked to me until mealtime, telling me every detail of Gasparenza that he knew because he could tell I was ready to think of anything but my leg, my plight, and the delay in seeking Cinda.

In a few more weeks I walked a bit and the itchy cloths came off for good. My leg was weak. Sancho said we must "dally" forth again, and soon. I was determined to work each day to regain my strength. Challenging me to spar, Sancho encouraged me to aspire to good health.

∽つ ∝

When I was greatly strengthened, I sent Frondo and Sancho for certain supplies so we could continue on our journey. I gave Frondo my ring to ensure the shop-keeper's payment from my father. Sancho proudly strapped on his new sword, and I gave Frondo my sword and shield for extra protection, though I knew he would not use it.

When they left, Miralda visited as she often did. I rose to greet her and offered her a chair. Instead she sat on my bed. "My husband is away." She sighed and pulled up her skirt above her ankles. She beckoned me with a finger.

"Nay, Doña Miralda." I ignored her behavior and sat on a stool, hands squarely in my lap as if to hide her from my second mind. "I dare not sit with you there, for with your beauty, too soon things would be out of hand."

She came to me. Leaning over and whispering in my ear, she said, "Yes, what I want."

I fell off the stool.

---

* Apprentices in Masters' studios signed works with the Masters' name. Marietta Robusti hid her initials in her paintings.

"Your gray eyes, your dark hair." She touched my chin. "This cleft." Her finger now stroked my cheek. "You are too handsome for words." Her voice was slithery, slinky, oil pouring from the spout.

That other part did rise as if he had been sleeping these long weeks and now was strong and well and wanted attention, and it was quite obvious.

As I scrambled to my feet, she said, "Don Christopher, I see you want me. You must know I want you as much."

My voice was weak and shaky. "You are being too familiar with me."

"And I intend to be more so." She opened her bodice, exposing her pear-like breasts.

My hands became magnets and were attracted, pulled . . . to touch her. Ah, to kiss her, to hold her. I wondered what it would be like. And this would be easy. She would not tell and I would not tell. No one was here to know. We could perhaps contrive to be alone again, and then I might discover more delights available to man and woman, until this urge was settled.

I sighed and turned my head. "Señora Spinozo, please cover yourself," I said weakly. "I hold my commitment to another higher than wanton pleasure."

She laughed, a seductive laugh, though she said sincerely, "I know of your Luscinda. I grieve for her, in fact, but surely she would not care if I were to comfort you." She pressed against me. I backed up. "If the situation were reversed, I would be grateful to her."

Her lips, her eyes, her shoulders, the scent of white lilies, her warm breath . . . and more invaded me, and I yielded to my longing. As I reached for her, I prayed, "God, please cure me quickly for I cannot help myself!"

Sancho flew in the door quite out of breath. "Robbed!" he cried. "The horses. Everything."

I quickly walked to him, hoping to shield the wanton Miralda as she covered herself. I pushed him out the door, saying, "Where is Frondo? Is he all right?"

"Battered some, but all right, I think." The lad's breath came in gulps. "Come!"

Miralda appeared at the door. I asked her for a horse and cart to go to my servant. She agreed.

Frondo was sitting up when we found him, but his arm was hanging from his shoulder and he could not move it. A barber in the little village deftly pulled and lifted the arm to put it aright, and though I knew the maneuver had pained the little man a great deal, he said, "It was quick and I am better." The barber firmly tied Frondo's arm to his body and told him to rest.

I left Frondo at an inn under the care of the innkeeper's wife, a sturdy, happy woman. I sent Sancho to retrieve the rest of our belongings from the Spinozos.

I knew quite well (I was not naive in everything—it is known that men are inconvenienced as are women) how Miralda's scenario would play out. Whether I left or stayed, she would sometime say I approached her with amorous designs. Her anger would determine to what extent she would declare I forced her.

My sword and ring (good heavens! how would I tell my father I lost a second one?), Sancho's weapon, and the animals were the focus of our search. I was able to hire horses, and Sancho and I went in pursuit of the robbers.

Within a day we spied Beleza (with the other animals) outside a tavern. All that seemed missing from the animals were my ring and sword. My squire saw the two robbers sitting inside at a table near the door, playing cards, with two other men. I instructed him to leave Beleza for me but to take himself and the other animals outside of town to wait. "If you do not do this . . ." I shook my hand in his face. I left my threat unsaid, for I could think of nothing that would make this lad mind me.

Inside the tavern, I went to the table of my interest and, as if to join the game, pulled up a chair next to the man who had my ring on his finger and my sword hanging on his chair. He looked up and graciously introduced himself as the duke of Gasparenza! flashing the ring as he spoke. I drew my dagger and impaled his hand—with my ring—to the table. He yelled, and as if obeying a musical conductor, everyone stood, knocking over chairs.

I reached over and took the ring from his finger, grabbed my sword, and backed out the door. Sancho was there holding his sword at the ready. We jumped on our horses and quickly left. By dark we arrived at the inn where Frondo was. I wished our search for Cinda would end so quickly and so happily.

Soon after, Don Hernando, my father, arrived. After checking on Frondo and dismissing Sancho, he turned to me and begged me to stop my "capricious" journey, my quest for Luscinda! He was a short but powerfully built man. The collar band strained around his thick neck. Yet I remained strong in my feeling and told him that it was not capricious! It was necessity!

In his booming baritone voice, he told me that Don Marco still had men searching for her. "What do you think you can accomplish?"

"Some peace of mind," I said. "I must do all that I can do to find her."

"All that can be done is being done," he insisted. His dark eyes narrowed. "Even Ruy Bonheur, only Luscinda's age, sneaks from their house, searching the streets of Seville for her among the gypsies and *picaros*. He puts *himself* in danger of being kidnaped. His parents talk of locking him in the house!" Because of his title and demeanor, my father was used to others obeying him. However, that day, I did not want to be persuaded to agree with him, so I turned from him to help keep my resolve.

Ruy was moved to action by his love for Cinda. I remembered the day he had announced his feelings to us all: A group of us, including Fernando, Ruy's sister Patrecia, and Cinda, were together. Ruy was ten and an odd child. Though he was small, his body was proportioned already like a man's and his voice had always been uncharacteristically deep. He announced to us that he wanted to be a tore-ador. He turned to Cinda and asked for a token to keep near his heart. She gave him a white handkerchief with a crooked black "L" embroidered in the corner. He turned to me, and—in his noble manner, no secrets there—said, "I love Cinda. I always will."

I had clapped him on the back. "Of course. We all do." I made an arc with my hand to include everyone. "I am pleased she has a friend in you." I respected his forthrightness, and I hoped he would love whomever his parents arranged for him to marry.

Was I moved in my quest, our search for Cinda, by love or duty?

My father moved into my line of vision and interrupted my memories. "You should return to the university."

Angrily, I said, "You would say that only if you thought her dead!" I thumped my chest and said, "I will not have it; I will believe she is alive and continue to search for her."

"You are not a knight of old going on a crusade," he said, waving his hand at the window where we could see Sancho flailing his sword at an imaginary foe. "You are a youth. Having a squire does not make you a man."

"This is my crusade!"

He shook his head. "My son, this is a regrettable turn of events. But tragedies happen to all of us." He placed his hand on my arm. "You must prepare yourself for a different life than you had once thought."

"I will not hear these things!" I cried. "I will search for her until I can no more, and quite, I wish, that will be my death if hers has indeed transpired."

"You are frivolous in this, Christopher." His voice mellowed as he added, "Yet I will support you in your desire—for now." He put his hand on my shoulder. "I understand your wish to have your life in order." He cleared his throat. "When you doubt this is the right thing for you to do, we can arrange another marriage."

"Alicia?" I asked softly, speaking of the sister next to Cinda. Then I realized I, too, thought of it, so perhaps there was a part of me that considered her dead. I hung my head. I wanted so to hold on to my fervor for this quest and for my belief that Cinda lived.

"Alicia lacks in many charms." My father shrugged. "Marco and I have always desired a tie through marriage between our families, but perhaps it will fall to other children." He pulled at the frill at his neck. "If only I could speak of your sister Luisa to Fernando. She is not as comely as Patrecia Bonheur." Patrecia, Ruy's sister, had been betrothed to Fernando as long as I had to Cinda.

I looked up; my cheeks grew warm.

"But Luisa is more docile. Patrecia is a pretty girl but lacks a brain and is disobedient," my father explained. The sun was setting and he removed his hat; his long day was coming to an end.

"How so?" I asked, surprised to hear ill of Patrecia; my own opinion of her being quite ardent.

"She persists in drawing. A frivolous past time. Birds and animals, I think," he said distastefully. "Her father thinks it beneath her station and insists she stop."

I turned from my father to hide my flushed cheeks. "Her drawing hurts no one. She is a kind and gentle maiden." I said. My voice was as flat and even as I could make it. "And she is promised to Fernando."

"Yes, but with the right money behind these matters, even King Philip can be persuaded to change his mind." The unions of all nobles were approved by the king. My father loosened his constricting collar. "You would be as good a match for Patrecia as Fernando."

My heart thudded in my chest. He gave me wrong hope . . . a terrible thing.

My father returned home with Frondo. Sancho and I began again to knock at every door we saw.

I tried not to let my mind think on the possibility of Fernando and Luisa. (Could we simply deal the cards another way? Luisa to Fernando, Patrecia to me, Cinda to Ruy?)

And did I want dark and troubled Fernando married to my sister? No more than to Patrecia.

Should I . . . would I let go my quest and seek the *other* for myself? And what of *her* virginity? I knew it nonexistent. Knowing this had scarcely squelched the ardor that rose quickly upon thought of her. Perhaps virginity did not have the importance we were led to believe. It is only paternity of children that was important. Surely there were ways to ensure that.

CHAPTER 7

in which the knight, Christopher, learns more of Honor

S I LEANED against a tree, contemplating the starry night, Sancho came upon me, Sosiego by his side. "It is nearly ten months that she is gone," I said. "She is twelve now." And Sancho was twelve also—he was nearly Cinda's age.

"How do you know you want to marry her?" Sancho asked. His sandy hair was ruffled.

A simple question, yet I reacted with anger. "How dare you question me?" I looked at him, my cheeks hot, my fists clenching.

Sancho stepped back from me, startled or afraid? Sosiego growled.

"Forgive me. It is hard." I took a deep breath. "Those born to nobility have no choice in such things."

He nodded and petted the wolf.

Where did this anger come from? My promises to her, even the contract, seemed dead (but binding).

He sat on a log, and I sat on a rock. He picked up a stick, took his knife, and aimlessly whittled. "What else would you do?" he asked.

"Stop this search; go back to school," I said. "Seek to marry another," I added quietly.

He sliced the last of the bark from the stick. "Is that what you want?"

"I don't know."

"You're the worst knight in all of Chrissumdom." He stamped his foot in the dust.

"Why do you say that?" I cried, angry again.

"You can never make a decision." He pointed an accusing hand, stick outstretched, at me. "I always make the decisions," he said. "As a knight you should know what is right, and you should fight for it." His knife took a sure stroke across the stick. "Mostly you are unsure."

"Once I thought right was easy," I said. "I remember saying to Cinda that right is right and wrong is wrong."

"What happened?" Sancho asked impatiently.

I shook my head. "It does not seem easy anymore."

"You are wrong," he declared.

He always seemed to understand things in a different way than I did. Was he too young to see?

There was wisdom there, I could see that. Yet what of his foolhardiness and pulling us into scrapes before knowing the situation?

And why was it hard when what I wanted most was to be good and honorable? *Dear God, Help me to always choose right and recognize it for that.*

♫ ♪

Sancho learned well how to handle weapons. In one day, he felled two deer with bow and arrow. We shared our bounty with some peasants.

Another day we happened on an orphanage. The roof had blown off in a storm and several nuns were working to replace it. We stopped to help and soon the job was finished. They asked us to stay, and I watched as Sancho played with the children. He was but a child himself, yet he took care of me. I saw so clearly then how green I was when I had begun and how helpless too. For being born to privilege, I had servants to do everything for me. I was glad that I had learned from Sancho and he had learned from me. He can do what I do and I can do what he does. For the most part.

♫ ♪

We were near Seville. Could she be near here? It was so far from Madrid.

When Cinda was seven, our families were in Seville at the same time. We went to an *auto de fe*, a ceremony of the Inquisition. We had known one of the doomed families, of which a boy Judah Abravanel, only seven, was Cinda's friend. The burnings took place that night near where we were staying. We went to the roof, and we could see—not the people—but we could see the torches. As the pyres were lit, we knelt in prayer. The air was filled with the peculiar smell of burning flesh, a smell that gagged the whole of me, a smell I will never forget.

A wind whipped up and swirled pieces of burning tinder and clothing through the air. One glowing coal came to our roof top and landed on Cinda's sleeve, which whooshed into flame. Her father threw her skirt over her head and smothered the fire. Her hair was singed and her arm was burned.

After that Cinda said she had to walk carefully—not from the burn on her arm, but from the ache, another kind of scar, in her heart.

That trip to Seville was not all dark and sad. We were there for the Celebration before Lent. When I spoke of that memory, Sancho made me tell him in great detail of the parade, which went by Ruy's and Patrecia's house. Sancho was particularly interested in the giants with large papier-mâché heads and pasteboard bodies; the men walking on high sticks, nearly as high as some of the houses; and the flaming dragon at the end.

Sancho cried, "Was it real?"

I shook my head and bade him go to sleep, but my thoughts went back to the Celebration when our families were visiting the Bonheurs. In particular to the evening of the Processional, when Cinda, just seven, first dressed not in a child's robes but in a new dress cut in the adult style, of red taffeta decorated with rubies and pearls and a bell-shaped skirt showing an underskirt befitting the finest of women. She wore pearls in her ears and in her hair. Patrecia's maid had painted Patrecia's and Cinda's faces and sprayed them with rosewater. Cinda was giddy from the attention; I tried not to laugh—she was a child. I was thirteen, clearly, I thought back then, on my way to becoming a man.

Yet she was transformed and here was a glimpse of what she would look like years later—the beauty of her birth evident, her brilliant smile, not dimmed by the reddened mouth, and in spite of shadowed eyelids, her own wide blue eyes, bright and clear.

In the yard, we waited for the parade. Nearby was a group of *hidalgos* from Castile. I could tell their station by their dress, and I heard them speak of La Mancha. One of the men in the group, a man older than my father and very thin with a gray *pickdevant*, kept looking at Cinda. Before I could ask him to look away, Ruy spoke up from the balcony. "Señors," he said loudly in his husky voice. "Your friend is rude with his staring." Ruy pointed to the strange *hidalgo*.

The men looked to see who was being singled out with Ruy's accusing finger.

"Alonso, you are disturbing these young people," one of the men said.

The gray-haired man bowed to Ruy and his sisters. "The señorita is most beautiful and unforgettable." He motioned toward Cinda. "She could have my heart forever."

"Do not look again, señor," Ruy directed.

The man said, "I only look from afar."

Ruy frowned at the man. I wondered what these men thought of this imperious seven-year-old, who looked to be a miniature man and ordered them hither and yon with the wave of a hand, but they said no more and walked away.

That man had seen in her something I could not, and that, I suppose, was the promise of her womanly charms. How can I doubt? I want to say that she will have my love forever.

๛ ๛

On our way out of Seville, Sancho and I stopped at the Cathedral. When he saw that the slave market was on the steps of a church, Sancho was angry, and I could see his point.

During our long-ago visit to Seville, Don Marco had intended to get Cinda her own slave, but Marco's priest brother, Father Andrés, argued against it. "Marco, the church says everyone should be enfranchised."

"Their opinion changed, didn't it?" the duke challenged his brother.

"Even the most unchanging can change," Father Andrés said, as if he were speaking about more than the slavery issue.

"And that only applies to those who embrace the faith," Don Marco said to his brother. "Infidels should be put into bondage."

"An excuse to exploit." The priest stood eye to eye with his noble brother, and the duke put off buying Cinda a slave.

Instead we went to Sierpes Street in the shopping district. We were in a small card and game store when a man entered. Don Marco studied him then said, "You are Miguel de Cervantes y Saavedra, are you not?"

"Your grace," the man bowed. "Don Marco. Yes. You have remembered." He was shabby looking and extremely thin. His hair was ragged and his clothing worn. He smelled of wood smoke—much better than he might have smelled.

"What is your story, señor?" Don Marco asked with concern.

"I have been a slave in Algiers for the past few years, but I was finally ransomed," the man replied.

"Praise be to God," Don Marco said and crossed himself. He explained they had fought together at the Battle of Lepanto, when the Christian nations, organized by the Pope, had destroyed Turkish sea power. The man had been terribly wounded and had been honored by the commander Don Juan of Austria, the king's natural brother, for bravery. Señor Cervantes showed us his badly mangled left hand.

Don Marco asked, "What will you do now?"

"I make my way to Madrid," he said. He fingered his full beard. "Seek a post. Perhaps write. I have five years of ideas in my head."

Father Andrés said, "I admire those who write. There is nothing like a good story of chivalry and the knights of old for filling in the empty hours."

"Surely chivalry is dead," the man said morosely.

"Do not let these past years rob you of your chivalric spirit," Don Marco said.

"I saw much of it at Lepanto."

Cinda, her voice clear as crystal, asked, "How was it? As a slave."

"I never gave up trying to escape and make my way home to Spain," Cervantes said. And he had only one good hand!

Don Marco said, "Allow me to make your way easier, señor." He reached in his pocket and handed the man several gold coins.

The man lowered his eyes. He licked his lips and looked uneasy. He took the coins. "Thank you, your grace." He saluted Don Marco, who did not return the salute but, instead, bowed to the man.

Cinda went to her father and took his hand. "Papa, I do not want a slave."

We were silent for a moment; I think we were all thinking of what it would be like to be kept from our homes.

And is it like that for Cinda now? Kept away against her will? Oh the anguish! May she never give up trying to escape.

Before we left Seville, Sancho and I stopped in a barber's shop. Sancho watched closely as the barber shaved me. The barber said he had never met a squire and asked how Sancho had become one, to which Sancho replied, "Through the Grace of God and of my noble master."

I thought, *I am a knight because Grace gave me a noble squire.* He has more heart than I, for would I have continued on this journey for so long? It has its hardships, certainly. And what of Cinda? What have her hardships been? When will I feel I have done my duty to her?

⁊◠

Near the end of October, we came to the town of Sandidad, some sixty miles from Madrid. Sometimes when we stayed in these villages I joined in gaming. I soon knew the rogue across the table was switching dice to his gain and my loss.

"Señor," I said in an even and polite voice. "Your play is not honorable. I will not continue until you dispense with the auxiliary dice."

"This is an affront," he said. "I insist upon satisfaction."

"The truth needs no proof nor is it an affront," I said, still sitting calmly in my seat. "Leave off your crooked way, and we will continue as gentlemen." I nodded to the others at the table. Dismay sat on their faces.

The man, one baron's son, though I was not concerned with who he was—only his honesty—stood and said, "I say you have affronted me and that is your precious truth. You owe me satisfaction." He drew his sword.

"I do not wish to be provoked into a witless duel," I said. "You mistake yourself to think I am so simple." I held my anger in check as befitting my station as a duke's son.

Sancho was by my side, whispering, "Master, he is well-reputed in the duel. The tapmaster told me."

I had no doubt of it. This kind of wretched man who honed his skills in underhanded gaming would have perfected his overhand in swordplay.

Still whispering, Sancho said, "Walk away. It's only a game."

I gave him an angry look. He, who was always spurring me on to right wrongs, to be a man of honor, wanted me to leave!

I joined the man outside.

The seedy place emptied of its clientele, who came to see the grim revenge of this silly man who thought he would best me, but I was certain I would win. And I did. But it was Sancho who changed my course of action.

I held my sword to the scoundrel's neck, his body prostrate on the ground. I took from a hidden pocket in his doublet the questionable dice, and after showing them to all, I pocketed them. My token, you might say.

I had him strip off his clothes and sent him out of town with nothing but the skin on his back.

In the evening Sancho said I wanted to fight the man, not for selfless reasons but, for my own gain.

"What gain!" I cried. "A few ducats."

"Exactly," he said. "What of starving orphans, homeless old women, crazy old men, and helpless girls!"

"I let him live," I cried. "Because of you! I thought you would be pleased."

Sancho was silent.

"That cheating man! I have no patience with his simpering type. He does not want to meet the world with honor; he only wants to meet the world with ease by leaving nothing to chance."

I knew this desire well. I wished to fix my life and leave nothing to chance. But uncertainty barked at my heels and urged me to find her.

Sancho was right.

I merely fought myself, and there was no honor in that. Being a duke's son, studying the tenets of chivalry, did not give me wisdom. My responsibility was to *know* right action. And while the duel was fair, I then saw it was a prideful act. It was for no good reason. Better to have walked away. *Dear God, Help me to shroud myself in humility.*

꩜

A few weeks later, Sancho and I were eating roasted rabbit and a fresh salad he gathered in the woods. He made a greensauce of parsley, mint, and cloves, maybe other herbs, for the meat.

When he finished his dinner, he threw Sosiego his trencher.* "Is there another you will marry?" he asked cautiously, as if he were not sure he wanted to know the answer.

His inquiry startled me. "I do not know," I said and looked away. "Why do you ask?"

"I sometimes think you simply want to know if she is dead, so you can ask another."

I got up and walked away. He followed.

After a while, I said softly, "I never want her dead." I paused. "Alive and safe in another life, perhaps." I squatted at the base of a tree and flicked at the moss growing there with the tip of my knife.

"And what of your life then?" His cap was smothering his sandy hair which made his green eyes all the more brighter in his face.

"I am attracted to another, but she is spoken for. Yet my father mentioned this might change."

He shook his head. "You cannot think of this other woman!" His cheeks flushed crimson. "What of chastity and what of your promise to Luscinda?"

"It is easy to say," I said sadly, "but hard to do. Wait until you feel the lurch in your loins that you feel when you see, or even glance at, a bare ankle or creamy crescent of a breast, and you will see how difficult it is to deny."

"Yet you do," he cried.

I smiled. "Yes, so far I have." I remembered Miralda's breasts at my chest and how Sancho interrupted us just in time.

He looked into my eyes and said impetuously, "I know you will be true to her, even if you wait a lifetime, for she is your beloved and you are her knight. Pray for it."

That was my intention, on that day anyway.

ᔆᦢ

Yet it was not long before I spent an afternoon, during a stretch traveling between towns, remembering the first time Patrecia awoke my interest. My father and I were in Seville staying with the Bonheurs. I was fourteen and Patrecia was thirteen, and as we often did when I was visiting, she and I walked to the Guadalquivir River to look for shells. I was thinking to add one to Luscinda's keepsake bag. A blue shell

---

* A trencher (plate) was sometimes made of a slice of old bread.

was what she wanted. I did not know if such a shell existed.

At the river's edge, I walked by the water, and Patrecia sat with her drawing paper and pencil. When I came back to her, she was sketching a nearby sandpiper. The drawing was well-shaded and lifelike. We sat on the sand talking. I noticed the curve of her ankle, without serious complication, merely noting how a woman's foot was smaller and more delicate than a man's. But when we were ready to leave, I stood above her to help her. It was then I saw a flash of her full breast. At thirteen she was a woman.

I found I could scarcely move or walk. I had to sit down to hide my state. And the pain! Oh, yes, the tightness, the fullness, the stiffness. It scared me so badly it went away, at least long enough for us to walk back.

And then there was the kissing game. I saw the others doing it, and when it was Patrecia's turn, I was the one to kiss. She whispered; a wisp of it echoed in my ear. "It's only a game. We will not tell Fernando and Luscinda." She shrugged off the kiss, but it left me whirling, unable to think or move for what seemed a long time, though the game continued. No one seemed to notice I was daft and blank and had to leave. It was good that on the morrow my father and I left for home.

We rode in the carriage, our horses tied to the back. He said, "I heard Patrecia and her friends were interrupted playing the kissing game." A smile played at the corners of his mouth.

That must have happened after I left.

"Her mother thought it was scandalous and dangerous at your age to be playing these games." He shrugged. "Yet in a group." He waved a hand to show it was a minor offense.

"Did you play them, Father?" I asked, curious.

He put his thick finger to his mouth. "Ah, yes, but not at parties." He laughed, his baritone filled the carriage. "Or when other people were around."

"With Mother?" I wasn't sure I wanted to know the answer.

"Before your mother and I were married," he went on to say, "I was available to help the maidens satisfy their wayward lusts." He smiled at a long-ago memory. He then told me the danger of disease and that I should never pay to woo a lady, for those who wanted money were more questionable women, and in my position, there were plenty who would be honored to satisfy my urges.

"Father!" I cried, not believing my ears. "What of chastity? What of the teachings of the church?" I asked. "How we must always be mindful of our weak flesh."

He nodded. His thick neck strained his collar. "Moderation," he said. "Our weak flesh wants it; do not give in all the time. That is all they are saying. A few times a week."

I called for the carriage to stop, and I rode Beleza the rest of the way. If this was what my father had to say, I did not want to hear it. I wanted more of tenderness, of love, of constancy.

Even though my second mind caught my attention most of that year, in my heart I desired that chastity be my way of life. And still do. I want one love for life, a love that will be my companion, sharing everything with me and me alone. I want that love to be Luscinda as I always thought it would be. I wish she were here and I wish I knew if it was to be she.

৯৹ ৫

In mid-autumn, several months after my father's last visit, Sancho and I happened on a local tournament, first signaled by a string of red, yellow, and blue triangular flags strung high across the road. Then we saw a field of horses grazing on the last of summer's grass, and also a camp of tents of varied sizes. My father's colors and Don Marco's were easily spied from the road.

Before we reached the tents, Fernando hailed us and took us to his father and mine. My father and Don Marco clapped me heartily on the back and welcomed me. They tried to send Sancho to stay with the servants, but I said he and I would stay near my father's tent.

Before supper, Fernando talked lifelessly of his betrothal to Patrecia that would end in marriage—but not until he was ready, he declared.

My heart sank. My father had not worked on his suggestion of shuffling the marriage partners a different way. "You do not seem contented in this arrangement."

Fernando's dark fathomless eyes met mine. "You would never understand." His voice was flat and hopeless.

"Do you love another?" If that were the reason, I thought, I might understand.

He stared at Sosiego, sitting next to Sancho, who was stirring a stew over the fire. "You have been traveling with a wolf."

"You had a pet fox, Salvar, once. It should not seem so odd to you."

He smiled slightly and shook his head. "I am too like the fox, too like that wolf." I waited for his explanation.

"I appear civilized, even as my father, but I do wild things."

"But once you are married . . ."

He interrupted me. "No. I cannot stop." He turned to walk away. "Lucky for your boy he has that wolf."

Surely, I had not understood him. How could he intend harm to Sancho? I watched as Fernando mounted Mercury, his chestnut stallion, and rode away.

As far as his marriage to Patrecia: Even though I had never spoken to her or for her, I felt as if Patrecia were betraying me! I even thought it just, that inconstant Patrecia should have inconstant Fernando.

Right. She was no virgin. Cinda had seen Fernando and Patrecia together—in the casket room at El Escorial. Still I had spent too much time thinking of Patrecia. I had put her on some kind of pedestal, but this pedestal was not of courtly love but of lust and I had to let it go.

Later that evening, when the stars were out and the moon, round as a ducat, was high overhead, Don Marco and my father tried to convince me to come home. Don Marco told me of the many messengers he had sent around the peninsula. He said, "Christopher, believe they did their best."

"I knew her. They did not," I said. "Perhaps they saw her and didn't know it."

"Just as easily," he said, his fingers ruffling through his hair, a familiar motion. "You could be in a house, and she be upstairs or in the back. You could pass her on the road and not see her face."

My insides writhed. How well I knew this! I thought of it every day. "I must trust that God is guiding me."

"Christopher, she is gone, I fear. It has been nearly a year." Don Marco's voice was husky and his eyes filled with tears. "We do not want it to ruin your life too."

He put his hand out to touch my shoulder, but I looked away from his pain, a mirror of my own.

"I must do this until I must not do it."

CHAPTER 8

in which Donza finds her voice

OU COULD SEE a difference in the womanly develop-
ment between the other girls and me. Though I was now
taller than Carlota, my flat chest held no hint of burgeon-
ing. It was as if they were leaving me behind in some way—
even Fredrica. I could not speak of this to anyone, so I
kept my sorrow to myself.

~

Aldonza had told us to stay on our side of the hills, but in the fall while looking
for a particular plant, I ventured a bit farther and crossed over the top. I came to
a small clearing in the dense woods, and I saw the most hideous scene—a mound
of animal bones—quite high—four feet or more. A pile of haphazard bones, skulls,
even antlers. On top were three carcasses in wretched decomposition covered with
flies, some writhing with maggots, though the bones were mostly picked clean
by the wretched scavengers, which had scurried away when I came upon them.
Dancing in the breeze from a nearby tree were blue satin ribbons, frayed and dirty.
The smell was too dense—suffocating, atrocious—and I gagged before I turned and
walked away.

I remembered the day Fredrica had said to me, "I like killing." I remembered
how her russet hair had been pulled back from her face, making her black eyes
appear all the larger.

How long had it taken her to kill these animals? And did she waste their parts?
What of the skins? I thought of the cold nights during this past winter. A fur cov-
erlet or two would have been welcome in our chilly little loft.

How angry would a person have to be to be so purposely wasteful? Or was it
something else? As always, with Fredrica, my mind would not stretch as far as flawless evil; I only saw her as less good, less kind. And more deceitful.

I left and only occasionally remembered I had ever been there, for I would not give Fredrica the power to disturb our peaceful existence; forgetting was the better way.

∽∂∝

"Donza! Wake up!" It was Carlota. Shaking me. Awake. "You were talking!" She was leaning over me, her hand on my arm. I heard Aldonza coming up the ladder.

Carlota looked at me wide-eyed, her mouth in a perfect "O." She grabbed my hands and said, "Donza! You talked."

I was only half awake, and I said in earnest, "You must save the fox! Now!"

"Fox?" Carlota questioned.

Confused, I looked around the loft.

"What is it?" Aldonza called. She sounded alarmed.

From below, Lorenzo asked, "What is the yelling about?" His voice was gruff, from sleep, not anger.

Fredrica, beside me on the mattress, stirred and rubbed her eyes. "Mmmffff," she said, coming out of a deep sleep.

Aldonza's head appeared at the top of the ladder. "Momma," Carlota cried. "Donza said, 'Salvar! Save him!' She can talk!" The little clicking sound, which sometimes accompanied her breathing, punctuated the words. "Who is Salvar?" Carlota asked.

But her questions got lost in the discovery of my voice. My hand flew to my mouth. "Hmm," I said. I felt my throat, my lips, vibrate. "Yes," I said simply—it seemed natural.

I remembered: I had been dreaming that Fredrica was holding her hand over a little fox's mouth, as if trying to smother him. And there was a boy, whose eyes were dark and fathomless like Fredrica's, who wanted to save the fox. I rubbed my nose. I needed to clear my head. Had it been a dream? Or a memory? Or some mixture of the two?

Aldonza was in the little loft; she had to crouch under the low ceiling. Lorenzo's head appeared at the top of the ladder.

I cleared my throat and said, "Momma." I looked at Lorenzo: "Poppa." That's how I thought of them.

Aldonza swooped onto the mattress and hugged me. Lorenzo laughed and said, "Now that was worth a trip up this rickety ladder."

Fredrica pulled away and sat against the wall, while Carlota held my hand and asked, "Why haven't you talked before now?"

I shrugged because I could not explain why I had not spoken or why it was I spoke this night. I did not understand that there were moments, and through my dreams, when my past reached a hand into my present and touched me.

Carlota hugged me, and I hugged her back—sister to sister.

"What is your name?" Aldonza asked. "Where did you come from?"

"The only name I know is Donza," I said. "I remember coming here in a cart."

"You must remember something," she said earnestly.

"No," I said easily. "I like it here."

Aldonza smiled; her eyes filled with tears. She patted my cheek, gave us each a hug, and said we would talk more in the morning.

But Carlota, Fredrica, and I whispered for a while. I wanted to talk about Meta and Enrique. Would they get married? When would we become aunts? Soon we quieted and went to sleep, but that was only the first of many times we lay on our mattress and talked, though mostly they listened because I discovered I liked to weave stories of dragons and knights and castles and princesses—and they liked to hear my fantastic adventures and no one ever asked why I knew about kings and nobility and castles or knights.

The next morning I felt particularly light and airy as if I might fly from the loft instead of climbing down the ladder. I looked at Carlota and Fredrica, still asleep, and whispered, *sisters.*

They were different, my sisters. Fredrica's creamy skin and russet hair promised beauty and kindness, while Carlota, her skin gray next to Fredrica, her mouth open for ease of breathing, appeared as if she would be querulous, unhappy. I thought of the word *transparent.* To look at Aldonza one rightly thought *fair, compassionate*, or Lorenzo, *intelligent, creative*, yet with these two sisters—one could not judge by appearance.

Downstairs Aldonza smiled warmly at me. She was kneading bread that we would have for supper. Lorenzo was at the fireplace scooping porridge from the pot. He handed me a bowl, and I poured a bit of milk into mine and his. He nodded his thanks then scratched his broad flat nose. I noticed, as I had the very first time I saw him, the small, deep scar on his temple.

I pointed. "How did you get that scar?" I asked, feeling the sounds tickle my throat.

"In a fight," he replied. "Before I met Aldonza, I was a raucous lad."

Aldonza met his eyes and together they smiled. She knew of his past but accepted all. I wondered if Fredrica's odd ways came from this extinguished part of Lorenzo. I felt hopeful that she might outgrow it too.

Meta, who had slept through the discovery of my voice, came in, and Aldonza and I sang a silly country song. Meta's face broadened in a grin, her eyes bright in her face. "Donza, you can sing!"

"I can talk," I said proudly. "Would you braid my hair like yours?" I could now find out the things I had been curious about!

She hugged me.

Our day was full of singing and celebration for my newfound voice. It sounded mellow, even musical, to me, and I tried to decide which bird I sounded like, the brown and spotted thrush, a warbling finch, a reddish nightingale, or a skylark. And I wanted to believe it was all of them, for how could my voice be more lovely than that?

The next day, Fredrica came to me. Instead of the dark demeanor she usually saved for my private audiences with her, she flashed her dimpled smile and asked in a confidential voice, "Are you going to tell?" She did not say what she was afraid I was going to tell.

I wanted to protect my family from Fredrica more than I wanted to tell, and if I told, would I not have to ask Aldonza if she'd ever thought I was from the devil?

I did not answer Fredrica.

"They wouldn't believe you," she said with conviction, touching one of her dimples as if to say the outer Fredrica was who everyone knew, not the inner.

I raised my eyebrows as if to say, "Are you sure?" Still I did not speak. I thought of the pile of bones in the little clearing over the hill marked by my old hair ribbons.

She walked away.

The lives of these simple farming people were dictated by the whims of the weather, the whims of God himself, and like farmers everywhere, they simply accepted what came their way. My beginning to talk was little fish in their pot, and by the new year, everyone forgot I had ever been mute. Now Fredrica seldom sought me out for company or tricks (though there was one on Father Jude that I was happy about). She spent even more time with Ana's son Julio.

CHAPTER 9

in which Christopher returns home without solace

HE DAY I stopped. The quest of house to house and village to village, of seeking orphans to help and maidens to save, ended. I lost my squire. Sancho was dead. Sometimes I got confused and thought it was Cinda who was dead and that my anguish of not knowing was over. And then I remember, no, it was Sancho, whose blood ran from mouth, nose, and ears.

After we had camped by a stream, I rode to a nearby village for supplies. He was going to fish for supper. When I returned to our camp, the first thing I saw was bloody Sosiego, panting, two arrows sticking out of him.

I jumped from my saddle. "Sancho! Sancho!" I cried, running to find him. There, on the ground thirty feet from me, was his naked body. His back, the old scars still evident, and his legs were bloody and muddy.

A wail came from low in my gut, and I rushed to turn him over. How can I tell this now? Sancho was a girl. Sancha. And she was dead. And badly used.

How had this happened? How had I not noticed that over the months she matured from a young boy into a young woman? How could our eyes deceive us so? Did they only see what our minds told us we are supposed to see? Was reality only what we believed to be true?

My ignorance cost her her life and cost me the dearest squire and friend a knight could have. Her aspirations in this quest had been my mind's inspiration. She grew me up from a green lad who took nobility and pat Honor for granted and taught me to think and see things from a wider view.

I did not even know where to find her family to tell them of their daughter. They would live with uncertainty, even as we did for Cinda. Even a father who beat and scarred his daughter. Even in him there must have been some good—did he remember how he galloped her on his back?—that made him miss her and want to know. And the red-haired mother who knew enough to heal all my bodily aches and pains (but not my heart), surely she would want to know what happened to her sixth child.

I returned to Gasparenza—home. Everyone was glad to see me, but I could barely talk to them. No one but Frondo asked of Sancho. Was this peasant child, the one who served me so well for many months, so anonymous to my family?

How very odd I must have seemed to them! Melancholy tied my tongue. I slept and slept and slept. Sosiego rarely left my side, which was just as well, as most were afraid of him.

As with when I broke my leg, I found wine numbed the pain, and Solariego wine was the best. Yes, the wine of Cinda's family: her father's, Don Marco's, vineyards. It gave me a strange connection to her. As if she were comforting me, even though her absence has brought on so much pain and now a death—or was it another death? Still, we did not know if Cinda lived.

Yet was there enough wine to deaden this pain? No. Enough to take the press of pain away? Perhaps.

I betrayed Sancha and she betrayed me. Not knowing she was a she, I left her unguarded in the woods. How careless! My virgin to protect—what kind of knight am I? Yet I did not know!

She, knowing I would be gone awhile, went bathing. They saw her there and she, without a weapon. They dragged her from the stream and held her down and beat and raped her. The three of them.

I want to forget what I saw and what I did afterwards.

Only a week before her death, Sancho confessed to me he'd run away from home. I was so angry. "You know what torture not knowing has been to me, to Cinda's family. How could you do this to your own?"

How green I was, only just beaten up by ruffians, not expecting more betrayal on the way to Santiago de Compostela! Then I had let this youngster tell me he would fix it with his parents. Oh, so much for me to learn, and I had, but not enough. Not yet. The truth might have saved this life, this life so precious to me.

That night when he told me he had deserted his family, I scolded him and he lowered his green eyes, and kneeling at my feet, begged, "Please don't send me home. I want to set the world a-right with better things."

I laughed.

The hapless rogue. A knight of chivalry at heart. A woman's soul.

———

My family grew impatient with my melancholic humor.* My mother came to say, "Come to Mass with me. You must act like the knight that you are. It is time to move on from Luscinda."

I obeyed. I went half dressed. My mother would not look at me. Nor my father. But he told me later, "You must act like my heir. It has been over a year and I will have no more of this."

They thought my actions were because of Cinda, but there was more. They were cruel to expect me to forget my loyalty to Cinda and to Sancha.

It was Lent. My mother, my determined mother, now sent Brother Diego from the nearby monastery to visit me.

"Don Christopher," the monk said, as he stood, tall and thin, by my window. "It is not fitting that a young man of your station lie in bed till noon and be intemperate with wine," he said. "Everyone has painful occurrences in their life. You. Must. Rally."

I groaned but rose from my bed and sat in a chair. Sosiego licked my hand that was resting on my knee.

Ignoring the wolf, Brother Diego sat on a nearby stool. He ran his fingers through his short dark curls. "Christopher," he said. "Everything I said, I was told to say by your parents. But those are not the words I would choose to say to you." His voice was gentle.

"I was a good person but God turned his back on me," I said. "I pray every day. Why does he hate me so?" My head in my hands, I slithered to the floor.

"Christopher, I have heard of your search for Luscinda." He shifted his weight in the chair. "Your devotion is admirable. Absolutely." He crossed his arms and looked casually at me. "But I am wondering if this behavior is from some other circumstance." The monk had large brown eyes that seemed to slant downward, giving him a look of perpetual sadness.

I nodded. I knelt beside him. Overwhelmed at the relief of being asked to talk of my peasant friend, my goodly squire, and my shortcomings, my inability to save her from harm, the words tumbled from my mouth.

I told of finding Sancho/Sancha. How I took the cord with the shell from Santiago de Compostela from her neck and put it around my own. And how, after I buried her body and marked her grave with rocks, I cut the arrows from Sosiego's shoulder. I sewed Sosiego's wounds, even as I had seen Sancha sew wounds. I put the weak wolf on a sled behind Beleza, even as Sancha had put me on a sled when I broke my leg. And taking everything, I tracked down the men who killed my friend.

---

* It was thought the four humors (sanguine, phlegmatic, choleric, melancholic) controlled body functions and governed a person's temperament.

It was before dusk when I smelled their stew and heard them. I stopped before they would see me and left the animals. Fully armed, I sneaked toward their camp. The three men sat around the fire and spoke of their recent attack on a virginal girl they discovered bathing in a stream. And each ravished her while the others held her down for she was a fighter.

I listened long enough to feel the anger push my sadness out and fitting an arrow in my bow, I sent it flying to the heart of one of the men. Quickly I sent another and wounded the second man, sending him backward and down.

I jumped to the front then, sword and dagger in hand, and the third met me sword for sword. I hacked at him until he fell. I felt the whiz of an arrow by my ear and turned to see the wounded man take aim again, but Sosiego saved my life. He crawled to help me avenge his mistress's death. Somehow he had managed to lunge at the man, making him miss. With my dagger, I killed him. I cut their bloody penises from their bodies and left all parts there for carrion.

At the memory, my stomach heaved and expelled all contents. The blessed monk held me, and I cried until I had no more tears, and then he ordered for me a bath and let me sleep.

ॐ

After that I was better, and I suppose I felt better, but I could not measure myself against the carnage I had perpetrated, no matter the reason, and only wanted to forget. About a week after the outpouring of my story, I visited Brother Diego. We sat on benches and talked. I tried to thank him for listening to me, and he said, "Christopher, I am a weak man, who seeks the good in everyone. I know that much goes on in this world that is not good, and we need each other to see our way through it." He smiled gently, his sad eyes brightened.

"I cannot forgive these men, and I cannot forgive me," I said. "I should have been more careful of her."

"Do you speak of Sancha or Luscinda?" he asked.

"Both." The answer was simple, my failures overwhelming. "I was not careful of them."

"How could you have been more careful of Luscinda?" he asked, leaning back on his bench and laying his arm across the top of it.

"If I had not had my mind on other . . . another woman, perhaps, I would have been more aware of what her life was like. Whatever it was that made her run away."

The monk shook his head. He put his elbows on his knees and leaned toward me. "There was nothing you could have done. It is the same with Sancha," he said in earnest. "You must pray for God to help you forgive yourself."

"I . . . my actions . . ." Before me, I saw three bloody men. Parts of them tossed aside. "That was not me."

"Your noble anger took over."

"There was nothing noble about such . . . viciousness." I burned with shame of wrong, my most horribly wrong, action. "Those base men did unspeakable things. And so did I. I knew better."

The monk was silent for a moment. "There is no crime so heinous that God cannot forgive."

"How could he forgive *them?*" I nearly shouted in my anger, then I nearly whispered, "How could he forgive me?"

"And there is no sinner so depraved that should not confidently hope for pardon, if they sincerely repent."

"I so regret what I have done," I said, the anguish twisting my insides.

"Accept that you are a weak man," he said. "Then let God do the work of forgiveness and love." He got up and we walked back. He was taller than I, and it was easy to think of him as my mentor.

I promised I would think on it, but I was reluctant to see myself as weak. I wanted to find my noble roots and cement myself in right action. I would begin going to Mass. I would resolve to never again allow myself to be pushed over the line of what is right. I would face my pain, not look to wine for comfort.

I willed the horrific scene from my mind, and in hopes of figuring out my uncertain future, I thought on memories of Cinda.

The last time I saw her was the day King Philip knighted me. My father hosted a grand celebration, though the evening was not all happiness, but full of unwelcome news and uncomfortable talk.

Cinda wore a sapphire dress, the color of her eyes, which sparkled, not with humor, but with righteousness in anger at Fernando who she had seen in the royal casket room making love to Patrecia—most unwelcome news to me!

With hands on her hips, she declared, "Patrecia says Fernando has promised to marry her soon, but he told me he will not!"

I was silent and could not look at her.

She asked, "Are you angry with me? For telling you."

"Patrecia deserves better." My chest was tight. *And shouldn't Patrecia have acted better?* I turned to Cinda. "I am sorry you were there. I think of you as my innocent Cinda." I took her hand in mine.

"Do not think of me as innocent," she said grimly.

"No?" I was surprised at her vehemence. "Then . . . Then I won't." I wanted to lighten our talk and so I laughed and hugged her. "We can do nothing about

Fernando's lies," I said slowly. "We can only think of ourselves." I tweaked her nose, my child wife, and I saw that the usual brightness in her eyes was still gone.

Then she asked, "Would you bed with someone before we are together?"

I put my hand to my heart. "Cinda, what a question!" I was stricken. "I am a true knight in my belief of faithfulness and chastity. No matter the pull of the outside world, I would go to a monastery first."

She smiled and we stood silently on the balcony, watching the dancers below make a symmetrical design of swaying skirts as the couples swirled in unison around the floor.

"I want you to be able to tell me anything," I said. "Come to me and we will talk it through."

The musicians began a new tune. A *pavaniglia*. She smiled at me and curtseyed. "May I have a dance with you, Sir Christopher?" And that was our last dance.

Oh, I thought, to go back to the time that fornication or talk of it was the worst thing. I was not the man I thought I was. I was worse than an animal, for they do not kill indiscriminately. There are laws.

As a duke's son I would not be punished for what I did to three common men. And the rationale would be they killed my servant, nothing about the unspeakable treatment of her.

Yet what I did was unspeakable. Was I no better than they? Or was it justification enough that I punished them for what the law wouldn't, for what they did to Sancha?

Oh, what kind of world is this? What kind of man am I?

CHAPTER 10

in which Donza sees Alonso Quesano, who is not yet Don Quixote

NE SUMMER FEAST day my path crossed that of Alonso Quesano, the future Don Quixote. The parish met after Mass on the village green, and colorful cloths were spread over the ground. While the women put out the food to share among families, the children played games, which included singing games, tossing metal balls for distance, and spinning tops.

After we ate, I climbed the new bell tower. I lay on my back and watched the clouds, as fluffy and billowy as freshly sheared wool, float through the sky. I heard voices at the bottom of the tower. I rolled over to see who it was: Master Nicolás, the barber-surgeon, and Alonso Quesano, who was dressed all in black. I had not seen him since my first day in Toboso; he and his niece had been in the shop when Lorenzo had stopped for goods and discovered me.

"It was good to hear our old friend Father Pero preach today," Señor Quesano said to Master Nicolás. "A good topic."

"Oh?" The barber's tone implied he didn't think much of it. The topic had been adultery. "Remember, my friend, that women are imperfect creatures, and we have to remove the obstacles in virtue's way, so they can achieve the perfection they lack."

I could see Señor Quesano straighten up, as if affronted. "But hold, friend, I cannot agree with you," he said. "There is no gem in the whole world worth as much as a chaste and honest woman, for surely women are the most beautiful and perfect creatures on God's earth. And were I to find the one—and I have seen her—whom I considered the most beautiful, I would go to the ends of the earth for her. I would fight for her. I would defend her against any adversary."

"My good friend," the barber said in good humor. "I think that the right pretty leg and smile would set your old heart a-beating and turn the whiskers on your chin black again."

Señor Quesano nodded. "One only needs something to live for, be it a cause or a woman, to put passion in one's life." The men's voices grew faint as they moved away.

I climbed down. It was windy, and being mindful of the sermon, I hoped that I did not show too much leg as I descended.

I found Meta and Antonia, Señor Quesano's niece, sitting by themselves under a maple tree making clover chains. I lay on my side on the grass beside Meta, facing them.

Antonia, a plain girl with straight, thin brown hair, said to Meta, "But why do you not come to school? Surely you want to learn to read."

"We have no books." Meta's braids wavered in the afternoon breeze.

"We've got dozens of books," Antonia said. "My uncle reads them by the cartload." None of us suspected these books would cause the frail Señor Quesano to one day sally forth as Don Quixote seeking adventures of a knight errant.

Antonia lowered her voice. "And what of the books Father Pero mentioned?" Picking another clover, she carefully knotted it to her chain.

"That have pictures of immodestly dressed women, you mean?" Meta asked. She finished a long chain. She looped it double around her neck.

Antonia nodded. "What do you think it does to men?"

"Makes them want to be with a woman, I guess," Meta said, starting on another chain.

Antonia leaned toward Meta. "I have heard there's an ancient book that shows men and women *together* in many different ways."

"How many could there be?" Meta asked, looping a clover stem around her finger.

"Dozens, I think."

Meta laughed. "I don't think so."

My throat closed, making it hard for me to breathe. I felt lightheaded. I turned my thoughts away from their conversation and let my fingers travel through the clover. *The flowers of clover need to be picked in late spring and early fall. They are used for coughs, bronchitis, skin rashes.* Meta reached out and set a circlet of purple clover on my head. She smiled at me and touched my cheek. *To help you sleep, and . . .* To the list I added necklaces, bracelets, and crowns.

"Will you be glad when I marry and leave home?" Meta asked, for marriage with Enrique was often on her mind.

"I will be glad for you," I said. "But I will miss you."

Without a word, Meta took the clover necklace from her neck and put it around mine.

———

That night I dreamed of an eagle. He soared high above, each wing feather stretched wide. He was strong and noble in the bright sky, but day became night and the regal bird dove toward me. As he came closer, he turned into a falcon—or was it a vulture?—with a hooked beak and swooped upon me, smothering me. I felt the weight upon my chest . . . I awoke, not talking, not screaming, but sweating and feeling frightened. I snuggled closer to Carlota, finding her familiar raspy breathing a comfort, and I thought of as many different ways to make salt pork as I could until I fell asleep.

Fall 1585

Meta married Enrique Traduccia. We made her a white velvet gown trimmed in beads—from the clothing in my satchel. Each of us had a new dress and even Lorenzo had new clothing. His hair glossed and tamed. His unruly red beard was trimmed in a spade, a very fashionable style for men (Master Nicolás, the barber-surgeon said).

The new couple moved into a little cottage on the neighboring Traduccia farm.

"She is only the first of my little chicks that will leave me," Aldonza said to me the day after the wedding. "I do hope she'll be happy."

I said, "But they're in love."

"Ah," Aldonza replied, "if that were all there was to it."

Soon after the wedding we got a letter—the first one since I lived there. Aldonza and I were in the yard grinding millet when Lorenzo brought it from town. Aldonza dangled it from two fingers and stared at it as it shimmered in the air. I could not stop myself: I took it from her, broke the seal, and opened the letter. Aldonza and Lorenzo glanced at each other.

"Who is it from?" They asked together, their voices timid but eager.

I read from the bottom of the page. "Margret Nogales Gautier."

"My sister." Slowly Aldonza's lips parted in a grin.

I was more surprised to find she had a sister, it seemed, than they were surprised that I could read.

"'Aldonza,'" I read, "'I hope this letter finds you well. I am without home and family. I hope to stay with you for a while. I will be there by year's end.'"

Aldonza took me by the hands and danced me around the yard. Lorenzo's deep laughter sprinkled the air around us. I was breathless by the time we stopped. Aldonza sat on the grass and was fanning herself with her apron when Fredrica and Carlota joined us.

"What is it, Momma?" Carlota asked, then made the little click noise in her throat that she often made when her breathing was difficult.

"Your Aunt Margret is coming to visit," Lorenzo said with enthusiasm.

Carlota and Fredrica cried, "Who!?"

"My sister," Aldonza said and told us about her. Margret was many years older than Aldonza. When Aldonza was three, Margret had married and left Spain, banished by her father and never to be heard of again. At least that was what Aldonza thought. Margret had stayed in touch with a neighbor and knew how to find Aldonza.

With the petite Margret came sunshine. She was quick and efficient; her tiny body seemed to bend any way it needed to accomplish a task. She wore her gray hair in an austere roll at her neck, but that could not hide that she was a person who smiled inside and out.

She was welcomed into the home, even as I had been. Now in the evenings, Lorenzo brought his woodcarving into the house, where the women sat quietly and sewed. Margret entertained us with stories of her life.

She had married a rogue, a dashing Frenchman Laurent Gautier, part gypsy, who had charmed her away from her family and had taken her on a merry ride of ups and downs. He had schemed their way across Europe and back several times. In Venice, they were welcomed as guests of the wealthy Cornaro family on a forged introduction from the pope!

Laurent was dead now and that did not stop Margret from speaking ill of him, though she loved him, I could tell. Each line of her face, each gray hair on her head, she said, was put there by a worry from her husband. "I am ready to settle into a normal life." She showed us a stiletto and a dagger, both weapons of defense that she had needed close at hand when Laurent was with her. Now she put them away, saying she never wanted to see them again.

She told us of dancing with the royalty of France: "We merely dressed as nobility—dressed beautifully—and we were never questioned. We could go to the theater without paying. Go anywhere. For nobility, it is easy."

In spite of her cheery disposition, Margret was sickly. From the first day, Aldonza plied Margret with herbal drinks. Within a few weeks, her color was better. She declared Aldonza needed to sell her remedies at Señor González's store.

Though Margret was small—I was a head taller—her presence was commanding. When she breezed in, you paid attention to her.

∽∾

Now I dreamed of a meadow with yellow flowers. A small girl, with auburn hair and amber eyes, skipped and hopped with me and made me laugh. She counted birds and sang songs and talked in a language I did not know. And always at the end of the dream, she became a songbird and flew up into a white-blossomed pear tree.

 барабан

One morning when Carlota was feeling poorly, Margret helped me hoe the vegetables. She was singing a song in French, and I began singing it with her. She sang another, and I knew it too.

She was dumbfounded. She shaded her face with her arm and looked up at me. In French, she asked, "Which would you rather hoe next, the asparagus or the carrots?"

I pointed to the feathery topped vegetables. "The carrots," I replied in French. I scarcely realized what I had done. It seemed natural to me—to talk back to her as she had spoken to me.

She knew Italian. Again I responded to her.

"But how do you know these languages?" she asked, her voice thin with surprise.

I shrugged.

She brushed moist wisps of hair from her forehead. In a low, serious voice, she said, "You know, Donza, that speaking tongues you have not been taught is a sign of the Devil."

The sun suddenly became warmer; the hoe dropped from my hands. "No, Margret." I said, but it was difficult to speak, my breath was gone. Fredrica had said I was from the devil too, but I could not ignore it so easily from Margret.

My hands shook as I picked up my hoe. *What of this past I have forgotten?* It did not seem I was from the Devil, but I did not *know*—the pages of my past were as blank as they had been.

Margret reached up and put her hand on my cheek. "I do not believe you are from the Devil, Donza, but others will," she said kindly. "Do you understand?"

I understood that I was not to speak in strange languages. Soon my breathing came more naturally, and the hoes skritched against the dirt and pebbles. I watched a worm curl, uncurl, and burrow again into the soil.

Margret's back was to me. Softly, she said, "Aldonza told me you can read." She paused. "And you have no idea how you know these things." She leaned on her hoe. I paused too and sat on the warm dirt. Reaching over, I pulled a weed and tossed it several rows away.

"I must have been taught," I said. I thought of the knife tossing, the ease of accuracy. And the cooking, baking, and sewing. I had arrived complete, it seemed, like Aphrodite rising from the sea. What manner of family (or demon) had so well prepared me for life?

Margret squatted beside me, putting her hand on my arm. "Of course you were taught." She laughed, tiny wrinkles around her eyes relaxed into sunbursts. "But by whom? Where? Why?"

I did not answer for I could not, and soon she stopped asking, but sometimes when we were working away from the others, we sang little songs she taught me or songs I knew in the other languages. One day I sang a song in a language she did not know. "I think it is Dutch," she said. "Or German. They sound alike."

That was four languages I knew. Were there others? I stopped myself from wondering. I only wanted to be in this life.

ɔɑ

After that when I dreamed of the little amber-eyed girl, I understood her songs, and when she became the songbird, the noble eagle came and flew overhead.

Spring 1586

Aldonza heard that the bishop would be in Toboso to do confirmations. She and Lorenzo, Fredrica, Carlota, and I went to church on Pentecost, the morning of the Confirmation. Father Jude, in the presence of the bishop of Toledo, said, "I do not think Donza is ready. We do not even know if she's been baptized."

I held my breath. Would he suggest I was from the Devil?

Lorenzo's eyes got bigger. "Oh, but surely she has been baptized. She has a rosary." He looked at me. "Show them the rosary, Donza."

I took out the blue-beaded rosary. The bishop, who was the tallest and thinnest man I had ever seen, took it and examined it. "Exquisite. Where would she have come by it?"

"I found her in my cart one day, your grace."

The bishop asked, "Donza, can you tell me where you got such a beautiful rosary?"

I shook my head and curtseyed.

Father Jude's ears turned red. "She's missing some of her wits." His right eye bulged a little more than his left.

Slowly, I let out my breath—he had not changed his first impression of me—I was forever an idiot to him, yet, thankfully, not a child of the Devil.

The bishop had kindly gray eyes. "I think her wits are intact." He gently touched my cheek with the palm of his hand. Looking directly at Father Jude, he said. "We will confirm her."

Now the scrawny priest's entire face turned red, especially his nose, but he was silent.

The bishop handed me the rosary. "If you ever want to sell it, I know a man who would buy it. A marquis, in Madrid."

I tucked the rosary away. I couldn't imagine selling it. I used it every evening when our family kneeled together for prayers.

∽ ⌐

Margret said, "Donza, do you know that Fredrica is jealous of you?"

My eyes widened and I shook my head. "But why would she be?"

"You are beautiful, you know."

"But so is Fredrica." I thought of her pretty smile—if only she would meet people's eyes.

"Fredrica is a restless soul and sometimes cannot help but do . . . hurtful things."

I nodded. "I will not let her hurt us."

Margret shook her head. "Donza, you must be careful. You do not see her as she is."

"She is better now that you are here."

Margret took me by the shoulders to emphasize her words. "She has not changed—she knows I understand her. She is more careful."

I hugged Margret. I would not listen to her for I believed I knew well enough what Fredrica could do.

But Margret was not content to only speak to me of Fredrica's ways. She tried to get Aldonza's attention.

"Where does Fredrica go when she is gone half a day?" Margret asked Aldonza one morning when we were hanging out laundry.

"Fishing with Julio, or checking her traps," Aldonza said easily. "She's never gone very long."

"Yesterday she was gone from right after breakfast to nearly dinner," Margret said.

"No," Aldonza said. "You are mistaken." She had stopped and looked at Margret when she said this. Her voice was blunt. She turned from Margret and picked up a wet skirt, and snapping it first in the air, she pinned it to the line.

"Aldonza, I beg your pardon," Margret said. "Perhaps Fredrica is too much like me. Restless. Wanting excitement—yet there's more. . . ."

Aldonza's eyes were cold. "You are our guest," Aldonza said. "You must love us as we love you." She put her hands on her hips.

Her hands fluttering to her chest, Margret said, "Oh, my dear sister, I do! But love can be blind—especially a mother's love."

The angered Aldonza and the staunch Margret stood looking at each other, the younger towering over the older. But soon, Margret bowed her head and fumbled with the wet towels.

I walked away. I knew Margret was right—that there was something unnatural about Fredrica, yet I saw that Aldonza could not see it. I was confused: I loved and trusted her and Margret.

I would keep us all safe.

⁓∾

Now the eagle became the raptor-beaked falcon, swooping down and seeking his prey. From the open meadow I took the amber-eyed songbird into the forest and we hid—but the trees would dissolve like wet salt, and the falcon swooped down again. I woke up sweating and breathing hard. I did not know if he were after the ethereal songbird or me—it did not seem to matter; I was equally frightened. Above all, I wanted to protect her. I longed for the dreams to be of only her, me, and our sweet-grassed meadow.

⁓∾

Carlota had grown into her neck and her body. No longer was she gangly and awkward, but pretty. Even though her health was still fragile, the circles under her eyes were less noticeable. She had turned sixteen and Fredrica would soon be fifteen. Both had the softly rounded figures of women, unlike me who was still planes and angles. I knew that it would be easy for them to "display too much in dress," as Father Pero would say, if, indeed, we had that type of dress available.

Fredrica liked going to Parado, which was less than a mile away. I thought she saw Julio Alonso there, and she shared her dimples with him as much as she could, though as it turned out he was interested in Carlota, not Fredrica, his long-time fishing friend. After church on Sunday, Julio now brought Carlota home in his family's cart.

I was beginning to worry that I was not going to grow the curves necessary to becoming a woman. I asked Aldonza about it one day.

"Every bird grows up in time," she said. "You must not worry."

"Is there some herb I can take?" I asked shyly.

She did not laugh as I was afraid she would. She merely looked as if she were thinking about it seriously and said evenly, "None that I know of."

I was sure, then, there were not any.

In body I was not ready, but in mind I wanted to know the nature of love. I asked Margret.

She began, "I fell in love with Laurent before I even saw his face."

"How could that be?" I asked, curious to hear her story. We were baking tarts, cherry, if I remember right. She had a ribbon of flour in her hair and a powdering of it on the shoulder of her blue blouse. I was carefully stemming and pitting the cherries.

"My father sent me to the blacksmith's." She continued mixing flour, lard, and a bit of water. "It was Laurent's voice—it was melodious and deep." She added a pinch of salt. (I always added the salt before I added the water.) Margret continued, "I peeked to see the owner of this voice which vibrated all the right places in me, and from the back, I saw a well-shaped man, dressed more elegantly than I had ever seen."

I carefully sliced into a cherry, so ripe and sweet it was nearly black. "But what did he look like?" I flicked out the pit and added it to my growing pile.

"He moved like syrup," she continued. "His hips carefully followed his broad shoulders as he turned toward me. I smiled, for as I say I was already in love with his voice, his body, and the way he moved." She slapped the dough on the table and deftly divided it into sections by squeezing it between her fingers. Section by section, she rolled it into a flat round of dough.

She took the bowl of cherries and added sugar. I watched as the sugar dissolved in the juice. "Yet he was sometimes full of lies for others as we plied our trade in roguery, but he never lied to me and always treated me as one would a kitten, with kindness and gentleness."

"Because he loved you?" I asked.

Margret spooned glistening cherries onto a ready dough circle. "He worked hard to live the large life he wanted us to have, but he would not work honestly to have a life like this." She looked sad and even then, tears welled up in her eyes, and she had to wipe them with her apron.

She folded the dough and crimped the edges of a pastry together before she continued. She cleared her throat. "You asked of love, and I would say, it is alchemical, something you feel that you cannot ignore, and then if, in time, you find, besides that inexplicable pull, you want to be truthful and careful with the other, then that is a devoted love."

"Like Aldonza and Lorenzo."

"Yes," Margret said. "They want to stand beside each other every day and instead of hardships driving them apart, they become closer." With her small fingers, she pressed the tip of a cloth into the butter and smoothed it on a tart. "In their hearts they hope to die together, for life without each other is too grim to imagine."

"Do you wish you had died with Laurent?" I asked quietly and did not look at her, for I did not want to think of Lorenzo's and Aldonza's deaths—or hers. My knife was still now, the cherries all pitted.

With her finger under my chin, she lifted my head to look at her. "At first, I may have, but now I know of other kinds of love, that I did not know or rather, had forgotten existed. Love of sister, brother, and nieces—that is rich and satisfying too."

"What do you call that kind of love?" I asked.

"Kindred love," she said without hesitation.

And I liked that because it spoke of kinship and kindness. Three kinds of love: devoted, alchemical, and kindred. It made sense to me. Margret put the tarts in the brick oven for baking, and we looked forward to supper, when we would eat them.

That night I dreamed of a family of birds: an amber-eyed nightingale; a stiff-legged, straight-beaked grouse; a black-eyed sparrow; a silent kestrel, and a skylark. Instead of wings, the birds had hands and made a circle. Again the regal eagle guarded us. I awoke feeling loved.

Over time, the dream changed, and soon the hook-beaked falcon was back. First, it came as a high-flying bird, the setting sun throwing its huge shadow on the ground. But in time, it got closer and closer. I ran from the other birds, wanting the hunter-bird to only come after me: *I would save them.*

CHAPTER 11

in which Christopher hears more about Cinda's disappearance

N THE GROUNDS of the monastery, which was situated on land carved from Solariego and Gasparenza more than seven hundred years ago, there was the Way of the Saints, which was maintained by the sad-eyed Brother Diego. Meandering through the forest, the path was lined with saints, dozens of them, that had been made by the monks themselves. Some in marble, some in clay, some in precious metals, some carved in wood; some were small and others were life-sized or larger.

My favorite place was a grotto with a life-sized Mary, dressed in blue and seated on a humble bench. She was posed in such a way that she appeared to be listening to someone, someone who was seated on another bench about four feet in front of her. So gentle was her demeanor that I always felt safe there.

Then there was St. Benedict, who was more than eight feet tall, as were the archangels in the Archangels Cove. When we were children, our mothers took us with them, and often we waited in Archangels Cove and swam while they walked the Way of the Saints.

Only days before his wedding to Patrecia, Fernando sent me a message by his servant to meet him in the Cove. It said, "Come alone. I must tell you the truth."

His message surprised me because he seldom sought me out. I went to meet him. I arrived first and watched as he approached at a walk on Mercury, his stallion. I recalled the evening Don Marco had presented to his son the large chestnut stallion. It was on the last evening of the Grand Tournament when Cinda was five. In a little ceremony, in the courtyard of the Solariego palace, Don Marco presented Fernando with the trappings of a knight. There was a blazing fire, and the servants had set up torches all around, and the courtyard was nearly light as day.

Standing in the center of the circle, Don Marco began, "In the beginning of the world, God planned for all humankind to love and fear God." His voice was deep and solemn. "But, sadly, there came a time when Honor became less well known than cruelty, disloyalty, and falseness."

My father Don Hernando stood up and joined in the story. "Knights were chosen to set an example for the people." His deep voice bespoke his pride at being a knight.

As Don Marco and my father presented Fernando representations of the clothing which went with knighthood—a sword, hauberk, the buckler,* the gauntlets, the spurs, and other things —they continued to explain the symbolism behind each article, for as each vestment of a priest has some spiritual meaning, so did each article belonging to a knight. Fernando accepted each solemnly and without emotion.

And last from a deerskin sheath, Don Marco pulled a silver-handled knife. The blade caught the glow of a nearby torch and flashed light over the faces of the onlookers. Don Marco said, "A knife is used up close when the knight has lost his weapons. He must place his trust in God." He handed the weapon to Fernando, who took it eagerly and nearly smiled. He thrust with it from his shoulder, as if going after a mighty adversary. The knife followed a true course. The duke continued, "A knight seeks Honor and if he loses his Honor, it is better for him to be dead than live with dishonor." I heard the women gasp at the harsh words.

Don Marco, then, nodded to a servant, who disappeared. When he returned, he was leading a large chestnut stallion. Everyone clapped. I could hear Doña Isabella murmuring.

Fernando smiled broadly. "I will name him Red Devil." Fernando's dark eyes flashed with pleasure, as he smoothed his hand over the flank of the horse. "He will take me as fast as the devil anywhere I want to go."

"Oh no, 'Nando," Doña Isabella cried, "you must not invoke the devil!"

"Then I shall call him Mercury."

The little ceremony was over, and Fernando fingered his dagger happily and helped the servant lead his horse to the stable.

About thirty feet from me, Fernando dismounted from Mercury. Fernando was dark with Don Marco's wavy and unruly hair, which was cut short to his collar. He had black eyes and though he was small-framed, one recognized him as a duke's son because of his noble demeanor. He seldom smiled; he and I were constitutionally different as I tended toward sanguine and he tended to choleric.

"Because of me Cinda ran away," he said. His eyes were dark pits in his narrowed face.

"To see me?" I asked, because nearly every version of my imagining of her running away was because she was coming to seek my counsel, just as we had agreed the last time we were together.

* Hauberk: a long tunic, usually made of chain mail; buckler: a small round shield

"Perhaps she came to find you. I don't know." The muscles on his neck were tight; his hands were fisted by his sides.

"Why haven't you told me before?" He'd known something all along. I felt the bile rise in me.

"She had seen me in the casket room with Feliciana and Patrecia."

(Cinda, you only told me of Patrecia!) "You were with both of them! Sisters!"

He swaggered a bit. "About an hour apart."

"You dog!" I cried and drew my rapier against him, but he would not fight. He raised his arms and would have walked into my weapon if I had not withdrawn it.

"I would end my own life," Fernando said. "But I am a coward. I thought if I told you everything, you would . . ."

He hoped to anger me enough to kill him! Was this a test from God for me? "We must choose to do good," I said quickly. I sheathed my weapon and crossed my arms in front of me.

"It is easy for you," he said, "but it has never been for me."

I shook my head. "It is not always easy, but we must try."

"I cannot stop myself," he said miserably.

I heard the pain in him.

"I thought you would be my friend and free me," he said, his dark eyes bleak. "A devil barks at my heels. I am *so* tired."

Those words could have come from me—I was still troubled by the tragic end of Sancha and my part in her tormentors' deaths. But I would not have said what Fernando said next.

"Killing me would be a service to so many." He sounded as if he believed what he said, and he lacked his usual bravado.

"I cannot help you. Speak to Brother Diego. He has helped me."

"God will have nothing to do with me."

"No one is so bad . . ." I began. It was not long ago that I had felt the same way.

"This is not going to work," Fernando said, as he walked to Mercury. "You will not help me."

"Wait," I called. "Is that everything? Do you know where Cinda is?"

He shook his head and galloped away.

I thought he must know something more. Cinda had not run away because of seeing Fernando in the casket room. She had recovered her good humor after talking to me about Fernando's dishonorable actions. There had to be more, but I had no expectations of getting more information from Fernando. *He had hoped that I would kill him!* Was it a sin to help someone commit suicide when that was their soul's desire? The question was too complicated for me to wrestle with. *Dear God, May Fernando and Patrecia have a happy union. May he find peace in his marriage.*

———————

Two weeks later Fernando and Patrecia formalized their union, and Patrecia moved to Solariego. A grand celebration followed, and the following morning Patrecia found a note saying Fernando had gone to Madrid on business.

"I'm sorry, Patrecia." I was sincere in my sympathy as new husbands did not go to Madrid on business. I was relieved to know my untoward feelings for her were gone, and I cared for her as I would for a sister, which she would have been were I married to Cinda.

"What can I do, Christopher?" Patrecia asked. "I had hoped he would settle in . . ."

"We must pray for him." I wondered if I could have done anything for him that would have helped. But I had my own devil tagging along with me.

Can I hide until Cinda is found?

To the monastery I will look. No, the university. As my father wishes.

CHAPTER 12

in which Donza travels to Madrid

Y DREAMS OF birds and falcons and eagles continued, and one night the wicked falcon swooped upon the amber-eyed songbird and, broken-winged, it fell from the sky to the ground. Then the falcon came after me, its feathers on my skin, attacking me, smothering me. I opened my mouth to get my breath, my much-needed breath, and feathers came pouring out of my mouth. I watched the feathers, which had been me, fly up into the sky only to fall down again on the house, making a great noise, as if it were raining pebbles.

I heard Fredrica yell, "Poppa! What is it?"

Carlotta screamed.

The noise was not in my dream. A clatter, a shaking, a trembling. We scrambled from the loft down the ladder.

Grasshoppers. Hundreds of them. Thousands of them. Clattering. Against the shutters. Coming in the slits and niches of the house. We stuffed every hole with cloth to keep them out. We went to the loft last and found dozens and dozens of them in our bed and in our clothes. Margret snatched up our sheets and stuffed them in the cracks around the window and roof. Aldonza shook out our extra clothes and clamped them away in one of Lorenzo's chests. Margret took the straw of our tick, now infested with insects, and threw it in the fire, the flames hissed and popped.

We huddled in a circle and prayed to St. Gregory to send them away; we prayed to Our Holy Mother, the Virgin Mary, to help us. We prayed to say we were sorry for whatever we had done to displease God so much. That night, in our circle, we believed we could defeat them.

But by daylight, we could see clouds of the militant insects, millions of them, swooping down on the trees, the fields, the house, marching onward. Inside or out, the armored winged beasts kept clattering, drumming, clicking; still the noise was deafening.

The leaves on the trees disappeared under their onslaught. Our entire stand of grain fell, eaten. Our entire garden. The insects invaded our fields and our sheds. Aldonza's herbs—yes, her fine collection of herbs, destroyed. Aldonza burned marigolds, which were thought to offend the pests and drive them away. But not enough marigolds existed in all of Spain to stave off these grasshoppers.

We swept buckets full of grasshoppers from the house the first day and the next; we fed the fire with hundreds of them, keeping it burning, hot as it was.

We could barely eat for whatever we prepared the army of grasshoppers attacked it. We stood around the cook pot and ate directly from it. Even as the very fabric of our lives was invaded, so were our clothes with tiny cuts and holes and foul stains. It was a consummate invasion of every minute of the entire day, our waking and sleeping—what little we could sleep.

I hated to close my eyes because I hated to open my eyes. I felt the hostile beasts crawling over me, whether they were or not, and knowing I could not endure another insect caught in my hair, I was driven to take one of Lorenzo's knives and cut it—short, shorter than a grasshopper. The constant thumping, tapping, whir and whizz, the dirty brown juice from their filthy bodies, those round insect eyes—I believed this instant was what insanity would be like, and I wanted no other glimpse of such a desolate life.

On the second day—we were exhausted and hungry. We avoided each other not believing such tiny insects could defeat us—we had failed to keep our home safe. Our farm had been pillaged and ruined, and we had been helpless to stop it.

The next morning we woke to sunshine, blue skies, and a strange stillness. The rustle, the hum, the clatter, the popping and ticking, and the noxious, disgusting multitude of hoppers was gone, though thousands of dead insect soldiers polluted the ground and stream. We still watched where we walked, expecting them to jump at us, fall on us. I felt as if they would flit against my body or on my head, at any moment, but the battle was over. The grasshoppers had moved on to greener fields, and we were faced with the barren aftermath of the war.

The taxes, the rents, and tithe to the church were still due. Our hope lay in the chest that Lorenzo was working on, but it was not finished.

We were fortunate in that the jumping beasts had not invaded our well, sheltered as it was by the windmill, so while we had little to eat, we had water. Each day, Aldonza and I went up in the hills looking for roots to eat. The grasshoppers had affected plant and animal life. Fredrica was having a hard time finding game, though she managed to get some fish.

We were eating one meal a day. At night I went to bed with a gnawing hole in my stomach. Each day at the table, I eyed everyone's food. I didn't want to; I couldn't help it. I saw Fredrica and Carlota were doing the same.

I went through the days lightheaded and empty; my hands trembled. When I was not out with Aldonza looking for food, I helped Lorenzo with the cherry chest, but it seemed far from finished. He had barely begun the carving, which was to be of mermaids and mermen. Yet the next day, the carving had progressed far more than I would have thought possible! And over the next night, another great advance was made again. Had I seen Aldonza and Lorenzo and Margret working on it together by the firelight? I could not be certain. We acted as if we were under some enchantment to make us dull-witted, but it was from lack of sleep and lack of food.

One night we all stayed up and worked on the chest, doing what we could, even if it was only to encourage Lorenzo. As the sun came up, I was buffing the last side and everyone had gone to bed, except Lorenzo, who was watching me and nodding. "Yes. Yes, rub more oil there."

The next thing I knew, I awoke on the floor next to where the chest had been, but it was gone! I jumped up and found it loaded on the cart. Lorenzo was bringing cloths to wrap it in to protect it on the trip to Seville. With every step, he dropped the carcasses of grasshoppers from the folds of the cloths. I helped him unfold them and shake them out. This day we laughed at the absurdity of having nothing in our possession that had not been invaded by the pests.

"Do you want to ride to Parado with me?" Lorenzo asked. He knew I could easily walk back. I was pleased to be offered this diversion.

Lorenzo and I climbed in the cart. I was reminded of my first ride with him. How long ago that seemed! Four years nearly. Everything had been so strange to me that day, and today everything here was familiar, yet not. The desolation made my heart ache.

Lorenzo clicked at the ox and slapped it with the reins. The cart rolled forward. When we met the stream, I looked in it. I could see a few grasshopper carcasses in the water, but it was so much clearer than a week ago. As we went up the rise, the stream got farther away, and I could imagine the grasshoppers were all gone as I could not see them anymore.

Suddenly there was a loud crack—the axle broke. The cart tilted. Lorenzo jumped. I was thrown toward the stream. The instant I hit the water I catapulted from that spot because I could see the cart, and the chest, coming down.

It seemed to happen very slowly, yet it could not have. The chest plummeted to the ground next to the stream and splintered, the pieces splashing like water. The cracking sounds echoing, echoing.

And then again with the cart, splintering, cracking, falling into the stream, barely missing me. The ox too had fallen, breaking its neck.

My back burned from where I had smacked the water, but I was unhurt. I ran quickly to Lorenzo. He lay moaning on the road, his leg broken. I could see Aldonza,

Margret, and the girls running. Lobo was barking and frantic. Someone must have been watching or the sound had been so loud . . . or maybe I had screamed.

The next day I was by the stream, picking up the pieces of our shattered hope. Lorenzo was bedridden. No part of the chest was salvageable. At least we (and our neighbors) had ox to eat for a while.

Lorenzo could do nothing but lie in bed and bemoan the fact he was laid up. Each morning and evening we knelt around his bed and said our prayers. One evening while I was holding my rosary, Margret said, right in the middle of the second mystery, "That rosary must be worth a lot of money."

Instantly, our tunnel that seemed to be getting darker, brightened.

I jumped up. "Yes," I cried. "I am certain," remembering that the tall and kindly Bishop of Toledo had said he knew a man, a marquis in Madrid, who would buy it.

As quickly as we could, we planned my journey to sell the rosary. Fredrica begged to go.

Aldonza shook her head. "One can travel faster than two."

Fredrica sat quietly for a moment. She turned to Aldonza and with a gracious smile she said, "It would be safer. For two to go."

With uncertainty, Aldonza glanced at Margret, but it was Lorenzo who decided. "Fredrica, we need you here." His deep voice was husky. "I am no help at all."

Fredrica looked at the floor. Her jaw tensed but she said nothing.

For safety I would travel as a boy (that would not be a problem). While Aldonza had been unhappy over my cut hair, she admitted my short hair would add to the boyish illusion. Margret and Aldonza worked to outfit me with the appropriate clothes. Margret was a master at these things! To sell such a piece, I must look acceptable; otherwise, it might be perceived I had stolen it.

From the satchel I had with me when I came, we took a nightgown. The entire front and sleeves were embroidered, white on white; it made a handsome shirt.

Fredrica reached in the satchel and pulled out the yellow brocade skirt and bodice. She fingered the flat shiny beads.

"Perhaps they can make something for you, Fredrica," I offered. "That yellow would be pretty on you."

She said, "It's too small," and threw the pieces back into the satchel and left the house.

From a full-skirted black velvet dress, they made breeches, a doublet, and a matching cap. Margret gave me a pair of suitable stockings which had some small holes, which were finely mended.

Isadora Princhez, the seamstress who bought my handiwork, provided me with a suitable castoff cloak. It was black velvet and had a silver thread in it. I could barely bring myself to touch it, it was so beautiful. The cloak was cut in the Spanish style, short with a deep hanging cowl, which could cover the head and face. (For intrigue, Margret explained. We laughed. Throughout our preparations our moods had lightened.)

For my travel and to keep the velvet clothes clean, they cut breeches from a skirt of Aldonza's and made me a shirt from one of Lorenzo's. Meta and Enrique loaned me his leather vest to wear over the shirt. With an old hat of Lorenzo's, my outfit was complete.

Except for shoes. I couldn't go barefoot with the velvet clothes.

Master Nicolás, Parado's barber-surgeon, solved this problem. During a visit he made to check on Lorenzo's leg, we told him of our plan. The next day he came with a handsome pair of black leather boots—a pair his son Garcia had outgrown.

Margret sewed straps on her satchel to make it into a pack I could carry on my back. She took me in her room to show it to me and gave me her stiletto. The blade was very thin; it looked delicate. "I hope you never have use for this but you must take it."

I understood that she did not want Aldonza and Lorenzo to know I had it but it was her way of keeping me safe.

She explained that the weapon was used to kill at close range. It could be slipped between the ribs, right into the heart. The heart would burst, and it would be over quickly. She demonstrated on an imaginary opponent. Her enactment was so good that I could visualize exactly what to do and how it would feel to thrust the narrow blade between two ribs, how it would hesitate at the heart, then go in smoothly.

"Thank you." I was glad to have it but could think of no reason I would ever have to use it.

Before I left, Margret advised me to ask fifty ducats for the rosary. Everyone gasped. That would last us a year! She also told me what the city would be like, how to ask for a room, where to find food, and other bits of information. "Remember you never know in what circumstances you might find yourself," she told me. "Always think ahead and anticipate the worst." I thought her advice was similar to Aldonza's "consider the consequences."

Lorenzo explained the route to Toledo where I would see the bishop, then on to Madrid, and home again by a more direct route.

"In Madrid," Aldonza said, "look for anything familiar, a street, a building . . . a person."

"Go to the shop where you may have climbed in the cart," Lorenzo said. "It's in

Grenada Street, owned by a Frenchman, Jacques Noblesse."

I shook my head. "I don't remember anything."

"You must try," they said together.

Aldonza lowered her eyes. "Maybe we did not do enough to find your family."

"Madrid is a long way," I said. "You did all you could."

"You deserve to have more," Aldonza said, her cheeks flushing pink. "We have nothing. . . ."

When I saw their sorrowful faces, my heart lurched. "We have enough." My hand swept an arc to include everyone: We had each other. "And I will bring home money," I said with more conviction than I felt.

"But look for them," Aldonza whispered because she was near tears.

"Yes," I said because she asked it, but I did not know if I would.

Lorenzo gave me one of his knives with a carrier for my belt.

"In crowds," Margret said, "keep it in your boot."

Aldonza crossed herself. "I hope you use it for bread and cheese only." She paused and grinned, something she seldom did now. "Maybe dig some roots?"

I smiled at that. But I knew, because of the knife games with Fredrica, I could defend myself if needed or even get a squirrel or hare.

After putting the fine clothing in the bag, Margret and Aldonza packed a bit of soap, a cloth or two, a couple of candles, a thin blanket to sleep on, some rice bread, and cheese. A goodly amount considering what little we had. I protested.

"We will be fine," Aldonza insisted.

I dressed my part—a lad. And what was my name to be? Aldo.

ꝏ

It was nearing evening on my first day of walking. I had passed several people, all of them friendly. One family invited me to walk with them. I remembered to say my name was Aldo. They had not seemed to think me anything but a lad. They shared their midday meal with me. Hot garbanzos and paella! Like a fish eager to get back into the water, I dove into the food, and though my stomach rebelled a little at the fullness of the meal, I was determined to keep it with me. Later I parted ways with them, but a couple of lads came into the road at Triccia and greeted me.

"Halloa," I said. "Where are you to?"

"Toledo," one said. "And you?"

"The same," I responded.

They were dressed similarly to me, though their clothes were more worn. I reminded myself to be careful. From Margret's tales, I knew how easy it was to be fooled.

"I'm Lothario," one said. "He's Anselmo." Lothario seemed the older. His voice was deep and he had a beard, though it was short and rather thin. I could see some chest hair through his open shirt. Anselmo, on the other hand, had none, and his beard was light and barely begun.

"I'm Aldo." We walked amicably along the road.

"What's your game?" Lothario said, looking me over with interest. His finger-nails skritched over his scraggly beard.

"My game?" I asked.

"You know. Your scam," Anselmo said. He was thinner and slightly taller than Lothario, who was stocky and short. "I've a few tricks with cards." He took a deck from his pocket. They were badly worn.

"Are they trick cards?" I asked, not knowing what he meant.

"I can pull an ace anytime," he said boastfully. Anselmo's voice had not yet changed, but it was trying to. He often slipped from alto into baritone. He flipped the cards through his hands quickly, shuffling and reshuffling, cutting them sev-eral times and, yes, always showing an ace.

"Ah," I said, for now I understood what tricks he meant.

"I can slice a purse string or pick a pocket with the best of them," Lothario said. He slipped up behind Anselmo pretending to cut the straps on his knife carrier.

We continued on our way—they did most of the talking, and at dark, we stopped in a little grove of beech trees. Lothario and Anselmo went to look for food. I took the opportunity to relieve myself, which I could see, would be a problem if I were to travel with lads. I certainly could not stand up with them and make pictures in the dirt!

The boys returned with five eggs—stolen from some farmer! I imagined the fam-ily was in the same straits I had left my family in, though I could see the fields here had not been devastated.

I watched as they built a fire and took out a small skillet. "Can you cook?" Anselmo asked me in his sliding voice. "I'm not so good at it."

I smiled and said since they had gotten the food, I would be glad to cook it. I added the rest of my cheese to the eggs and, though some seasoning may have helped, they were quite good. My new friends agreed. We finished off the bread I had brought with me.

At dark, we got ready for sleep. I stretched out on my blanket and used the pack for a head rest. I felt the rosary in my pocket, and I placed the knife under the pack. Though Lothario and Anselmo had been friendly, I would trust no one.

Lothario rolled over on his side to face Anselmo and me. "Have you ever done *it* with a girl?"

When I caught on to his meaning, I, truthfully, said, "No." My heart began to beat more rapidly. *Careful, now,* I thought.

"One showed me her melons," Anselmo said. His voice cracked when he added, "She leaned over, and they popped right out."

"What a story!" Lothario said.

"It's true," Anselmo declared.

I rolled over, not wanting any part of this conversation.

In the morning I gathered my things and wandered off into the bushes, hoping Lothario and Anselmo had already seen to their morning toilet. I squatted and as I finished, Anselmo came through the bushes and said, "Taking a dump? Me too." Before I could think, he'd pulled his breeches down and squatted a few feet away. I had my wits about me enough to realize my shirt covered me; perhaps if I squatted here until he left. . . .

Lothario came and let his stream go noisily. I tell you truly, dear reader, that, though I had not thought to evacuate my bowels at that time, I did. The morning breeze cooled my sweating forehead. I did not want to be found out. Could I trust these lusty boys?

But right then I found out I had more courage than I would have thought. I arose from my squatting position, making sure my shirt covered my front and walked away while buttoning my breeches. After all who would not walk away from their morning job, leaving it to fertilize the wild lettuce?

♄ ♋

In Toledo, I took leave of my fellow travelers. I had to wait three hours at the cathedral before I could see the bishop. The old deacon, who was large and gruff, led me to an office.

"And what brings you here?" the kindly bishop asked as I entered. He was sitting on a stool near a wooden desk and was clothed in a plain robe.

I reached in my pocket and pulled out the rosary. I explained my mission.

"What is your name?" the bishop asked gently.

"Aldo," I said without hesitation.

"If I remember correctly, the girl who had this rosary was named Aldonza Lorenzo." The bishop unfolded from his stool. I remembered his tall, thin body. "And she had your blue eyes."

He remembered me! I knelt before him. He leaned over and put his hand under my chin, raising my head. Smiling, he motioned for me to stand. I remembered his soft gray eyes.

"And why are you dressed as a boy, Aldonza?" he asked.

The whole story came tumbling out: the grasshoppers, the ruined crops, the splintered chest, Lorenzo's broken leg, the hunger (which I was beginning to feel again, not having eaten since last night), how I now wanted to sell the rosary.

"Take a breath, my child." His eyes were amused and friendly. He wrote a letter of introduction to Señor Sebastian Boscan, marquis of Dierba, who lived in Madrid.

He held out a small pouch with coins in it. "Here. Take this to your family. It will help for a while." He walked me to the door. "Go home and have someone take you to Madrid. It is too dangerous for you to go alone."

I took the pouch and the letter and curtseyed. The bishop said wryly, "Most young men bow and leave the curtseying to those in skirts."

I smiled and bowed.

"Yes, your grace."

After he said a prayer for my safe trip home and for my family, I said, "Thank you," and left. But I had no intention of going home.

✧✧

Long before I got to Madrid, I encountered dozens of pack mules on their way to and from the city. Few carts were on the road, but as I walked by one, the carter, a lad who looked to be about Lothario's age, hailed me. "Ho!"

I looked around.

"You look hot and tired." He patted the seat beside him. "You might get there faster walking," he pointed at the distant city wall and the line leading up to it, "but you'll save your feet this way." He brushed a shock of straw-colored hair from his eyes.

I paused and then decided, *why not?* I climbed into the cart and put my pack under my feet.

"My name is Jesus," the driver of the cart said.

"Aldo," I said, patting my chest.

"Where are you from?" he asked, again brushing his hair out of his eyes.

I cleared my throat. It was dry from the dust on the road. "Toboso, in La Mancha."

"What brings you to Madrid?" he asked.

"I wanted to see the city." *That sounded good,* I thought.

Jesus looked me over. "A tourist," he said and laughed. He had snapping blue eyes. "My friends are in the cart behind us." With his thumb he motioned backwards. I looked and waved; the two young men acknowledged me. "The darker one is Ferandez, and the other is Pieter. He looks Flemish but he's from Basque country." Again, Jesus brushed his hair from his face. Jesus, too, looked Flemish.

"So you work together," I said, not knowing what to say.

"We work for a carter in Madrid," Jesus said. "You can see there aren't many carts," with his hand he indicated the long line of pack mules. "Madrid is situated where everything has to be brought to it," the young man continued. "It is quite behind the times. Not as in Paris."

"Have you been to Paris?"

"No, but my boss has," Jesus said. With his whip he flicked at a large fly, which was worrying his mule. "He saw the need, so he started a carting business."

"That makes sense," I said. A cart could haul more than three or four mules.

"Someday, I hope to be his partner. Or maybe have my own business." His light hair and blue eyes were startling. It was hard not to stare at him.

Jesus told me quite a bit more about carting before we got to the city. I watched him as he talked. He was very friendly. I found his little habit of brushing his hair back charming, and when the shock fell back in his face, he looked like a little boy.

By the time we got close to the city walls, I knew I would not make it to see the marquis. Anyway I needed to find a place where I could clean up and change to the better clothing. I had picked up too many layers of dirt along the way, not to mention a few crawly things. I was grateful for the coins from the bishop.

"Have you got a place to stay?" Jesus asked.

"No." Would he invite me to his place? My heart fluttered; the thought excited, yet alarmed me.

"Try José Jérez's on Amiata Street. He has a *pension* next to a *bodegón*,* so you can get a room *and* eat," he said. "If you'll go with me to drop off the cart, I can show you."

As we neared the walls of the city, I saw policemen looking closely at everyone and asking questions. Some people were asked to produce passports. But when we got to the gate, the policeman waved us through.

Jesus drove the cart to the place of Ernesto Carretillo, Carter. It was a large barn-like building at the end of a short street. After leaving the carts, Jesus and his friends showed me the inn—it was only a block from the carter's—and left, saying they would be back for dinner. The place was a half-timber, three story. It was not too clean but not so dirty either.

I wanted a single room so as not to give away the secret of my true self. The innkeeper, José, was good-natured enough. He said he did not have any private rooms, but I could stay in the corner of a store room, if I liked. He only charged me for the bath, saying with a chuckle that he only rented rooms and not closets.

He showed me a miniature room, from which he first had to clear out some

---

* Hotel and tavern

small casks and stack others to the side. He handed me a broom to sweep it out, which I did. Then he gave me a rolled up tick, well-seasoned, and a worn quilt and left.

I shook out the shirt Aldonza had made for me from the clothing of my previous life. I tried to smooth it, the velvet pants, doublet, and cloak. I hung them on hooks along the wall.

Someone knocked on the door. When I opened it, I saw a girl about my age, a little older maybe. She was a filled-out young woman, nothing boyish about her.

"Good day," she said with a thick accent. "Want . . . bath?" It took me a minute to understand what she said. Her accent and clipped words were strange to my ears.

"Where are you from?" I asked, curious about her speech.

She paused as if trying to understand. "Italia."

"Ah. You're learning our language."

In Italian she said to herself, "If only people could understand me."

Her speech triggered some reflex in me. "I understand you," I replied in Italian.

She smiled in the most grateful way. "My name is Daria. I am from a very small Italian town near Florence with no prospects for a peasant girl. I came to better myself." The words tumbled from her, like a spring cloudburst. "I came with my brothers, but they have gone off to fight for King Philip in the Armada." She sighed as if this saddened her a great deal. "I am lucky to find José who will let me work when I hardly speak the language," she brushed her straight brown hair from her eyes with her forearm, "I hope to do better than this someday."

"This is honest work," I said to her in Spanish, forgetting to speak in Italian. "Better than threshing wheat or butchering pigs." I sat on one of the up-ended casks.

She looked at me with disappointment. I repeated the words in Italian, and she brightened. "Yes," she said. She was glad to speak her native language. "Everyone tells my parents that I am very pretty." She smiled and I agreed. "They say the *hidalgos* in Spain are more likely to take a poor girl who is beautiful than in Italy, where they want a large dowry." She asked, "How do I find the *hidalgos*?"

I shifted on my perch and told her I did not know. I thought of Alonso Quesano. He was the only *hidalgo* I knew. I wondered if Daria could be the woman he would fight dragons for.

"I work here to save enough money to buy finer clothes." She touched her coarse blouse and skirt. "To attract a rich man's eye, I must dress nicely and take care of myself." She looked away for a moment then shyly looked back at me. "I am a virgin and that is important to the rich men. Is this not so?"

I told her I was from a taxpaying family, and I knew nothing of noble gentlemen.

"But you must," she insisted. "You are educated. You speak Italian."

To divert her attention from the question of this odd bit of knowledge, I said, "Now is fine for the bath."

She got up to leave.

"Wait," I said, standing. I touched her arm to delay her. She looked at me through her eyelashes and smiled. I quickly removed my hand. I had better be careful! "Where do I go?"

"I'll bring the tub to you."

I helped her move the tub into my small space. I was pleased to have this bath in private. From a barrel behind the building, we filled the tub. After she poured in one last bucket of hot water from the kitchen, she left. I removed my dirty things, and my spirits lightened.

I climbed in the tub and slid down into the warm water. Had I ever in my entire life had a bath in the privacy of my own room? I did not know. At Lorenzo's, baths were in the pond or not at all. Using my bit of soap, I washed my hair, sadly, for I still missed my long locks. Yet only one of many losses caused by the wretched insects. Then I lathered my body and watched the dirt dissolve from the lines on my skin. Even from under my fingernails, the dirt floated away in the water. I could feel the grit on the bottom of the tub.

I sat on the edge of the tub, dripping dry. In the morning, I would find the marquis's place and, in my most confident manner, present the letter. The thought of giving something back to my family excited me.

I brushed the dirt from my breeches, shirt, and vest the best I could, dressed, and went to eat. I hoped that Jesus would be there. I felt eager to see him—was it only because it would be a familiar face?

The taproom was full of men, eating and drinking. I felt sorry for Daria. I could see that serving tables was hard work, and many of the patrons were too familiar with her, which only made it harder. I admired her because she knew what she wanted and she was willing to work hard for it. The three carters soon arrived and sat with me. Jesus across the table, and Pieter and Ferandez on either side.

Over the course of the evening and with the help of a few glasses of wine, I came to know them better. I was initiated into the ranks of being male in a way I had not yet experienced.

Pieter had hair the color of hay and a scar above his right eye. He had been in Madrid for three years and had worked several months with Ferandez and Jesus. They drove goods from Madrid to nearby places and back every day. Ferandez, to my left, was small and dark. He was very nice looking until he smiled and showed that half his teeth were gone or rotted. He seldom smiled; in fact, he seldom talked.

Then there was Jesus, so good-looking with his straw-colored hair. Like a cool scent, his confidence floated around him. His blue eyes attracted me and for the first time I wondered if my own blue eyes could be appealing—was that what had attracted Daria?

Jesus smiled easily and often used his hands as he talked. When he spoke, we listened. I had noticed this afternoon that he knew how to tell a story in a way that kept you interested and eager to know the ending. I could see, of the three of them, he was the leader.

Daria was waiting on our table. Jesus flirted with her. Daria was merely polite to him, though she greeted me warmly.

"That Italian is a winsome wench," Jesus said. "Bet she's a great kisser. Italians are."

I felt my heart lurch. I wished he were not interested in her, and I wondered if it were because I saw Daria was not interested in him or because I wanted him for myself!

I asked what else they carted.

"Different things. Wine, bolts of cloth, foodstuffs," Jesus answered. "Once in a while we cart animals." He caught Daria by the sleeve as she whirled by, nearly upsetting her tray, which held plates of paella and beans. "Daria," he said, indicating the empty glasses. "Pour for us. Four," Nodding at all of us, Jesus held up four fingers. "And when you come back, bring me a kiss, beautiful." With the now familiar gesture, he brushed his hair out of his eyes.

I wanted to get away from here. I was not ready for the loudness and crudeness of manhood. *Keep me a boy*, I prayed, then laughed to myself. I should be praying to be home and be a girl again.

"It's getting late." I hiccoughed; the room seemed to tilt. The three friends giggled, then Ferandez hiccoughed also. I was so tipsy I did not know if I could walk. I knew I had to leave before I said or did something that was not in character with Aldo. What if I, in my befuddled state, were to reach out and touch Jesus's hair!

Unsteadily, I rose from the table. Jesus said, "Yo, Aldo. Take it easy." Pieter kept me from falling. Mumbling thanks, I staggered out.

I could not stop thinking about Jesus. I could never have predicted how my first infatuation would end, but I was already dismal about it—he did not even know I was a girl, and I certainly lacked the curvaceous charms of Daria.

Before I got to my room, I was headed out back. In the alley, I threw up, it seemed, more than I drank. (*If Aldonza were here, she would remind me about moderation.*) Daria had followed and helped me sit on the steps.

"Too much . . . drink," Daria said in her broken Spanish.

"Yes," was all I could say, but it occurred to me that later I could help her with her Spanish. It would help her in the taproom with the customers. I could teach her how to say, "Hands off." But not at that moment, I was heaving again.

Daria helped me back to my room. Spreading my tick and blanket on the floor, she said in Italian, "Do not be shy. I help my brothers when they have too much to drink." She began to help me undress, but I was shy for a good reason and wanted to be left alone. My head was pounding, but I thought if I stayed still I would be fine. I lay on the mattress.

"Let me sit with you for a while," she said in Italian. "I miss my family."

"Please leave me in my misery," I pleaded and weakly motioned toward the door. "Good night," I said in Spanish. I closed my eyes and rolled over. She covered me with the blanket, a gesture I greatly appreciated. In a moment I heard the door close.

CHAPTER 13

in which Aldo learns more of the world

HEN I AWOKE, my head felt big as a cow. My tongue felt swollen and mossy. Slowly, unsteadily, I got up from the floor. After I righted myself, I managed to walk across the little room to the door. I found José's wife, Juana, in the kitchen and asked if I could have some water and bread.

"Is this your first time in Madrid?" she asked, as she poured me a tankard of water and sliced me a piece of bread on which she put fresh butter. I sat on a stool and devoured it, answering her with my mouth full. "Yes." I was hungry: I had emptied my body of everything.

She motioned for me to help myself to the bread. Holding a headless chicken by its feet, she plunged it in a bucket of scalding water. "I noticed you made some friends last night: Jesus, and his friends. They are here often." She retrieved the scalded fowl and began plucking its feathers. "They have rooms down the street." The kitchen smelled of wet feathers and blood.

I wanted to ask her about Jesus but did not want to appear too interested. I cut my second slice of bread and added the creamy butter.

She picked up the thread of conversation: "They are steady young men."

"Yes." Breaking a piece of crust from my bread, I chewed it slowly.

"Daria would not do badly with Jesus. I think he has an eye for her." She rubbed the de-feathered body with fat.

"But Daria wants better," I said, forcefully enough to start my head throbbing again; as well, my heart was giving those little flip flops.

Juana squeezed some garlic on the meat and shrugged. "We take what we get. She could do worse."

Daria came in with a broom in her hand.

Juana said to her, "I was telling Aldo that Jesus would be a good match for you."

Daria did not answer right away. She had to decipher what Juana said. "No, not match." She shook her head. "Want better."

Juana looked offended. "We have good clientele, Daria. Who are you to hope for more?"

Daria said, "What is 'clientele'?" She looked at me, but I was not going to speak Italian in front of Juana.

"The people who come here," Juana said. "Daria, look, even here's a nice young man." She waved a hand at me.

Daria smiled and walked near, brushing her hip against me. "Yes, Aldo nice."

I swallowed but said nothing.

Daria shook her head and said, "Want rich *hidalgo*."

Juana laughed and skewered the chicken to ready it for the spit.

Daria asked me how I was.

I did not answer in Italian. "Better." I thanked Juana and went back to my room.

Daria followed. "Why won't you speak Italian?"

"Juana will wonder why I can speak it," I said, now speaking in her language. "I was glad for your help last night. Thank you." I flushed remembering Margret's admonition about not speaking other languages, but I wanted to help Daria. "I will help you with your Spanish if you have some free time today."

"After we serve lunch," she said, looking pleased at my offer.

I should have sold the rosary by then, but I would stay the night before starting out in the morning. Perhaps I would see Jesus again.

After dressing in my fine clothes, I found my way to see the marquis. The house was made of stone on the side too. Most houses in Madrid were brick or cob; even the homes of the most wealthy were only fronted with stone. The marquis must be very rich.

I walked around to the side door and spoke with a servant, an old man, and discovered that the marquis was not in attendance in Madrid. He was in Valladolid and would not be back until late that night. The old man coughed—a lung complaint, I thought. He continued, "I don't know your business with him, lad, but I suggest you be careful."

I frowned. "I must see him. The bishop sent me."

"Then look for me—Vittor." He pointed to his chest. "Tomorrow."

I walked down the muddy street. Maybe there was someplace else to sell it? But I did not know, and the old Bishop had said to try the marquis.

Because Aldonza had asked me to, I asked for directions to Grenada Street. At the end of the street, I walked into Jacques Noblesse's shop, where I might have climbed into Lorenzo's cart years ago. The store was no longer a furniture store but arrayed with shelves and shelves of crystal: goblets and chalices, stemmed, flat-bottomed, fluted, etched, blown, gold-rimmed, silver-rimmed, beset with jewels, each piece different than the last. And crystal animals, crystal earrings, crystal plates and bowls.

I asked for "Monsieur Noblesse" and found that he no longer owned the store, though the sign outside still bore his name. I left the store and sat on a tree stump in a small yard across the street from the store.

I was surprised that I was disappointed. And why? I was not sure, except that having left Aldonza and Lorenzo's, I could turn my thoughts more toward my past, and I found that I was curious about it.

How was it I happened to curl up in Lorenzo's cart? I had always thought that I must have run away because of some terrible happening or that my family was dead, but today, after seeing the crowded streets of the city, it occurred to me that I might have gotten separated from them. Perhaps they were a nice family, maybe even a wonderful family, and they wanted me back—had even looked for me but could not find me.

Unexpectedly I became consumed with the thought of finding them. I entered and asked at every store on that street, and the next and the next, if anyone knew of a family who had lost a daughter four years before. But after a couple of hours I had learned nothing, and I returned to José's and changed out of my fine clothes.

Daria meant for me to keep my promise about helping her with her Spanish. When she was free, she and I walked to the square. The streets, which were muddy sludge in the morning from the slop poured in them the during the night, had been dried to dust by the Madrid sun. Luxuriantly blooming plants were everywhere. The fragrances of these blooms seemed to mask the malodorous streets. I loved the purple stock, a tall flower of delicate blooms, sweetly scented. And the chamomile, in clusters so white they seemed to be alight, even in day. Also tall hollyhocks, pink soapwort, and others.

As we walked, I pointed to things and told Daria the Italian word and the Spanish word. Sometimes I formed sentences for her. I made her repeat everything. Some words of the two languages were similar and she caught on quickly.

In the stores I saw things I had never seen. The idea of what was available opened up the world to me. One store had ten chests, all of them different, such as Lorenzo might have made. Another had dozens of pairs of boots, each one more elegant than the last and all nicer than the pair I had brought with me. I felt the pull of these luxurious things but, a bit sadly, knew they were not for me—or were they? What if I found my lost family?

What would it be like, I wondered, to have so many choices all the time? What would it be like to have the money to buy these various items, to fill one's home with soft, colorful, and elegant things? But I shook myself to remind me that my family, the only family I knew, was destitute, that every single *maravedi* we had was needed for taxes and sustenance.

Daria and I passed a *bodegón de puntapié*, a stall where *empanadillas* were sold. We each bought one of the hot meat pies. In the plaza we sat by one of the fountains. While we ate, Daria told me of her family. Her father was a shopkeeper in Florence, and when the farmers had a good year, he could feed his family of nine children and Daria's grandparents. But in recent years, there had been a drought and it had been harder and harder for the family to survive.

"My father can't say *no* to anyone, and because he extends credit, he gets nothing if the crops fail." Daria pulled a handkerchief from her pocket and wiped a bit of meat sauce from my chin. "My mother works every hour of daylight, and beyond, taking care of my little brothers and sisters, working in the shop, cooking."

"I'm sure you helped her," I said, picturing her doing the same for little brothers as she had just done for me.

"Three of my brothers and I thought we would be more help if we left."

In her eyes I could see sadness and a much younger Daria, one who wanted her mother to have time for her. My life would be much different if I had to share Aldonza with more family members.

"We planned to find work and send money home." She took the last bite of her *empanadilla* and reached in the fountain to rinse her hands. "My brothers enlisted in your king's service, and I worry about them every day."

The king was an abstract idea to me, the *me* from a farm in La Mancha. I didn't know any soldiers. "But just as much your mother must worry about you."

Tears came to Daria's eyes. "Juana helps me write a bit when I send the money." She dried her hands on her skirt. "I hope to hear back from her someday." She swallowed. "But she is so busy."

I touched her hand in sympathy and Daria looked at me. We both looked away—something had been in her eyes that I had not expected.

"That is why I want to marry a rich man. To help my family."

"Of course. I wish you good luck." And I prayed silently for good luck to me, too, in helping my own family. "Now, back to work," I said in Spanish.

Near us, an elder tree waved its lacy, white branches at us. She asked me the names for the clothing: gown, vest, hat, shirt, stockings, shoes. She asked me about the clouds and the sun. Looking at me through her eyelashes, she said maybe we would come back at night, and she would learn about the stars and the moon. I decided it was time to go back to the inn.

That night in the tavern I sat next to Jesus. I knew I could not reveal my true gender to him, at least, not until my task was done. I would not do anything to endanger my crusade to get money for my family, and he remained interested in Daria, who appeared as I would have liked to appear. She wore a red dress with lace around the neckline, which, though not immodest, left no doubt that she was a fully developed young woman. Her slender waist made her bosom seem even fuller.

If Daria had any free moments, she would come and sit at our table next to me away from Jesus. He was not pleased. When she was out of earshot, I insisted I had no interest in her. But he only brushed off my protestations. Since he was attracted to her, he assumed everyone would be.

As for me, I swam in the nearness of Jesus. I leaned within inches of him. I thought I could feel the heat of his body through our clothes. I felt as heady as if the glass were filled with the best Andalusian wine. This situation was impossible, yet I wished for more time with him, and my wish came true.

Jesus asked me if I wanted to go with him, Pieter, and Ferandez that evening. "Of course," I said. Finally, I would have some time with Jesus without Daria.

He said they had a way to make some extra money, if I was interested. Why would I not be? I was here to find money for my family.

Daria overheard the conversation and asked to come with us.

The fellows laughed and Jesus said, "Another time, for certain." To me, he said, "Why don't you get cleaned up? Meet us at the plaza."

I said I would and they left. Daria would not speak to me even when I spoke to her in Italian. I was having enough trouble understanding my female heart, much less hers.

I dressed in the soft velvet clothes and long boots. I put the rosary and the letter deep in my pocket—for I would not chance leaving them anywhere. I felt taller and fine to be dressed so. I joined my new friends and we walked, or swaggered, through the streets, a quartet of fine lads, looking for some fun.

The lanterns were being lit and thick ropes of smoke rose from them. We arrived at the playhouse as the theater-goers, all nobly dressed, exited the doors. Some climbed into waiting carriages. Several men, a particularly jocular group, walked down the street and turned into a nearby alley.

With his hand, Jesus motioned for us to follow. "Down here's a gaming club for the grandees. Sometimes the king himself comes." The alley was narrow and smelled of old milk.

"The king?" I repeated. I had gone years in La Mancha without hearing of the king and now the idea of him seemed omnipresent.

"Yes, the king," Pieter confirmed, rubbing the scar on his forehead.

"What are we going to do?" My eye twitched. I was having doubts about our fine evening.

"They'll pay us to spend an hour or two with them," Pieter said. "And pay us well."

"I don't understand," I said.

The handsome Ferandez broke his usual silence: "Surely even country peasants know about getting paid for certain favors. You ever do it with some fellows?"

My stomach felt worse than the night I drank too much.

"Come on, Aldo," Jesus said. "Don't look so surprised. It's an easy way to make good money." He brushed his straw-colored hair from his forehead, the gesture no longer endearing.

"Easy?" I choked on the word. My throat closed; I pulled at my suddenly too-tight collar.

"Yeah, a couple of hours and you get a week's wages."

Before we could talk any more, a group of people came down the alley. Even in the dusky light I saw they were some of the finely dressed men and women from the theater. Their brocades and velvets littered with jewels were gleaming in the dark by the dim glow of the lanterns. I heard the laughter of women.

To Jesus, I whispered, "They have women with them." My tongue stuck to my lips, my mouth so dry I could barely speak.

"Yes, some have women," Pieter whispered. "But some like boys."

Some like boys. I was not a boy. *My God, I have to leave.*

"I cannot do this," I whispered, but they did not hear me.

"Look." Pieter said. "Princess Catalina is with them." He nodded toward the one with diamonds in her hair.

One of the noblemen, who was no taller than the princess, approached her and said, "Princess Catalina, I have not seen you here for a long time." He was graceful and regal and dressed completely in purple.

"I come for the sport, Don Fernando." She pointed with her folded fan to the tavern. "Will you join me at the table?"

"Not just yet."

Catalina glanced our way. I moved behind Jesus.

"Does not Patrecia grow impatient with your waywardness?"

"She is content. We have an heir on the way."

"From what I hear, you may have some already," another woman said.

The members of the group laughed, and the young man pulled himself taller. "None that we are aware of." His voice matched her humor.

"He plants his seed where it will not grow," one of the men said and again they all laughed.

"I plant it anywhere I want," the man in purple said; his hand went to his side. His voice now had an edge to it; he had become uncomfortable with the banter.

"No trouble here," the princess said and waved her hand as if to clear the air of any tension. She smiled. "But if Christopher were here, he would prevail upon you to behave and stop your wicked ways." She did not say this as if the ways were wicked, but as if they were amusing to her.

"He would never come here. You know that."

"*He* is an honorable man." The princess smiled and looked around their little circle. "Unlike the lot of you! Or should I say the lot of *us*?" They all laughed and she walked on. Everyone followed except the man she had called Fernando.

He walked toward us, his long cloak rippling around him.

Jesus quickly said, in my ear, "He is the duke of Solariego's son. And very wealthy." But that was all he could tell me because the young man was beside us. He was shorter than Jesus, more my height.

"Jesus," he said. His plumed hat shaded his face in the dimly lit corner of the alley, but I could see he had dark hair and a neatly trimmed beard. "Good to see you." The duke's son touched Jesus's face. Cold sweat rolled down my chest.

A woman—not one of the nobles—came over and pulled on his hand. "Don Fernando, come with us." She pulled his head to her mouth. Her tongue flicked in and out of his ear. Her gown was cut so low that the dark circles of her breasts could be seen, a hint of nipple. I breathed in sharply. Nonchalantly, he looked at me. As the woman continued her ministrations on his ear, her hand made its way down his chest. His hand on her buttocks, he pulled her closer.

Nodding in my direction, he asked, "Who is this, Jesus? Someone new for me?" Where the richly figured velvet cloak opened, I could see shiny purple stockings below his paned trunk hose. On his finger was a heavy, gold crested ring.

"This is Aldo. He can use some money."

I could not talk, could not swallow.

The nobleman pushed the woman away. "Later, pussycat." The woman meowed good-naturedly at the duke's son and walked away.

"Aldo, he will pay us well for a good time," Jesus said earnestly to me.

Another man was kissing Ferandez. Yet another had approached Pieter. I saw money exchange hands and they walked off together.

The duke's son angrily grabbed me from behind by the waist and pulled me to him. I pushed his hands away. Jesus grabbed my arm and pulled me from the noble-man. Jesus said, "He is not ready. I am sorry."

With his hand the nobleman dismissed us; his ring glittered in the flickering lamplight. I thought I read the words *Truth, Mercy, Honor.* He turned away.

"Let's go." Jesus waved his hand for us to leave. We walked hurriedly along the alley out into the street. My thoughts were in a jumble. It seemed so ugly to be a boy, a man. Crudeness in the taproom, crudeness in the streets. My new friends taking money for favors. Men with men. I did not understand. Why did they do this? Surely it was more pleasurable with women. Women had a place for the male part. Aldonza had told us about men and women together, how babies were made. What did a man make with a man?

How elegant the nobility had looked in the light of the street lamps as they had exited the theater. The women were bedecked with sparkling jewels and beautifully tapestried cloaks. Their servants helping them, the people looked genteel and graceful as they entered their carriages. The men looked charming in their brocade jackets and trunk hose, their calves smooth and muscled in their stockings, intricately embroidered clocks* on their ankles.

Oh, I was glad I had not found my lost family, for what if they were like these men and women I had seen tonight! And wasn't it likely?—they were wearing clothing much like the clothing in my satchel.

Jesus said, "I was like you the first time. But you get used to it. I save the money to start my own business."

I remembered he had mentioned his plans during my ride in his cart—was it only yesterday I had arrived in Madrid! "I'm sorry," I said tentatively, though I was not sorry to stop him from such an evening. I looked up at him. His good looks seemed dimmed and not only because it was now dark.

He waved his hand to show it did not matter. "Come on," he said, "I've got to water the mules for Señor Carretillo." He referred to his boss, who was out of town.

I helped him fill the water troughs in the carter's barn, clean out the stalls, and put out hay and grain for the animals. Before we were finished, Pieter had returned. He tousled my hair. "Not quite ready for the city, heh?"

Jesus growled at him. "Leave him alone." Then he flashed a grin. "Did you bring a jug?"

"No. Ferandez went after it. To José's." Pieter fanned his money—to me he said, "Don't worry about getting caught. The police turn a blind eye."

"But surely," I said, "it is the nobles who would get arrested."

Jesus and Pieter shrugged. "No, they would say we have enticed them. We could be sent to the stake."

Burned. I did not understand this. Burned! I was speechless. I began sweating. My hand went to the scar on my arm.

Ferandez slid open the barn door; he was carrying two wineskins. Daria was with him, carrying a jug. I was sorry to see her. I no longer thought these lads were good company to keep.

"Daria, let me walk you back," I said.

"No." Jesus took her arm. "Come, we'll share." He took the jug from Daria and motioned for us to sit on the dirt floor.

I sat on the other side of Daria. Jesus held a wineskin high and spewed a goodly

* Decoration to hide the gusset of a stocking

amount into his mouth. He passed it to me. I took the jug and pretended to take some. I wanted to keep my wits about me. These fellows seemed sinister, no longer friends, here in the dark barn.

Giggling, Ferandez fell backwards. His eyes wandered and would not stay straight.

"I need to get some rest," I said. "Daria, let's go back."

But she refused and took my arm to keep me there and said, "Let me sit with you awhile."

Jesus shared his wineskin with her and passed the jug back to me. "When are you leaving Madrid?"

"Tomorrow." Again I pretended to take a drink. "It's time to go home."

"Hey, beautiful," Jesus said to Daria, "come sit by me." He patted the floor next to him.

Daria moved closer to me. "Do not go." She began crying. "Take me with you."

"No," I said. That was it; that was all I said.

"Hey, Daria, he doesn't want you." Jesus made kissing sounds. "Come here. A kiss, maybe two."

"No," she said.

He scooted next to her. He touched her face and then reached for her bodice.

"No, Jesus," she said. "No!"

"Who do you want to touch you?" he said, taunting. "Aldo?" He took her by the neck and pushed her toward me. "Kiss her, Aldo, kiss her."

I got up and moved away. "Jesus, no. Please."

"What is it, Aldo?" He put his arm around Daria and pulled her to him, though he continued to talk to me. "Too young for girls too?" Pieter and Ferandez chuckled. Jesus put his hand over her breast and squeezed. Their laughter was ugly.

Daria tried to get up, but Jesus held her down.

It happened so fast.

I could not move.

I could not speak.

Jesus pushed her back, while Pieter and Ferandez held her and pulled up her skirts. My hand rose, stopped in mid-air as if to halt them, but it froze. I saw the light flash on Jesus's naked penis, white like the underbelly of a fish, before it dove into Daria.

To silence her, Pieter jammed part of her skirt in her mouth. When Jesus finished, his member did not shine white, but was dim and glistening. I gagged, though I did not, could not move, could not speak as Pieter took her next, then Ferandez.

I *felt* everything that happened, as if it were happening to me. My lungs were heavy and heaving, as if their weight were on me. Each breath hummed acutely in my ears. *Hww. Hww. Hww.* The sound of flapping wings. I wanted to say *horror, horror*, but I was all air and no words. Then there was not even air; I felt I was being smothered, choked.

Daria had stopped struggling; maybe she was dead. Was it only a minute of time or was it an hour? How long could it have taken?

"Now it's your turn, Aldo."

Daria's eyes were dull, the whites wide with fear and loathing. She was on the floor and unmoving; tears oozed from her eyes and ran down her temples.

I do not know where I got the breath to speak, and why I spoke now and not moments before. "Of course," I said as smoothly as I could, "but you must leave. I want her to myself."

Jesus laughed, a lustful laugh. "Sure," he said, with a wave of his hand. He led them toward the door. "I gotta piss. Leave the lovers."

With the closing of the door, Daria was up. She slapped me, twice.

I tasted blood. "Wait, Daria. Wait," I said, as loudly as I dared. What if they returned?

She was at me again, pummeling me with her fists. Swearing at me. Kicking at me. A stomp to the foot. She tried to run to the door.

I reached for her hand. "Not that way!" I pulled her toward the window, trying to dodge her flailing hands. One hit my eye and false light flashed around my head.

I caught her wrist. "The window." I said firmly. "Let's go." I helped her through the window, and we ran through the streets of Madrid. *Where could we go?* We could not leave the city—the gates were closed at night.

We needed to hide, needed time to think. José might not take her back at the tavern. I thought of going to a church. But would a priest say it was Daria's fault? Say she enticed the boys? Want to burn her?

I pulled her into an alley out of sight. She sat crying. I watched the alley and I watched her. What was she thinking?

"You could have stopped them." She hit my arm. "Told them to stop."

I agreed with her. I could have screamed. I could have protested. *I could have pulled a knife.* Why hadn't I thought of these things? "It happened so fast."

"It was an eternity," she said with intensity. I heard her irregular breathing, the staccato sighs of someone who has cried a lot. Then a deep breath and she said, "Men are pigs." She spat in my face. "You think you own women." She wiped tears from her cheeks. "I have lost my jewel, which was mine to give."

Tears stung my eyes but did not fall. What right had I to join in her sorrow?

Now she was angry. "You'll do this to some woman sometime." Now she was crying. "You'll be jealous."

Quietly, I said, "No." *Do I tell her the truth? Or let it go.*

She spat her words at me. "How can you be so sure?"

"B-because I'm a g-girl too." I stammered; my teeth were chattering. I could not move, as if my insides were frozen. "For my protection my family thought it safest for me to travel as a boy." I winced—perhaps I had been saved her fate only because of how I was dressed.

She sat quietly beside me. The moon moved during her silence. I was clearheaded now and I was determined to protect her.

"Why tell me now?" Her voice was tired, very tired.

"Because I feel like it happened to me too . . ."

"It did *not* happen to you," she yelled and hit me again. "*You* don't know what it was like! *You* didn't feel them grabbing you and pushing you and shoving at you. You weren't hurt. You didn't help."

"I was afraid. They . . ."

". . . might do it to you?" she finished the sentence I did not want to finish.

I looked at the ground. *Why hadn't I . . . done something?*

"Hah! I hate you!" She got up and left the shelter we had found.

I went after her. She was walking fast to get away from me. I walked faster to stay up with her. "Where are you going?"

"Back to José's," she spat out at me.

"But what if Jesus is there?" I asked.

"José will beat him up."

"José is a man too. He seems to be a good man, but he may not . . . protect you or take you back." I thought how easy it would be for José to turn her away; Daria had no power to make him protect her. I thought of the wealthy people in the alley; the very way they dressed and walked showed *they* had the power.

She stopped and leaned against a building. Her voice weak, she said, "What am I going to do?" I put my arm around her. Furious, she pushed me away. "No one will help me, and no one will want me." Her anger returned. "You . . . you . . . you . . ." She did not finish.

"Yes." I disgusted myself.

"What am I going to do?" she said again.

We went to Daria's church, which was next to a convent. The priest, Father Jaime, offered us shelter. He put Daria in the care of Sister Cecilia and found a small room for me to stay in. I was grateful for a bed and a safe place to rest. As he left, he said, "Things always look brighter with the morning light."

How could that be? I hoped that tomorrow would offer some choices.

I did not see Daria the next day. Sister Cecilia told me that they had sent Daria to a convent east of Madrid where she would be welcomed. The nun reached in her pocket. "She asked me to write you a note." She handed me a piece of parchment. The handwriting was narrow and straight. "I do not know your name. You were kind to me and you hurt me. I will pray for you. Pray for me too."

I had let Daria down. I hoped she would still find a way to help her mother. I wanted to say, "I'm sorry," one more time or as many times as it took for her to forgive me—if she ever could. But I did not deserve forgiveness: I had put her in harm's way because of her attraction to me and my attraction to Jesus.

Fear, too, was inside me. I had seen how quickly safety dissolved and people became dangerous. Yet I had to go on, had to sell the rosary, had to leave Madrid, had to go home. With the help of Sister Cecilia, I washed up and brushed my clothing. I removed the mud from my boots and polished them. I wanted to appear as presentable as I could at the marquis's. Margret had stressed it.

My hair combed neatly under my cap, I arrived on the marquis's block by midmorning, the silver thread in the velvet cloak glinting in the sunlight. I found a broad limber leaf and rubbed off my boots again. I had the rosary in my pocket and the letter from the bishop in my hand.

I found Vittor. He motioned me to wait, took the letter, and left. In a while he was back, beckoning me to follow him. After leading me through the kitchen, a hallway, and a couple of large rooms, we found the marquis in the largest I had ever seen. Like a church, it was richly decorated with wood trim and large tapestries. The windows were glass with wrought ironwork on the outside and were draperied with red and gold fabric.

The marquis was bald on top. His fringe of hair hung scraggly on his flat, limp ruff. He had a "Z" scar on his cheek, which made him appear more peasant than noble. "Let me see," he said, not at all kindly. "Don't waste my time."

I pulled the rosary from my pocket but words failed to come. The rosary swung like a pendulum from my shaking hand. He grabbed it, holding it toward the window. Taking his time, he looked at each stone individually. I stood swaying from one foot to the other, using the rhythm of my body to help regain my composure.

"Flawless. Quite rare," he murmured, then barked, "How did you come by it? Only nobles and kings can obtain blue amber." His haughtiness reminded me of Father Jude.

Taking a deep breath, I said, "My family. Hard times." I stood as tall as I could. "We hate to part with it."

"Oh, yes," the marquis said sarcastically. "I know these sob stories."

"La Mancha," I said.

Squinting at me, he said, "You stole it."

To this comment, I could firmly answer, "No, señor."

A scowl on his face, the marquis narrowed his eyes. While he studied me, he fingered the rosary. "How much do you want?" he said gruffly.

"One hundred *ducats*," I said with more confidence than I felt. I was ready to bargain.

"I cannot deny that this is exquisite." He scratched his beard thoughtfully. "You could easily find a buyer for it."

"Yes, señor. Exquisite." I repeated *exquisite* in the same rhythm, same inflection, he had said it.

"Do not take it!" He laid the rosary on a table. "I will be right back."

He walked through curtains into the next room. I heard him call, "Pablo!"

Wanting to know what he was doing, I followed and saw him enter yet another room, through another curtained doorway. I peered through a crack between the curtain and the wall. Quickly, he sat at a desk in a small room and opened a box full of money! He would buy it . . . but for how much? He had not even tried to bargain.

While he was counting the *ducats* in stacks of ten, a large manservant entered the room.

"Ah, Pablo. Good," the marquis said. "I will be giving this money to a lad." He put up a hand to indicate my height. "When he leaves, you are to follow him and retrieve my money. *In whatever manner is necessary.*" The marquis continued, "Do you understand? I'll send him out the front."

Pablo pulled a knife from his boot and wiped it on his pants before he replaced it.

The marquis smiled and nodded.

So that was his plan to obtain the rosary. He would have it for nothing!

Pablo left as the marquis finished counting his tenth pile. One hundred *ducats*! I would take the money and run. I knew what Pablo looked like; surely, I could escape.

The marquis clinked the money into a pouch and put the box away. I skittered back into the other room and tried to look bored, as if I had been waiting there for him. Sweat ran down my back.

He entered, his eyes checking the table to be sure the rosary was where he left it. Still, he examined it once more, a certain sign he was a duplicitous man. He handed me the pouch. "Your one hundred *ducats*."

"Yes, thank you, sir."

I took the bag and bowed but cut it short to run out the back, the way I had come in.

"Wait! Leave by the front!" the marquis roared. "Pablo! Pablo!"

I rushed by the old man servant nearly knocking him over. I pulled open the heavy door and was out the back. Putting the pouch of money firmly in the crook of my elbow, I ran through the streets of Madrid.

I made a quick turn and nearly ran into Pablo, who was asking someone if they had seen me. *Not good. Not good.* I pushed a cart in his way, dumping its contents. I ducked under the merchant's arm and went down a squishy alley. It was a dead end. I jumped onto a stack of crates and tied the bag of coins at my waist. I pulled Margret's stiletto from its holder and tucked it in my sleeve. I made myself as small as possible, hoping Pablo would not see me.

His big head loomed over a box, and he grabbed my left arm and pulled me down, pinning me to the wall, one hand firmly on my chest, pushing my breath out. With the other hand, he reached for the money. Easing the stiletto out of my sleeve, I planted it between his ribs.

It entered so quickly, so smoothly, only one slight hesitation. I thought I could feel the heart burst, but maybe not. He fell, taking the stiletto with him, its hilt sticking out. The large body collapsed on the hard-packed earth. The head bounced from the impact, not from any will of his own. Pablo was gone.

I pulled the stiletto from the motionless body and cleaned it off with Pablo's shirt. I felt in his pockets and found some coins and put them in my pocket. I took his knife too and slid it in my boot.

Then I carefully walked through what seemed like miles of alleys to get far away from this part of town. I decided I would take some of the money and buy a cart—we needed a new one—and horse. I would not have to travel by foot, and I would arrive home sooner. A cart would enable me to carry supplies home.

In an extreme part of town, I found a livery and bargained for a cart and horse and was pleased with what I got. The man had been glad to get rid of the horse, a rickety nag, but I found it to be a sturdy horse and obedient. I called it Hope, something I needed.

I snapped the reins and the horse headed for the gate. The traffic was backed up and moving slowly. I fingered the knife at my side. It was a mortal sin to kill, and now I had done it. It mattered little to me that it was kill or be killed. I saw *life* evaporate from a man's eyes because of my actions and was shaken by it.

Were there things worse than death? Was killing a human one of them? Was being raped one of them? Could I have killed Jesus last night, or Pieter, or Ferandez? Perhaps it would have been a better choice to kill Daria or myself. At the gate I passed through without anyone taking particular notice of me.

Once outside the walls, I pushed the horse as much as I could. I wanted to leave Madrid and unpleasant (and unthinkable) thoughts behind. The storytelling Jesus, who had charmed me at first, had taken me away from the nobleman in purple, only to later turn violent with Daria. His actions painted him two-sided, not one way or the other. As Daria had written to me, I was two ways with her. The Church wanted us to be perfect and only good, but it also knew we would sin because God offers forgiveness. It was confusing.

There were people, like Aldonza and Lorenzo, who seemed only good. I knew Margret had broken laws with Laurent; still I knew her to be a good person. Now here I had killed in order to live and stolen from the body. I had stood by and watched as a young woman was defiled, an irreversible act.

I stopped in a village outside the pest-infested area and filled the cart with supplies. The shopkeeper told me where I could procure small amounts of several herbs—lobelia, dried dandelion, echinacea, and a few others. The woman I bought them from told me where I could find a stand of plantain not far from the road. I also found daisy, broom, and some other medicinal plants and piled them in the cart.

I passed through Parado and followed the stream, the water flashing and rippling over the rocks. The fish waggled through the water. I stopped and lying on my belly, drank from the clear stream water that came from the waterfall above our house. I felt refreshed and continued toward home. When the precious hills behind Lorenzo and Aldonza's house appeared on the horizon, I began to sing. It was a solemn song, but a song nonetheless.

It had not been a week since I had left. What had changed here? I could not yet measure the changes in me. Seeing those nurturing hills made me aware of how tired I was.

What would I tell Lorenzo and Aldonza of my search for my first family? I thought of the wealthy man that night with Jesus in the alley. That man had certainly been debauched. I would not be proud to be in that family. Yet if I were still in the family to which I was born, I would not have had to disguise myself as a boy and travel to Madrid. Then I would not have betrayed Daria and not have taken a life. And who was that man I killed? Loved by someone? A ruffian for hire only, willing to kill. Only that? Or more?

Hope whinnied. I shook myself from my reverie and saw that I was on the last rise from home, the very place the cart and newly carved chest had plunged into the stream. I could see Meta's cart. She must be visiting for the day. Her baby would be coming soon. Lobo raced to greet me. Margret was by the pond, washing clothes. When she saw me, she stood and waved her hand high. I returned the wave. By the time I reached the house, they were waiting for me, even Fredrica. Lorenzo walked with the help of crutches.

They all spoke at once, and I was reminded of my first arrival here, but this time I understood every word. "How was it?" "Did you sell it?" "Look at the cart and horse!" "Are you all right?" "We've been worried." "What a load you have!" "What did you bring?"

I gave the bag of coins to Lorenzo and collapsed in Aldonza's arms—too tired to talk, too tired to cry. I was home, where I no longer had the final say, the last word; home, where someone would take care of me.

Aldonza patted my head, stroked my hair. "Donza, we are glad you are home."

Never had I been so happy to hear my name. I could put Aldo aside. But what of his deeds? Could I put them aside also?

CHAPTER 14

in which Donza confesses to a priest

HE MONEY I had brought did not lessen the work on the farm. Lorenzo still could not help. But I was glad to work from before sunrise till after sunset.

Margret became ill within weeks of my return from Madrid, and all thoughts of the trip, which I had kept to myself, were buried under worry and work. We took turns sitting with her, even Meta, who came often. As Margret lay in her bed, I patted her hand and stroked her hair.

Aldonza soon used the herbs I had brought from my trip, and she fretted over not having more. I walked the hills hoping to find some wild lettuce or echinacea, but there was very little to find on the still barren hillside. I began having headaches myself, but what herbs I found, I gave to Aldonza for Margret. Each day she seemed a bit frailer, a bit paler; her eyes had less sparkle.

And finally one day she was gone. Empty spaces . . . empty spaces were in our home and lives and in my heart. In my grieved mind, I felt that losing her *was* my penance for not protecting Daria and for killing Pablo.

I prayed through Mary to let Margret's loss be enough to make it right with my soul, but I could never bring myself to discuss my experiences in Madrid with Father Jude. Because things became better, I willed myself to forget my misadventures. As if Aldonza had an herb the opposite of forget-me-not. Or maybe because I knew one could completely forget the past, I decided I could choose what I would forget.

∽◌◠

Within four months of my return from Madrid, Aldonza and Lorenzo had a grandchild and I had breasts. My monthlies started. Aldonza shook her head at me. "This is what you've been wanting, and you can't have one without the other."

Perhaps, I thought, the persistent headaches had something to do with these changes. I came to expect them.

Hair appeared on me in new places, and the new curve to my hips and narrowing of my waist was more evident. I joined my sisters in the state of womanhood. For Fredrica, Carlota, and me, it was a time of exploration of our bodies. We now often bathed in the waterfall up the hill, rather than the pond where we could be seen by anyone who came to visit or get herbs from Aldonza.

When we stretched our arms up, our breasts seemed bold on our bodies. Fredrica's were pale with brown and narrow nipples. Carlota's were the largest, and the colored part surrounding the nipple was nearly pink with the nipples broader and flatter. As for mine, I could not see them from the same angle as I could theirs, but I could tell my breasts were creamy and round, the nipples, pink. They often looked different, changed colors, changed shape. Under the cold water of the falls, they stood out, got firmer.

When I looked at Fredrica and Carlota, stretching and bending in the water, I felt curiosity between my legs. I wanted to touch myself there. Once I did, and I found I was wet with something other than water, for the texture was slick and smooth and stayed as I rubbed my thumb to my fingers. It had its own smell too. I know now that this is how the body prepares for *amour*, but this did not happen then because of a desire for Fredrica or Carlota, but from my desire to be a woman, to be a mother, from my desire to experience all my body had to offer in my life.

By mistake, I think, Fredrica discovered the best secret of a woman's body. She lay on the upper ledge of the waterfall and spread her legs, opening her secret parts to the air and the sunshine but mostly to the water, flowing against her.

"Fredrica," Carlota cried. Her wheezy voice was shrill. "You must not."

But Fredrica only laughed and said, "Why not wash this hair too?"

I giggled and wondered if she were right. We watched Fredrica and saw her aspect change. A gentle rocking of her body began which became more urgent, a searching for the water, it seemed. Her eyes glazed then closed. A cry rose in her throat, and then she was panting, lying there barely moving.

I started to go to her. Carlota was concerned too and cried, "Fredrica, what is it!?"

"That was delicious," she cried, when she opened her eyes. "I want to do it again."

"What happened?" I asked.

"Try it," was all she said. She moved and pointed to her place. Carlota would not, but I did and soon I, too, found this funny action of our bodies that caused me to lose myself, lose control for moments, before I could gather my wits about me.

Carlota finally tried it too, and though she thought it felt good, she said she knew it must be a sin and would not do it again.

Now the three of us were of courting age, and the bench in the front yard was seldom free from a couple. Julio still visited Carlota and was very solicitous of her fragile condition, never letting her walk to Parado and often doing her chores. I sensed Fredrica was unhappy with Julio's attentions to Carlota; he had been her friend first—but perhaps he was unable to see her as anything but his fishing partner.

Alberto, the young man keeping company with Fredrica, was a cousin of Julio, who was living with the Alonso family. I thought he was even more handsome than Julio. Seeing Alberto gave Fredrica the opportunity to be near Julio, something that made me uncomfortable, for Julio and Carlota were happy together, and I did not want Fredrica to disturb their growing love.

Bernardo and Garcia Nicolás, the sons of Master Nicolas, the barber-surgeon who had set Lorenzo's leg, vied for my attention. Aldonza thought it was unkind for me to encourage the brothers, but I could not choose. It was fun being courted by two at once, though I thought it might have caused trouble between them.

∽◌∝

Carlota came to me one day with the embroidered bag I had had with me when I first arrived. "Donza," she said. "I found this. Is it yours?"

I had not thought of it in years. "Yes." I took it from her. On it were some dark blots from the grasshoppers, and when I dumped the contents on the table, three dead and very dried-up ones fell out.

"Ugh," Carlota said. Her hand flew to her mouth.

I grimaced and threw them in the fireplace. I sorted through the things. Four rocks—one opaque pink, the others cloudy with murky colors: red, green, and gray. And a shell, which was an orangey brown, cupped and ridged, fan-shaped.

"That shell is symbol of the pilgrims who go to Santiago de Compostela," Aldonza said.

Also in the bag were two ivory combs with red stones in them. "These are pretty," I said. I picked them up and held them out to show Aldonza. "I could wear these, if it's all right."

Aldonza nodded and smiled. With gentle fingers, she placed them in my hair.

Picking up the locket, she said, "What's this?" She opened it.

I did not remember at this time that the pictures were turned backwards. We only saw the back sides, which were facing out. On one side the word "Topher" was written. "Top-her? To-pher?" I said. "What an odd word!"

I took the locket from Aldonza and closed it. On the back it said, "Tintoretto," but we knew of no such word. I put the locket in the bag with the other things.

Fredrica came to the table to look. "Where was it hidden?" she asked.

In her breathy voice, Carlota told her, so instead of hiding the bag, I began carrying it with me in my pocket or hooking it at my waist as it had been when I arrived in the cart. It felt nice to have it with me, as if my life did not start when I came here but had existed before, and I had been a small child, a baby once, somewhere.

ᔕ ᘓ

Meta's baby was a fair-skinned boy. They named him Rique. I often walked over to see him and played with him while Meta worked around their little one-room home or outside with Enrique.

If Meta was outside doing chores and I was left with the baby, I pretended their little home was my home. I pretended Rique was mine and I had a husband, who I called the funny name inscribed in the locket we had found in my bag—*Topher*.

Neither Bernardo or Garcia Nicolás made my heart flutter the way I remembered it had for Jesus in Madrid (before he revealed his true self). When I walked to Parado or went to Toboso, I would look for new faces, new neighbors, hoping to find a face to put on my imaginary husband.

ᔕ ᘓ

I did blackwork embroidery for Isadora Princhez, the seamstress in Parado. I made bands,* wristbands, smocks, and pocket handkerchiefs for her. This brought a steady stream of coin into the family. Things had begun to ease for us since my trip to Madrid. It was as if my traveling to Madrid had opened everyone to new possibilities, and things were going well. Now, if only the headaches would stop.

Because Lorenzo's broken leg had not healed well, and he walked with much pain, he had to turn more and more to his woodcarving, which, we found, paid better than farming.

Our fields were rented to others to farm, and while we kept our gardens and the house, our income was earned in other ways. As the herbs on the hills began to grow back after the infestation, Aldonza and I refilled her shelves. I was glad to see the wood betony return. It helped my headaches the most.

As Margret once suggested, Aldonza grew herbs in the garden, no longer leaving

---

* Falling detachable collar

them to chance on the hillside, and made ointments for the skin and herbal mixtures to sell in Señor González's store in Toboso. Carlota made small coil pots to put the ointments in. She fired the pots in the ground and seemed to have a knack for working in clay. Soon she sold pots of various sizes at the store.

Fredrica discovered she could sell the excess animals or fish she had, so she, too, added to the family's income (though I knew she did not give over all the money she earned as Carlota and I did).

⌇∽ ᦉ

When my horse Hope needed new shoes and Aldonza had business with Señor González, I was glad for a reason to go to Toboso for the day. Recently, I had noticed I was restless—lonely, I think. I wanted new people or something different in my life. Aldonza had her herb business; Carlota had Julio and her pots; Lorenzo had his woodcarving. Meta had the baby and Enrique. Fredrica spent much time in the hills or in Parado.

On the morning we were to go to Toboso for the horse's shoes, I awoke before dawn and washed in the pond. I used an herbal preparation of Aldonza's that seemed to soften my hair after I washed it. Wrapped in a sheet, I sat by the pond and combed my hair, fastening it up with the ruby combs. I could see in the early morning sun, how my hair shone from the herbs. My hair had grown considerably in the nine months since my trip to Madrid, and it was more than halfway down my back again.

Inside the house, I put on a new blue baft* dress. Around my neck, I added a falling band, which I had embroidered myself that was as wide as my shoulders and fell over the front of the low-necked dress. The sleeves were tight below the elbow and full above with bombast to fill them out—stuffed with cotton, not hair. It was not necessary to dress up so to go to Toboso, but I wanted to wear my new dress and collar and maybe swing my hips, just a little, not immodestly.

In Toboso, I let out Aldonza at Señor González's store, and I drove on to the blacksmith's. As it turned out, Señor Rufo, the farrier, had a few horses before Hope. The big man put Hope in a stall next to a horse, which was the ugliest horse I had ever seen.

"Whose beauty is this?" I asked lightly.

"Quesano's," Señor Rufo said. "Shoes." He turned back to his bellows.

Señor Rufo was a man who practiced economy of words. I wondered if Don Quesano's niece and Meta's friend, Antonia, was in town.

I walked through the marketplace and looked over the fruits and vegetables

---

*   A coarse cotton fabric

displayed at the stalls. I thought about how much smaller this marketplace was than Toledo's or Madrid's. At a stall of leather goods, I fingered a cordovan bag. When I turned around, I saw Antonia.

"Hello, Donza," she said, smiling. "How are Meta and the baby?"

I had no trouble telling her about the latest smiles, burps, and giggles of little Rique. She laughed with me. I noticed she was carrying three books. "What are those?" I asked.

"Books for my uncle. He asked me to hold them while he went to do some business." She held them out for me to see. "They are about chivalry."

I had to squint in the bright sunlight to read the titles: *The History of the Famous Knight, The Knight of the Cross,* and *Knighthood's Mirror.* "They are nearly the same," I commented.

"All he does, night and day, is read books about knights and giants and damsels in distress," Antonia said, petulantly. "He sells bits of his land to buy these books." She lowered her voice. "I do not know what I am going to do. It worries me so."

I tried to reassure her. "He must know what he is doing."

She smiled and looked distracted. "He sometimes does not care for himself well. His beard is becoming longer and unkempt." She saw her uncle across the square. He did not seem to see her; he was in conversation with the priest, Father Pero. Antonia said, "Give Meta my greetings. I would love to see her baby." She turned toward her uncle and walked away.

It was nearly noon and I met Aldonza on her way to the green where we would eat. As we walked by a doorway, we heard a voice say, "Good day, señora and señorita." It was Xavier Padua, the sheriff. He replaced his hat, which he had removed to greet us. Aldonza knew him and his young wife, Rosa Camila.

We nodded our greetings.

He gazed at me, and I was uncomfortable, wishing instead I had the attention of a young man—none of whom had chanced my way that day.

Aldonza asked, "How is Rosa Camila?"

The sheriff smiled a grim smile. "She expects our third child."

"May you have a blessed boy," Aldonza said.

The sheriff bowed and doffed his hat again. I felt his eyes following me as we walked down the street.

My throat filled with bile and I spat out, "I do not like that man!"

"Donza!" Aldonza said. "What is wrong?"

I was shaking, my shoulders, arms, and hands. I could walk no farther and sat down at the edge of the green.

Blinking back my tears, I cried, "He looked at me!"

"Yes, he leered at you." Aldonza frowned. "It was not seemly."

I was silent. I had not expected her to agree with me—she had been so civil to him.

"But, Donza, men look at beautiful girls—he did not hurt you."

She opened the little basket of food and gave me some salt pork and bread. I put them back in the basket. I was not hungry. I was confused. My mind was filled with thoughts and images—of beating wings, of not being able to breathe, of Jesus, of the dark alley, of Daria, of a trickle of blood from the hole in Pablo's shirt—and I could not settle them.

Again Aldonza surprised me. "What happened in Madrid that you have not told us?"

I gaped at her. *How had she known?*

"I just know," she said, as if she read my thoughts.

The story spilled from me—from my meeting Lothario and Anselmo, to lying to the Bishop, to meeting Jesus and my feelings for him and Daria's feelings for me, to the rape of Daria. It seemed I told it all without taking a breath.

Of Daria, she said, "I am glad it was not you." I opened my mouth to protest, but she put her hand up, saying, "I cannot help it, Donza; I am glad you are safe and home with us."

"But Daria . . ." I felt angry—yet glad Aldonza cared for me.

"We should not have sent you."

"But that is not all," and I told her of killing Pablo.

We sat in silence, her food in her lap, untouched.

"You learned of danger. You were able to defend yourself when you needed." Aldonza touched my hair, which curled down my arm. She patted my cheek and looked grim. "It is a terrible thing. But you are here now and for that, I am most happy." She urged me to talk to a priest. We hugged. I walked down the street toward the Toboso church, much larger than the one in Parado. I knew she was watching me, and I knew the difference between her watching me and the sheriff's watching me. I felt safe.

Toboso's priest Father Jerome was kind and gentle. I told him the story, the telling all the easier because I had told Aldonza. He patted my hand. "There is no crime so heinous that the Church cannot forgive, and there is no sinner so depraved that should not confidently hope for pardon, if they sincerely repent."

"I do!" I cried. "Please tell me what I can do to make it right."

The priest was silent for a moment. He folded his hands in his lap. "What a lot for one so young to keep locked away inside!" He smiled.

I smiled too. I noticed a lightness in my body that I had not felt for months. Had I been so burdened then? How had I kept it all in? I even laughed a little. The priest did too.

Though I did not agree with him, he saw no sin in my actions with Daria. He blamed Daria. *If he had been there,* I thought angrily, *he would not.* I wondered why men were too often ready to blame victims.

Of Pablo, Father Jerome said that it was self-defense. "You have suffered enough."

"Truly?" A slice of hope appeared. "I took a life." And I had been terrified, and I had felt the heart burst. The heavy body had fallen in the alley and settled there, unmoving. I had erased the life from his eyes, and I did not like knowing I was the one who had done it.

"Truly."

Cautiously relieved, I said, "Give me a penance anyway, in case it is not."

He laughed, but he was ready with an answer for me. "Do you know Ana Alonso?"

"Yes." She was Aldonza's friend, the midwife. "She helped deliver my nephew."

He nodded. "I want you to see if you can assist her. Bringing lives into the world would please God."

This penance was to my liking, and I was not sure that was as it should be, but I did not question it.

I left the church. Outside, the clouds looked like a plowed field—rows of rounded fluff. At the fountain in the square, I splashed water on my face. Then I went to the farrier's to wait for Aldonza.

Señor Rufo was not yet finished with Hope. I climbed in the back of our cart to wait. I watched two birds in the tree. They seemed to be having a conversation. First one, then the other chittered away, as if one were confessing to the other. When one flew away, I thought that was how I felt, as if I could fly, float up into the air. The lightness I had noticed since my confession was still with me. My head was vacant of pain. I lay down and closed my eyes to rest.

Soon I heard two men talking. I peeked over the side of the cart and saw Señor Quesano and Señor Rufo. I could not help but listen.

Señor Quesano was doing most of the talking. "It's all in the blood, Rufo. From our mother's blood we are formed and from our mother's blood, we are fed."

"Yes," the blacksmith agreed.

"I have my *executoria** gilded with my family's coat of arms. True, I am on the lowest rung of the ladder of nobility, but still I am of noble blood."

"Noble," the blacksmith interjected.

A leaf fell on my face. I brushed it away.

"And pure," Señor Quesano said proudly. "My great-grandfather fought for our Faith, our Mother Church, in foreign lands." He added, "I have his armor still, the whole of it, save the helmet, which has been missing for some years now."

---

* Literally, letters patent, which guaranteed rights to those of noble blood, i.e., exemption from direct taxation, immunity from debtors' prison, and exemption from hanging.

"Missing." The blacksmith was holding up his end of the conversation in his own way.

"I found some books today, quite to my liking, and I am afraid to say it, but I have bought them," Señor Quesano continued.

"Books."

"And of the greatest kind," the *hidalgo* said with enthusiasm. "Of knights and their quests for Honor. That is the sole purpose of life, to keep one's Honor."

"Honor."

I could imagine how these two men looked talking to each other. Señor Rufo had been facing the sun. Perhaps he was squinting, seeing the older man haloed like a saint in the afternoon sun.

"They all have horses. Bucéfalo is one, belonging to Alexander," the older man paused. "Perhaps you have heard of him."

"No."

"Then what of Babieca, the horse of El Cid." He referred to the greatest Spanish hero of all times. Everyone had heard of the Cid.

"Yes." Señor Rufo did not disappoint me.

"Of course there are those who do not have horses. Take Morgante, the giant, and even though he was one of that gigantic race—they were all arrogant and rude—Morgante was pleasant and well-bred."

"Rude."

I was beginning to feel as if I needed to giggle, but I did not want to be discovered. I covered my mouth with my hand.

"I must be going. I want to begin reading my purchases today!" the old man said eagerly. "I'll get my horse."

"Money?" Señor Rufo asked.

"Gone," Señor Quesano said sadly.

I heard them walk into the barn, and I rose up. I saw Señor Rufo give the old man the reins, and he led the horse out into the sun. I ducked down again. Antonia came, for I heard her uncle say, "Just in time, dear."

I peeked and saw her give some coins to the blacksmith. He clasped them in his hand and walked back into his shop. I heard them drive away. Perhaps Antonia had reason to worry about her uncle.

By the time our evening meal was over that night, I had unburdened my soul again of the happenings on my trip to Madrid. At least I told the skeleton of what happened. I did not tell how I had felt the nobleman's hands on me or how Jesus's skin had flashed pale like the underbelly of a fish or how Pablo's head had slapped the ground.

Lorenzo sat at the table and listened without eating or without comment to the entirety of my story. When I finished, he got up, came around the table, and hugged me. He was sobbing. I held him tightly.

So great was the experience of purging my soul that during the next few days, I remained headache free and continued to feel as if I were floating. However, it was as if I had taken my burden and broken it into pieces, giving it to them; a cloud remained over the house for several days.

Only Fredrica questioned me, "How did it feel to kill a man?" "Was there blood?" "What did it sound like?" "How did the body fall?" and about the night in the alley, "How do men do it together?" and about Daria, "Was she really a virgin?" "What if she had kissed you?" "Do you think you could have killed them?"

I seldom responded to her questions, though I knew the answer to the last—if I could go back to that night I would defend Daria—even if it meant harm to me, even if it meant hurting or killing her attackers. Action, through fear, would have been the right thing to do.

But I did not share these thoughts with Fredrica, and maybe I should have. Maybe I should have described each gory detail; maybe that would have satisfied her. Maybe she would have learned from my experience and not have to continue having unnatural experiences of her own.

One day she came in to the herb shed and began poking around the baskets. She laughed a humorless laugh and said, "We would have been better off if Momma were a wizard who tried to make gold from dross." She shook a basket of blessed thistle.

"I'm sure that cannot be done," I said. "If there were a way to make gold, everyone would be doing it."

Fredrica picked up a basket of lobelia and smelled it. She wrinkled her long nose as if she did not like the smell and put the basket back on the shelf in the wrong place. "It can be done! You merely need the right substances," she insisted, speaking of the wizards' search for gold. "They keep the recipe a secret."

I moved the lobelia.

She changed the subject and began asking me about the different herbs. "What does that one do?" "What if you took too much of this one?" "Can you overdo it?"

I answered these questions until I saw the strange pattern. It was as if she were looking for poisons, another ware of wizards. *Did wizards have long noses, shifty eyes?*

After that I began watching the containers of lily of the valley, male fern, foxglove, and others to see if any of the herbs were missing. "Do not think this way," I said to myself, but I had to, for I remembered the prank on Enrique and Meta, when I had misjudged the amount; I knew Fredrica had a dark and queer spirit.

About a week after I had told my story, Lorenzo and Aldonza came to me while I was doing laundry by the pond. They sat with me and told me how sorry they were for my misadventures, that they should not have sent me alone.

"I learned much from the adventure," I said. "And I am here, safe, with you."

Aldonza patted my cheek and looked into my eyes. "Are you certain nothing about Madrid was familiar? Did you remember anything?" Her voice dwindled away, and I barely heard the last question.

"Nothing," I said firmly and squeezed her hand. As I had told them shortly after I returned from my trip, I had found no clues to my first family—and I was glad. We hugged around.

I told them of the funny conversation I had heard between Señor Quesano and the Señor Rufo. I thought Fredrica would have told it better than I, but I did my best and we all laughed.

After this, things seemed to go back to normal, as if sharing my burden had finally dispersed it to the wind, and we were all free of it at last.

CHAPTER 15

in which Christopher honors his squire

N MAY 1588, my studies at university were complete. The endless tests, the graduation parades, took place. An ending, but I saw no bright beginning. My life was aimless, pointless, and I did not want to continue. I was tired of numbing my brain to sleep and dragging myself out of bed in the morning.

I finished my studies by removing myself, for the most part, from the society of my fellow students. I felt so much older than they, and I was, but only a year or two. I had often escaped to Brados, the estate of my father's friend Alphonse Mentos, duke of Terraria. His son, Carlos, was a kind friend also. Without judgment—for others, my father, for one, still said, "You must forget Luscinda; you must move on"—the duke and Carlos gave me a place to wander with trusted Sosiego, my only confidante, at my side, through their grounds.

I hear what people say. "There goes Christopher Solidares. He was once the bright hope of his father."

Even after all these years, since the quest for Cinda and its terrible end, everything about me feels raw, as if I were burned all over and all inside from sorrow and shame at my failure to find Cinda, to defend Sancha, and at my barbarous actions. Often I tell myself I would do the same thing—to revenge such dishonorable actions against my faithful squire, but then I remember my talks with Brother Diego, and I pray until I, once again, remember vengeance is better left to God.

Years ago, at the church in Santiago de Compostela, where I was a supplicant to St. James, I had felt ardent devotion for a God who could create adulation in so many people. I had hoped He could help me and, at times, I had felt his presence through prayer. I thought of myself still, as Sancha had called me, the Knight of the Seeking Heart, but now I sought solace and direction, for what would I do now? My father wanted me to go on my Grand Tour,* but I felt too unsettled to leave Spain.

---

* After graduation, nobles' sons spent a period of time traveling the continent.

On my knees I prayed for what seemed like hours and then an answer came to me. I yelled for my servant. "Frondo!" I reached over and scratched Sosiego's ear.

"Yes, Don Christopher." The little man came through the door to the bedroom.

"I am going on another *pill grimace*," I said and laughed, a laugh of hope.

"Señor?" he asked, as if he wanted me to repeat what I had said. "You are thinking of Sancho." Remembering the irrepressible Sancho, he smiled, showing his bright even teeth, but he quickly sobered.

"Yes. A pilgrimage to find Sancho's parents."

I had never told him Sancho was a girl.

"How will you do that?" he asked earnestly.

"I cannot know if Cinda is alive or dead, but these parents can know of their child, and I will find them," I declared. "Sosiego will help." I wondered why I never thought of this before and was grateful for the Divine intervention of that day.

"Don Christopher, what a wonderful thing for you to do!" I remembered how Frondo had helped Sancho when they first met and how sad Frondo had been to see the scars on the youngster's back.

I packed my bags and sent word to my father to arrange for my trip. I would leave from Gasparenza in a month's time.

Whether I was successful or not in finding Sancha's family, whether I would ever give up hope that Cinda would be found, I knew I had to take action, to appear to move forward.

With Sosiego at my side, I followed the trail as best I could that I had followed in 1583 to Santiago de Compostela. It was a different time of year and everything was in leaf now, but I was sure I was in the vicinity of my attack—where Sancha had frightened off "those whackers." What a formidable young girl she had been; what a naïve boy I had been!

At a small village, I made some inquiries. Though I did not know a last name, I knew there were twelve children (several years ago) and that the mother had red hair and knew about healing, often with rose hips. At the third house, my sketchy description brought directions to the homestead I hoped to find. As we neared, Sosiego took off through the woods. I followed him as best I could, though I was on horseback.

I thought I had lost him; then I heard shouts and laughter, and when I entered a clearing, there was a little house with many people in the yard. A woman—with a cap—not so very old, but worn from a hard life, was kneeling on the ground with her arms around Sosiego. Several children surrounded her. No sign of the father.

I approached the group slowly on Beleza. Looking at me with gaping mouths, the younger children hid behind the older ones.

The woman got up and said to me, "Señor, did you come with Sosiego?" She looked at the wolf, who was sitting and panting, waiting for more attention. "Do you know of my Sancha?"

I dismounted Beleza. I removed my hat and bowed to her. The words stuck in my mouth. I thought to bring them news that would put their worry to rest, but I did not consider how devastating the words were. Yet I knew I could not prolong her wonder a moment longer.

"If your daughter was the owner of Sosiego and if she disappeared in November five years ago, then yes, I know of her," I said. "Though she came with me as a boy and called herself Sancho."

"But why did she do that?" the mother asked. Wisps of her faded red hair escaped from her cap and framed her face and shoulders.

"To be my squire," I answered. "She told me she wanted to be a knight's squire."

Her mother smiled a bit, though worry clouded her face. I was sure she knew where this was leading. After all, her daughter was not with me.

"She would like that," her mother said.

I cleared my throat and said, more loudly that I wished, "She died while in my service."

The mother gasped and fell to her knees. The older children grabbed at her and all began to keen, whether from relief or sadness, it was hard to tell. I knew that were I told Cinda was dead, I would cry from sadness and relief that my waiting was over.

I helped up the mother and settled her in the shade of a large tree nearby. She smelled of roses. Oh, dear, Sancha, just as you have said.

One of the children ran to get the father.

We sat beneath the tree, and the father held the mother's hand. I told them everything I knew of Sancha, and every adventure we had, but I did not tell all about how she died, for I could not bring myself to tell a mother of such horror, only that it was robbers—and they *had* robbed her of life.

It was nearing dark and they asked me to stay for supper, but I could not. I told them that Sancha saved her salary from me to give to them, but she died before she could send it. I gave them a bag of gold coins. The father said, "Where can I spend this?"

"Anywhere you like."

He held one of the coins in his hand and looked at it. "What is it worth?"

"About four hundred *maravedis*," I said.

They gasped and their mouths opened, but no sound came. They fell to the ground and kissed my feet.

"Please do not," I begged. "I have brought you terrible news."

I have killed your daughter.

"Our daughter is dead," the mother said, with tears in her eyes, "but we are living and this will help us."

I nodded. I understood. They had more worries than a missing daughter. That was their lot in life. Mine was to live well on the outside and live poorly on the inside. But now I could put Sancha to rest, and perhaps I could move forward a bit.

It saddened me greatly to leave Sosiego with them, but the youngsters took to him and he to them. I cannot think of a more noble animal companion than that particular wolf.

∽∾

Before I left for Italy, I visited Brother Diego. He seemed happy to see me.

I began, "At first I could not think of myself as a weak man."

Brother Diego nodded. "It is very difficult for those who have been brought up to believe they are perfect because of their birth." His sad eyes added gravity to everything he said.

It was true. As nobility, we were expected to be good and honorable men, but it was difficult in an age where honor was defined as the way we lived and not as the way we should act. Few people spoke of charity, piety, chastity, or loyalty. I was now certain I needed God's help to live a just life. "I am relieved to feel God's forgiveness when I cannot forgive myself." By giving finality to Sancha's family, as hard as that had been, I had been given a gift from God: hope for the future.

The tall man put his arm around my shoulder and squeezed. The rosary hanging from his belt tapped against my leg. "Ah, you have come a long way. Come see me when you return."

CHAPTER 16

in which Donza discovers she is Quixote's Dulcinea

WENT TO VISIT Ana Alonso. I explained to her, not that it was a penance, but that I wanted to help bring new life into the world. She said she thought I would be a perfect apprentice because of my knowledge of herbs. She showed me her own collection. While not as extensive as Aldonza's, Ana had the herbs needed for her trade.

I got to help that very day, for as we stood talking, a young man rode up and asked Ana to go to Pronto Real to be with his wife. Ana grabbed her satchel, and we followed the young man, Alejo Sentera, to his home, which was a one room cob hut. His wife, Chastain, greeted us at the door, but she quickly doubled over in pain. We helped her to the mattress which was on the floor in a little alcove behind a curtain.

The hut was quite dirty, and Ana was upset by this. While she sat with Señora Sentera, I tidied the main room, raking up the smelly rushes and spreading fresh ones on the dirt floor. I made Señor Sentera get water, so I could wash the few dishes they had, as all appeared dirty.

"Don't you have anyone to help?" I asked.

"My mother lives in Toboso but would not come," he said bitterly. "She says she is sick."

"You watched me tidy up just now, didn't you?" I asked.

"Yes," he said.

"Then you see that it continues to get done."

"But I can't."

"Yes, you can."

I heated some water, and at Ana's direction fixed a mild drink with golden seal for the woman. I helped her take a few sips. The pains were coming close together. Ana was rubbing lily oil on the woman's distended stomach, but the woman was rolling this way and that, and Ana had to stop. The woman's legs drew up with each pain.

"There," Ana pointed, "the baby's head."

It was tiny yet, a circlet of pink between the woman's legs.

"Help me," Ana said, and together we lifted the woman to her feet.

Ana called for Alejo. He helped me hold Chastain in a squat. Ana explained calmly that without a birthing chair this was the best position. Within five more pains, the baby slid into Ana's waiting hands. "A boy," we all cried.

Ana showed me how to bind the cord and cut it, how to wipe off and clean the baby, and how to deliver the afterbirth and clean Chastain. Alejo, to my surprise, helped in all this. I helped him wash the bedding, which, when it was dry, he would have to stuff with clean straw. In the meantime, we made a bed for Chastain of a quilt on the floor. She held the baby and put him to her breast. Chastain looked so pale and worn out that I did not know how she could look so happy at the same time. So much happened and quite quickly that I wondered how Ana ever managed by herself. She told me later she seldom did: "Often there are too many hands wanting to help."

Before we left, we fixed some gruel for the couple to eat, enough to last for a couple of days. It was sad they had no one to help them.

On the way back to Ana's, we arranged that I would come to apprentice with her two or three days a week.

As I rode home that evening—clouds partially covered the full moon—I realized I was not ready to have my own baby and my own home, but I was eager to help Ana. *I saw the baby take its first breath.*

ৡৢ

The next several weeks passed quickly. I assisted Ana at several successful births, learning something new at each one. It was a Thursday in the summer of 1588 when we went to the gypsy fair near Parado. I dressed in my blue dress. Instead of the blackwork collar, I wore a white embroidered vest, which cinched my waist and formed to my body. The neckline of the dress was scooped to the hint of the curve of my bosom—still modest, I thought. In my hair, I put the ivory and ruby combs. I splashed myself, Aldonza, Carlota, and Fredrica with rosewater, which made us all laugh. I waxed our lips and blushed our cheeks, something we rarely did. I decided I must do it more often for Carlota. More and more I noticed her with blue-tinged lips and fingernails.

At the gypsy camp, we pulled up our cart next to the Alonsos' cart. Pedro, Ana, and their son, Julio.

Julio and Carlota walked away, slowly, arm in arm to the ring of tents. Fredrica, making full use of her dimples with Julio, walked with them, even though I asked her to come with me.

Bernardo and Garcia Nicolás soon found me. I was contented to have them accompany me, but I still could not decide on one of them, which merely told me neither was for me.

As the three of us walked off together, Aldonza said, "Be careful." Lorenzo's farewell was, "Have fun."

The brothers and I watched the dancers, though they were hard to see because of the large crowd. The dancers performed a medley of carols and then danced a *seguidilla*. Their feet and arms kept perfect time to their tambourines and snapping fingers.

In front of us was Xavier Padua, the sheriff, who had stared at me and made me uncomfortable in Toboso. He was with another policeman, Manuel Montemayor.

Montemayor licked his lips and look longingly at the dancers. "What a hen house full of legs and breasts," he said. "Quite a feast to look at."

Xavier agreed with a lascivious laugh. "Yes, but once the rose has been plucked from the bush, it quickly fades." He paused, then added, "I should say, 'once the Rosa has been plucked'. . ." He looked across the circle, where his wife, Rosa Camila, was standing with Ana.

Rosa Camila looked to be twelve months pregnant; her face was swollen and pasty, and her ankles looked like tree trunks. (Not a kind thing to say, I know, but truthful.) Xavier sighed. "I am a thirty-five-year-old stallion married to a puffed-up old mare." He shook his head; then the men moved and I was glad. Their rude ramblings had made me uncomfortable.

The dancing was over, and a man with three trained dogs and a half dozen trained birds entertained us. Next a man in an elegant black outfit, embroidered in white, recited a poem of how the Christians regained the land from the Moors. Each performance was greeted with a shower of coins, and the gypsy children scurried around and picked up the money, putting it in their caps or in felt pouches. After the recitation, the performers stopped for a while to give everyone a chance to throw their money in other ways: to fortunetellers or for gypsy goods, such as bracelets, belts, bags, jewelry, and almond cakes and other foods.

Bernardo, Garcia, and I walked over to a knife toss game, and I stood next to Carlota, who was already there with Julio. Small circular targets were painted in rows on planks several feet away. Bernardo paid for us to play. The brothers' knives hit the boards, but the knives were outside the target. My toss went straight to the center of the target. The boys gasped. The old gypsy removed the knife and handed me a braided leather bracelet and looked for someone else to play.

He handed the knives to a stranger, a handsome young man, who was dressed in brown velvet, threaded with gold. The gypsy took his money. The man's knife went straight to the same target I had hit.

Bernardo paid the gypsy for me to throw again—three knives. Again I hit the target each time. Another bracelet, which I gave to Carlota and helped her tie it on her wrist. She was pleased.

The well-dressed nobleman paid again and hit the targets—again the same ones I had hit.

"Sir," I said boldly, "you are not from this area."

"No," he said, "I am traveling." His golden brown eyes crinkled with humor. Displaying a head full of short golden brown curls, he swooped his hat and made a sweeping bow. He replaced the hat, the brown and yellow plumes still shivering from their flight. "I did not know I would find a princess."

I blushed at his words.

He was only slightly taller than I, broad-shouldered and narrow-hipped. His clothing was finer than anyone's, more like the men I had seen leave the theater in Madrid. I shuddered to compare him to them.

He looked at Bernardo and Garcia and asked if they minded if he paid for me to throw again. I bristled but did not want to embarrass my friends by saying he only needed my permission. The stranger paid the old gypsy man enough for each of us to have five throws. A small crowd had gathered to watch.

"Please, señorita, go first," the stranger said gently. He seemed strong and gracious at the same time.

I was intrigued. I threw the first knife into the far left target. I then threw each successive knife into the next target. When I was finished, it was as if five soldiers were lined up in a row.

The stranger followed suit, and in the row below, he plunked an opposing row of soldiers.

The onlookers applauded. Even Bernardo and Garcia did, though they looked a bit unhappy. Carlota was bouncing on her toes. "Donza, that was perfect!"

The stranger looked puzzled. "You are very good, Doña Donza." By using this title, he accorded me an honor I did not deserve. It felt wonderful.

"Señor, you have me at a disadvantage," I said. "Your name?"

He removed his hat again and made another sweeping bow. I saw the plumes on his hat were fastened with a large button, a coat of arms. "Carlos Mentos of Brados, the first and only son of the duke of Terraria. At your service, señorita." His eyes shone brightly. Yes, one could see he was of noble birth, and a duke's son, too. He would know the king, himself! "And you?"

I laughed. "Aldonza Lorenzo, the last daughter of four of the house of Corchuelo of La Mancha." I curtseyed. The crowd laughed. Carlota poked Julio in the ribs with her elbow and nodded my way. Fredrica was now there too, but her look was inscrutable.

"Another round, Aldonza Lorenzo, beautiful lady?" he asked. He had a wonderful smile. His teeth were perfect, gleaming white.

"Why not?" I knew I was flirting outrageously, but all of Parado was watching, so I was well chaperoned.

He paid the old gypsy, double what he had before for the ten knives.

This time I threw one at a time, letting him throw right after me. *Pflank!* Five times my knife hit. *Pflunk!* Five times his knife hit right next to mine, sharing the same landing spot. Not soldiers this time, but lovers. The applause was even louder. The music began, and the crowd moved away to watch the dancers.

The stranger leaned over and said in my ear, "As close as those knives are, that is how close I want to be to you." Looking into his golden eyes, I felt my heart leap, something it had not done since my infatuation with Jesus—but this was more exciting, infinitely more exciting. He took my hand and kissed it. He had a small ruby ring on his little finger. He removed it and said, "Here is the prize, for you have won."

"I did not win," I said.

"Ah, but you did. You have won my heart," he said, oh, ever so smoothly. He slipped the ring on my finger. "It is a ruby, as you have in your hair." He touched one of my ivory and ruby combs. His touch, a touch that was dangerously personal, left me breathless and flushed.

"But I have nothing for you," I cried, "for you have won too." I smiled coyly. I would not say he had won my heart—but he might choose to think it.

When I smiled, he touched my dimples. "Ah, how fetching you are, my lady." He closed his eyes and clutched his heart and pretended to swoon. In fun, I caught his arms and pulled him upright again. He looked happy at my touch. I removed my hands.

I untied the braided leather band I had won and tied it on his wrist.

"An honorable token." He twisted the band and rewarded me with his shining grin. "I shall always keep this. I will never forget you, señorita of the blue eyes."

"You are like no one I know," I said. "But you have not turned my head." I lied, oh, yes, I lied.

"Then we shall bide our time, until I must leave, by watching the dancers." He offered his arm, and I hooked my hand in his elbow. Placing his other hand on top of mine, we walked to the circle. I saw the difference his noble presence made for the crowd parted, and we walked to the perimeter right in front of the dancers.

He was not at all surprised by this, had grown up expecting it, but I felt awkward.

If this is only for now, if this is only for this minute, I thought, *this feeling is what we are made for.* The heady feeling I was experiencing was unlike any I had had before. I could scarcely watch the dancers for looking at him. His beard was trim and neat, quite short.

"Your grace." A man I knew to be from Toboso, Jaime Jorges, wanted Don Carlos's attention. Señor Jorges bowed until the duke's son acknowledged him.

"What word of the Armada, your grace?" The local man's eyes looked at the ground.

Those around us were interested in the answer and pressed forward. Here was a chance to get news straight from the king's court.

"The king has ordered daily prayers for the success of the expedition, for the victory of Spain," Don Carlos replied. "With God's grace all will go well." Then he turned from Señor Jorges and pulled me closer. We again watched the dancers.

The gypsy band was playing a *sarabande.* The dancers moved gracefully. The music and the swaying of the dark gypsies with the rhythm stirred my inner fires. I wished it were he and I dancing there in the circle.

As if he read my mind (and why not, we were in a place of fortunetellers and magicians), he threw a half dozen gold coins into the ring and motioned the dancers to step aside. He guided me to the center of the circle. The music began slowly, and I watched him closely to follow his every move, for he was a courtier and surely knew more about dancing than I, a poor peasant girl. But he danced as we danced at our festivals, and I knew well what he was doing. As the music picked up, we swirled and swayed together, brushing each other as we spun, touching fingers for an instant.

At the end the crowd burst into applause, and I was breathless. He tossed down more coins and called for a partner dance for everyone. This time he held me as we moved together across the circle. The other dancers were as incidental as gnats. I was so intoxicated by his nearness that I did not know how I was even moving, much less standing.

We danced until he said, "I must be on my way, Aldonza Lorenzo."

Then I stopped and knew, in that instant, that this was all I could expect, that what I had experienced *was* just a moment of my life, a sensual memory to always have, the most a peasant girl could ask. In fact, I was lucky, as most peasant girls could only *dream* of such an afternoon.

"A compassionate God will see we meet again." Don Carlos bowed, swooping his hat one last time, the dancing golden curls on his head bobbing at me. He kissed me on the cheek and was gone.

I was not sure how long I stood at that spot, my heart pounding, but soon Meta and Antonia found me and asked me a dozen questions about the stranger. I answered them all, the ones I could answer and hoped they would ask me again, so that I could savor the moments we had together. For when I talked about it, I felt his presence beside me and his touch instead of the sorrow of his leaving.

I was at Ana's when a servant rode up and said Rosa Camila Padua, the sheriff's wife, needed us. She grabbed her bag and I grabbed mine. On the way there, Ana told me she was very worried about Rosa Camila. I remembered how swollen and pasty she had looked at the gypsy fair. "Rosa Camila is a woman who does not do well in pregnancy. Her body holds too much fluid and her heart is overused."

"She looked . . . uncomfortable," I said, not wanting to list her many symptoms.

"That was a fun day for you, wasn't it?" Ana said.

I blushed and touched the ruby ring, which I had on a string beneath my clothing. I did not want to wear such a precious ring on my finger. "Yes," I said.

"What advice would you have given Rosa Camila?" she asked.

I was glad she was changing the subject. I had now talked enough of that day, and I began to realize that I relived it in my mind for nothing. What happened with Don Carlos (Carlos, a name I had decided I wanted to whisper across the pillows) *was* a dream, and nothing would come from it but having had the experience.

"I would give her dandelion leaf, elecampane. . . ." I named a few more herbs and told how to prepare them.

"Good. That's what I suggested to her," Ana said. "She would do nothing. I visited her often in the past months, and she would not help herself."

At the Padua house, we found Xavier and his old mother waiting for Ana. The mother looked worried and Xavier did, too. Two small children were near their grandmother, both sitting and sucking their thumbs.

We heard Rosa Camila cry out in pain. In her room were two servants holding her hands. The servants stepped out of our way as Ana and I each moved to a side of the bed. I looked at Rosa Camila's hand. In it and around her wrist was an exact hand print of the servant. Ana squeezed her ankle and I saw a like phenomenon.

I rubbed lily ointment on her stomach, but Ana motioned for me to stop. Rosa Camila was nearly unconscious. She checked Rosa Camila internally and said, "I cannot feel the baby move." She whispered, "I may have to take it." I sucked in a breath; I felt my palms grow warm and wet. "Go tell Xavier to get a priest," she added firmly.

Quickly I gave Xavier the message and returned to the bedroom. Within minutes Rosa Camila had died. She had not opened her eyes. She had not spoken to us. Great quantities of liquid and waste poured from her body. I gagged at the odor and stepped away, but Ana said sharply, "We must get the baby. Quickly, the knife."

Numbly, I got the knife and watched as she cut Rosa Camila open with a long and straight cut over the fullest part of her stomach. The skin pulled back, and the baby popped out like a morning glory greeting the sun. Ana plucked the baby from his mother, the stem of cord trailing behind.

The baby trembled and gasped, then cried a tiny cry. She handed him to me. I tapped the bottom of his feet to see if he would open his eyes. He did for a moment. He seemed to look over my head, at his guardian angel, I hoped. Then he died in my arms.

I did not go back to Ana's for more than a week. Then Aldonza took me, and she, Ana, and I sat in the front yard under an elder tree and talked about how it felt to have someone under your care die.

While we sat in the cool breeze of the afternoon, I listened to these wiser women, who had seen much more death than I, talk about how they learned to accept the times they could not help and the times they may have made mistakes, deadly mistakes.

"Why did God wish Rosa Camila dead and for the baby to die in my arms?" I asked.

Neither had an answer. Finally Aldonza said, "What you are doing with Ana is beautiful. I want you to continue."

৯ ৎ

One evening I was sitting alone on the bank by the pond—it was still light—and Fredrica came and sat by me. I watched the water swirl into dimples as we gently swished our feet back and forth.

Without looking at me, she handed me a scrap of paper. "Would you read this to me?" she asked, smiling prettily.

Warily, I looked at the paper. It was a recipe that called for fox lungs, kelp, roach allum, coriander, pollen of bees, skin of a rooster foot, damiana, panax. . . . I asked, "What is this for?"

"A love potion," Fredrica said, rubbing her unfortunate nose. "I got it from the gypsies. To make Julio love me." She kicked a foot out and flipped water at a nearby duck. Her foot plopped back into the water.

"I think it's clear he loves Carlota," I said gently. "Alberto thinks highly of you."

She frowned and picked up a stick to dig into the ground. "But Carlota doesn't love Julio as much as I do."

"How do you know?" I pushed the loose strands of hair from my eyes.

"She's sickly. I'm much prettier." Fredrica dug in harder with the stick. "I loved him first." The stick snapped in two. "I want him to spend time with me."

"I'm not going to help you try to change what is."

"You're getting even with me for all the things I have done to you," she shouted at me. "You don't want me to be happy." She pulled her feet from the pond and stood up.

"That's ridiculous," I said angrily, also rising. "Let me help in another way."

She stomped her foot and punched me with her forefinger. "Everything happens to you. You get to do everything. I hate you!" She ran off.

I stood there wondering what I could have done for her, what I could do for her. But I did what I always did about Fredrica—nothing.

A few days later, at night, I was in the loft alone. Since Margret had died, Carlota and Fredrica slept in Meta's old room. I woke up to a loud scream—Fredrica!

I flew from my mattress and stumbled down the ladder.

In the little alcove Aldonza was leaning over Carlota shaking her, talking to her. Fredrica was crying frantically. Aldonza was crying. Lorenzo was stunned.

Carlota was unresponsive. Still warm, but dead. If she would only breathe. *Breathe,* I thought. I watched her chest, hoping against hope. But—nothing. She grew colder and bluer.

After the funeral, as she was being lowered into the earth, I took a handful of pink lilacs and showered them on top of the box. Aldonza added a rose, and Lorenzo picked up a handful of dirt to throw in.

Fredrica was stoic but looked the most troubled I had ever seen her. I watched her every move to see if she did anything to back up my suspicion that she had poisoned Carlota. Had she become an alchemist, mixing potions, which did not heal as her mother's herbs did but that killed? Sometimes you cannot know the truth. My suspicion, my anger, held back my grief for Carlota. I stood watch over everyone—to be sure no one else died.

Aldonza and Lorenzo went about their days as if all were normal: laundry this day, feeding the cows and pigs in the morning, and at night, cooking, carving, weaving, sewing. What I saw was that silent grief came to live in our little home and wrote itself in their faces. Late at night, I heard their muffled sobs, and I imagined them in their bed, arms around each other, wishing and wishing and wishing Carlota was here again—just as I was wishing it.

One afternoon, Fredrica came to me. She did not look at me as she said, "I know you think I killed her, but I did not."

I said, "Yes."

She looked confused. "Yes, you think I killed her? Yes, you think I did not?"

"Yes," I said again and walked away. I believed both, and I did not know the truth, nor was I ever likely to. I wished Margret were here to talk to; she, I believed, understood the possibilities of Fredrica in a way that I did not.

I ran up the hill alone, slapping branches out of my way and saying every wicked word I had heard in the streets of Madrid as I went, and wanting, *wanting* Carlota with me, wishing that we were going to the falls or going to pick berries or stopping to look at a spider's web or climbing trees. *I wanted her back.*

I picked up a fat stick and hit it against a tree. Something expanded inside me. I hit the tree again and again until I shattered the stick. Then I picked up another and yelled with each *whack*. My lungs filled and felt large and full. I attacked the tree again and again. I should have protected Carlota (I should have protected Daria). When I was out of breath, the anger left me, and I fell to my knees and cried. For Carlota. How I missed her!

After Carlota's death, Julio moved to Toledo. Ana was grief stricken, though she never talked about it, other than to say, "He can't forget Carlota. He said he had to leave."

Fredrica became more and more withdrawn from all of us. She began making pottery as Carlota had done. Because Fredrica fired the pots in the ground, she had the opportunity to start many fires with my old mirror, something that still seemed to fascinate her. She was very good at the pottery; her pots sold better than Carlota's. I never knew what Fredrica did with her money, and she was gone more often than she had ever been.

Fall 1588

As I continued to work with Ana, I spent more time with her. If I knew a baby was soon to come, I would ride or walk to her house and wait.

I was at Ana's late one night when Pedro came home with a story. "I found old Alonso Quesano out on the road badly hurt," he began.

"How awful!" I cried. "Is he all right?"

"I'm not sure, but he is home and a-bed," Pedro said. "I've seen to it myself." Then he launched into his tale. It seemed the old gentleman's mind had finally gone. He fancied himself a knight errant—Don Quixote, he called himself—and had left his home to find adventures. Pedro had found the *hidalgo* badly beaten with some armor on and with the ricketiest old horse Pedro had ever seen. I remembered the horse from the blacksmith's shop.

"I found him this afternoon but waited until dark to take him home," Pedro said. "He was in such bad shape I knew he wouldn't want the neighbors to see." Pedro shook his head.

I said, "Poor Antonia," remembering how she worried about her uncle.

I did not go home until the next evening. On my way, I passed Señor Quesano's house. There was a large bonfire in the yard, which seemed very odd to me. I stopped to see if anything were the matter. As I drew closer, I could see the fuel of this brilliant fire was dozens of books.

I pulled the blanket from Hope and began beating at the flames, though surely this would be in vain, as I saw the flames curling the covers and pages of book after book.

"Stop!" Antonia cried. I looked and saw her and the housekeeper. "We have set the fire on purpose." She had to speak loudly for the fire whooshed and gushed before us.

"But, oh, how awful. You are losing your wonderful books," I cried, for I thought to have this number of books would be quite fine.

She explained to me how the books had muddled her uncle's brains to gruel. "He thinks he can right any wrong, protect orphans, and preserve virgins."

I remembered Daria and how I had failed her, and I wished that Antonia's uncle might be able to do what I could not. "But surely they are not bad books," I said. "Why would printers waste their money printing bad books and why would readers read them?" Neither woman answered me. "A book should transport you to someplace you have never before been."

"But that is the problem," Antonia finally spoke. "My uncle went someplace he should never have been and came home wounded. And who is to say he will not go back?"

I could see she was too upset to understand what I meant, so I climbed up on Hope and left the crackling fire behind me.

The next morning I told Aldonza, Lorenzo, and Fredrica of the fire of books.

"Was the fire close to the house?" Fredrica asked, her dark eyes gleaming as she looked in the fireplace.

"Rather," I said, "though not dangerously so."

"Who started it, the housekeeper or Antonia?" Her thick russet hair waved around her pretty face.

"I don't know," I answered. "The flames rose high into the air. I saw it from a long way."

"I wish I had seen it!" Fredrica said vehemently; she turned to look out the window.

Aldonza looked concerned. "Will poor Señor Quesano be all right? Perhaps

I could help him." She pulled off a piece of bread and put some berry jam on it.

Lorenzo's dark and bushy eyebrows nearly met. "I imagine Master Nicolás will ask if they think you can help."

∽∾

More distressing events happened that fall. The Spanish Armada had suffered a grave defeat in English waters. It was not the English fleet itself that felled the Grand Armada. But their attack, from which we suffered a loss of only eighteen of 130 vessels, drove the Armada into the North Sea and forced it to go around the British Isles. Then at the mercy of Atlantic storms and at the hands of the Irish, who showed no compassion for our brave Spaniards, the Armada returned with a handful of the 18,000 men who had embarked on this expedition.

In our little church in Parado, Father Jude prayed, "O God in Heaven, whose anger toward us is justified as we are merely most lowly humans, what is the message for Spain? Do you disfavor our king? Our mighty conquerors continue to spread Your Word throughout the New World and in Flanders and other places, yet you punish us in this manner. Show us Your Way."

The defeat of the Armada did not cripple Spain's capacity to launch new armadas or new armies, but it severely undermined the confidence of many Spaniards in the king. It was rumored his health was poor. The defeat of the Armada created much hardship on the taxpayers of Spain. Our little enterprises kept money trickling in, yet it trickled out at about the same pace.

For me, life was good. I helped Aldonza, Lorenzo, and Ana and embroidered for Isadora Princhez and found pleasure in all of it. Sometimes in the evening I would touch my blue dress and look at the ring on the cord around my neck and remember dancing at the gypsy fair with the golden-eyed stranger. Nothing in my life was as exciting as that afternoon. I felt I was a rosebud waiting to bloom into the rose. Things would change for me, but when?

Summer 1589

The next summer, in Toboso, Antonia told me, "My uncle has left home again." Her eyes sparkled with tears. "This time with Sancho Panza as his squire." She explained her uncle now wished to be known only as Don Quixote and was desirous of more adventures.

In less than two years of the book burning, Don Quixote and Sancho Panza returned. I was riding home when I met Sancho as he walked home from Señor Quesano's. The old man had died.

I was surprised to see Sancho's face streaked with tears, his voice breathy from his crying. He was a sturdy man, yet here was a love and tenderness I would not have thought of him. Every few words, the tears would well up in his eyes and spill down his cheeks, plopping in large droplets to his shirt.

Sadly he said, "I w-w-want to hear him say, 'Sally f-f-forth again with me, Sancho!'" He stuttered in his grief. "And when I was to be the governor of Baratario, he gave me such good advice." He looked down the road toward his little farm. "He told me to be honest, compassionate, and to always remember where I came from. Though it be from peasants, I was to be proud and humble. Qualities of a good knight."

I nodded. I was not surprised when he said he was a governor, for Teresa, his wife, had had me read her the letters from Sancho. I knew something of his story.

"He said to keep my nails pared regularly and not to eat too many onions or too much garlic. He said to never get drunk." He added, "I seldom do, you know."

I agreed, for, indeed, I had never seen him or Lorenzo drunk.

"I would give ten thousand governorships for one more adventure with Don Quixote," the little man declared. He was a good man because of his simpleness.

I saw the change in him then, some belief in an unseen ideal, but I did not know until years later, when I read the manuscript by Miguel Cervantes that was found at a market stall, what the change was in Sancho, how he learned the mystery of faith, which, without believing, believes. For Sancho knew windmills were not giants, sheep were not armies, puppets were not Moors; he knew that a barber's basin was not a golden helmet. He knew the difference between fantasy and reality, yet, at some point he had discovered the gap between the two was not so far, and the illusion of external appearances was not stronger than the internal vision of never-ending hope for a better world.

He sniffled and two large tears fell on his knee. "I begged him to come with me once again to search for, to fight for, My Lady Doña Dulcinea, but he said, 'I was mad and now I am sane.'"

"And what of the beautiful Dulcinea?" I asked because I did not know this name and did not think she was from around there. "Have you let her know of his death?"

And most amazing! Sancho Panza cried, "She is you!" Looking at me as if he just realized who had been talking to him. And indeed he did get down on his knee and bow to me!

"Get up, Señor Panza." I pulled at his arm. Shaking my head, I said, "You are confused. I never met Señor Alonso face to face."

"Nor he, you," Sancho cried, sitting again on the log. "But he admired your beauty from afar and loved you. He chose you to be his inspiration that spurred him on to noble deeds. Dulcinea del Toboso, he called you."

I laughed. "I am no noble lady. You know me. I am Lorenzo's daughter."

"He said, 'I paint it in my mind as I want it to be.'"

This news was beyond my understanding. How could it have been my beauty that was the inspiration for Dulcinea? Why would he have traveled the country risking his life for a dream love? I did remember hearing him say, while I listened from the bell tower: "Were I to find the woman whom I considered the most beautiful, I would go to the ends of the earth for her."

Sancho cleared his throat. "Because he is dead, the world is deprived of its righter of wrongs, its protector of orphans, its preserver of virginal chastity, its patron of all widows and supporter of women still married, and many other matters of the same sort."

"Surely there are others who perform these good deeds," I said. I did not understand his view of the crazed old man. How had Don Quixote achieved such great good?

But Sancho said sadly, "I think honor has become about self and what is easiest. Not about protection of others. Chivalry might have died with my master."

We got up. He patted me on the arm and then hugged me. He walked away, leaving me to ponder what I had heard.

And yes, perhaps one could blame the books; I could not decide. Don Quixote acted from a belief that the world was worth fixing, that wrongs were worth righting. He sallied forth to do good deeds. At least, that was his intent. From what Sancho said this sometimes went awry. Yet in the end, Don Quixote gave Sancho a changed outlook on life. It was not as if the old man read books of indiscriminate murder, inordinate brutality, and random mayhem (but why would these even be written?) and went out and aimlessly murdered people. Would one blame such atrocities on books too? Unthinkable. Have we not minds of our own?

ᔕ ᘉ

It did not take long for the story of Don Quixote and his Dulcinea to be passed around the countryside. Also the rumor that I was the inspiration.

One afternoon, Fredrica found me in the pond gathering water lilies, which I would press for scented ointment.

She splashed into the water by my side and grabbed my shoulder, nearly knocking me over. "Now *everyone* thinks you are special. That *you* are the most beautiful."

"This is a fable," I said. "Why do you listen to it?" Trying to stay upright in the water, I stiffened my body.

Her fingers pressed into my flesh. "Why did you come *here?*" She was looking over my shoulder, not at me, but I saw cruelty and hatred in her eyes.

"What would you have me do?" I felt my feet slipping in the mud at the bottom of the pond, and I struggled to free myself from her grasp, but she pushed me under and held me there. Instead of fighting, I pulled myself lower in the water and flung myself away from her, heading for the bank. Grasping at my clothing, she followed me.

My clothes lifeless against my legs, my hair straight and streaming with water, I stood on the bank and said, "I did not ask for him to love me from afar."

"I did not ask for you to come here," she said, as she plowed out of the pond.

"I do not know what made him. . . ." I could not acknowledge her wish that I had never been found in Lorenzo's cart.

"You," she said with venom. "You made him. You are a bewitcher," she cried. She flung her head and water flew from her sodden hair.

I became cold beyond the day. I shuddered and wrapped my arms around me. "What do you mean?" I cried. She was again saying I was from the Devil.

"One look at your blue eyes, those dimples, that black hair, and men fall in love with you," she cried, pointing at me, jabbing her finger at me. "Like Julio did with Carlota." She rubbed her long nose with the back of her hand; water droplets fell from her fingers. "I can stop you too!"

Was this an admission of guilt? Had Fredrica—O wicked wizard—used errant alchemy, our herbs as chemicals, to take our precious Carlota away?

"Fredrica!" came Aldonza's voice from behind me. I turned and saw her and Lorenzo standing there. Lorenzo's red and wild hair made him look thunderous, and Aldonza stood straight and stern. "What are you saying?" she cried. "What have you done?"

Fredrica looked uneasy. "I have done nothing." She pointed her finger at me. "It is she who came and ruined our lives." Fredrica was trembling, her hands in particular.

Aldonza came and put her arm around me. I felt her fingers, warm and gentle, on my shoulder. She said, "Do not think she speaks for us. You have been like a daughter."

Wishing Fredrica had not heard, I flinched. Her mouth twisted; her dimples flattened into the lines that I called Cruelty, plain for all to see—if they looked.

Aldonza stayed by me and said to Fredrica, "What happened to Carlota?"

Fredrica did not look at Aldonza and did not answer.

Aldonza's lips quavered. "Did you do something? To her?"

"You care for all of them more than me," Fredrica said.

Aldonza shook her head. "No, I love you all." Tears were in her eyes.

"But since she came . . ." Her finger shaking, Fredrica pointed to me.

Lorenzo, his deep voice gruff with anger, said, "Fredrica, say no more. Donza belongs here."

Fredrica's eyes narrowed, and she looked from me to Aldonza to Lorenzo, staring with hatred at each of us. I shivered and Aldonza held me closer. Lorenzo moved to stand between us and Fredrica. Then she ran.

I stood in silence, my face in my hands, the faint odor of the water lilies at my nose.

It could never be set aright. For how could I forget her words, her hatred, her jealousy? Now I saw that I had known how she had felt all these years. I had known, and as long as I had kept it hidden from Aldonza and Lorenzo, I had been able to ignore it. But now, how could I let Aldonza and Lorenzo berate her and favor me? In the end, I was not their daughter and Fredrica was. I knew I must prepare to leave. A wreck of family lay before me.

CHAPTER 17

in which Christopher makes a decision

EARS AGO, I overheard a conversation between Doña Isabella and my mother.

Doña Isabella was lamenting how much she missed her children when she traveled without them, and my mother replied, "I seldom think of the children when I travel. I am more enamored of the new places than anything else."

"But how could you forget them?" Doña Isabella asked.

"It is not that I forget them, they are simply recessed in my consciousness," my mother said, "and I have little thought of them. I enjoy my life in a different way."

I had not understood her meaning until on Grand Tour, away from Spain for many months, I discovered what she meant. It was if I were in a different life and the burden of my losses fell away, and I was able to enjoy myself and enter into daily activities without the pall of the events that filled and seldom vacated my mind while at home. There were days upon days when I thought nothing of Cinda or Sancha or my future, and looking back to the trip, I saw I was able to be a typical young man of noble birth, one without guilt or shame from inaction or wrong action or failure at not solving the mystery of Cinda's disappearance.

In the two years I was gone, I spent a few months with Marietta, Tintoretto's daughter and our old friend; some time in France; and a few months at the Hapsburg Court (the Hapsburgs were cousins of our king), where I found myself involved in a few brief flirtations with women of the court.

The time was an exercise in exploring my manhood, unexpectedly giving up my virginity one night when my senses were overpowered by an earl's widow. Bella was my senior by ten years and easily shared her knowledge of pleasure. I came to understand that that sort of enjoyment was natural, and in those foreign lands, it was as if I were under a sort of spell, a Glamour, that brought my senses to the fore and banished my usual turn of mind.

Yet soon I saw that the luster of lust was dimmed by lack of commitment, the lack of caring, and even as I began to think of home, I received a letter from my father who said he would not live forever, and I must be prepared to care for the estate.

It only took the few minutes of reading my father's letter to pull me back to my mindset of the past several years. When I told my lover that I must leave, she said, "You have learned much from me, but I think an older lover would suit me better."

Feeling happy as if freed from a trap, I laughed, intermittently, for several miles in the carriage headed for home. Even though her words humbled and deflated me, I found it was a relief to be gone from her. Once at home, its familiarity recalled my constant self, and I was content to forego further lovers while I determined the course of my life.

As for my father's concerns in regards to my taking over responsibilities for Gasparenza, I had little taste for it, yet I was the eldest son and heir and needed to participate. I had never given much thought to my four dead brothers, two who died at birth and two, Miguel and Juan, who died in a quarry accident (thankfully Tomás was only injured). If they had lived, the pressure would not be so much on me. But I only had two surviving brothers, and Tomás, though a good and steady youth, did not have the temperament to oversee the lands, and Franco was only thirteen, too young to tell.

After attending to the affairs of the estate with my father for eight months, I found I needed respite from the outside world. Too many temptations. Too much pressure to wed. Too many people wanting to order my life; too many reminders of what my life was to have been.

I decided to go to the monastery for a time: the decision of orders to be made later. Brother Diego agreed to continue to be my mentor until I had chosen my life's path. From there, I could still work on the estate with my father but without the pressures of a secular life and with the comfort of a loving God who accepted my weaknesses.

I believed in his forgiveness, though forgiveness for myself I was unsure of. The failure of my quest to find Cinda, the failure to keep Sancha safe, the horrendous actions at her attackers still caused shame in me. It sat at the base of my stomach, a little to the right—a little lump—and I carried it, a burden, everywhere I went. I did not speak of it for Brother Diego would only remind me I was a weak man, and I had resolved to become a good and honorable noble man with all right action.

Seven years since Cinda's disappearance. How had she changed? I had resolved myself to never think that she was other than alive—in another life. I hoped she had embraced her world in a way I couldn't embrace my own. I hoped she was free of shame, anger, and sorrow. The monastery was my solace.

CHAPTER 18

in which Fredrica starts a fire

THAT NIGHT I dreamed of the eagle with a fierce raptor beak. He ignored me—he was busy chasing down mice in the meadow. Soaring up and soaring down; pouncing on the russet-furred mice and taking off again. I played spinning tops with the amber-eyed girl, and she did not change into a songbird. All night long, nothing bothered us.

⁂

Through some sort of unspoken agreement, everyone acted as if the scene at the pond had not happened. Quietly I pondered my options. Could I live with Ana? Should I leave Toboso? But by Sunday, Fredrica seemed to be over her anger, and I saw no sign of further revenge, though I was watching for it.

After church, Fredrica came to me, smiling, her disarming dimples in full bloom. She asked if I wanted to go up to the falls as we often had on Sunday afternoons. By what alchemy had drossy Fredrica been spun, this day, into gold—for she was all innocence and grins, not the hateful hag of a few days before when she had sprayed her bitterness on us all.

I agreed, for Sunday afternoon had always been Lorenzo and Aldonza's special time together, though I wondered what Fredrica had in mind. I remembered how only a day or two ago she tried to hold me under water—but I decided I would act as if I believed all was normal.

She packed bread, cheese, and grapes, and we walked to the falls. It was a hot August day, and the sun was bright, but on the hillside it was cooler. We stopped and laughed at the squirrels chittering and chasing each other in the oak trees.

At the falls we splashed and swam. When we were finished, I took my bejeweled comb and brush from my little bag I carried with me and combed her hair. Her russet hair was straight and smooth; it readily behaved at my touch. We were sitting by the water's edge, and we could see ourselves reflected in the water, our bodies shining and young in the sunlight.

When I finished, I asked, "Do you want your hair braided or hanging?"

She smiled shyly, her eyes ducking as they often did, and asked, "Could I wear your ruby combs today?"

I was surprised by her request, and how could I refuse? Would this make her feel I was her sister? I wanted to make everything right. I wanted my family to be easy and loving. Was there hope that I could stay?

I fastened the jeweled combs in her hair. "You look beautiful!" I said. "Never have I seen you look so lovely as you do today."

For an instant she looked in my eyes. "You are the beautiful one," she said softly. "Everyone sees it in you." She touched her nose. "My nose is ugly."

"No one would notice if you would meet people's eyes," I said. "You could be enchanting." I took her chin in my hand and tilted up her head. "See, like this." I smiled at her and she saw, in my eyes, that I admired her.

"You do think I'm pretty," she said. Her eyes met mine.

"I think you are beautiful." And I meant it. I was happy she had taken my suggestion so readily.

"Beauty has . . ." she seemed to be searching for a word, ". . . power."

"No," I said, puzzled, not understanding what she meant.

"Julio loved Carlota because she was beautiful; Antonia's uncle was inspired to take wild chances because of your beauty."

"Julio loved Carlota for more than her beauty. Señor Quesano," I paused, "he was . . . confused."

For a moment her expression reminded me of when she had said, "I like killing." I wondered if killing made her feel powerful—I did not understand how, maybe a sort of control. Being powerful was for kings and priests and noblemen—what did it have to do with Fredrica; what did it have to do with beauty?

She smiled merrily and said, "I will comb your hair." While she did, she talked of different things, of a neighbor's new horse, of Meta having another baby on the way.

She did not mention her tirade of a few days before and later talked of our younger days when Meta and Carlota came with us to the hill. The sliding wooden bowl and the other games we often played. She seemed quiet and at ease. She braided my hair down my back, using her ribbon to fasten it.

She curled up in the shade to take a nap, and I thought I might too, but before I put the comb and brush away in the bag, I looked briefly at its other contents and wondered of my previous life, perhaps, because this one seemed tenuous and had been so recently threatened by the now sleeping Fredrica. But still these things held no clue for me. I put the rocks and locket back with my comb and brush and hooked the embroidered pouch under my skirt. I looked over at Fredrica to see the combs, now tucked in her hair. Where were they from? And me. Where was I from?

I felt happy I had handed Fredrica the key to her beauty. I did not know how she would use that key, and I did not know that that day she had honed her evil arts so finely that she could do her deeds while fast asleep. I, the sister of innocence, near at hand had no idea Fredrica knew the alchemy to turn gold to ashes from a distance.

Smoke! I smelled smoke. I looked up and saw a column of gray and black rising from the bottom of the hill.

"Fredrica!" I cried. "Wake up! Fire!"

Why hadn't her long nose detected the fire sooner? Where was it? The house? *No!*

I raced down the hill as fast as I could, stumbling and falling along the way. Fredrica soon caught up to me and together we reached the clearing. I could hear Lobo barking frantically. It *was* the house! And before we could reach it, it was a roar of flames! What crackling! The thatched roof and sides aflame!

"Momma! Poppa!" Fredrica cried. She raced toward the door. I was close behind her. The flames snapped and popped. A ceiling of smoke hovered above us, and smoke filled the air around us. It seemed to band my lungs and choke me. It clouded and burned my eyes. Still barking, Lobo was racing back and forth before the house. Hope was neighing and kicking, and the other animals were making a dinning racket.

Thank God! There was Lorenzo at the door with precious Aldonza in his arms. Fredrica and I rushed to help him. He was stumbling, stumbling, falling.

Aldonza rolled from his arms. The smoke was nearly too thick for us to see them. I grabbed her arms and pulled her away from the snapping flames, the wall of heat. Fredrica was trying to get Lorenzo. I raced back to help her. Together we dragged him to Aldonza's side.

Lobo came and licked their sooty faces. I knelt beside them shaking them and shaking them. Fredrica, too, was yelling for them to awaken. They were not burned, no flames had licked their clothing, yet they did not move.

I put my lips to Aldonza's, then Lorenzo's and tried to suck the smoke from their lungs, tried to blow clean air down their throats. Fredrica moved her lips, calling for their lives, I thought, but I could not hear her words for the thunderous gush of flames from the burning house. Her face was contorted.

I pushed on their chests, my parents' chests. I would have them live again. But

I failed and life for them was not to be. And if I could have held it—life, that is—in my hand that instant, I would have tossed mine aside to have them bright and breathing again.

Oh, Lorenzo—poppa, friend.

Oh, Aldonza—momma, teacher.

I would never see Lorenzo take his knife delicately to wood. I clasped his hand—already warmth of life and warmth of fire were leaving him. It was no comfort to me—the pain so great I thought I would burst apart—that they died together as Margret had said they would want. I felt flushed and faint. I found myself taking gulps of air, the air deprived from them.

Soon others came. Meta. Enrique. His cousins. Neighbors. The smoke had been a signal to the countryside. It would be hard to tell you how it was then. Rushing. Jostling. Crackling thatch. Pitiful buckets of water from the pond. The gush and whoosh of flames. Chaos. Questions. Sloshing buckets from the well. Coughing. Slapping wet blankets. Falling timber. Showers of sparks. The scrape of shovels digging, throwing dirt. Tears. A nightmare.

I was no help. They were dead. My momma and my poppa. They were dead and who cared if the house burned.

Let it.

ᔓ ᕕ

It was early evening before most of the people left. "Come home with us," several of our neighbors said to Fredrica and to me. I merely shook my head, not knowing what I would do.

Because I would not go with her, Ana took me to the pond. With her handkerchief she washed my face, arms, and hands, and I wondered if one could wash the burning grief away by beginning on the outside.

And in my mind, I saw Aldonza on those first blooming days of spring; you know what that's like—the air has a certain crispness and smell about it; the sun has a certain clarity—and she threw open the doors and windows and swept the faded herbs and odor-drained cuttings out and spread new ones around—lavender, mint, juniper, cypress. It lifted our spirits after gloomy winter. I sat docilely and let Ana dab the soot away. I hoped she would find that one right place to wipe away the brutal pain. But it was not to be that day; it was too soon.

When her own pain became more than she could hold inside, Ana covered her face and said, "My friend. Oh, Aldonza." We held each other and cried.

Pedro came and urged us to leave. I told them I would go to their house after Lorenzo's and Aldonza's bodies were moved to the church. Ana hugged me and they left. She looked back and said, "If you do not come, I will come back for you."

And I knew she would.

A few people were still there. The sheriff Xavier Padua, for one. A few other men. All waiting to be sure the evening breeze did not kick up the embers.

Fredrica was sitting, patiently, under a tree, watching the heap of house.

And then it was in the sun's waning light that I saw a spark of light on the ground beneath a shrub. I looked to see what it was—not an ember—but my mirror! The one I had given to Fredrica. I reached for it and turned to Fredrica, knowing, then, what she had done, that she had placed the mirror *just so* to start the fire.

She looked steadily in my eyes. Feeling afraid, I gripped the guilty mirror more tightly, and it bit into my flesh, bringing blood, bright as flame: a slash where my thumb began.

She was beside me and grabbing my hand, took the mirror.

"Look!" she called to the sheriff and the other men.

"What are you doing?" I whispered.

"Anything I want," she hissed. "Watch!" Her fingers touched one of my combs! The combs I had put in her hair a few hours ago. Her black eyes were no longer bottomless, but clearly iniquitous and relentlessly meeting my eyes. I had not foreseen the depths of evil she could plumb. Had I understood, would I have maintained silence about her deeds all these years?

Yet can those of us with any goodness believe in such strong evil? That is why I failed to protect them, and in the end I had betrayed my parents because I had been unable to believe there was no spark of redemption in her. And my pain of loss included pain of shame for I had failed them; I had failed Daria, and who had I failed in my first life?

I should be dead, I thought. Why not me along with Lorenzo, Aldonza, and the old man, who had seen some beauty in me that did not exist, for if I were a good person, a beautiful and good person, could I have not stopped these deaths? The deaths of Lorenzo, Aldonza, and, perhaps, Carlota. (And Margret, what of her! She suspected what Fredrica could do.)

And still Fredrica was not satisfied. She wanted me to be blamed. *Kill me*, I thought. My family gone. My home gone. Burn me. I thought of how it would be—the hot and hotter flames licking at my legs, my arms, crackling in my hair, the sweat pouring from my face, my body. *Yes, please God, take me too.*

When the sheriff came over, Fredrica carefully met his eyes; then one by one, she looked into the eyes of all the men. "Thank you for your help. My family . . ." She smiled, though it was a smile calculated to convey her sadness. "It's time to take them."

Was she including me? Would they take me?

She pointed to Lorenzo and Aldonza. "To the church, please."

In a sisterly manner, she took my arm, her fingers digging into my skin, bringing more tears to my eyes, as we watched them move the bodies, my parents, into the back of the cart, side by side, just as I hoped they were in whatever afterlife there is.

But I did not want to die, and I did not doubt what she could do. I would not wait for her to indict me for a crime she committed. I *knew* she could charm the men. With my one suggestion, she *had* discovered the power of beauty. I *knew* she could turn them against me. I *knew* she would win. She had *no* remorse, *no* loyalty. My loyal Hope was standing by, twitching her tail, waiting to be hitched to the cart. . . .

I pulled Fredrica's hand from my arm. My eyes on Hope, I walked to her. As I had lost my voice long years ago, I, then, lost my hearing, and if they called out to me, I didn't hear. It was as if I were encased in a glass box, its own steady wind swirling around me. I grasped a fistful of Hope's mane and jumped to her back.

I rode the old mare over the bridge where years ago the carved chest had fallen and shattered in the creek, still scattered with grasshopper carcasses. I rode toward Parado, the small town that was no longer my home, and turned the plodding Hope north. By morning, my cut hand throbbed, and my head ached, but I was far away. I was safe.

Hope stopped and I slid to the ground, glad to stop, glad to rest, wanting water, but instead I slept.

CHAPTER 19

in which Aldonza awakens as Dulcinea and keeps a journal

HE CALLS ME Dulcinea because that's what I whispered in my feverish state.

"You said, 'He called me Dulcinea,'" La Corona said this morning when I had gained enough strength to ask why she was addressing me by the name the old knight called me.

I did not correct her. What difference did it make? Aldonza was not my name. I could not remember the name I was given at baptism. I was with Lorenzo and his family for nearly seven years. How long had I been with the family of my birth?

It has been three weeks since I ran from Fredrica's treacherousness. It was only this morning that I became aware of my surroundings. I found a journal, quill, and ink by my bed. The woman, La Corona, agreed I could have it. Tomorrow I will write more.

La Corona tells me her slave, Blalock, found me along the road. The cut in my hand, from the deceptive mirror, festered, and I have been quite ill. My head aches. We are miles from Toboso, she tells me.

Today I forgot they are dead. It seemed as if I were away and would go home when I got better. Then I remembered the reality; my breathing stopped and the pain came. How is it possible that I could lose Lorenzo and Aldonza in one day?

I hear Lorenzo say, "Hold the knife this way." His nimble fingers flip the short-bladed knife into the proper position to address the wood, the blade coming from the heel of his hand. I imitate him and he says, "Good, Donza. Good."

I see Aldonza when I first called her "Momma." She hugs me.

And I see Fredrica standing there and touching my combs in her hair. O the treachery.

I am left alone much of the time. I tire quickly.

September 19, 1590

I met La Corona's son today. Luis, he is ten with wavy sandy hair and green eyes. I sat up for a while, and we played cards. I beat him the last hand. Then I had to lie back in bed. I asked him where we are.

In his cherubic voice, he said, "We are east of Madrid, fifteen miles or so." I told him I was in Madrid a few years ago.

I hear women's voices—laughter and talking, especially at night.

This room is large and grandly furnished. Rooms adjoin it, but I do not yet have the strength to explore. My bed is a four poster with blue silk curtains. There is a dresser with a mirror and stool, a chest, a bench, and a wardrobe for clothes. Why would anyone need more than a couple of hooks for clothing? To have more seems extravagant.

September 23, 1590

Today I opened the wardrobe. (The scent of flowers and fresh grapes escaped. Ah! Could I duplicate it? I smelled lavender and lily.) The cabinet is full of colorful dresses! A dozen, at least. I closed it quickly, as if I had intruded on some secret rendezvous. Whose clothes were they? I could not ask because I should not have looked!

Yet I opened the wardrobe again. I picked up handfuls of fabric and held them to my nose. And like that night in Madrid when I had too much to drink, I felt giddy and off balance, this time from the luscious scent and the gaudiness, the colors, and the showiness of the fabrics. I took a dress of gingerline samite,* threw it over my head, and looking in the mirror, swirled the skirt back and forth around my legs. My hands sought the feathery fabric, and I rubbed it again and again against the back of my hand.

Removing the first dress, I put on one of amber-colored brocade. I twirled, and the skirt, heavier than the silk, plumped up, bell-shaped. I laughed out loud, and the laughter sounded strange to me for sadness is so much with me now.

Next, I found a bright green dress of lawn, a type of linen fabric that was semi-transparent and new to me. Its skirt had several layers of fabric, each cut in different angles so when I put it on, the skirt resembled the petals of a flower. The bodice

---

* Reddish violet silk

was decadently low and the fabric was filmy. The full tops of my breasts showed, and through the fabric I could see my nipples.

From sheer delight, I sashayed around the room. The insubstantial fabric caressed my legs. The sleeves were wide and loose and pulled the shoulders even lower. Thinking of Father Pero, I knew this dress was immodest, but I did not feel immoral. Instead I felt as if I had been transported to some strange world where such delights were permitted. I was a beautiful bird, a swan with bright green plumage, who merely wanted everyone to look admiringly at it and point and say, "Have you ever seen anything so beautiful?"

I took the ruby ring, the one from the handsome Don Carlos of the gypsy fair, from the string around my neck and put it on my finger. Here, I would wear it.

I continued my explorations. I opened the low chest: again the scent of flowers—gillyflower, carnation?—and grapes. I found several smocks, quite finely finished. Some of gauze, some of cobweb lawn, some of borato or cambric. I touched each one to my cheek, purring with contentment at their fineness.

At the bottom of the chest, I found a set of eight flawless clothing brushes. Hand carved and rubbed. Cherry wood handles. At Lorenzo's, we'd had one brush for all, and it had been quite worn. But eight? For one person? And each brush was slightly different. For different clothing? Different parts of clothing? Different fabrics?

How grand this life seems! I feel a princess—like the ones in the stories I told at night to Carlota and Fredrica. Only in the stories the king-father gave the wealth. I will have to find a way myself to have things like these. And what else is out there? For in my narrow peasant life I never imagined such luxury, only glimpses of it in Madrid. And could it be mine? I was happy at Aldonza and Lorenzo's. Then, I wanted no life but that one, but now . . .

I remember that Sancho Panza talked about the two families, have-much and have-little, and though I was content having what we had at Lorenzo's, why can't it be my turn to be a have-much? Surely, there is no shame in a life of extras—if I am kind and good to others still.

September 25, 1590

I slept all day yesterday. Today, well rested, I am ready to explore. Through large curtained openings in the wall—each the size of two doors—the bedroom opens to two rooms, one on each side. My three rooms are like its own high-ceilinged house. Yes, as big as Lorenzo's.

The sitting room, which has a door that opens to a hallway and one that opens to the outdoors, has several floor cushions and a couple of stools. It has two windows, like the bedroom. Through the windows—glass ones—I see a flower garden. Beyond the flower garden is a wood. When I am better, I will walk there and search for herbs.

The other room holds a large tub for bathing, a chair which has a chamber pot, and a washstand for a pitcher and bowl. A door opens to the outside to carry in (and out) the water. What lavishness this all seems! Whose room was this? Could it become mine?

Mine! What a dreamer I have become.

I have seen six people. La Corona and Luis, of course. Sarai, the old wild-haired cook who checks on me often. Another woman, Braden, helps too. She wears a veil, and I cannot see her face. She does not talk, and they tell me she cannot. I remember what it is like to not speak, but to understand what is being said. Braden is at my side the moment I need anything. She sleeps in a loft above my bedroom. A tall ladder fastened to the wall leads to a square hole in the ceiling.

I have also met Moravia, who is about my own age, I think. She is from Africa. Her skin is smooth and chocolate dark, and her arms are tattooed with many strange, repetitive markings, like rows of bracelets. She wears a ring on every finger and jewels in her hair, which she fixes in elaborate ways, often in finger-thin braids. I am fascinated by her sparkles.

Soon after Moravia came today, the slave Blalock—who found me sick along the road—joined at my bedside. He is the largest man I have ever seen. His head is as bald as a top. I thanked Blalock for rescuing me. He smiled, showing large white teeth, and said, "I'm glad you are recovered."

Moravia and Blalock spoke to each other in Italian, so I spoke to them in Italian. They were surprised. It reminded me of Daria in Madrid. Ah, Daria. What has happened to you?

September 26, 1590

La Corona is not beautiful nor even pretty, though her body is perfect, rounded, yet willowy. Her chin is long, and her nose, crooked. She has the longest fingernails of anyone I have ever seen. She said she can keep them that way because all she does is pick up money. I was puzzled. But she said it and laughed her jolly laugh, which reminds me of tinkling coins or silver bells. I suppose she is rich and has many more servants than Sarai and Blalock. She smells of lavender, the scent which is like the color of her eyes! Her eyes! They are full of laughter.

Her skin is creamy and soft, even her hands. Her coarse hair is long to her ankles with white mingled in the black. She wears it pulled back at the neck. It is not braided, but loosely tied with colorful cloths at her neck and waist. Some short strands pull loose from the binding and frizz around her face like the tiny roots of golden seal.

She is regal—queenly—and always wears purple. Though she appears to be stern, she is quite compassionate to me. In that, she reminds me of Aldonza. Oh, Momma, that I have lost, I carry this empty ache inside, a vacancy. Please return.

September 27, 1590

This afternoon I left my room. Moravia gave me a beautiful yellow satin dressing gown to wear. It is embroidered with bright birds and trees. Even now, back in my bedroom, I keep it near me to touch. It is cool and smooth. It gives me much pleasure.

Moravia helped me put it on, and I watched her bejeweled fingers tie the cord. She held my elbow to steady me in case I became shaky. Along one side of the hallway, the side my rooms are on, are several doors. To my left, the windows look out on a courtyard. I could see the other wing of the house, a mirror to this one. I say house but it must have dozens of rooms, more like a castle or palace. It is U-shaped. My rooms are at the end of one wing.

At the other end of the hallway, where it turned to the left, we went straight into the morning room. In it were two dozen or more women, mostly young, most in smocks, some long, some short, some open to the waist. They were laughing and talking, though they became quiet when I entered, and I felt sad, the odd one. I remembered how Lorenzo and Aldonza had welcomed me, a stranger, immediately.

For a while, I sat and listened to the music. Chalsea, a tiny red-haired, freckled woman from Madrid, played the harpsichord. I watched her closely and thought I might be able to play it too. Tressa, a tall blonde, had a guitar. Chalsea kindly asked me to sing with them and I did. She helped me with the harpsichord; I found it familiar and plinked out a few melodies. We laughed together, and music, that day, was our common language.

It seemed strange to see so many idle women in the middle of the day. They must be very wealthy and have many servants. Think of the laundry for so many people! And the cooking!

Moravia introduced me to the women as Dulcinea, and I did not correct her. How could I claim Aldonza as my name? Aldonza was dead. So Dulcinea I will be. I do not feel like Dulcinea, the lofty, even perfect, beauty of Don Quixote's madness. Worthy of being admired, adored. No, not now. I am too sad. Too broken.

September 30, 1590

This place is called Le Reino.* Many men come and go in the evenings. They are students from the university in Alcala (which is near) or fine gentlemen from Madrid and the king's court. I remember the gentlemen I saw with Jesus that night. One was a duke's son. These visitors dress as he did, but it seems different. I remember the other duke's son, Carlos, of the gypsy dance. I touch the ruby ring on my finger. How different these two noble sons were!

All this I discovered when I ventured one room farther than the private sitting room. No one seemed to notice me and no one told me to leave. The room, a sort of greeting room, is very large and full of floor cushions and some small tables with stools. Down the center is a counter from which wine and other drinks are served. On it are baskets full of fruit and breads and platters of large crescents of cheese. One side is for the grandees and the other for the students and the common men.

Even in the evening, the women dress much as I see them in the morning room. In shifts and smocks, though sometimes flowing gowns, tied at the waist, sometimes open above and below. Red-haired Chalsea was playing a harpsichord near the door where I entered.

Slowly I began to understand the nature of this place, and I remembered that night in Madrid, when Jesus pulled me from the dark alley, but here it does not seem the same. The large high-ceilinged room is bright and cheery even late at night, thanks to multi-tiered candelabra and polished metal mirrors placed on the ceiling and throughout the room. A fragrant blue haze hangs in the air from cigar smoke. The candlelight catches the many jewels of the noblemen and throws sparkles and flashes on the walls and ceiling.

Couples dance. Sometimes Tressa plays the guitar. One evening she played a chaconne. Chalsea got up from the harpsichord and pulled at a student who was sitting on a cushion. I sat at the harpsichord and soon was playing. The tunes entered my head and came out my fingers! I played late into the night. This music seemed to help heal my pain of loss, and I will seek it often.

What I see here are good people working for a living. Who am I to judge? It is not like living with thieves or murderers or betrayers, of which I could count myself among. No, I will not judge them, for I, too, have broken God's laws, and I see there are shades of good and evil and most are not only one way or the other (except Fredrica; she is unremorsefully evil).

---

* French for "the kingdom"

October 2, 1590

I went to the morning room, where the women collect to talk and laugh. They were quiet when I entered, but soon this one or that one spoke to me. I helped one hem a shift. Moravia was there. In my sitting room is a picture of a faraway place with colorfully feathered birds. Moravia is like an exotic bird with her multifaceted jeweled hair and fingers, and when she laughs, her many braids clink together, the jewels tapping against each other like a bird calling to a friend.

In the early afternoon Luis and I went on a picnic. Though the leaves have begun to turn, it was still warm enough.

Luis knows I am sad. "Everyone here is sad, at times, but then it goes away," he chimes.

No one is sad at night. Music and gaiety and bright colors abound, just as painted faces, bare bosoms, rouged cheeks, and waxed lips and, they tell me, much pleasure.

October 3, 1590

La Corona told me these rooms belonged to a woman named Melisandra, who was the most sought after woman here. She brought much money to Le Reino. A man proposed marriage to Melisandra, and everyone had been happy for her. She had believed he was wealthy, and he had told her to bring nothing but her jewels as he would buy her new clothes, new everything.

Melisandra went with him, as had her servant Braden. Soon after leaving, the man killed Melisandra for her jewels and slashed at Braden several times, even cutting off part of her tongue, but Braden escaped and returned and now always wears a veil.

I saw tears fill La Corona's lavender eyes, though they did not spill over. She told me that no one wanted these rooms because everyone had known Melisandra.

Perhaps they feel these rooms are cursed. But not I. They have become home to me. If only the people here could accept me, as I had accepted this place.

I touched the ruby ring on my hand that the gallant noble had given me at the gypsy fair. I wanted to add jeweled rings to my fingers. I could have a rainbow on my hand.

October 7, 1590

I have been wondering about my childhood again. I have lost my middle life, and I yearn to know more of my first. I have so much time to sit and think. Memories prick at me, but they are too often of sadness from my losses. Sadness from

Fredrica's betrayal. I am numb because I do not understand. How could she?

Often, to quell my unsettling memories, I take out my embroidered bag and look at the contents—the garnet and blue topaz comb and brush, the locket, the rocks, the shell—thinking one of the items will be the key to unlock the past.

Once La Corona saw me looking at the contents of my bag. Of the locket, she said, "Tintoretto is a famous painter of Venice." A clue, to my past, but what could I do? I could not go to Venice.

Three of the stones, she told me, are uncut jewels. A diamond, a ruby, and an emerald. The other stone, a small pink one, is just a rock. Oh, Lorenzo, if we had only known I had wealth hiding in your house. What miseries I could have saved us!

I opened the locket, and this time it occurred to me to try and remove the paper. With my fingernail I flicked at it, and the miniatures fell out. I stared at the pictures, willing myself to remember who they were: a father? a brother? Neither had my blue eyes. What of the boy with dark hair and gray eyes? He looked to be a little older than Luis, perhaps twelve. If not a brother, then . . .? My intended? I pressed the pictures in the locket the right way, so I could easily look at them. I finger the locket, even as I write. Perhaps one day the wall that somehow divides my mind from remembering the past will crumble from my relentless looking and wishing, and the memories will come.

What if it is a terrible story? Perhaps I was a slave girl who stole the bag. Perhaps my family perished in an accident—even as Lorenzo and Aldonza had—and only I remained. Or maybe I was the daughter of a wealthy duke or king. The rosary of blue amber: "Only nobles and kings," the wicked marquis in Madrid had said.

I know different languages. I can read. I could believe I was a princess. When I think of the comfort I am living in, it seems I live the life of one.

Though I do not go to church, I pray daily to Our Lady Mary, Queen of Heaven, to help me remember my original family, and I pray too, for the comfort of my second family, those in Heaven with our Queen.

October 8, 1590

Blalock supplied me with a shovel and an old knife so I could dig roots. La Corona found me washing them. She was interested to learn of my knowledge of herbs and that I had been a midwife's assistant. She said they sometimes need a midwife here and maybe I can help them.

"The women have babies?" Then I felt silly: of course, they could.

"Yes, it happens." She smiled and tossed her head, sending the scent of lavender my way and making her tail of hair sway against her ankles. "Perhaps you know of a way to avoid it." She pointed to the roots with a long fingernail.

"I can make a drink of fenugreek, blessed thistle, cinnamon. . . ." Slowly I listed herbs that were contraindicated in pregnancy—perhaps they helped avoid it. "I would be guessing for I know nothing of this. But it won't hurt anyone to try it." I also suggested that she have Sarai use parsley liberally in salads.

La Corona nodded her head. "Do what you can," she said. "Your knowledge of herbs will be very helpful." Then she left, leaving the scent of lavender with me. I feel encouraged by her words: she had suggested a way for me to give back to her.

October 16, 1590

I sometimes wake up thinking I should feed the pigs or gather eggs. I stretch out on my silken sheets and laugh at my old habits—then feel sad. I cannot have the wealth of family back. It is a sorry trade—the richness of this place for family. Yet could I have both?

I have not been to church in many weeks! La Corona said some women walk to church four miles away on Sundays. I do not have the strength to do that yet. Soon I hope. I kneel and pray every morning and night.

October 21, 1590

I have found another way to be useful here. I translate for some of the clientele. I know five languages: Spanish, French, Italian, English, and Dutch.

I have met Gabriel Santo, an Italian duchess's son with black hair and snapping eyes, the color of lapis, darker than my own. He studies at Alcala. He shows two dimples when he smiles and that reminds me of Fredrica, so I am hesitant to trust him. (Though I know I, too, have dimples.)

Gabriel enjoys enlarging my Italian vocabulary. He speaks close to my ear, and I feel it deep within me, as if tiny soft feathers were tickling my insides. He has taught me many new Spanish words too; words that describe things that I did not know men and women did together. And I have learned the word for what Fredrica did at the falls. He laughed—his laugh was deep and carefree—when I asked him if it were a sin.

What could be wrong in it? I wondered. Overindulgence perhaps. I am always moderate.

Gabriel waved his hand in a wide arc. "Is not all this a sin?" he said and winked.

"Why do you think that is?" I asked.

"The Church decrees it," he said simply, tossing his head, setting his black hair waving at his shoulder.

"But surely it is God who says it is."

He shook his head. "The Church does not want us satisfied." He spoke in a confidential tone, his voice deep and whispery in my ear. Certainly what he said was heresy, but I enjoyed every word. He was something I had never been, nor did I think I could be—a rebel. And he made it appear to be a good thing. (How is that?) "If we become satisfied in our lives," he replied, "then we do not need the Church. And the Church needs us to need it."

"Do you think passion can satisfy us?" I asked. For though I thought of passion in many ways, I knew Gabriel would only see it one way.

"A man always thinks so." He smiled broadly. His fingers played with the curls on my shoulder. "Coupling takes up a dribble of a man's time," he said. He pulled the curls to his face and breathed in their fragrance. He found the scent of carnation there, I knew, and oleander too. "Yet lusting takes up a mighty river of a man's time." He laughed. An intriguing laugh, I thought. "And that is all you need to know to work here, Dulcinea," he said.

"I do not want to work here! In that way."

"But it would be easy to dam the river of a man's thought and direct it to you. It only takes this: the fragrance of your hair." He touched my hair again. "Or the flash of a smile." His finger circled my mouth and touched a dimple. "Even the slightest curve of your breast." His hand cupped my breast. I drew back at his boldness. He laughed his infectious laugh. "Remember this: It only takes the promise of satisfaction to arrest a man's attention." Pragmatic Gabriel added, "Of course if you want money, it takes a bit more."

Here, they say that one's career is not a sin, for one needs to make a living and God wants us to live and eat and have shelter. It is a legal business. In fact, La Corona, with her good humor, declares this a noble business. A client is called a *rey*: king. His cock, *cetro*: scepter.

As for what the women call themselves? "Princesitas." Never whores. What the "princesitas" do to bring in money is referred to as "making the treasury."

La Corona, who oversees all, is the "Crown," the symbol of power.

What shall I think of this? Can I live here among prostitutes? But I have transgressed. I see myself as no better. I do not wish an existence of man after man after man, for I have talents to make my treasury and may have other choices.

October 25, 1590

I am laughing so hard I cannot stop.

I asked La Corona if I must leave, and she said I may stay if I pay rent for the rooms. She rubbed her long chin as if thinking, then named the rent. I felt my eyes and mouth fly open. It was an amount per month that would have kept Lorenzo's family for nearly half a year.

She will pay me to be a hostess or to play the harpsichord, and when I can provide herbs or other services, she is glad to not have to send to town for help. I tell her I sew and embroider too. She says the women will pay me for the herbs or for the handiwork.

Then La Corona gave me Melisandra's clothes and all her things.

"What did Melisandra look like?" I asked Braden as she helped me begin alterations on the dresses, which were slightly too big.

Braden held her hand above my head to show me Melisandra was a bit taller. She said, "Weh he."

"Red hair?" I asked.

She nodded, happy that I understood.

Melisandra must have been a striking woman. I am one of the tallest women here, and she was taller. Larger too, but then I am so thin now after my illness.

Three of the dresses are blue—my favorite color.

"Come with me to see Serenity," La Corona said, her eyes clouded with worry. "It is near her time, and she is not well."

We walked through the woods together to a house, a large, square house (though they call it the "little house"). Here was where the children were born and kept, if the mothers wanted to keep them. Living in the house were three women and eight children, ages one to eight.

I knew at once what Serenity needed. She was keeping too much water, and her complexion was yellow. I looked around to see if they had anything to help, but I found nothing.

La Corona drove me to Alcala. Her long hair whipped around in the wind as we drove in the cart down the road. We found the herbs I needed to begin my pharmacopeia—lobelia, dried dandelion, lily of the valley, plantain, and bilberry. Licorice, hawthorn, yarrow, Echinacea, and broom I had already found and dried. It seemed that I was in business.

By evening Serenity was better, but I could still see my thumb print in her ankles. . . .

October 28, 1590

On my way back from seeing Serenity, I took a different path and found a tiny chapel next to a cemetery, which had three dozen or more markers. All noted 1580 as the year of death. An epidemic. In particular I noticed six well-kept graves, identified by specifically carved wooden markers. The markers were carved in the images of a person, perhaps the person who was buried there? What a strange idea! The markers said: Belle, our mother, 1554-1580. A small and delicate woman was carved on this marker. Her face was turned to look over the other smaller graves. Juan, 1572-1580; Raquela, 1574-1580; Charles, 1575-1580; Juanita, 1576-1580; Maximilian, 1578-1580. The markers were so personal; I felt I had known them. Had the father made the markers? How had he escaped this death—whatever it was?

Inside the chapel, the woodworking was finely crafted, the ends of the benches—there were only two—elegantly carved. The statues were plain wood, not painted, and were perfectly appointed life-sized representations of Jesus and Mary and Joseph.

I thought of Lorenzo. Whoever built this chapel in the forest was a craftsmen beyond Lorenzo, beyond my experience. Here is the church for me until I can go to church. I will visit this chapel daily. I will continue my prayers.

October 29, 1590

Serenity delivered today. The boy is fine. I stopped at the chapel to give thanks. Does anyone else go there?

I cannot help but think of home—yes, I still call it home. Of the day Meta gave birth to Rique. I remember Aldonza and the way she looked holding Meta's baby. "It is different," she had said, a light in her eyes, a grin on her face, "to hold the baby of your daughter than to hold your daughter." And what of Meta's second baby? Was it a boy or girl? Whichever, it would never know its grandparents.

Dear God, I miss my home, Aldonza, Lorenzo, Ana, Meta. . . .

October 31, 1590

Last night, Luis joined me, and after reading, we played cards until very late. We were so tired, we lay upon my bed and fell asleep, fully clothed. The first time Luis stayed the night in my room, he had asked shyly, "What if I fell asleep here? I am too tired to move."

I ruffled his wavy hair and said, "Then you will be here in the morning."

It is not so lonely to have him by me when I awake. His hair falls across his forehead into his eyes. He sleeps with his arm thrown over his head. I pretend he is my brother; I long for a family again.

I cannot remember when I was ten. Maybe that is why I feel so close to him. He exudes the naiveté and freshness I must have had at that age. Here, everyone protects him and keeps him safe. I want to lie back down beside him and put my arm across his shoulders and pray for him to always keep the innocence he has now, at this moment, safe, asleep in my bed.

November 2, 1590

I feel in me a stirring, an opening up of possibilities. Am I becoming a rebel? It is not a rebelliousness like Fredrica! I now see her as evil. What I feel is more like a child disobeying his parents. A reshaping of the definition of what is good and what is bad. How can I live here if I do not shift my vision? I want to see both sides, make my own choices. Perhaps I listen too much to Gabriel Santo, and I begin to think like him.

Gabriel has an air of mystery about him. He is tall and broad-shouldered, already quite a fine and noble-looking man, though, as I say, underneath he seethes with some desire, some longing, something I am attracted to yet do not understand. His uncle is a diplomat from Italy, in the employ of the duke of Savoy, and Gabriel has spent much time in Spain.

Born to an Italian duchess ten months after her duke's death, Gabriel's life has been one of privilege, but not of belonging. He had been close to his older brothers before they learned the truth; now they shun him. His mother told him of her indiscretion with a noble Englishman—twenty years her junior. Gabriel hopes to someday find his father.

He belongs nowhere—is this how I feel? Yes, we have things in common, but in other ways we are opposites. He wants to know when I will take him to my room. Knowing that it will not happen, I take this suggestion in good humor. I want to stay here, but I will find another way to earn the money I need.

November 5, 1590

Today I walked on a different path west of Le Reino. I came upon two barns and a large vegetable garden.

"Good morning," I said to Blalock, who was brushing one of the horses. "Want help?"

"If you like," he said and opened the gate so I could come in. "You're not afraid?"

I walked through the gate and up to one of the mares.

"Marchioness," he said. She was a beautiful bay with a black mane. I wanted her as mine right then. She was nearly as big as the gray stallion, Olivares, next to her. I brushed her. Blalock watched for a moment.

"You seem to know what you are doing," he said. He wiped the sweat from his forehead on the back of his sleeve. It wasn't a hot day, but he had been working hard.

I nodded. "Does La Corona let the women ride the horses?" I asked.

"You will have to ask her," he replied. "If it were up to me, you could."

"How do you come to be with her?" I asked boldly, thinking how her long hair looked like the stallion's tail, which nearly trailed the ground too.

He continued brushing Olivares. "She won this place from a debauched nobleman. Then made it a bawdy house."

"Won it!" I cried in disbelief.

"It was overrun with vines. The mice were kept in control by the ferrets!" he said in his smooth voice; his bald head was glistening in the morning sun. "Everyone had died in an epidemic and nothing had been touched since their deaths. No one had lived in it for months, except one man, Rudolph—a German prince—he still lives here. That was ten years ago. Now Le Reino is the best in Castille." He said this proudly. "And beyond."

Rudolph, I thought, must be the husband of Belle and the children in the cemetery. Did he stay here merely because his family was buried here?

November 7, 1590

I think of home, of Meta and Carlota, how we frolicked up the hill, laughing and pulling at each other. Or in the evenings, by the firelight, how we sat and sewed and talked in low and confidential voices, telling of the news from Parado. I remember how with time, I began to think their memories were mine, to think of Aldonza as Momma. Ana welcomed me as her partner in midwifery. Can I find again that type of home? Here?

To stay, I must find the money for the rent. I have brought in some, but not enough. I need to sell the jewels from the keepsake bag. I do not think this will be hard; there are many wealthy men to ask.

CHAPTER 20

in which Dulcinea arranges her new life to her liking

WANTED TO GET the most I could for the uncut stone, so I dressed carefully. (I saw how beauty swayed men—was this what Fredrica had meant about the power of beauty?) I wore a soft white shift, the skirt of which was trimmed with rows and rows of white lace. The sleeves were finely embroidered. Over the shift, I had an outer corset of blue velvet, which pulled in my waist. I added a blue velvet skirt which opened in an inverted V to show the lace of the underskirt. I wore my hair half down and half up. I wished I had my ruby combs to wear, but I would not let myself think of Fredrica and her treachery. Or sapphire combs—they would look good! Perhaps I would buy some sapphire combs after I sold the jewel.

To finish my dress, I put on a blue velvet loose-fitting gown with paned sleeves, through which one saw the delicately embroidered sleeves of the shift. I sprayed myself with rose water, with a hint of cinnamon. I had not found the right combination for Melisandra's scent yet. As for my face, I merely darkened my already long lashes and waxed my lips. Some of the girls painted their faces, but I saw how this was bad for their skin and teeth.[*]

In the greeting room, I welcomed clients as usual, occasionally sitting at a table to wait with one or the other of them. I poured wine and even played a little dice. The door opened and in came the man. I knew he was my best choice. He was in his fifties, gallant and graying. His hair and beard were trimmed close, though his moustache was narrow and long—to his chin. His shoulders were broad, and he was impeccably dressed. My eyes were drawn to the purple plumed hat, a style I was fond of. Two servants accompanied him, and they stayed near the door to wait.

---

[*] Lead was the base for makeup.

My skirt swept around me as I walked to greet him. We were the same height; I looked directly into his eyes. "Good evening, your grace."

He bowed. His short purple velvet cloak swept forward. The plumes on his hat nearly brushed my face. I caught a whiff of peppermint.

"A glass of wine, before other pleasures?" I asked.

He scarcely looked at me. Taking in everyone, he slowly scanned the room. His eyes stopped on Chalsea and Moravia longer than on anyone else. He started to walk by me, but I put my hand on his arm. He looked at my hand and then me, for the first time. His eyes were brown, his skin firm, yet weathered from many hunts. I saw his demeanor change.

"And do you have pleasure to offer, my dear?" he asked, raising his eyebrows a bit and looking at my bosom.

I felt a little nervous and I blushed.

"Ah, modesty," he said, now looking at my face—we were eye to eye. "A trait I find exciting, but too often absent."

Taking his arm, I led him to a small table with only two chairs. After he sat, I procured some good wine and two glasses. He had many fine lines around his eyes (from laughing or worrying? I wondered). He smiled, and I sensed they were not from worry. He watched while I poured the wine and handed him the glass. "Our best wine, your grace," I said. "My compliments."

As he took a drink, he looked at me. "And are you the best, señorita?" he boldly asked.

"Alas, señor, I do not know, for I am untried in bed," I said, looking carefully at the floor.

"Ah?"

"I am merely a musician, sometimes a hostess," I added. "Call me Dulcinea." I supplied my name, hoping to gain his also.

"A lovely name." He pointed to himself and said, "Call me Alphonse."

"Don Alphonse . . ." I said coyly, hoping to learn his title, for it was obvious he was a grandee, but from where?

He ignored my hint for information and changed the subject. "A nice ring," he said, indicating my ruby ring. "How did you come by it?"

"A young nobleman gave it to me." I fingered the ring. "He had paused in his journey one afternoon at a gypsy fair," I explained. "We threw knives together in a game. He matched me knife for knife. We only had a few hours before he continued on his journey." I brushed my hair off my shoulder then said, "We danced together. He called me a princess." I picked up the wineskin to top off the man's glass, but he waved it away.

"For an afternoon of casual company he gave you a precious ring?" Don

Alphonse seemed skeptical. With a bent index finger, he smoothed each half of his moustache. An action, I noticed, he often used.

"It was a chivalric courtesy."

"And did you give him your token in return?" he asked.

I laughed. "I had nothing to give him but a leather bracelet I had won at the knife toss."

"A pretty tale." He took another drink of wine and looked around the room.

He seemed to have nothing more to say; in fact, seemed to have lost interest in me. I played my cards, so to speak. From a pocket I took the uncut diamond, ruby, and emerald. "I have these to sell, Don Alphonse. Are you interested?"

He looked at the stones as I placed them on the table, *one, two, three.*

"What of the ring?" he asked, looking at me. "Would you sell it?"

I was taken aback. "No," I said. "It means something to me."

"Pray tell me what that is." His hands, fine and gentle, rested easily on the table.

I struggled to put in words why it was important to me. "He made me feel beautiful, and I want to always remember that." (And had *he* not said he would wear the bracelet always?)

The man nodded and patted my hand. "Yes," he said, as if he understood.

"But these are for sale." With my hand, I drew his attention to the uncut jewels.

"How does selling me a stone please you?" he asked; his dark eyes crinkled into a smile.

"I would be able to stay here," I said. "To have a home."

He looked surprised. "But you said you do not ply the trade of those who live here."

"No, I am an herbalist and midwife," I said. "A seamstress. I earn my keep in other ways. But not enough. The rent is high."

He laughed; the lines around his eyes seemed like petals to dark centers. His kindness was evident. "But why do you want to stay?"

"La Corona found me in poor health and has nursed me to good health. She and the others are kind to me, and I like it here."

"Have you no home?" he asked. "No family?"

"No," I said, sadly.

"And you want this to be your new home?" he asked.

"Why not? I am here and they have need of me."

He raised his purple plumed hat from his head and smoothed his wavy hair. The purple plume dipped toward my face, nearly brushing me. He replaced the hat and said, "To help you out, then, my fair and blue-eyed señorita, I will buy one of these."

———

One by one he picked them up, and after examining each, he replaced them on the table. (Could it be true that if these dull stones were cut, they would be faceted and sparkly?) He pointed to the ruby and made his offer, then to the diamond and offered twice as much as the ruby. Both offers were much more than I had hoped for! I would only sell one stone for now. Next, he held the emerald and named a price.

"But, your grace, that is as much as you offered for the diamond."

He reached out and dropped the stone between my breasts. I felt it fall to the constriction of the corset. Leaning over, Don Alphonse looked for the stone. Again I noticed the faint odor of peppermint. His smiling eyes were still kind and gentle, though there was something more in them now.

"For the emerald and the *pleasure* of retrieving it," he purred. Before I could protest, he took my hand in his and kissed it, then added more kisses up my arm as he swept my sleeve upward.

What shivers he caused in me! As if my insides had jumped to the outside—I cannot explain it. Where was my strength to stop him?

And now in my ear, he whispered, in his rich voice that echoed in my body, "Dulcinea, will you please me?"

And that was what I wanted to do—please him. I could not have said, "No," even if it had occurred to me to say it. I whispered back to him, "Sold."

Don Alphonse was a slow and steady lover. So gentle was he that I did not bleed.

"I am not the first," he whispered, though without reproach.

"Yes," I said, "you are."

He smiled and shook his head—the moonlight had brightened his gray hair— and we continued. . . .

The next morning, I lay in bed remembering the night before. He had left the faint smell of peppermint on my sheets. It had not been difficult. It was even pleasurable. From the first moment, I divined how to move and how to act and what to do. It was a most natural thing. *Why, this fits me like a glove,* I thought, as if I were born knowing the information I needed to arouse a man, to tease him to full pleasure.

I got up and went to the dresser. On top were the coins from Don Alphonse— and the emerald. Before he left, we had stood together by my window, looking at the garden, and eye to eye, we struck a bargain, and now I could stay here without worry about paying the rent.

And nothing about it seemed wrong. I remained the same person I was yesterday.

I sat on the bench. My shift from last night was thrown over the end of it. I remembered how Don Alphonse helped me out of my gown. I untied my skirt and helped him loosen it, letting it fall to the ground. Slowly I let down my hair and gently shook it. Picking up the tresses, he held them to his face, breathing in the fragrance.

He looked with dismay at the laces on my corset but patiently unlaced it, and when the garment fell to the floor, the emerald fell too, but we did not bother with it then. He must have found it later and placed it on the dresser.

There was a knock at the door. It was La Corona. I handed her a month's rent and even more. "For your generosity."

She added the money to a pouch at her waist, and merrily she said, "Get dressed. The girls are waiting."

Waiting? I threw on the shift that was beside me. Simple and easy. I now understood the common dress of the morning.

We walked down the hall to the morning room. When I entered, clouds of fabric came flying at me from all sides! Shifts, skirts, chemises, stockings, corsets, robes, gowns, cloaks. Red, green, blue, yellow, orange, black, purple, white—a rainbow of garments. I caught whiffs of different spray waters—carnation, rose, cinnamon, vanilla—of garlic, of cigars, of sweat, of recent sex, of flowers. I was pelted to the floor and covered completely. The women were laughing and clapping, so I was not frightened, but I did not know what was happening.

"Come out!" they cried. "Come out!"

Slowly I pushed my way out of the mound of clothing. So much! As if every article of clothing they owned were piled on top of me. And so it was—their ritual to welcome me as one of them. They said it was the most clothes I would ever have on again!

I blushed at their attention, but, oh, how good it felt. I knew they were wrong, of course: I was not one of them. However, I did not correct their impression because I wanted to be a part of them and this place.

Moravia came over and hugged me. Then Chalsea and blonde Tressa. These three became my fast friends. Once again it was as if I had three sisters.

"And how was it?" Chalsea asked; her loose red hair made a shawl around her shoulders.

But I felt shy and could not say. They all laughed.

"She did well," La Corona said. "Don Alphonse has spoken for her exclusively."

She knew! I heard gasps. I would not have announced it so; it was personal information.

Tressa said with admiration, "You will be like Melisandra." Her pale blue eyes picked up the sun from the window. She did not seem jealous but happy for me.

"You can see this about her." Moravia brushed my hair back from my face. "She is good at everything she does. Are you not?"

I blushed. "No," I said without hesitation. I would not be so immodest as to agree with her. I was afraid I would make enemies like Fredrica.

"Ah," Chalsea, the tiny Madrilene who shared the harpsichord with me, said kindly, "then you will learn better how to please him. It takes time."

I did not like what she said. I knew I had pleased him.

"Do not be mistaken, Chalsea, Dulcinea knows what she is doing." La Corona laughed. "As if she were born to this."

Chalsea smiled and nodded at me; she accepted La Corona's assessment.

La Corona gave us more information about my new position. "His son has recently married. His wife will allow him to, in fact wants him to, have a *princesita*, but it must be the same one." Some of the girls nodded. I frowned at her use of the word *princesita*.

"The wife is wise," Moravia said.

"Because of the French disease," Barcela, the older Italian woman, said. Everyone nodded. I knew she was referring to syphilis and that some of the women had their men wear sheaths of washed pigs' intestines to prevent disease; some thought this prevented pregnancy too.

Sarai, the cook, brought in oranges, candy, almond cake, and chocolate to drink. It *was* a celebration! Everyone took a treat and found a place to sit. I found myself sitting on cushions with Moravia, Chalsea, and Tressa, who collapsed her long body down to the floor, like a folding fan.

"It is fitting you have Melisandra's rooms," Tressa said.

I was not happy with the conversation. They did not understand. I had agreed to please the kind-eyed Don Alphonse and his absent son occasionally, and he agreed to pay my rent. It was not the same as what they did—going with different men at any time.

Chalsea broke open her orange and began peeling the skin away from the fruit. "Where are you from, Dulcinea?" she asked.

Til now, no one had asked me of my past. I smiled. "Toboso in La Mancha."

Stirring her thick chocolate, Tressa asked, "How did you come to be here?"

I told them of the fire that had taken Aldonza's and Lorenzo's lives and had caused my departure from my home. They expressed shock and sympathy.

"Is there no one else, then, but Fredrica left?" Chalsea asked, taking a handful of her long red hair and idly pulling it over and through her fingertips, as if brushing it.

"An older sister, Meta," I said. "She is married with a baby." I felt a ripple of sadness remembering how Rique would toddle toward me and giggle as I picked him up. I thought of the new baby I would not help deliver and wondered if it would be a boy or a girl. "Maybe Fredrica lives with them now." I felt sick to my stomach to think of her.

"Why don't you write Meta?" Tressa asked. A crumb of cake popped from her mouth, and she quickly brushed it from her breast. "And tell her you didn't start the fire."

I had not thought of writing Meta. She could find someone to read a letter to her. Antonia, maybe.

"Do not write," Moravia said. "We are glad to have you here." She touched my cheek and smiled. Being susceptible to suggestion and happy they wanted me, I decided to put the thought of writing out of my mind for now.

I had wanted to sell a jewel, but I had procured a better price, secured my staying here. And he had returned the emerald. Living at Le Reino did not make me a *princesita*.

Don Alphonse did not return for several days. I went into the greeting room now only to play the harpsichord. My friendship—or was it flirtation—with Gabriel ended. I spent my time sewing, helping with ailments, keeping up my music. I still wore the ruby ring and sighed as I thought of my gallant nobleman. I knew that it was unlikely that I would find my own true love while living here, but I was content for now. If I ever wanted something different, I could leave.

We arranged for Don Alphonse to send the money for the rent directly to La Corona, so I scarcely thought of it. The rest of the money, he put in an account in a bank in Madrid for me. The money I made from my other ventures, small in comparison, took care of daily needs.

ᔥ ᕍ

La Corona and I went again to Alcala where I bought herbs and other supplies. I had plenty of room to add shelves to my bathing room for herbs and unguents. La Corona told me there was a carpenter, Rudolph, who lived at Le Reino. I remembered Blalock had mentioned him.

She said, "He came to Spain to marry his true love."

"And she died!" I said, remembering the six well-groomed graves in the cemetery. It was this man of noble birth who carved the markers for those graves and built the little chapel, my haven for daily prayer.

La Corona nodded. The wind brought her lavender scent into my face.

I felt sad for this Rudolph. "Why does he not return to his homeland?"

"He will not leave his Belle . . . or his children." La Corona shook her head as if she did not understand.

But I thought, *here is a loyal and honorable man.*

ᔥ ᕍ

Sitting by the pond in the center yard one crisp afternoon with Chalsea, Tressa, and Moravia, I exclaimed, "There must be nearly sixty rooms in the two wings!" I had never been to the other side of the house, the wing across the courtyard, and I did not know of anyone who lived in that wing.

We were bundled in our cloaks, but the sun shone brightly down on us. The two kittens I often saw here were watching the fish. The kittens' tails switched in unison as they stood together, one all gray and one all black, as if one were a shadow of the other.

"Probably," Moravia said in response to my comment about the number of rooms. Her braids fell forward—today they reminded me of little bells, and my feelings toward her grew warmer: How glad I was to have her as a friend! She drew pictures with a stick in the dirt. A house. A tree. Two people.

"But there are only two dozen or so women," I said, looking at my other friends.

Chalsea pushed her long red hair behind her ears. "About that on our side and as many men on theirs," she answered.

"What!" I exclaimed. "I have not seen any men."

"They stay on their side, and we stay on ours. La Corona does not allow mixing."

"Mixing of what?" I asked naively. The kittens curled beside me in two juxtaposed balls, a funny figure eight.

"Employees. Coupling," Moravia said sadly. Her dark skin was smooth like the thick chocolate old Sarai made. Moravia had no need of my unguents.

"The other side is for different clientele," Tressa said. "Women."

"Women?" I asked, incredulous.

Chalsea, who was always kind, said, "Many noble women come here and from long distances too. Ones who do not get satisfied at home."

Moravia added, "Then there are the men who want to be with men."

I thought of the dimly lit alley in Madrid, how Jesus had had to pull me away from the angry duke's son, how the nature of men with men had become known to me. Here, it simply seemed like another kind of spice in the *olla podrida** of humanity.

Tressa started a discussion of the nature of love, which fit in with my thoughts. I told them of Margret's idea that love came in different kinds—*devoted, alchemical,* and *kindred.*

Moravia nodded. "All you need to know is love of God, true love, and friendship. For though I join with many men, that is not love. It is a part I play." With her jewel-laden fingers, she brushed her braids behind her shoulders.

"A job I do," Chalsea chimed in. Her freckles were bold in the sunlight.

---

* A stew, highly seasoned, to cover the taste of old meat and vegetables

Tressa, her pale eyes calm, agreed her job was not of love.

I did not have the same experience as they, for one would scarcely call what I did a job. It was not work, but play. "I think, perhaps, I am friends with Don Alphonse." What I did was merely a mutual agreement between congenial people.

"Do not think it," Moravia said. "It does not work that way."

"Men do not know of friendship with women," Chalsea said. "Friends to them are men who hunt and game, not women, whom they seek to bed."

Tressa, her long arms curled across her body in a hug, said, "A swinging skirt must make them hard or they walk on by."

I would be more to Don Alphonse than an open pair of legs. I would encourage our friendship, suggest sometime we play chess and talk. We would have more than bed time when he was here.

"Have you ever been in love?" Moravia asked me. She cupped her hand and took a sip of water from the pond.

I told of Carlos and showed them the ruby ring. I told them I had been sad and forlorn when he left, and how I once checked at every crossroad to see if he were coming. I reached over and rubbed the gray kitten's cold ear, warming it with my fingers.

"It takes time to know if a seed planted in one afternoon blooms into true love," Moravia said. "Will you stay together when life is usual life? Life is not always dancing to a gypsy band."

"Love is for the rich." Tressa said matter-of-factly. Her blonde curls wavered softly in the timid breeze.

But I did not agree, for Lorenzo and Aldonza had it. Margret and Laurent had it.

Moravia replied, "Not always. They often marry who is chosen for them. It is hard for anyone to find true love and have it free of obstacles."

"I wonder if Don Alphonse's son loves his wife?" I asked.

"She does not love him," Moravia said. "Or she would not allow him to come to you."

"We have only to worry about satisfying our reys," Chalsea said. "It is not for us to think of love. Remember Melisandra. She thought she found true love, but it was death to her."

We were all silent. They remembered Melisandra; I thought of Braden's scars.

"Then we will love each other," I cried in generosity. "For friendship is open to us." I reached out to squeeze their hands. They smiled and returned my gesture.

The kittens stirred from their nap and began to chase each other. Chalsea said, "It's as if one were the shadow of the other."

"I thought that too." I laughed. "But which is the shadow?" I got up and walked over to them. Now they were wrestling with each other. "Which?"

Chalsea laughed too. "Either. Shadows can be black or gray. This one or that one."

"I want to make them mine," I said. With sadness, I remembered Piccolo and his ill-fated end after our prank. I thought of Carlota, a pure soul if there ever was one.

"Take them," Moravia said, nodding, causing her many braids to clink together as they swayed in the sunlight. "Blalock complains of too many cats."

I took them to my rooms and fed them clabbered milk and bits of cheese. I called the black one Midnight and the other Misty, because he was the color of the mist that comes just before sunrise.

Ꙅ ꙇ

Don Alphonse came every few days. Sometimes, he spent the night. Between times I stayed busy with all my activities. I bought some blue figured velvet fabric and started a new dress.

I decided to seek out Rudolph, the carpenter La Corona had mentioned, about building shelves for baskets of herbs and rafters for hanging herbs to dry. I asked Chalsea how to find him. Chalsea told me more of his history: His mother was a Hapsburg, a distant cousin to King Philip. His wife's father was the man, a duke, who had lost all his property and money to La Corona. Everyone—servants, family, including Rudolph's wife and children, had died from *cartarro*, a very contagious disease, which nearly depopulated Madrid and killed Queen Anne, King Philip's last wife. Rudolph had asked if he could stay on as a carpenter, and La Corona readily agreed.

The kind-hearted Chalsea said, "He lives among dozens of women, yet he has eyes for none." She wrinkled her freckled nose. "He is like a father to all of us. They say he was a priest before he married."

"He must have loved his wife very much to leave the Church," I said. Perhaps he wished he had died too. "I've seen the chapel he built. I have never seen him."

"He goes at dawn," Chalsea said.

The next morning, before sunrise, I went to the chapel. Inside I stood eye to eye with the Virgin Mary. "Help this man find happiness," I said to her. I had been saddened by the story of Rudolph, who was once prince, once priest, once husband and father, but no more. I could see the six graves out the window.

The door to the chapel opened and I looked to see who entered. A man—possibly the most handsome man I ever saw. He was nearly as large as Blalock, and perfectly shaped. His hair was blond and cut straight at the shoulders. He was clean-shaven with chiseled cheeks and a strong chin. My breath came quickly, and I was surprised at how readily my body responded to him. *No, I must not.* I was attracted to Don Alphonse—but it was not the same. This seemed more magnetic, the alchemical pull Margret spoke of.

"It is a fine morning. I did not think to see anyone." His voice was deep, almost a purr, seductive. I remembered how Margret told me she responded to Laurent's voice, even before seeing him.

"I-I was l-looking for Rudolph," I stammered. "I am afraid he is not here." I sidled toward the door, hoping to get away from this man who affected me so deeply.

"I am Rudolph," he said, pushing his longish hair behind his ears. His eyes were brown, a contrast to his blond hair. His skin was bronzed from the wind and sun.

My knees buckled and I sat awkwardly on a bench. "They said you were old." I flushed at my rudeness. "I was expecting someone older." Still I bumbled. My neck was hot.

He laughed, a laugh as delightful as the rest of him. "I am old compared to others who are here," he said lightly. "They think of me as their father."

Chalsea had said as much. Could it be they did not see how handsome he was? Or did they see past his looks? I did not think he was forty. His manner of speech was odd; it was uniformly correct. Our language was not his native language, but he had learned ours perfectly.

I swallowed but could not speak.

"You come here often," he said.

I nodded.

"I did not know who came, but I recognize your scent. It is here when I come in the morning," he said. "You are Dulcinea, are you not?"

I was so discomfited that I did not wonder how he knew my name. "I come to pray," I said. "I-I lost my family too." I regretted saying this. Surely his loss was greater: Lorenzo's family was not really mine.

"I am sorry," he said. "It is a great loss."

He sat on the other bench, and we talked. He told me of his Belle and his children.

I spoke of Margret, Carlota, Lorenzo, and Aldonza. He prayed for our lost families. After that, I told him I needed some carpentry work, some shelves and rafters.

"I did something similar in the desire theater," he said. "Shelves and rafters."

"The *desire* theater?"

"You are not familiar with the other side?"

I shook my head for even after I learned of it I had not ventured there.

He went on, "Did you ever wish to be rescued by a knight?"

"Rescued?" I asked. *Would this knight be blond? Beardless?* I wondered how it would be to touch his straight, light hair, to caress his sculptured face.

"Maybe you have imagined a giant kidnaped you and took you away to ravish you and a knight rescued you."

"I see," I said. "A story."

"On the other side, they fulfill desires. People, men and women, come with a *desire*, which is played out for them." He said all this evenly, but his mouth was tight. "Come," he said. "We will go to see the carpentry work."

I did not understand what he was talking about, but I was most willing to follow him. He led me to the other wing and into a large room. On the wall inside the door were shelves which held pillows and coverlets. Around the room, twenty low platforms held very fat down ticks, like having twenty narrow beds in a room. On some were men and women. Rudolph whispered, "Oh, they are beginning. We can talk after the play." Rudolph pulled me by my arm (I shivered at his touch) to one of the mattresses.

At the front of the room was a large stage. Polished mirrors helped reflect the light of many candles. Looking up, I saw the rafters he had mentioned—it was no surprise; they were rubbed wood, beautiful, quite like the maker.

A woman, dressed in fine clothing, came out on the stage. She was pretty and shapely. Before she walked across the stage, a "giant" came out and grabbed her. The giant was a tall thin man dressed in ghastly clothes and a mask. She screamed; he pulled at her. She screamed again. He tugged at her clothing—which seemed to be fixed to come off easily—ripping it and exposing one breast, then her back, then a thigh. She struggled. He grabbed at her again, and her hair fell to her waist. "Do not hurt me," she begged.

My mouth dropped open. I looked at the couples in the audience. They, too, were in various stages of dress and undress, various stages of amorous play. I glanced at Rudolph, for these were thoughts I could easily have of him. He was not watching; instead he had taken a knife and a piece of wood from a pocket and was carving a short finial—the top of a bedpost, perhaps.

On the stage, a knight with helmet, pasteboard armor, and sword appeared. After a bit of swordplay, the giant ran off. The woman collapsed into the knight's arms, and the rest of her clothes fell off, as did his. After a bit of kissing and nuzzling, they were coupling on the stage, and the event was replicated over and over in the many mirrors and by many of the audience.

I could not get my breath. I *had* to *leave* this room. I pulled at Rudolph's hand, and when he looked at me, he dropped his things, picked me up, and carried me out. He took me to a little room with only a bed and washstand in it. He sat me on the bed.

"What is it?" he said. "You are as white as salt."

I began to shake. Sobs came from deep inside.

Rudolph sat beside me. He held me firmly, stroking my head, and said, "Be easy, child. Be easy. You are safe here." It was as if that was what I needed to hear. The sobbing stopped. I was calmer and began to talk.

"I saw a girl raped," I said in a low voice. "By three men."

"Oh, my child," he said. "You must have been terrified."

"I wanted to stop them."

"Yes," he said. "There is no stopping a man from doing what he wants. Even harder to stop three."

I looked at him in surprise. What an odd thing, I thought, for a man to say. "But I should have done something."

"You did the best you could." He patted my arm. "You have got to believe that," he said with intense emotion.

"But you do not even know me," I said, with exasperation.

"I can see it in your eyes." His hair fell across his brow, and he brushed it back with an easy gesture. "I should not have brought you."

"I had a knife," I said, still thinking of the night in Madrid.

"You were scared." His eyes seemed wise and sad. "Pray for peace about this, Dulcinea," he said gently in his baritone voice. "If you had pulled a knife against three of them, you would be dead."

I sighed. There was no right answer about what I should have done, because the situation was wrong. And I could not go back and change it. "It should have been me," I said quietly. "I deserved it."

Tears filled his eyes. "Now do not say that," he said firmly. He took my chin in his hand and made me look at him. "Nobody deserves to be hurt like that, hurt in any way."

"I deserve to go to hell."

He laughed, which was not the response I expected.

"You are going to be all right," he said. "Before you die you will know you do not deserve to go to hell. If there is a hell."

I drew back shocked. "*If!*"

As he shook his head, his hair swayed around his shoulders. "Unless it is hell on earth."

"But do you not believe in God?" I said, thinking he might be from the Devil, which would explain his good looks.

"Yes, I believe in God. I once studied for the priesthood, but I have learned to see things in a different way." Thoughtfully, he rubbed his cheek. "I believe in what I see," he said. "What I know." He looked at me. "I see you in a hell of your own making because you did not help your friend."

This talk of no hell was such a new idea to me; he might as well have been talking in Portuguese, a language I did not know. "I need God to forgive me."

"God always forgives," Rudolph said with such surety that I almost believed him. "You need *you* to forgive you." He went to the washstand and dampened a cloth. He washed my face and hands. He was—had been—touching me, but the attraction to him *was gone*. And the seeds of friendship stood in its place.

"Dulcinea, everyone here has done bad things and has had bad things done to them. We are fine," he said. "You will see." Again I noticed the way he said his words, so perfectly and evenly. I believed him when he said I was fine.

I pointed back to the desire stage. "Who would do that? In front of others?" I was still trying to wipe the images from my mind, the images that had brought up memories of Daria with Jesus and the others. "Who would watch?"

He laughed. "Some people like it. I do not care for it. Pride of my work is my sin," he said. "I should have waited to show you." He told me more of this side: "That woman on the desire stage is a client. She is from Madrid, the wife of a count. She dreams of being rescued. She acts it out."

I touched the ring on my finger. I remembered I had dreamed that the man I had encountered at the gypsy fair would come and take me away. Yes, I had dreamed of his return, but I had not taken it this far. At that time of my life, a kiss on the cheek was far enough, maybe a peck on the lips, some cuddling. "The problem with wanting to be rescued," I said, "is the waiting. I want more than that!"

Rudolph grinned. "Yes, I see that in you."

And I had been the inspiration for a knight, one who had jousted windmills and freed convicts. I wondered what the old man would think of his Dulcinea living in this place.

Rudolph swung a handcuff hanging from a nearby shelf. It clanked against another. I noticed other paraphernalia in the room. He said, "Much on this side I do not understand but accept." He told me of The Barnyard. A place where they kept animals. My head reeled. Dogs, mostly, he said. A few chosen sheep, large birds . . . I put my hands on my ears. I did not want to hear the whole of it.

"But not hearing does not mean it does not happen," he said. "I am saddened by much that goes on at Le Reino, yet I stay not only because of my family," he looked grave, "but to add beauty to this life." His handsome face was bathed in sorrow. "I know the people here are good at heart. I share some of their experience."

"How is that?" I asked.

"Many have had experiences like your friend in Madrid." He was talking of Daria. "I was three the first time. But it was my tutor."

"How could he?" I was appalled.

"Sometimes I think this place is a mirror of our past, and we seek it or it finds us."

"As if we had no choice?" I asked.

His brown eyes were somber as he nodded.

I had not sought this. But had it found me? What of when I was three? I remember the first night I had gone with Don Alphonse. How easily, as if in some trance, I had responded to his voice in my ear, "Please me," his hand on my arm. How easy it was to be with him, as if it were familiar. I had not bled. I shook my head to stop my thoughts. Out loud I said, "What a silly notion! It is not like that for me."

CHAPTER 21

in which Dulcinea hosts Don Alphonse and meets his son

ATER AS I bent over some sewing, I thought of following Rudolph's example. I would reconsider my faith—the one fed to me by others. Even with his original ideas, he professed to be a devout Catholic; he found forgiveness easy and accepted everyone as they were.

After all, I reasoned, Holy Eucharist encourages us to think of the world as one body for the many grapes are made into one wine and the many grains of wheat are made into one bread. Does that not make us all brothers and sisters in this world without exception?

∽∾

Don Alphonse brought some wine with him for me to have on hand. "It is good Andalusian wine of Solariego," he said. "The finest in all of Spain, I think."

I poured him a glass, and he sipped it after we settled into a tub of hot water, prepared for us by Braden. Melisandra had understood that preparing for love is important. The tub was a double tub. Imagine two narrow ovals set together, not symmetrically, rather like a lopsided eight. Each person sat in a curve of the tub facing the other. This arrangement put their torsos closer to each other.

Before joining in other activities, Don Alphonse and I relaxed in the warm water. For the first time, he told me about his business interests. He had a large estate outside of Bradosina about ten miles from here. His serfs mostly raised grain, but he also dealt in lumber, there being many hills on his land filled with trees.

He said, "Trees are like people; it takes years for them to mature." He explained that he was careful not to cut all the trees from a hillside because that would be disastrous, causing mudslides and damage to the surrounding farms. "Europe uses much wood for cooking and heating," he said, his eyes serious.

"What do you like to do?" I asked, pleased that my plan of getting to know him better was working. I took a cloth and washed his chest and arms. "I hunt," he said. "And I paint pictures." He pulled at the end of his long moustache and in his rich voice said, "Would you like to see some of my paintings?"

"Of course," I said, now washing his ankle. "And I would like one for each of my rooms."

He looked mischievous. "I know what I will paint—for in here," he indicated the bathing room and laughed. "And the bedroom. I will think of something for the sitting room."

After our pleasure, Don Alphonse sat up in bed, smoothing his long moustache, and said, "My son will return home within a fortnight from his wedding trip."

"Tell me about your son."

The moon was shining in the window on his face, and I could see he looked pleased. "I have three daughters and one son. My daughters are vain and proud, seldom obedient, but my son is all that a man would want in a son. I am blessed indeed."

"And his wife?" I asked boldly.

"She is young and noble, a wonderful match for my son, but uninterested in the bedroom. Though there will be an heir. Or two," Don Alphonse said firmly. He touched my thigh and ran his hand along it; the familiar smell of peppermint reached my nose. "With any luck Matilde will be pregnant by their return."

"Are you a grandfather already?" I asked.

"I have four grandchildren," he said proudly. ("I" he said, not "we." *He must be a widower.*)

It seemed his daughters did not have an aversion to marital duty. I did not say this out loud, but he did. "My girls and my son are as lusty as I." He pulled me to him. Before he left, he said sternly to me, "No falling in love, Dulcinea. Not with me or my son."

I nodded, too full of myself to consider that I might love anyone else but me.

∽ɔ ɔ∾

On an unusually slow afternoon, I was in the greeting room. The women were dancing—some needed practice! some were having fun—to the music from the harpsichord and guitars. Luis was there too.

I stood on a stool while Moravia checked the hem of my new blue velvet dress. It was nearly completed, though I had not yet finished the sleeves of the shift which were hanging below my wrists, nearly covering my fingers.

Moravia glanced over at Luis dancing with Tressa. "Luis is learning skills he needs."

I took in this information slowly. "Do you mean . . . so he can work here?" I asked.

"Of course," she said casually. "La Corona will expect it."

I thought of how his hair stood up on his head in the morning, making him look young and vulnerable. "I will hope for something different for him."

The door opened and four young grandees entered with their servants. All were wearing plumed hats. Two of the young men went straight to the dancers and found partners—Tressa and Modesta, a new and pretty Italian girl. Another bowed to Moravia and led her to the dance floor.

"But what of my hem?" I called, disappointed that she left.

"Tomorrow," she said over her shoulder, and she put her hands on the man's cheeks and pulled his mouth to hers briefly to let him know she was committed to him.

"Perhaps I may help, señorita," the fourth young man said. He was tall, broad-shouldered, narrow-hipped and dressed all in scarlet—even the plumes in his hat, which hid his full face from me. He threw off his cloak, ready to help.

"She was checking my hem," I said, looking down on him from the vantage point of my stool and wishing I could flirt; he was that appealing, for as meeting Rudolph had shown me, there are feelings stirred in women by men and it was natural. Now the dancing seemed attractive. I imagined his hand on my waist, my velvet skirt whispering against the floor, brushing against him. I felt like a married woman must feel turning her back on romance. I had to be faithful, not to my husband, but to my patron.

"I fear I cannot do much about that," he said. "But these sleeves could use tying up." From a nearby table, he picked up a ribbon from among my sewing articles, and gathering the material near my elbow, he pulled it up until my hand was visible and then he quickly gartered the material around my upper arm to hold it in place.

"Señor," I gasped, as my heart raced. "You are too bold."

"Is that possible?" He laughed and added, "Here?"

"Do not mistake me, señor," I said, short of breath, for his brief touch had quite affected me. "Please help me down," I begged. I meant to leave the room. But I merely confounded myself more for he put his hands around my waist to lift me from the stool. When my feet touched the floor, our eyes met.

Carlos! I thought. *Yes, see his golden eyes. But can it be?*

He took my other hand in his and rolled back the sleeve and there was the ruby ring. He pulled back his sleeve to show me the leather bracelet, quite weathered now.

"Aldonza," he said quietly, touching my cheek, finding my dimples, for I was smiling broadly. "But how is it you are here?"

I could not speak, for joy and quite its opposite were in my heart.

He requested Chalsea to play a *fandango,* and as we had before at the gypsy fair, we danced together. There was no applause this time, for the others were not watching us, and the seduction we danced was not worth noticing but was the expected.

In my sitting room, we sat on cushions. He removed his hat and when I saw his golden-brown curls, every detail of that foreign day came back to me.

"Perhaps you are married," I said timidly. "Many who come here are."

He shook his head as if to say he were not. But then he said, "No, I cannot lie. I am."

I felt disappointment and anger. "It's just as well," I said, hoping to hurt him a little. "For I am committed to another."

We sat with our hurt feelings for a bit, looking longingly, a little bitterly, at each other.

"Tell me what has happened," he said. "You are a long way from La Mancha."

I briefly told him what had happened between the time he left me at the gypsy fair until I had gotten here, and he told me some of what had gone on with him. From time to time we stole a touch—I, his curly hair; he, my dark ringlets. I touched his noble hands and he kissed my ruby-ringed finger. Soon we were silent. Was there no more to say? I could not betray Don Alphonse for I had made a promise. If I did, I was sure I could not stay here, and Carlos was married. There was no hope that things would come right for us to be together.

As bravely as I could, I said, "I think you must leave."

"Yes," he said. His eyes looked moist, but my own vision was blurry because of my tears.

He took my chin in his hand, brushed a kiss against my cheek, and left. I threw myself on the floor. I was disconsolate, and that was how La Corona and Moravia found me.

"But what is it, Dulcinea?" La Corona asked, grasping my wrists to help me up.

Moravia asked, "Did you not get along?" She led me to sit on the bed.

I shook my head, my breath coming in gasps. I could not speak.

"He looked wonderful," Moravia said, leaning close to me. "Did he hurt you?" Her braids clinked a little tune.

"No!" I could be emphatic about that, though I was certainly hurting.

They were silent for a moment. La Corona took my hand and patted it gently.

"He is the one. Who gave me this ring. Years ago," I said, still breathing unevenly, the words coming in spurts. I sighed, remembering our moment of recognition. "When we looked into each other's eyes, he called me 'Aldonza.'"

"Aldonza!!" they both said at once.

I nodded. "That was my name then." I did not care if they were confused. How could I tell them I slipped into new names and new identities as easily as a chemise? I told the story for La Corona and finished by saying, "And as he rode off from the fair, he said, 'A compassionate God will see we meet again.'"

"But that is true and wonderful," Moravia said and hugged me. "Why the tears?"

"But why bring us back together again, only to keep us apart?"

"Apart?" La Corona said. "You should have been together in this bed." She patted the quite straight covers.

I looked at her in disbelief. "How can you say that? I promised to be Don Alphonse's exclusively!"

Her lavender eyes solemn, she said, "Or his son's." As if she needed to remind me!

"I know," I wailed, flopping back on the bed. "It is hopeless."

They seemed to be hiding smiles. But why? I jumped up. "I thought you were my friends," I cried. "Have you lost your hearts?" I flounced into the sitting room and threw myself on a cushion.

I heard them murmuring together—La Corona's tinkly laughter sprinkled in. Soon Moravia joined me. She asked, "Do you know Don Alphonse's son's name?"

I thought for a minute and realized I did not: how was it Don Alphonse had never mentioned it? But no matter. I shook my head and continued sulking.

"Carlos," Moravia said quietly.

ᔓᘰ

I was full of energy. I finished my dress and began on a blackwork corset for Tressa. While I sewed, I found my mood swinging from happy to forlorn. Happy that we could be together, forlorn that we could never be more than lovers, for I knew the truth of the situation. Still, could I not love him? Did I not love him? I thought of nothing but Carlos, the touch of his hand, every word we had said here and at the fair.

One afternoon I took the locket, which I now kept on my dresser, and opened it. If that boy were my intended, I hoped he would find another, for I wished for Carlos and Carlos only. To be with the boy would be wrong, it seemed, for would he not always seem young like this picture, never a man?

I put the locket back on my dresser and went for a walk in the woods. Unexpectedly—or perhaps in my pitiable state I was completely oblivious to my surroundings—it began to rain. I saw a little cabin among the trees. As I approached, I saw smoke coming from the chimney. I thought the fire was there for my convenience—

when one is in love, isn't everything done for them alone?—so I opened the door and walked in.

I heard bustling and scrambling. Then I saw Moravia naked on the straw tick near the fireplace. She laughed. "It's Dulcinea! The love-struck!" I looked around and there was Blalock! covered with a blanket, presumably as naked as Moravia. I was speechless. I sat on the mattress next to Moravia, looking from one to another. I could not help but think her regal, dressed only in gems, her hair in dozens of colorful braids, her arms braceleted by tattoos. The fire was warm, and steam rose from my wet wool skirt.

They told me their story. They were lovers. Here was their meeting place, and no one had discovered it until now!

"I won't tell," I promised soberly. We sat in silence and then I asked of Moravia, "Why don't you buy his freedom?"

They had never thought of it, and this idea gave them hope that one day they could leave here together. As we were walking back, Moravia took my hand and said, "Thank you, Dulcinea."

"Maybe there's hope for a happy ending," I said, but silently I wondered if love was always for people who could not be together.

I spent part of that evening, as was my habit, playing games with Luis.

"What do you think of God, Dulcinea?" he asked me.

"I believe in a compassionate God."

"What of hell?" he asked. "In Alcala today, I heard a woman say that those like us would go to hell." He rose from his cushion and accidentally knocked over the stool which held the game board and pieces. "Oh, no," he said with chagrin.

"No matter. You were winning." We laughed and he began to pick up the pieces. "You are a good lad, Luis, and must not ever think that God does not love you enough to take you to heaven with him." I remembered what Rudolph thought of hell, but I did not tell Luis. I did not yet understand Rudolph's ideas.

Later, when Luis had fallen asleep, I asked myself how I had so easily shed my cloak of religion—I had not been to Mass for many weeks and I had not missed it. My daily visits to the little chapel easily took the place of church. Yet I knew Father Jude—or any other priest—would not agree that I could replace Mass with my own prayers. I searched my heart and found I believed in a good God who wanted our lives to be as simple as possible.

I fell asleep and dreamed that Luis and I were angels who lived in the little cabin. And day and night, we gathered flowers and herbs to dispense to those in need, healing them. Most everyone I knew, dead and alive, came to see us includ-ing Daria and Fredrica. I was happy, for in my dream, I healed Daria and she forgave me, and I healed Fredrica and made her a kind person, not one whose soul blazed like the fires she started. Before I woke, I saw Antonia and her uncle. He was dressed as a knight in beautifully buffed white armor, and he asked me for an infusion of Eyebright to help him see clearly. I gave him what he wanted, and I said, "We all must try this." I went back to everyone and gave them some. But there was not enough for me.

⁓ↄ ∼

The afternoon I saw Don Alphonse and Carlos enter the greeting room, I felt very shy. Carlos did not look happy to see me. Holding my head high, I walked slowly toward them.

I heard Carlos say, "But Father, you said I could only see Dulcinea."

I laughed and called out, "I am Dulcinea!" and ran to his arms. We nearly fell to the floor in my enthusiasm. We got our balance, and I decided I needed to behave with better decorum; after all, I was not to fall in love! As if one had control in that!

The fine lines blooming at his eyes, Don Alphonse laughed. "You two have made a muddle of this!"

We hung our heads, though our hands held fast together. Don Alphonse explained that he had known who I was from the very first night because of the ruby ring; it had belonged to his mother! Years before, Carlos told his father the story of the gypsy fair, the knife throwing, the bracelet, and the ring. Don Alphonse said to me, "He came home from here long-faced and unwilling to tell me what happened." He clapped his son on the back.

Carlos grinned. "How could I tell him I did not want the beautiful Dulcinea because I had found my Aldonza!?"

Don Alphonse smoothed his long moustache. "Now that I have put you two on course, I am off to Madrid." He kissed me on the cheek.

Carlos stayed two nights. After waking up together the first morning, he reached over and took his knife from its sheath. He held it. "To think, it was a knife that brought us together."

I quoted him. "'As close as those knives are, that is how close I want to be to you.'" I felt quite grown up, as if I knew everything there was to know about life, as if I had already suffered every misfortune. And now I was ready to settle in, sit back, and enjoy what was left.

He flung his knife at a knot on the mantle then retrieved it. He handed it to me. I did not quite hit the knot. But I went to stand beside him and said, "I am out of practice, but let me show you how I can make this bold knife," I caressed his *cetro*, "ready to find its target."

"Aah. Then I will sheath it," he said lightly. He closed his eyes to my well-placed touches. And true to his honor, for he was among the most honorable of men, he sheathed his *knife*, and we found our *little death* together.

When we could breathe normally again, he rose from the bed, took his knife to the mantel, and asked, "Shall we fill it with notches of our lovemaking?"

I said, "Lovemaking! What a glorious word!" I repeated it slowly, feeling it in my mouth, my tongue against my teeth, the arch of my tongue.

He laughed. "Yes, though we speak not of love."

"Yes," I said, thinking he referred to his father's edict that we not fall in love.

He asked, "Can we get something to eat?"

On the floor in the sitting room with a stool for our table, we fed each other apples. Then we played chess and that day set our habit: our days were full of love-making, games, and food.

After the new year when the weather became milder, we moved our games outdoors. Carlos insisted I take up my knife throwing again, and we often staged contests, making our own private wagers on who would do what to whom when one or the other won. Sometimes he brought a bow and arrows and set up targets for that too. Carlos arranged with La Corona for me to ride Marchioness.

ဩ ૪

At Easter time Don Alphonse took me to Madrid. The morning of our departure, I woke at dawn. I had Braden fill the tub and help me wash my hair. Then I sat in the hot water and relaxed.

Luis, who had slept in my bed as he often did, came in to use the chamber pot. The warm smell of urine briefly filled the air. He sat on a stool near me.

"When do you think I'll be old enough to work here?" he asked me, rubbing his sleepy eyes. "My mother says it may not be for a year or more!" he cried. "I can barely think of waiting so long!" He spoke with the impatience of a child. His sandy hair was styled in its usual haphazard in-the-morning way. His green eyes were eager and desperate. He stood up tall, stretching as high as he could. "When will I be big enough?" he asked.

I was glad to hear La Corona was going to wait until he was a bit older. "It has more to do with when you are ready to shave," I said, "than how big you are."

He sat again and looked at his *cetro*. He picked it up and it wavered, then flopped in his hand. His groin was as clear of hair as golden apples.

"Do you think I will be able to pleasure women?" he asked. "It's not as big as some."

I was not happy to have this conversation. "Luis, I think you will be able to do whatever you want to do."

"Will you teach me what a woman likes?" he asked eagerly.

"No, Luis, I cannot teach you that," I said. "I will always think of you as my brother."

"But can we not talk about it?" He knelt by the tub, speaking to me in earnest. I shook my head.

Bringing her fresh lavender scent, La Corona arrived. She sent Luis to help Blalock and sat on the stool where Luis had been. She coiled her long hair in her lap.

"You'll have a good time on your trip." She clasped her hands confidently in her lap, as if this made her pronouncement true.

"I am afraid I will do something wrong." I got out of the tub, water dripping from my every part. I had no confidence that I knew how to act in noble society.

"You could do nothing wrong."

"Of course I could!" I cried, as I dried my body. "I could draw attention to myself. Bring a shadow to Don Alphonse's honor." I rubbed on lotion before I dressed. I had finally duplicated Melisandra's scent—the right combination of flowers and grapes.

"Men, like Don Alphonse, who have women such as us," she explained to me, "delight in our unexpected nature. He will cover any mistake you make."

"I would rather not make the mistake."

She shook her head. "Trust your mind to tell you what to do." She tapped her forehead with her long fingernails. "Simply act confident."

I remembered Margret saying as much before I went to Madrid as Aldo. But this trip seemed to require different information.

"You worry for nothing. Your beauty gives you an entry wherever you go." That seemed a flimsy thing to rely on, though I remembered Fredrica saying beauty had power. But I saw my power in my ability to give pleasure, my ability to help others.

My experience of Madrid as courtesan was very different than my experience of Madrid as Aldo. We stayed in a house near the center of town and were busy with parties, the theater, shopping, and more. Whenever we went out, I covered my face with a veil, which was the custom of many women.

Each day we went to Mass. Each day I contemplated going to confession, but I was not sure what to confess. My life did not feel sinful—I had no headaches, no guilt. My way of life was simply for convenience; I was alone in the world and had to make my own way. Surely I could find nothing better than what I had. I decided the worst sin was going to the little chapel and not to a church, but I did not intend to change. Confession would be pointless.

Carlos arrived in our second week in Madrid.

Surprised, I said, "I did not expect you."

He kissed me on the cheek.

"Yes, yes," Don Alphonse said. He greeted his son with a hug.

Carlos asked me, "How do you find Madrid?"

"Exciting. Exhilarating. Exquisite." I thought of the lilacs on the corner that were fragrant with plump white blooms, the shouts of merchants in the market square, and the herbalist shop in which I had found new herbs: ginseng, gingko, wild yam, also sassafras, a herb from Florida in the New World. We had been to the theater and court, though the king was not in residence, but at El Escorial, north of Madrid.

Don Alphonse said enthusiastically to Carlos, "Today—the bullfight!" He clapped his son on the back.

The morning brought a nice spring shower, though by the time we left for our outing, the rain had stopped, leaving the day pleasant and cool. I wore red with black accents. I carefully covered the lower part of my face with a red scarf. Don Alphonse dressed in black and Carlos in red.

The bullfight was held in the main city square. The nobles sat on festively draped balconies. On our balcony, just above ground level, Don Alphonse and I sat in front. Carlos sat with two friends behind us. Carlos's friends were introduced as Jovi Bonheur, the second son of the duke of Melancon, who lived in Seville, and Tomás Solidares, the second son of the duke of Gasparenza.

Jovi was the brother of Ruy Bonheur, who was one of the *toreadors*. Ruy was a bullfighter of renown and would someday become duke. Tomás was married to Jovi and Ruy's sister, Sonora. I liked Tomás immediately. He had brown eyes fringed with thick eyelashes and a broad grin. On his handsome face was an L-shaped scar below the left eye.

We could not yet see the bulls but could hear them snorting and thrashing. The crowd was growing larger.

Grand and glorious, the music began. A dozen *toreadors* entered the square wearing multicolored plumed hats and short capes, swords and daggers at their sides. They rode grandly caparisoned horses that marched to the music.

Jovi leaned forward and said to me, "My brother is the third one."

I nodded. "I understand he is very good."

"He is!" the proud Jovi said, thumping his fist on his knee. "Ruy thrives on danger," Jovi declared. "He is danger."

I smiled at the boy's pride. Jovi seemed younger than the others, maybe even as young as sixteen.

As Ruy came closer, he raised his hat to the crowd, and I saw his engaging, white-toothed smile and dark flashing eyes. I believed in him. I believed him to be the best. Approaching our balcony, he and his horse bowed before us. He acknowledged his brother and brother-in-law with a wave and then looked at me. He urged his horse closer. "Don Alphonse," he said; his voice was deep, rather husky. "I would like to meet your beautiful blue-eyed companion." His smile was even more engaging close up. My cheeks grew warm; I was glad for my veil.

"Ruy Bonheur of Seville, son of the duke of Melancon, number one *toreador* in all of Spain," Don Alphonse said, "this is Doña Dulcinea."

"I have a weakness for blue eyes." His own black eyes twinkled, but then they became sad. "My first love had blue eyes."

"And you lost this love?" I asked, interpreting his sadness this way.

He nodded. "She disappeared some years ago. But I have always hoped she would return." He added sadly, "Though she was another's."

Don Alphonse nodded. "Yes, Christopher Solidares's Luscinda. She was promised to him from birth." He spoke sternly as if Ruy could not love her too.

I was enchanted with Ruy, and I did not know this Christopher, so I said, "I hope she does return to you, Don Ruy, for you are a brave and gallant man."

The attractive *toreador* took my hand. "May I ask to fight for you, señorita?" Don Ruy asked. "I would carry your token."

"It seems you have enough tokens," I said lightly, pointing to the several brightly colored scarves tied near his shoulder.

"Doña Dulcinea," he said gallantly, as he sat tall in the saddle. "These are old ladies'." He leaned toward me in a confidential manner. "I will wear your colors close to my heart, if you allow it. Only one other's token has found its place there."

"I have no scarf," for I could not remove my veil, "but I have a handkerchief."

He nodded. I handed my white lacy handkerchief to him. I laughed merrily when, with exaggerated show, he tucked it inside his red jacket, and to show where it now resided, he patted his hand above his heart.

"You turn a lady's heart, Don Ruy," I said, smoothing my skirt with my hands to cover my breathlessness.

He pranced his horse and moved closer. "I wish that I could do more," he said. His voice was much too intimate in tone. What a rogue! "But I do not wish to dishonor my friend Don Alphonse." His hand rested on the rail of the balcony. "But surely, Doña Dulcinea, when I am finished today and have won the most *réjons*, you will grace me with your full visage, for I wish to see more than your eyes."

"It would be my honor, señor." I settled in my seat as he rode away to join the others. The crowd cheered and clapped.

I leaned over to Don Alphonse, catching a whiff of peppermint even today when the air was filled with a medley of smells of a thousand people, food, bulls, and spring rain, and said, "Now you must tell me what the *réjons* are."

"Wooden spears with steel points." He pointed to the containers of spears around the plaza and also to special holders on the sides of each *toreador's* horse. "The object is to embed the point in the rump of the bull and break off the shaft, the *réjon*. The winner is the bullfighter with the most *réjons*."

"It is very dangerous," I said, quite concerned for Don Ruy.

Jovi laughed. "For amateurs. The *toreadors* show their noble blood by their skill." His hands jabbed the air in his enthusiasm. "It's terribly exciting!"

Thinking of Luis, I felt certain he would enjoy this spectacle.

The music sounded the entry of the bulls. The center of the plaza was cleared of everyone but the intrepid *toreadors* on their horses. A dozen huge charging bulls entered, their feet flying. Everyone jumped up! The noise was deafening. One of the huge creatures immediately came close to our balcony and paused. His body glistened with sweat, and snorting, he pawed the ground with a front hoof. Don Ruy was on him quickly and planted his first *réjon*, competently breaking it off and leaving the spear head. The bull swerved, and Don Ruy, anticipating the move, elegantly turned his horse away. I could see why he was the best. Compared to the others, Don Ruy was a virtuoso, an artist, a master dancer.

And it was a sort of dance. The *toreadors* moving in, the bulls moving away. The bulls moving in, the *toreadors* moving away. Rhythmic and predictable, or somewhat predictable. Yet, there! The first *toreador* was down, and the bull, before the *peons* could distract him with their capes, had trampled him.

The crowd moaned and held its breath waiting to see if the young man moved.

"It's Don Paco," Jovi cried, wringing his hands. "From Segovia."

Don Alphonse whispered at my ear, "I know his father. He's a fine and noble man." Nervously, Don Alphonse fingered his long moustache. His eyes were solemn as he stared straight ahead at the still body on the ground. Carlos and Tomás prayed quietly. I prayed too.

The *toreadors* and *peons*, with their waving capes, worked to give a clear exit path to two rescuers, who carried the injured man out of the way of further harm. As they reached the gate, the injured *toreador* lifted his hand. The crowd cheered in relief.

I watched as several more *réjons* were planted and broken off. The crowd cheered with each one. The *toreadors* raised their trophies high, and the trumpets sounded triumphantly.

"Ruy is ahead," Jovi said loudly. "He has ten so far." He held up all his fingers.

The crowd roared and I stretched to see what had happened. A *toreador* had been knocked from his horse by a bull. This time the *toreador* was up quickly—unhurt. Now he was honor bound to kill the bull. He pulled his sword and dagger.

He was quick on his feet, dodging the angry bull. With his first thrust, he struck the mortal wound. The crowd erupted with cheers as the bull fell heavily to its knees, then to the ground, spilling out its life in the dirt. The *toreador* raised his arms in victory, but only for a moment, for he quickly remounted and had soon claimed another *réjon*.

Ruy was near us again. He had his eye on a bull that was coming toward him, and he did not see the other one, which hit his horse in the hindquarter. This assault downed the horse and flung Ruy ten feet.

I gasped as he fell head over heels and landed near our balcony under the galloping feet of another horse and *toreador*. His body, prone, ricocheted, without will, off the ground and back again, first his head landing, then his feet. Jovi, Tomás, and Carlos leapt from the balcony and pulled Ruy to the side before more damage could be done.

Don Alphonse and I made room for him between us. Two men jumped beside us to help, and they leaned forward, reaching for Ruy.

A bull threatened the rescuers and Tomás pulled his sword and dagger and attacked it! Here was another brave man! Two *toreadors* were quickly there to help. I heard cries of consternation, but I was distracted by the men placing Ruy on the floor beside me.

I knelt and took his head upon my lap. Don Alphonse took his cloak and covered Ruy's broken body. Using my underskirt, I wiped the blood and grimy sweat from his face. He moaned; his breath rattled in his throat, into his chest.

Blood inched from his nose and his mouth, the trickles meeting and rolling down one cheek. His brow furrowed and his eyes squeezed shut, but he forced them open to look at me. Slowly, his hand trembling, he reached into his jacket for my handkerchief and tried to pull it out, but his arm fell limp and he could not hand the handkerchief to me.

I pulled down my veil and smiled at him. His dark, tortured eyes flickered and stared. "*Toss the bones?*" he whispered.

I stared at him, not comprehending. *Why a reference to knucklebones now, as if nothing were wrong?*

He smiled, not feebly, but with some inner passion for life. Then he died: His head rolled to the side, his eyes now staring at nothing. I covered his face with the cloak and solemnly replaced my veil.

I saw my handkerchief, still partly in his jacket and I reached for it. With it came a small, white square with childish blackwork. In the corner was the initial "L." The token from the missing Luscinda. I tucked the little handkerchief in my pocket along with my own.

Much more happened that day, as you may guess, but what I would most remember was a man, who I did not know, dying in my arms, who had touched my life in a profound way. The frightful amount of blood shed when the bulls were killed simply could not eclipse the importance of that event.

In the evening Don Alphonse excused himself and left Carlos and me alone in the house. For what purpose? To give his son a chance to bed me? To give himself a chance to ponder on the mortality of young sons?

Our lovemaking was urgent, the kind you experience when you have recently been touched by death, the kind you experience when you need to affirm that you, yourself, are alive—fully alive. By the time Don Alphonse returned, I was asleep in his bed.

In the morning, he told me our trip was being cut short, that he and Carlos were to ride with Ruy's body to Seville. He kissed me gently on the cheek and told me that when I was packed, three servants would accompany me back to Le Reino.

After he and Carlos had gone, I realized I should have sent the childish handkerchief that I had taken from Ruy yesterday, but I tucked it away and soon I had forgotten it.

When I returned to Le Reino, my friends gathered to hear about my trip. Tressa and La Corona asked many questions about fashions. Chalsea, Rudolph, and Moravia were interested in hearing about the theater. I obliged everyone. When I began the narrative of the bullfight, Luis sat up in full attention. I told of the horses and colors and grand music. Chalsea and Tressa listened intently to every detail of Ruy's elegance and banter; both sighed heavily, clutching their hearts, not yet knowing his sad end. There was not a dry eye among them by the time I finished, for I revealed all and did not spare them the death of the young man who had loved "L."

CHAPTER 22

in which Dulcinea, disguised as a nun, delivers Don Carlos's son

T WAS FINALLY spring and I could begin collecting herbs and flowers in earnest. Braden helped me and I taught her about the different herbs and their uses. We carefully dried them in the sun and left most in bound bundles which we hung from the ceilings of my rooms on the hand-hewn and hard-carved rafters put in place by Rudolph. What a wonderful multicolored and fragrant cover over my head!

⋰⋱

Several weeks passed before Carlos came to see me. When we were satiated, we lay in bed talking, I on my stomach, as he idly rubbed my back with a fragrant oil.

"Matilde is great with child now," Carlos said. "For Father, I hope it is a boy. For myself, I only pray it is healthy and lives."

He sometimes spoke of his wife. Matilde had obligingly gotten pregnant on their wedding trip, relieving her from fulfilling her marital duty.

I turned over and sat beside him. "But if she has a boy, you will have an heir, and you will never have to sleep with her again." *Only with me,* I thought.

"Yes," he said quietly. "I suppose."

"What is it?" I asked, turning to him and touching his cheek, so he would look in my eyes. I felt he had more to say.

"But you must know, I love my wife."

"No." I sat up quickly. "And she does not love you!" I cried, thinking of how we suited each other and got along without quarrel.

After a silence, Carlos said, "Why do you think she does not love me?" He answered his own question, "Because she does not want to sleep with me."

"Yes," I said bluntly.

"Do you also, misguided child that you are," he, too, sat up in the bed, "think that this," he waved his hand at our naked bodies and the curtained bed around us, "is love?"

"Yes." I felt my chin begin to quiver, for I saw he did not.

"Do you think," he began, "because I brush your breast and your nipple puckers," and he demonstrated, "that this is love?" Tears fell on my cheek. He sighed. "Or do you think," he continued, "that because you wave your hand and my cock rises that this is love? This," he pointed to our moving parts, "is momentary. And that is all it is." His eyes met mine. "But Dulci, I like coming here and seeing you." He used the shortened name he had given me.

"But you wore my bracelet; I wore your ring." My voice was shaky. I was thinking of the years we fired our imaginations with the memory of that one afternoon at the gypsy camp.

"And I knew I would marry Matilde all along. Anticipation. Excitement," he said, "does not equal love. A dream of a clandestine affair holds charms for any man. Maybe it is the dream of the unattainable."

I saw I had moved to the attainable and Matilde was the unattainable. My throat hurt.

"Matilde is a good match for me." Carlos smoothed his curls. "She is beautiful and of good blood." (Wasn't I beautiful, too?) I pulled away from him. He did not see he had hurt me. He continued, "I knew she did not want to share our bed, but I thought that would change."

"You thought you could charm her," I said flatly. He had easily charmed me.

He nodded. "I hoped she would fall in love with me." He swung his legs over the edge of the bed and sat next to me. "On our wedding trip, I devoted all my time to her. We did everything she wanted, but she never warmed to me, and I merely wanted her all the more. And that desire continues to grow." He paused. "I pray for the day that she will declare her love for me. That would make me the happiest of men." He looked at me and smiled. "I have much love for her. I want to make her happy."

"And what of me?" I asked.

"Why do you think this would change?" he asked, puzzled. He looked at me intently. "I still need you."

I felt more tears spilling over. Surely he would wipe them away and tell me he did not mean what he had said. But he did not touch me or speak. I had bestowed more importance on his attention than he had ever intended, even on that very first day when we had found ourselves matched in the knife contest.

I walked to the window. I was a convenience for Don Alphonse and Carlos; they both had made it clear. Now I saw my choice was to stop or to ride the wave—it was not one-sided—of convenience and congeniality.

I would merely change my view of this. Yes, a shift in thinking. Perhaps I was not in love with Carlos. Never did I miss him, or Don Alphonse, when they were not here. I had plenty to keep me occupied. Indeed, it must not have been true love for him I felt. I knew I did not want to give him up either. Had I grown to need him? Was "handsome, entertaining"—love?

I touched his hand. "I am sorry," I said sincerely, "that she cannot love you the way you love her." I saw that he was stuck in wanting what he could not have. But I resolved to be content in having what I had, not unhappy over not having what I wanted. And while Carlos hoped Matilde would change, it was I that did change. And it was this moment that confirmed our friendship, and while we still played at being lovers on occasion, it was incidental and convenient.

ꝏꝏ

A week later—it was May 1591—I was summoned, for the first time, to Don Alphonse's house in Bradosina, the village near his estate, Brados. Don Alphonse was confined to bed with an injured knee and shoulder, caused by a fall from his horse as it jumped over a stone fence. He had sent two servants for me—could I help his discomfort?—and La Corona had granted that I could ride Marchioness back with them. Uncertain of what was expected of me, I packed to stay a week but thought it would scarcely be that long. I took the herbs and salves I thought might help.

At his house, I was taken upstairs by his servant Risio. Don Alphonse instructed Risio to tell the other servants to do as I instructed. The stooped old man nodded and went to put my belongings in a downstairs room.

The injuries seemed mostly strains and sprains, so I fixed him daily baths of certain herbs. I carefully helped him to the tub after I supervised its filling. I found, too, that I could order the kitchen to cook the foods I thought best for the duke. The servants did my bidding quickly and without resentment. Was it because Risio had told them to or was it because of my beauty? Was I more beautiful than Matilde?

Some days while Don Alphonse rested, I wandered through the grand house and imagined what it would be like to be the mistress here, not an impostor. *What am I doing here?* A simple peasant girl, trained by a simple peasant woman in herbal remedies. *Act confident,* I heard La Corona and Margret say to me.

The house was three stories and straightforward in design. The top floor was one large room perched on the top of the house with large shuttered windows all around, which could be flung open to the light as it pleased Don Alphonse as he painted. Dozens of canvases were lined up along the inner walls, in some places six or eight deep.

One was of Carlos and me sitting on cushions playing chess; Don Alphonse had never seen us do this so the scene was from his imagination. Carlos was outfitted in somber black and I, in yellow. Carlos's hand was hovering above a knight, which would be moved to capture a vulnerable bishop—oh, how had I allowed that to happen? Though now I saw it was a sacrifice to put me in a better position. But would the ploy work? Only in Don Alphonse's mind would one find the answer.

In another stack of paintings, I found pictures of a young gray-eyed nobleman, dark hair, a narrow beard covering his chin and jaw. His hands were large and generous, his fingers long. In one painting he was walking in a woods as if in deep thought. His head was down, and he was unaware of his surroundings, even of a group of hares, easily killed had he been paying heed. A wolf accompanied him in the posture of an obedient dog.

In another painting the same young man sat, reading, in a rude cabin in front of a blazing fireplace. The wolf was curled nearby in the warmth of the fire, again like a pet. I looked for other paintings of him, curious as to his character and his identity. A friend of Carlos's perhaps.

Ah, there was one, a large painting of Carlos with four young men in their short capes with rapiers by their sides standing in a pose of comradery near a stone wall. I looked closely and saw that three of the companions were young men I had met at the bullfight in Madrid—Tomás Solidares and Jovi Bonheur, and the bullfighter, Ruy. He was shorter than the other men but regal and sturdy. I imagined that as a child he had looked like this, a child with a man's body.

And there was the young man with the wolf. How did he come to have a wolf as a pet? Perhaps he was a brother of Tomás. I saw a resemblance, the same noble cheekbones and square chin, though Tomás was not so broad-shouldered. The stranger had kind gray eyes, while Tomás had brown.

Within a few days of my arrival Don Alphonse was better, though he still hobbled on his painful knee. One afternoon, I had fixed the warm water with his dose of herbs and had settled him into the tub. He pulled me in with him, clothing and all. Carlos, just arriving from the country, discovered us so.

"I was hinting for her to join me," Don Alphonse said jovially to his son.

"A strong hint," I said, struggling to get out of the tub and be upright again. I stood there dripping, my dress clinging to me, while both men looked at me with longing in their eyes. I shooed Carlos away and did what I could for Don Alphonse—to ease the pain. His several pains.

Later I found Carlos, and we spent the night together in my downstairs room, which turned out to be his room.

"Where's Matilde?" I said, as I moved astride him and felt him slip inside. "Mmmm," I murmured. "I like this part."

"Uh," he groaned. "Yes. A little faster, please." Then he answered my question, "At Brados," he said. "My mother is with her."

My eyes flew open. "Your mother!?" I cried. "I didn't know you had a mother." I stopped moving.

"Later," he said, with a moan, as he tried to guide my hips. "Talk about it later." He tried to roll me over and capture me there, but I was up too quickly.

I left the room and went to Don Alphonse's. He opened his eyes when I walked in. "What is it, Dulcinea?" When he realized I was naked, he said, "It's a bit soon for me, I think."

Carlos was right behind me. He had a blanket wrapped around him and had my shift in his hand. I ignored his offer.

I said to Don Alphonse. "I never knew you had a wife."

"Why does it matter?" he asked.

I knew it was not supposed to matter. I was surprised by my anger. "Why is she not here nursing you?" I asked. "Why am I?"

"Because you are a better nurse," he said. "And more concerned."

"Do you have another bed for me?" I asked haughtily. "I wish to be alone."

"You will have to figure it out, my dear," Don Alphonse said. He sighed and waved us out of the room.

But Carlos would not have me angry, and he picked me up and carried me downstairs to his bed, to our first floor room.

Why had I been so upset to find out Don Alphonse had a wife? And why had I never known this before? Of course, they neither knew nor asked of my history. Carlos knew I had left La Mancha, but they did not know I was lost from the first dozen or so years of my life. We only lived in the present.

Why weren't my feelings simple when it came to these men? They seemed to clearly understand how I fit into their lives. Were they friends? Did I love Don Alphonse? Carlos? Why did I waver in my feelings?

Every morning when I arose from Carlos's bed and stood at the open casement window, breathing fresh air from the night, I saw the wall around the convent next to the house. From the third floor windows, I could see over the wall. Often I saw nuns walking across the courtyard, in groups of twos and threes. I could hear bells as they chimed the hours of the day. Behind the convent was a lake, and I enjoyed watching birds flying over it and seeing in its stillness the reflections of flowering trees.

During this time, I began thinking about church, how I no longer went, what

218

that meant to my immortal soul. I even thought of going to the convent to see if I could get clear on my chosen way of life and reconcile the different ideas floating around in my head and heart.

I did get to visit the convent, but not in the way I had anticipated. One night, Carlos and I were awakened by a commotion in the hallway. He, more awake than I, got up to see what it was and as he opened the door, he exclaimed, "Mother!"

A woman's voice said, "Carlos, cover yourself!"

My first thought was to go out the open window, and I did. I wish I had remembered to cover myself! Here was a comedy for the stage (and maybe I have seen it there). I walked beside the convent wall. I came to a stream and found a way under the wall. Inside, I crouched shivering behind a bush. I saw a cloaked nun walking to the building on my right, which appeared to be a dormitory.

I softly called to her as I peered over the bush. "Hello."

Looking my way, her eyes widened when I showed myself. Her mouth gaped open. She put her hand before her as if to keep me away.

"Please help me," I said. I walked forward, hunched and trying to cover myself more completely with my hair and hands. My teeth were chattering. She removed her cloak and gave it to me. Putting her hand around my shoulders, she took me to her room.

Her room was stark. A narrow shelf in the wall for a bed. Chamber pot. A few cushions. One stool.

She motioned for me to sit on the bed. I pulled the cloak closely around me.

"Now tell me, señorita," she said in a soft voice. "How have you happened to be here?" She looked concerned. "Has a man tried to have his way with you?"

I could not speak, though I was beginning to feel some warming. How could I explain?

"Let me get my friends. They will know what to do." She disappeared out the door.

On one wall was a crucifix and on the other a charcoal drawing of the Madonna and Jesus. A few hooks lined a third wall; from two of those hung a towel and a night garment.

The door opened and three nuns entered the room. The nun who had brought me here said, "I am Sister Teresa; this is Sister Martha, and," she pointed to the third, "Sister Daria Brigida."

I nodded, still not knowing what to say. Perhaps I could get by without speaking, as I had at Lorenzo's.

Sister Daria Brigida came to sit on the bench bed beside me. "I know how it is," she said. "To be ravaged by men." She put her arm around me. "I am so sorry for you." She patted my shoulder. I looked at her kind face.

It was Daria! from Madrid!

"Daria," I said. "Can it be you?" I wished I had not spoken so quickly. I should have waited. She had left not forgiving me. Being naked under someone else's cloak, in a strange place, was not a good time to bring up bad memories.

Startled, she searched my face for something familiar. "Do I know you?" The other sisters stood silently watching our little drama.

Giving myself a moment to think, I swallowed and cleared my throat. "You know me as Aldo." I repeated what I said in Italian, though she was speaking Spanish.

I waited until this connected with her. For a moment she looked blank, then, "Aldo, how wonderful!" She hugged me.

I was surprised by her warmth. I had jumped out of one house, only to be welcomed into another. "You left hating me."

"Yes, I remember, but I have changed." She looked at the sisters. "It was a miracle." The sisters nodded in agreement. "I was bitter and so unhappy because of what had happened to me. I blamed you."

I hung my head. Now living with dozens of women, I saw a sisterhood among us; I often thought of my failure to help Daria.

She explained, "Through ardent prayer and a deep desire to rid myself of hatred, I have been blessed by the Holy Virgin Mother, by the grace of God, with forgiveness and peace." In her eyes was a freedom I had seldom seen in anyone's eyes.

With a sigh of relief, I said, "I am so happy for you, Daria." After a silence, I timidly asked, "Do you think I could stay here tonight? I can sleep on the floor."

The three nodded.

I was relieved. We talked for a while. I was truthful about how I came to be in this situation. They, too, could see the humor of it.

Martha said, "We are all sinners."

"But surely I am more so," I said, aware of how my behavior must look to them.

Martha smiled. "Though the Church differentiates by degrees, I do not," she said. "I only know none of us is perfect."

Daria said, "In God's eyes we are." But I saw the other nuns did not agree, and I was sure the priests I had known would not.

Teresa said, "If we were perfect, we would not need forgiveness, and I'm sure we always need forgiveness."

Daria laughed a merry laugh. "The church would have us believe so." She reminded me of my conversation with Rudolph about hell. Imagine, knowing *two* people who expressed their own opinions about their faith.

This convent welcomed itinerant travelers and prided itself on hospitality. In that I was fortunate, for they accepted me as a visitor, and they supplied me with a postulant's robe to cover myself. I could not sit with my friends at meals. Guests were fed beforehand. But often I tarried in the dining room. When the bell chimed for the nun's mealtime, doors opened and in poured nun after nun, dozens and dozens—three hundred in all—in their brown habits. Like a colony of ants, they followed one another down the stairs and filled the tables as they came.

In the evening, before the sisters went to bed, I sat with them in Teresa's room, and we talked of God. "It is too contradictory for me," I said, deciding I could express an opinion of my own. "I cannot truly see how a God of love can be an angry God."

"For our safety," Teresa said. "As a mother keeps you from walking behind a mule."

"For our soul's safety," Martha said. "He is angry if we do not let Jesus save us."

"He is ever loving and accepting," Daria said. "I, too, do not have an angry God."

"Do you think God has a sense of humor?" I asked, thinking of my misadventures.

"Yes," Martha and Daria said. But Teresa was unsure.

꩜

On the afternoon of the third day, Daria came to me and asked if I would walk with her. She took me out the back of the grounds and along the lake.

I asked of her family and she told me her brothers had returned safely from their stint in the military. "A miracle," she said. "And a miracle I came here. I have found my calling."

I could hardly comprehend that something so good had come from something so bad, but she was at peace and happy.

"And your mother?"

"She is happy that I am happy."

She told me more of her life here and of the visions that she had had that helped her reach her newfound state of peace. Daria's hair framed her face like soft feathers. She ended with, "And do you know what I've discovered?"

I shook my head, for I could not fathom what other news she might have.

"In Madrid, when you were Aldo, I was attracted to you because somehow I knew you were female." She explained, "I have found that I am a woman who loves other women." She said this proudly, as if it pleased her to so understand her nature. "I have a lover here." As if she thought I would question her actions, she added, "I do not think the Church is very serious about us being celibate," she said. "You have only to hear of the many priests who are not."

We only hear what we want. I, too, justified my behavior, even as she did.

I knew of such women. I had come to see it as neither right nor wrong, sweet nor bitter—though I wondered how she had thought she could have divined Aldo was a woman, as if some scent defined our gender. Well, that could be.

The next morning, Daria found me in the chapel. She beckoned me to follow her. "We've had a request for a midwife."

I agreed to go, though I had nothing I needed with me. Daria led me to the double wooden gate, which separated the convent from the town. There I saw a servant of Don Alphonse's and realized that it must be Matilde who needed the midwife. "God does have a sense of humor," I said to Daria.

I pulled the cowl of my borrowed robe over my head and low on my face, glad that I had tightly braided my hair and wrapped it around my head. The servant led me to Don Alphonse's house and showed me into Matilde's room.

She did not seem too far in labor but was restless and unsettled. I could see she was quite pretty, though her face was puffy and furrowed in pain.

"Doña Matilde," I said softly. "You may rest well now. I am here to help you." I put my hand on her stomach. She moaned. "Did that hurt?" I asked, lifting my hand.

She had chestnut hair which curled about her face and made a cloud around her on the bed. "No, Sister," she said a bit sheepishly. Her hazel eyes were fearful. "I am afraid," she whispered.

"Be easy, Matilde," I said, using Rudolph's phrase. "Relax. You are healthy. It should not be so long—or so bad."

She leaned back, though she did not seem reassured.

"How old are you?" I arranged the blankets, making it easier for me to examine her.

"Sixteen," she said.

I covered my surprise by smiling and saying, "May you have a blessed boy." She seemed but a child; no wonder she did not know what to do to be a wife.

"Will you pray with me, Sister?" Matilde whispered, her fearful eyes round as sundials.

"Yes," I said, knowing that the best comfort was to agree in words, but, in action, do what is best for the mother and child. "You begin and I will be back shortly."

Covering my face with the hood, I left the room and found Carlos in the sitting room. He thanked me for coming. "I am Carlos Mentos of Brados. This is my mother, Carmella Mentos, the duchess of Terraria. The duke lies injured upstairs and cannot be with us."

I nodded, though I did not look up at either of them.

"Don Carlos," I said. "It would be well if your mother sat with your father."

"I want to be with Matilde," the duchess said sourly.

I shook my head. "Perhaps later. His grace, the duke, will want to share his joy with you, your grace."

Reluctantly she left.

"You are powerful, Sister," Carlos said after she had left, and we were alone. "My mother and father have not spoken to each other for sixteen years."

I looked at him in surprise, the hood falling from my head.

"You! Where have you been?" he hissed. He took me by the arm and led me to his room, exactly where I wanted to go. I did not speak but instead found my bag of herbs, and after replacing my hood, I took them to the kitchen. There, I gave the cook instructions on preparing a drink. I tripled the amount of lobelia that I would normally have used.

Carlos was at my arm. "Will she be all right?"

"Yes," I said simply. Another thing I had learned from Ana. Why ever say, "No," in answer to that question? And in Matilde's case, I had every reason to believe I was telling the truth. "Come with me, Don Carlos."

He followed me, but when I got to the door of Matilde's room, he stopped. We could hear her moaning. I motioned him in. He hesitated. To everyone, I said, "I insist the father be present." The duchess (had she gone and returned or was I not as influential as Carlos had thought) was in the room and looked surprised at my announcement.

I motioned Carlos to Matilde's side. "Take her hand and keep telling her everything will be all right. Pray with her."

Matilde looked at him. "G-g-go away, señor," she said and pulled her hand from his.

I went to her and held her face between my hands. Gently, but firmly, I said, "He is your husband and the father of this baby. He loves you very much and wants to help."

After a while, she arched her back and pushed, screaming now with every pain.

"Matilde," I said, looking at her, then to Carlos for help. "Do not arch your back. Lean forward at the shoulders and push."

With the next contraction, Carlos put his arms around her shoulders and helped her sit upright and push. After the birth I gave the boy to Carlos to hold, though the duchess was protesting, saying she wanted to hold her grandson.

Matilde was crying, though not loudly. I saw from her eyes that the drink I had given her was working—finally, I thought, her recent screams still shattering my own calm. "Good, Matilde. Good. Everything is fine," I said, wiping my brow with my sleeve. "Doña Matilde, you were wonderful." A lie—ah well, one does what works best.

She smiled weakly. I saw her look at Carlos, and in her eyes I saw not dislike but ambivalence. I thought this experience might not endear her to Carlos or to her marital duty. Though she was not unduly young for a wife and a mother, she seemed completely unprepared for it. But she would forget how bad it was; I had learned that from Ana too. So, for Carlos, there might be hope.

I finished with Matilde. I made sure the servants put her in a clean bed and then saw that she got another drink, which would help her sleep.

To the duchess, I said, "Perhaps you would like to show the baby to his grandfather."

She recoiled and did not answer.

"Then I shall accompany you, señor," I said to Carlos. The duchess turned her back. Together we walked to Don Alphonse's room. Inside I quickly closed the door. He was quite surprised to see me and delighted with the baby.

"Carlos," he said jovially, "give our midwife a bag of coins." He pointed toward a chest.

I accepted it and said, "Thank you." I checked his aches and pains and found his knee still painful. I left some herbs and gave his servant, the old hunched man, Risio, who knew me but did not let on, instructions.

The baby was crying. Carlos gave him to me. I put my finger in his mouth. He latched onto it. "What of feeding him?" I asked. "Will Matilde?"

They looked shocked at the suggestion. I would nurse my baby, even if I were queen. *What better way to show one's love?* I would trust the milk of no one else.

Carlos said, "The wet nurse is below." He took the baby from me. I showed Carlos how to hold the baby with one arm and use the finger of his other hand for comfort.

After Carlos left, Don Alphonse's eyes crinkled with humor. "Do you wish to go home, Sister Dulcinea?"

"I think I shall stay next door for a while." I smiled. "You will know where to find me."

He did not question this, merely took his index finger and straightened his moustache.

～♂♀～

I knew I would be displeased by the monetary comparison I would make between the delivery of a grandson and our monthly arrangement, which allowed me to stay at Le Reino. When I got back to the convent, I counted the coins in the bag. Both ventures were profitable, but I felt a bit sick.

Was it because I had seen the naked consequences of my chosen role? Was it because I had deluded myself into thinking I was different from Moravia or Chalsea? Daria had deluded herself by thinking she was still celibate because it was a woman she loved.

It was unclear how I would proceed with my life. Did I want to leave Le Reino? It was convenient for me to be where I was. Did I want to give up seeing Carlos and Don Alphonse? I could refuse the money, but why should I? He had plenty to give.

I liked my situation, except this new feeling that because I was exclusively with these men, because I did not have to sit in the greeting room waiting to be chosen, because I had other means of making money, did not, in the end, make me different than the other *princesitas*. This idea was a bitter herb for me to swallow, and I ingested it slowly, for I did not like having to change my idea of me.

Ah, but the mind can work out any problem to suit it. (As Don Quixote said, "I paint it in my mind exactly as I want it to be.")

So, I thought, it was not *quite* the same. I was faithful to my *reys*. How wrong could it be? I was not married. Besides, I helped out at Le Reino providing medicines for the inhabitants, administering to their ills. Why should I give up my pleasures with Don Alphonse and Carlos?

And the secrets that I had carried with me when I helped Matilde give birth to my lover's son; when I forced the duchess to leave the room so I could talk to Carlos; when I, face hidden, walked into the kitchen, risking recognition by servants who knew me; when I coyly accompanied Carlos to see his father, ah, those secrets! What a *thrill* it had been! I had *not* been the stranger nun the duchess and Matilde thought, but their husbands' companion!—and a hand's breadth away from discovery. I thought of my old friend Gabriel Santo, his talk of intrigue and danger.

No, I did not need to give this up. I would continue. It hurt no one. The choice was mine to make, and I would see what other *excitement* lay ahead for me. I did not see my actions as extreme, so Aldonza's admonition of moderation did not come to mind.

∽∝

I stayed at the convent, peacefully, for two weeks. When I left, I knew I would be back. I sent a note to Carlos telling him what time I would get Marchioness. Though I did not expect it, both he and Don Alphonse were waiting.

"I am sending servants with you," Don Alphonse said.

I asked after his health and the baby's. Carlos was full of information about his son, Alphonso Carlos.

I did not know if or when I would see them again. For though I had determined

I wanted to continue with my life as it was, there was no doubt in my mind that Carlos loved Matilde and wanted her to love him in the same way. Why wouldn't sharing the miracle of the birth of a child cement the love of any couple?

As for Don Alphonse? Perhaps my intrusion into his everyday life had not been the thrill for him that it had been for me, but then I could not know his thoughts, only mine.

☙ ❧

It was three weeks before I heard from either of them. Carlos arrived one day at midmorning. I asked about the baby, and over a game of chess, he told me every bit of infant information he could. His eyes shone with pride. He showed me how the baby waved his arms, told me about his transparent hands and tiny fingernails, and tried to imitate his toothless coos and grins.

"And Matilde?" I asked.

I could see his face change, as if he did not want to talk about her, yet his eyes brightened. "Dulcinea," he spoke what was in his heart. "I love her more each day. She has given me the greatest joy of my life. Before it was in the golden tone of her voice, the light in her eyes, the sometime touch of her hand, but now, through paternity, she has given me eternity."

"How nice," I said, quite underwhelmed by his ardor and enthusiasm for Matilde, though it gave me hope that one day I would find someone who would light up to speak of me, and I, of him—yes, to even *think* of him.

I saw Carlos had been right: What we had shared was not love. Matilde, he reported, avoided him, and he was lonely for her. He loved her as the old knight had loved me, from afar. I could see that neither, an ideal love from afar or breathy undulations between sheets, was the kind of love that would last.

Carlos seemed to want my company in other ways than bed, and I wanted his company too. He was eager to include me in the activities of a man's world—riding, fishing, even hunting.

What became our habit over the next several months, when he came for a day, which was, yet again, once or twice a week, was for us to ride out together—he purchased Marchioness from La Corona for me.

For our outdoor excursions, I wore breeches—I had had some experience with that. Rudolph, who knew everything about Le Reino, found a chest of gentleman's belongings, clothing, boots, and weapons. The clothing needed little alteration. At the bottom of the chest I found leather riding boots and other footwear which easily fit me.

I showed Carlos the rapier and dagger that came with the clothing.

"Shall I be your Master of Defense, then, Dulci?" Carlos asked.

"Yes," I said, not certain what he meant.

"We will begin your lesson." He told me of the Four Governors of swordsmanship: perception, distance, timing, and technique. "And as far as distance," he said. "All you have to know is 'out of reach,' 'within reach,' and 'too close.'"

"And do you avoid 'too close?'" I asked, smiling.

He laughed. "Yes, unless you know you have the best of your opponent." He showed me the blade of the rapier. It was diamond shaped and only sharp at the point. He explained that with the rapier one killed by thrusting, not by cutting, like the stiletto. I did not mention that I understood what he meant.

I took the rapier from him and whipped it into a ready posture. I did not know why I knew this—again the hand of my unknown past reached out to grab me, as if I had been more boy than girl. How strange it was to meet his parries, to know the fighting stances, the guard positions and more. He shook his head and laughingly said I was his most apt pupil—that I learned without a lesson. And it did not occur to him to question if I were from the Devil as my once sister Fredrica had. He accepted me as I appeared before him.

In time, we became evenly matched in the rapier, for my strength gained with each lesson, and though he was slightly taller, I could hold my own against him.

ᔭᐤ

Don Alphonse brought me two paintings, signed coyly with only an A. In the one for the bedroom, I was standing, dressed in blue, in front of my long mirror, the full front of my dress and my face visible only as a reflection. I held my jeweled brush, poised ready to brush my hair. The painting for the bathing room was of me stepping from the tub. Only a picture for a house of *princesitas!*

CHAPTER 23

in which Dulcinea discovers La Corona is ill

A CORONA DISCOVERED the love between Blalock and Moravia. At Moravia's insistence I went to La Corona's room, which was on the second floor above the greeting room, to speak for them. La Corona was wearing not her usual purple but an orange gown, and when she turned, I saw that her hair was cut. It now hung not to the floor but to her waist and was in a long braid, tied by a gold ribbon on the end. I noticed a strange smell in the air—orange blossoms.

"La Corona," I said, "you have cut your hair!" (I could think of nothing original to say.)

She laughed her tinkly laugh. "It was time." She poured me a warm raspberry drink—one of my own concoctions. "If you want things to change, then you have to change things."

I nodded. "What do you want to change?" I asked, situating myself on a cushion carefully, so I would not spill the drink.

La Corona sat near me. "I need help. Someone I can trust." The afternoon sun shone in a window and lit up her face. The lines seemed more pronounced than usual. For the first time, I noticed she looked sickly. Had her joyful laugh and laughing eyes masked this from me? Her color was poor, yellow, even the whites of her lavender eyes, an indication of serious illness. "What can I do?" I asked, knowing that one thing I would do was to give her some healthful herbs.

She said, "You are educated."

I nodded, though said nothing. I seemed educated, but I did not know how. I had not sprung a dozen or so years old into Lorenzo's cart. I watched how the dust floated in the sun rays from the window.

She stared at her hands, as if thinking. "Maybe Moravia." *Now here was an idea.*

"You have found out about Moravia and Blalock," I began. "Perhaps you should free Blalock, and the two of them can work together with you to help run this place."

"Why ever would you think they could?" she asked, surprised.

"Moravia is canny. Together she and Blalock know much about the business."

"I will think on this," La Corona promised. "Come with me." I followed her to a large rectangular painting. It was rather narrow but five feet tall and hung about eight inches off the floor. With some effort, she lifted the painting from the wall. "This is getting harder to do," she panted. I helped her steady the painting and set it down. Behind the painting was a portal big enough for us to go through.

There was no furniture in the room, unless a piece or two was completely covered by coins or jewelry, and the secret room was full of money, stacks and piles of money—and jewels. Oh, yes, King Midas would have found this room quite to his liking! With each step, coins—silver, gold, Spanish and foreign—shifted, slid, and dribbled out through the entryway, jingling to the floor in La Corona's apartment.

La Corona walked to a pile of gold *ducats*, as high as her waist. She ran her fingers through the pile and scooped up two hands full. Her long fingernails did help her hold more! She let the coins fall one by one to rejoin the pile. Yes, her laughter was like the sound of falling coins.

My eyes feasted on the contents of this marvelous room. High in one wall was a window with enough light to cause the jewels to sparkle, making the piles seem to quiver in the dim light as I, gingerly, walked around.

Like a conspirator, La Corona whispered, "Go ahead. Touch it."

I put my hand in a pile of the shimmering jewels—emeralds, diamonds, amethysts, rubies, pearls, lapis lazuli, garnets, amber, sapphires, agates—every gem imaginable, and seed-sized, pea-sized, cherry-sized, nut-sized! Not one caught my eye in particular for there were too many. Bracelets, earrings, tiaras, necklaces . . .

I dove into a pile of coins and filled my hands as she had. I held them high and watched as the coins rained down. Three times I did this, watching in silence as I listened to the melody of the jingling coins. Then I laughed and took two handfuls of jewels, tossing them into the air and watched as they flew up and down again, like a raining rainbow. I heard her laughing too.

"Can you count this for me?" She sighed. I could see how tired she was. "Can you see that it gets to Madrid?"

"You need medicine and herbs." I took her arm and helped her sit on one of the piles.

"Yes, later." She brushed me away. "But will you count this?"

I was filled with love for this woman who had taken me in and cared for me, who had shown me a new way of living beyond my imagination, and who now trusted me more than she trusted anyone else. "I will do anything for you." I said, feeling the force of sincerity behind my words.

She smiled wanly. "Ah, yes." She motioned me to sit too. I looked around and chose a pile of jewels. It was an unsteady seat, but once it finished shifting, I sat well supported.

She explained about the room. "When the room gets too full, when coins slide out,"—as I had noticed they did as we had stepped in—"I put those in a box and take them to Madrid." We all knew she sometimes went to Madrid alone. She began to rub her hands together. A nervous gesture, I thought. "I have decided it is not good to keep this here." She patted her damp forehead with her sleeve. "And it will grow with the right investments."

"Then we will count it and take it to Madrid," I said.

It was the chore of more than a week. I showed Luis and Moravia how to count and add. Like Luis, Moravia caught on quickly, and I thought the tattoos on her arms seemed no longer to be bracelets, but an abacus. We spent every moment of light counting and bagging the coins or putting them into boxes or chests. At the end of each day of counting, our hands and clothes were black. And Luis! Ha! But for his sandy hair, you would have thought him Blalock's brother.

Here is what we worked out. Moravia and Blalock were offered positions as, I guess you could call them, managers. For a while every day, then twice a week, Blalock and Rudolph took chests of money to Madrid. If any problem arose, these two giant men could handle it.

And you wonder, what of me? Did I get a wage? Not exactly, but I got the church's tithe of the money, and I added this money to my other investments, hoping it would grow and stand me in good stead if I came to need it. You may wonder why I did not stop my arrangement with Don Alphonse, but it had become important to me, and I do not think I could have stopped—I liked being wanted; I liked being a duke's woman; I liked bringing in more money than any of the other inhabitants of the house. I was ensconced in my life here and did not see the wisdom of making any changes.

I nursed La Corona daily, giving her herbs to clean out her system and make her stronger. She improved some, but her health was damaged, and we all were aware of it.

Knowing her money was being taken care of did not ease her mind. Over the next few months or so, not all at once or right away, she began to become stern and somber. Her sense of humor faded. She pressured everyone to work harder. She encouraged every client to spread the word about Le Reino, and she filled the rooms with women and men. It was as though, now that her money was invested and growing, and not close at hand, she could think of nothing but wanting more.

I was unhappy with this change in her, and I was sorry for it. I had hoped when she talked about wanting things to change, it would be for the better. But I guess there are two ways for things to change—for the better or for the worse, and sometimes you have both. The good change was Blalock was freed, and he and Moravia were together in their little cabin.

∽ᴐᴄ

In early December I rode to Madrid with Rudolph and Blalock. I wore my blue velvet dress with the low square neckline. I did not add partlet, ruff, or collar, but took my cloak in case it grew chilly. My hair was in curls down my back, though I wore a hat and my face was veiled with a transparent gauze scarf. Madrid was dry and comfortable, so I left my cloak in the cart and headed for the herbalist's.

As I came around a corner, I collided with man. When he righted me, I cried, "Carlos!" Immediately I saw Matilde by his side and was shocked into silence.

Carlos was as discomfited as I, and looking at me as if he did not know me and without even so much as tipping his hat or saying, "Pardon," he took Matilde's arm and walked on.

"Who was that?" I heard Matilde ask. She looked back at me to see me staring after them. Quickly, I turned and walked away.

I felt confused by the incident. I told myself there was often cloudiness in every bit of sunshine, and so I merely reconciled my life this way and would not consider there might be wrong in it.

Because of this incident, I did not get what I wanted in Madrid and so had to go with Rudolph and Blalock on their next trip. I was still feeling out of sorts with Carlos. I kept seeing his vacant eyes and how he had taken Matilde's arm and pulled her with him. This time I dressed in my breeches, shirt, and jerkin, and tightly braided my hair and hid it under a floppy cap. I carried my dagger. After all, we were carrying chests of money—perhaps it was wise for me to be armed; perhaps, now that I thought of it, it was dangerous to travel with them as a woman. Blalock and Rudolph sat on the cart seat, and I sat in the back on the chest.

In his perfect speech, Rudolph said, "Why are you dressed like that?"

I told them about running into Carlos and how he had acted.

Blalock nodded his bald head and said, "It is that way with rich people." His big hands flicked the reins at the horses.

Rudolph said, "It is about being ignoble—not noble."

"What do you mean?" I asked, tucking some hair, which had escaped, under my cap.

"If you are of the nobility, you are included anywhere," Rudolph explained. The wind caught his cap and he grabbed it, pulling it lower on his head. "On the other hand, if you are not noble, you are excluded. You are an outsider." He continued, "These are the people Jesus was kind to."

Slowly, I nodded. I thought of Jesus' stories about Zaccheus, Matthew, the lepers, of the prodigal son, the woman at the well. "He treated all the same and with respect."

"Always," Rudolph said. "Always."

The wind was cutting today. I got off the chest to sit low in the cart and fell asleep until the cart stopped. I looked up and above me were trees: We were not in Madrid.

A gruff voice said, "Get down from the cart." From my prone position, I watched Rudolph and Blalock slowly get off the cart.

Another voice said, "Give over your swords." I heard the swords slide out of their holders and then thud to the ground. There were at least two men. "'Fredo! 'Raldo! Get the swords and move them away." Three? Four?

I slid my dagger from its holder and maneuvered myself until I could see Rudolph, but he was not looking at me. I knew they were carrying knives but would need the right moment to get them.

"Get their knives!" a man cried.

No! I thought. I peered over the edge to see who was giving the commands. A man on a horse, holding a musket. I raised my knife and took aim. It flew like a javelin, hitting him in the chest, felling him from the horse. His gun went off as it hit the ground. I jumped from the cart. Three highwaymen left and a *woman*.

Rudolph and Blalock pulled their knives and faced the foes. I picked up a sword from the ground and approached the woman, thinking I was taking her prisoner. She surprised me by pulling a short sword from a holder at her back and there we were, two women, sparring in earnest. She was an enemy, yet I could not bring myself to fully attack her.

She matched me blow for blow, and I knew I had to stop her before I was worn out and became careless. She drove me back and back, and I tripped over the dead man and dropped my sword. Flat on my back, I watched as she closed in for the kill, the point of the sword coming close to my throat.

I glanced to the side and saw my dagger, sticking out of the man. I pulled it out and threw the dagger in her eye. My life too precious to reprieve her life. Her sword pounded on the ground, and as she fell, her hair, a wig, flew off, and then I saw she was a man! A false decoy for this group of ne'er-do-wells.

I turned. The other three were dead, my giant friends, Rudolph and Blalock, standing over them and panting. I sighed in relief.

We hid the bodies in the woods under much brush and limbs.

"She looked like a woman," Blalock said over and over. "I thought she needed help."

"I thought so," Rudolph said glumly. "I would have stopped too."

I had thought the man a woman too, and had I known the truth, I think I could have dispatched him much more quickly. I resolved that in a fight gender should not matter.

Back in the cart, Blalock snapped the reins. We rode in silence. I realized I had killed. Again. While masquerading as a man, I had taken two more human lives. I heard a moan and I looked at Rudolph. *He was crying.*

I sat on the chest behind him and put my hand on his shoulder. "What is it?"

Looking at him with concern, Blalock said, "You were handy with your knife. You are well trained."

I gave Rudolph my handkerchief.

"I have never killed anyone before," he said. "My heart will not stop thudding." With a shaky hand, he wiped his face and blew his nose. "Are you not upset?" He turned in the seat and looked at me.

"It is not my first time," I said. They both looked at me in surprise. I told them quickly of the circumstances surrounding the murder of Pablo. I had again acted in self-defense.

Blalock said he had never killed before, but he felt justified today.

I said we were outnumbered and sometimes the choice is to get or be gotten. "Why not say a prayer for them?" I added, "And for us."

The big blond man sighed. In an unsteady voice, he prayed for forgiveness for us and for blessings on their souls. When he was finished, he looked at me again. "Are you not a bit sorry for their deaths?"

I felt triumphant in my actions to protect us, and I could not find it in me to be sorry for these thieves. I thought of Fredrica and remembered there were people in this world who were pure evil, and it was only hesitation in doubting they were so that caused tragedy for good people. After that day I scarcely gave the incident another thought.

∽∝

The new year, 1592, came and Don Alphonse presented me with another unsigned painting for my sitting room. This painting was of me on Marchioness in a soft blue and yellow brocade riding outfit, sitting tall in the saddle, the full skirt nearly enveloping the horse. In the background were many flowers and a wood.

I spent time with Luis, and I continued to watch over La Corona, but sadly I could tell something was happening in her mind that I could not help. She got in a temper and forced the older women to leave. She took in several new young women.

Tressa, Chalsea, and the others were disturbed by this, and though they did not voice it, I felt they knew that one day they, too, would be too old. Moravia was fortunate that she and Blalock, now married, had some savings, and if La Corona decided to send them away, they would be all right.

I saw the pain other *princesitas* suffered of ill use and long hours, and I knew for me, I had found a better way. Finally I was reconciled to say, perhaps, I was halfway a whore. I did not know the worst of being one, nor ever would; even so I traded my body and that made me a whore, and no matter what, my circumstances put me near the bottom rung on the ladder of humankind, for you do not hear of *noble whores*. Yet I still continued and enjoyed nearly everything about my life.

ᔕᔓ

In the spring, Carlos brought me a letter from Don Alphonse, who was again unwell. The paper smelled faintly of peppermint, and I smiled as images of Don Alphonse flashed through my head.

"Why do you smile so?" Carlos asked. We were on floor cushions of my sitting room, near the window.

"I think of good times with your father." I held the paper to his nose.

"Oh, peppermint," Carlos said. "It makes me think of one particular feast day when I was eight. My sisters and I were outside. At the end of our lawn is a hill of peppermint." He looked out the window as he told me the rest of the story. "The four of us rolled down the hill, over and over." His hands followed the description of up and down and over and over.

I nodded and with a pang of sadness, I remembered the sliding bowl on the hillside at Lorenzo's and how much fun we had with it.

"Our mother and father walked out to find us. We saw them and went running up to meet them." Carlos's eyes were seeing his parents, not me or my room. "We crowded around them, and Mother said, 'Get away! You all smell of peppermint!' And she walked into the house."

"Why did she do that?" I leaned over to straighten a crimp in his ruff.

"I do not know," he replied. He caught my hand before it returned to my lap and held it for a moment. "But since that day they have not spoken to each other."

Someday I will ask why: why would two people live together and choose not to speak to each other, choose not to work things out? I tried to imagine what it would have been like to live with Aldonza and Lorenzo if they had not spoken and were always angry with each other.

Carlos's eyes were sad. "I come here, Dulci, because my home seems so empty. My father has taken to his bed. My mother is sulking. Since the baby, Matilde can barely look at me."

Impulsively I hugged him. "How can you bear it!" I thought of my life here, how there was always someone to talk to, something going on, something to do. "It must have been awful for you and your sisters growing up." I moved closer to him and touched his shoulder.

"My father and I were gone much of the time," he said. "We traveled everywhere."

"But that is exciting! Where have you been?"

"Europe, England, India," he said. "The Holy Land." He smoothed his moustache, a gesture like his father's.

"Tell me about one place."

He leaned against the wall, and I lay down with my head in his lap. He told me about Venice, making it seem as real to me as if I had been there, as if I had walked the bridges over the canals or rode in the gondolas, hearing the *swoosh* of the pole in the water. I could see the candles in the windows of the houses along the Grand Canal at night and hear the pigs snorting in the streets in the day. He talked into the evening and did not go home that night.

The next morning he said, "Come home with me."

I laughed, but the secret thrill, my fondness for adventure, welled up in me, and because of that and because it was such a silly idea I said, "Yes, I will."

He told me how we could manage it. And I loved his idea—I would masquerade as a young man.

From the actors of the desire stage, Rudolph got for me a suitable moustache and beard, and the gum to hold them in place, and also a brown wig, rather longish for the style.

We looked through the chest of nobleman's clothes. The doublets were already padded to broaden the shoulders and fill out the chest, so this did as much as anything to hide the shape of my body.

It was decided I was to be an Italian: Guido Scherzaro from near Venice. I felt I had heard enough of Venice from Carlos the night before to think of myself as being from there. Carlos made up a titled family, said I was a second son of a duke. My father had died (so now I was the brother of the duke), and my brother sent me away, threatening to kill me if I returned.

I laughed and shook my head. "Too dramatic!"

In his deep voice and formal speech, Rudolph said, "You found out your father slept with your sisters." He added, "So you have run away from home forever."

"No," I said, shaking a finger at both of them, "that's all too dark. I need something simple." But after a moment, I said mischievously. "Maybe I found out my father and brother were sleeping with the same woman."

Carlos scratched his head and sounding puzzled, said, "There's nothing wrong with that." He laughed. "Oh." His eyes filled with humor; he shook his head. "I will say you are a friend of mine from school."

"In Italy?"

"Yes, I went to school there for two years."

Together we made up details about my "family," so we would both have the same story. The rest, Carlos said, we could make up as we needed.

"Speak Italian; you won't have to say much," he said.

I remembered the way Daria had spoken Spanish in Madrid, and I thought I could speak like that or with the perfect intonation of Rudolph, though his birth language was German. Rudolph explained to me that if I took deep breaths it would help to lower my voice. I practiced speaking in a lower, more masculine tone.

I asked Carlos how as Guido Scherzaro I would be able to prescribe herbs for Don Alphonse. He thought for a moment, "Tomorrow we will ride to Bradosina. Disguised as the nun, you will come with me to Brados. Another day we can arrive with you as Guido."

In the morning, I tossed my clothing and other necessities, including my bag of herbs, into two tapestry bags, and we left Le Reino on our horses. On our ride to Bradosina, Carlos said how delighted he was to think of pleasing his father with the gift of me.

I laughed. I knew I was smiling broadly, my eyes gleaming in the morning sun, for there was the thrill in this adventure that I savored.

When we arrived in Bradosina, I went to the convent to see Daria, who found the postulate's cloak for me. I paid her several *ducats*, which she deposited in the alms box in the church. I spent a short time visiting with my sister-friends.

Daria said, "Come back to tell us your adventures."

Carlos took us in a carriage for the two-mile ride from the house in Bradosina to the estate of Brados. Brados was immense. Of course, Le Reino was large also, but not in the same way. The castle on the estate of Brados was begun in 1157 A.D., and various wings had been added over the ensuing years.

Before we reached the entrance doors, I could see several people. They seemed to be gardeners working in the yard. As we rode up, they bowed. When the carriage halted, four servants appeared. One took my bag of herbs. The other took my arm to help me up the many steps.

Carlos said, "She is here to see my father."

Inside, the entry hall was enormous, three stories high. Along the walls of the balconies to the second and third floors were portraits of the Mentos ancestors.

Carlos took the bag and dismissed the servants. "Come, I will take you, Sister . . ." He whispered to me on the steps, "We forgot to give you a name."

"María," I said, for it seemed many nuns were named María.

Carlos took me to Don Alphonse's room. I saw at once his steel gray beard and hair were unkempt, quite uncharacteristic. He was propped up in a large four-poster, curtained bed. The posts were oak and carved in an ornate grape leaf. Lorenzo, and certainly Rudolph, could have done better, I thought to myself. Carlos motioned for the stooped Risio to leave.

"Father," Carlos said, "I have brought you a visitor."

Don Alphonse seemed to brighten up. "Someone who can play chess, I hope. Everyone is too busy for me."

"They are not too busy," Carlos said. "They will not play with you for they never win."

"Dulcinea would play with me," he muttered. "How is she?"

"You may ask her yourself, for she is who I have brought." Carlos stood aside, and there I stood in my disguise as nun.

"So it is!" Don Alphonse cried, though weakly. He reached to take my hand and pulled me to him, kissing me soundly on the mouth.

I was alarmed by his appearance but tried not to show it. His face was bloated and splotched. He reported that his body would not act properly. I knelt to check the chamber pot, and seeing the dark urine, I was certain how to treat this. I asked to see his ankles. He threw back the covers. He was clad only in a short shirt. I could see from his knees down that his legs and ankles were swollen.

Carlos summoned Risio, Don Alphonse's servant. Risio nodded without expression and without a show of recognition. "Do as Sister instructs," Carlos said, then left to visit his son.

In one bowl I put measures of herbs, including broom, lily of the valley, hawthorn. "Pour boiling water over this and let it stand, while you take these herbs," I put other herbs in a second bowl, "and put them in water until it boils. Boil it a few minutes. Strain them both, and bring the liquids back to me."

He nodded and within the hour, Don Alphonse had his first herbal drink. Through Risio, I instructed the cook to fix with every meal a salad with a variety of leaves and seeds. Also a greensauce of sheep sorrel, horseradish, and garlic.

I told Don Alphonse, "You must drink water, as much as you can." I knew he preferred wine. "It's very important," I said. "You could feel well enough to go hunting by week's end if you do."

"That's impossible." He looked much older than his fifty years. "You do not know how bad I feel."

No, I didn't. How could I know how someone else felt? I smiled and kissed him lightly on the cheek. "You must trust me." For as Aldonza had taught me, a belief in a cure sometimes worked better than the cure itself. I stayed with Don Alphonse for a while, and even before I left, his body had begun releasing water. I told him of our plan for me to be able to visit him. He was pleased.

I left an assortment of herbs for him to take and put a basket of foxglove on a higher shelf than the herbs he was to get daily, giving Risio explicit instructions on its purpose, hoping he would not have to use it, but I deeply feared Don Alphonse's problem began with his heart.

I waved a hand at the duke as I left the room. I went downstairs looking for Carlos but found Matilde. She was dressed in a brown linen dress, elegantly embroidered in white. All signs of the pregnancy were gone, and there were no signs of another one.

"Doña Matilde," I said, adjusting my hood. "How are you?"

"Are you the one who delivered my boy?" she asked, peering at me. "Carlos said he brought you for Don Alphonse."

"Yes," I said. "Sister María."

She looked around. "Perhaps you have time to help me."

"In what way?" I asked. Carlos was not in sight; I had nothing to do but wait.

She motioned for me to follow her and led the way to a corner sitting room off the entryway. There were four slit windows in the two outside walls. It was gloomy and there was no fire. We sat across from each other in two straight-back chairs by one of the windows.

She nervously twisted her handkerchief in her lap. "Do you know of love potions?"

"Love potions?"

She began crying. As each tear spilled from her eyes, she wiped it away. "My husband loves me very much."

I sat upright and nodded. Though this did not hurt me as it had once, it was not easy to hear from this child, who did not appreciate the fine husband she had. *I must remember I am Sister María.* "That does not sound like something to be unhappy about," I said gently.

"He brings me flowers from the gardens every day," she said, the tears still coming. "He says, 'I am yours, Matilde, and I patiently await the day you will be mine.'"

I swallowed. "Any woman would be happy to hear this." Then glancing at my habit, I added, "Nearly any woman. Not one promised to God, of course."

"You would not know of men and women together, sister," she said. "It is horrible." She made a face as if she had to take bitters without sweetener. "I cannot bear it. I had to endure it after we were married, but I do not want to ever again."

"But surely, Doña Matilde, you wish for more children," I said. "Or to please your husband. Or fulfill your marital duty."

She wrinkled her nose and raised her haughty chin. "I told him from the very beginning I did not want anything to do with sharing a bed."

"But you miss out on so much," I said with enthusiasm. "I mean," I added, "from what I hear of it. Of course, I do not know." I chastised myself for my ardor.

"No matter, I told him to find a mistress to keep, as I would not satisfy his vulgar lusts," she declared. She shuddered, "Yet I cannot stand thinking of him being with this tawdry creature."

"Tawdry?" I said, surprised. "This woman, you mean?"

"I saw her once. The whore." She whispered the word.

I felt light-headed in the face of her characterization of me. "You seem jealous. Of this woman," I said flatly. "Perhaps that is a sign that you do love him."

She shook her head sadly.

I tried again. "But sharing yourself with your husband is a wonderful thing. Perhaps you could look at it differently."

She eyed me warily. "Why are you so enthusiastic about . . . this?" She fingered her lace ruff. "You are sworn to be chaste."

I stammered for a moment. "I-I am, oh, I am very chaste," I said. "As I am supposed to be." I thought hard for an answer. "I celebrate my celibacy. It is God's will for married couples to enjoy the wonders of each other's bodies."

With distaste, she said, "Surely you are mistaken."

"I do not think so." I said, though I was a bit addled at the moment. I remembered her first question. "But what of the love potion?" I asked. Once Fredrica asked me to make a love potion; I refused to help her and Carlota died.

"I would like to be happy," Matilde said and sighed. "But I am not, you see. Here," she waved her hand around, "and in this family."

I nodded. She was young to have been thrust in her role.

"I thought," she continued, a bit desperately it seemed, "that if I could fall in love with my husband it would be better."

"Ah," I said. "Yes, that would be the answer, of course." My opinion of her shifted. She was trapped in an unhappy situation and was looking for a way to make it better.

"So you can give me a love potion?" she asked.

I wanted to help her, but I did not know how. I gave the wrong answer. "No," I said, "I do not know of love potions." This time forgetting Aldonza's teaching that belief in a cure sometimes worked better than the cure itself and forgetting Ana's teaching that sometimes it does not hurt to lie, if it gives comfort.

"You do not know," she sighed, "what it feels like."

And, again, I had to acknowledge that I did not know what it was like for someone else.

"I hope it becomes easier for you," I said sincerely.

"My son will be duke someday," she said and brightened a little. "I can endure for him." But her voice was low as if tears were near.

Would that I had an answer to help her, but none came. And I chose that moment to say something worthy of a nun. "I suggest you pray every day for this to happen and it will." I meant for her to fall in love, not for her son to become duke.

She looked down with a frown. Then very sweetly she said, "Yes, I will."

Carlos walked in then and said, "Sister María, I was looking for you."

I rose and said, "Doña Matilde, your answer will soon come to you."

Her lips pressed together in a thin line, she looked out the window.

In the carriage Carlos said sadly, "Did you see how she won't look at me?" His golden brown eyes, now more brown than golden, were sad. "She will never love me."

"I think she wants to love you." Could I tell him what she had said to me? No, I decided. I would let things go on as they would—without my interference. I did not know it was too late.

CHAPTER 24

in which Guido is challenged by Honor

HE NEXT DAY, Carlos and I, as Guido Scherzaro, rode out to Brados. As before, four servants came out the door and helped us with our bags.

"Please take my friend's belongings to the garden guest room," Carlos said, barely looking at the men. "Come, Guido. We're in time for midday meal, I believe," he said, looking at the sun.

I found my heart was beating erratically, and I thought of running back to Marchioness and riding, at a gallop, to Le Reino, but I remembered I, at least, needed to see the ailing Don Alphonse. And truth to tell, though I was nervous, I would not have given up this adventure.

"Carlos, dear, you are home," the duchess greeted us. She stopped when she saw me. "Here is the guest you told Risio to prepare for," she gushed. To Carlos, she said, "I was disappointed you were here and did not see me."

"Forgive me, Mother," he said. "Someone must see after my father."

She looked wounded. "He has made it clear he does not want me to help. "

Carlos introduced me to his mother.

I bowed as she curtseyed low. "Your grace," I said, in my low voice.

"Welcome, Señor Scherzaro," the duchess said warmly. "I am pleased to meet Carlos's friends, always." She took my arm and asked, "What is your business in Spain?"

I was silent; my heart beat unevenly. My mouth was completely dry.

Carlos again answered, "Mother, Guido does not know Spanish well. He is going to join us in the hunt. I saw him in Madrid and asked him to come."

"Good. Good," she said. "You will meet Carlos's friends. Perhaps you know them."

She had said nothing that set me at ease.

Carlos introduced me to his oldest sister, Elena, and her husband, Alejandro.

"How is Father?" Carlos asked. Elena was plump, pretty, and dark.

"He is better today," she said. Her voice was soft and slow, like honey. "The nun helped him, it seems." She seemed truly happy that her father was better and I decided I liked her.

"He will be glad you have brought a visitor," Alejandro said. He had light brown hair and a square-cut beard. "He is lonely and bored."

Carlos took me to my room. I saw that my belongings were already unpacked, so I suggested we go to his father's room.

The duke greeted us cheerily and swung his legs over the side of the bed. His ankles were not nearly as swollen. Since Risio was there, Carlos introduced me as Guido Scherzaro, though I doubt if we fooled him.

"Tell me about yourself, Guido," Don Alphonse said. "Do you play chess?"

Carlos excused himself. I spent the rest of the afternoon with Don Alphonse. He showed great improvement. I insisted he continue to drink water. Grumpily, he agreed.

As I left to go to the evening meal, I said, "Tomorrow you must join us downstairs."

"Perhaps I will," he said, nodding his head. "Will you come later?"

"I will try," I said, knowing I would, but it turned out to be quite late.

After the meal, the men, Carlos, Alejandro, and the other two brothers-in-law, Bernardo and Ramón, retired to an evening room for cigars. As for me, I did not have one. That was one skill I did not choose to develop.

The first thing Bernardo, husband of Carlos's youngest sister, did upon entering the room was to remove his wig. Underneath he was completely bald! He was a short man with a curly bushy beard. Quite a sight now without hair!

I discovered the passion of the brothers-in-laws—Alejandro, Bernardo, and the third, Ramón—was dice, and soon Carlos and I were caught up in a game with them.

"Carlos," Bernardo said, picking up the dice in his small hand, "how about changing your mind the next time you visit Dulcinea—let us go too."

I choked and started coughing. Ramón pounded my back and exclaimed, "Guido! Guido!" to see if I were all right. He motioned to a servant to bring a drink for me. To Carlos, he said, "She is not so busy now that Don Alphonse is laid up. It is not quite fair to us, is it?" He tapped the ash from his cigar. Ramón was very tall with greasy brown hair.

Carlos, without looking at me, said, "My father would not approve of his daughters' husbands going to Le Reino." He picked up the dice and before rolling said, "I do not think any of you are deprived in the bedroom arena."

Ramón skritched his fingers against his scraggly beard. "I hear you can do about anything there. *Even see it on a stage*," he whispered this.

Without looking at me, Carlos grinned and said, "They have men there who pleasure unsatisfied wives. You had better save yourselves for your performances here or my sisters will be asking me to take them."

Bernardo had a long scar on his cheek. Fingering it, he frowned. "You jest, Carlos."

Carlos shook his head. "Make your wives happy or you may find out if I jest."

"I am most content," Alejandro said sincerely. He turned his dark eyes toward Carlos. I smiled to myself to think of pretty, plump Elena and how her husband loved her. "Please, do not think otherwise."

Carlos smiled at him and said, sadly, "Would that Matilde cared for me as Elena does for you." He rolled the dice and then passed them on to Alejandro.

Alejandro patted Carlos's shoulder. "I think she is trying to." He earned a second roll.

Ramón said, "No, she is not. She is still as cold as ever. You can see that." He took another puff on his cigar.

Carlos frowned. Alejandro rolled the third time. My pile of coins was not increasing.

"Perhaps," I said, in my careful Spanish, "we should speak of other matters." And soon after, I excused myself and went to see Don Alphonse.

"I fell asleep waiting for you," Don Alphonse said sulkily, rubbing his rumpled hair.

"I was playing dice with the fellows."

He eyed me warily. "Do you plan to be one of the fellows as long as you are here?"

"When you are ready," I said, "we will see what we can do."

"I hope that damned beard comes off," he said. "I am afraid your blue eyes will not be enough to make me forget it."

"It will come off when necessary." I smiled at him. Then I kissed him on the mouth, beard and all. I made him drink some water and told him to go back to sleep.

After breakfast the next morning, Carlos and I rode out to gather some more hawthorn berries. I pulled up Marchioness by a hawthorn full of the small showy fruit. We cut several branches, and Carlos showed me a small, empty cabin in the woods.

"What is this place?" I asked, as we entered the small cabin. "It hasn't been used for many years."

"No, it hasn't," Carlos agreed. "Not since Christopher Solidares used it." He pulled a table away from the wall and dropped the hawthorn branches on it.

"Related to Tomás?" I asked, recognizing the family name of one of Carlos's friends from the bullfight.

"Yes," he replied. "His older brother. He sought a place for solitude while he was at the university, and my father let him come here." I now recognized the cabin from the painting in Don Alphonse's studio in the house in Bradosina. In it the young man was reading before this fireplace, the wolf-pet by his side.

"Were you friends?" I asked. I began pulling berries and leaves from the stems, showing Carlos how to do it too.

"Yes, of course," Carlos said. "He had lost his betrothed." That explained the look of sadness he had in the paintings. Carlos continued, "He traveled around the country for more than a year seeking Luscinda."

I remembered now that Luscinda was the same young woman that Ruy, my gallant bullfighter, had loved: the "L" on the handkerchief he'd kept with him for so many years. I thought of Alonso Quesano—Don Quixote, and I asked, "Is this Christopher a knight?"

Carlos nodded, pulling the last of the berries and leaves from his stems. Gathering the stems, he tossed them in the fireplace. "Yes," Carlos replied. "On his quest he had a squire, Sancho, who accompanied him."

Another similarity to Don Quixote, I thought. "And was his Sancho a full-bellied, middle-aged man?"

"No, a young lad, who had a wolf for a pet," Carlos said.

Ah, the wolf of the paintings.

"And he never found his lady?" I asked.

"I believe she is nowhere to be found," Carlos said solemnly, which made me think the maiden must have died. "But he could not be persuaded otherwise. He lives in a monastery now still hoping she will return."

Yes, like Don Quixote, unsure of reality. *At least Christopher Solidares is not dead.* In my mind this unknown young man took on the qualities of the old knight—a righter of wrongs and a seeker of a vanished love. But my thoughts turned to spreading the berries and leaves on a shelf to dry. "I'll come get them in a day or two."

The next day Carlos's friends arrived: the handsome Tomás Solidares with the ragged L-shaped scar on his cheek and young Jovi, brother of Ruy. But there was no recognition of me in Jovi's or Tomás's eyes, which settled my unease in seeing them again.

In the afternoon, Carlos took us out to the archery field, and we practiced shooting. The next day we were to hunt for deer.

I asked Tomás about the scar on his cheek. "How did you get that?"

"In a quarry accident. I was a child," he said. "I was lucky. Two of my brothers, Miguel and Juan, were killed. They were eight and five."

A picture of two young boys came unbidden to my mind. The older one with a limp and the younger with a crooked smile. My imagination was too active, I thought, and shook the picture from my mind. "I lost a sister once," I said, thinking of the night Carlota had died—I did not know that statement was also true of my first life, and now it would be true for Guido!

Tomás murmured his sympathy.

"I love Venice," he said. "My first visit was when I was seven."

I nodded. I was beginning to feel nervous. What if my false life was discovered?

"I think it's your turn," I said, pointing to the target, and we continued our practice.

Don Alphonse insisted I come to his room after our evening meal to "play chess." It was more like "playing chest." But I was happy he was better, and I was glad to be a woman again.

I rolled on my side, head propped up on my hand, and looked at him. "Tell me, Don Alphonse," I said, twisting the gray hair on his chest, "why it is you do not speak to the duchess?" I could not believe my own boldness, but surely I could ask, and he could answer, or not, as he pleased. "Has it truly been sixteen years since you spoke?" I asked. We sat up. "You make everyone uncomfortable." I remembered when he had first joined us in the large sitting room before an evening meal. It had felt a bit like trying to toss an egg without breaking it. Who did you speak to first and when? It would not do to show disrespect to the duke or the duchess.

"We do not make everyone uncomfortable!" Grumpily he smoothed his rumpled hair.

"Will you not tell me the symptoms of your illness with your wife?" I said in my role as healer, solemn and firm. "Perhaps I have a cure."

"She affronted my father," he said, bluntly, looking at the window and no longer at me. "She said he always smelled of peppermint and that it made her sick."

I wanted to act dignified, be sympathetic, but I could not stop myself from laughing.

He looked at me as if *I* had affronted him. "So I defended my father's honor by wearing the same peppermint oil that he did and swearing on his grave I would never speak to her."

Still I laughed, covering my mouth as best I could, but I could not hide it. "But for so long!"

"My father's memory is worth the keeping of my vow. I do it for Honor."

"I do not understand this idea of Honor," I began. "Is it supposed to make sense?"

He glanced at me. "Of course. It is worth dying for."

"May I suggest that your wife said this as no affront to your father. Sometimes, smells cause people's stomachs to react adversely. It is no one's fault." I saw that he was listening to me. "This is particularly true with pregnant women. They become nauseated easily. But it happens at other times also."

I got up, dropping the blanket, and went over to a hook which held the shirt he had worn that day. As I walked over to him, I held it to my nose and breathed in deeply. "When I smell peppermint, I think of you, and I have this reaction." I took one of his hands and placed it between my legs.

He came closer to me, and bringing his nose to my hair, he breathed deeply. We watched the reaction of his *cetro*. His face broke into a smile, the crinkled lines of his kind eyes showing.

"It is not your wife's fault that her reaction is different than mine," I whispered in his ear. "Be glad your father did not affect her this way."

Surprised, he pulled away.

I returned to the bed. Perhaps he needed time to think about this. But, no, he followed me.

My conversation with Don Alphonse caused no change. When we gathered before dinner, the room divided into odd little groups of conversation because of the presence of the duke and duchess. Everyone had to be careful to engage with only one of them at a time.

I sat at the harpsichord and played until dinner was served. It became the habit for me to play before dinner, and often Matilde or Elena sang along.

Don Alphonse improved greatly. Soon I asked to go turtle hunting with him and Carlos. The weapon used was a three-pronged spear. Each point was shaped in a triangle, like an arrow, giving it more cutting edge.

We stopped to eat, and Don Alphonse announced to Carlos, "I am thinking of speaking to your mother." He did not look at me when he said this.

Carlos seemed surprised. "That is good, Father."

Don Alphonse hesitated and then said, "Do you think I would be breaching my honor if I speak to her?"

"How do you mean?" Carlos asked.

"Perhaps speaking to her now means I have been wrong for not speaking to her," he said. "I would not want to have been wrong."

"But people make mistakes," I said, joining in the conversation.

They both looked surprised, and Don Alphonse said, "No, it is God's will that we do not."

Exasperated, I said, "We are promised to be forgiven by God. Does that not mean that he expects us to err?"

They were silent.

"You do not understand. A man is stronger and wiser by nature than a woman," Don Alphonse said slowly. "We have been born to nobility."

"We do what is right," Carlos said. "Always."

"What delusion is this?" I shook my head. It seemed to me that all humans were the same in that one set was as fallible as another. Certainly the nobility had no leg up on the rest of us.

They did not speak; both were angry.

"Simply admit that you made a mistake and go on from there," I said. "If God can forgive you, then you must forgive yourself."

"Something is wrong with what you say," Don Alphonse said. "But I do not know what."

"I see a man who has not spoken to his wife for sixteen years. Where is the good in that?" I spoke sternly as if he were a child. "You have grandchildren to share and talk about. Why miss this part of life?"

Don Alphonse thoughtfully scratched his cheek. "It cannot be wrong to forgive Carmella."

"No," Carlos said. He seemed pleased with the conversation.

I shook my head and watched the wind ruffle the high trees. I thought Don Alphonse's conclusion self-serving—but the result was what I wanted. It was like winning the skirmish but not the war.

That evening while we were all in the sitting room before the evening meal, Don Alphonse came in, and walking up to his wife, he said, "Doña Carmella, I wish to speak to you."

As if this were the most normal thing in the world, she replied, "And I wish to speak to you." He took her arm and together they sat on a bench at the window overlooking the garden.

Everyone was silent at first, and when we began talking again, it was not about this event, but other topics of conversation, and never in my hearing did anyone comment on it. The duchess began sitting next to Don Alphonse at meals, and they seemed to talk unceasingly. During the afternoons now they began gathering their grandchildren in the garden with them.

Their speaking did not stop the interlude of my playing harpsichord for a bit before dinner, and often Matilde found me at some odd time during the day and asked that I practice this song or that with her. She, too much, liked to sit with me on the bench, though it wasn't quite long enough for two people. Still she squeezed up next to me and often hooked her small hand around my elbow, which made playing so much more difficult.

She had a lovely singing voice, but having the family present seemed to thwart her, as she was always more melodious when it was just she and I in the room.

While the speaking of the duke and duchess to each other again gave me pleasure, I was a bit nervous about how this change would affect my arrangement with Don Alphonse, an arrangement I was quite attached to. One night, I asked, "How are you and the duchess getting along?"

"Quite well," he said, smoothing his moustache. Then he whispered. "Not in bed. She's rather dried up, I think."

"Dried up?"

"It is well known that the woman needs constant moisturizing from the man or it dries up," he said matter-of-factly. "That is why women have a constant need for amorous relations, though some deny this need."

I laughed and shook my head. "And did you ask the duchess if she denies her need?"

He looked offended. "Not in those words." His voice was gruff. "No, it is too late for her." He took me in his arms and kissed me. "I am glad you are well in touch with your need."

I liked wooing for its closeness and its gentle and not so gentle delights. It warmed the blood. I was sure it was good for one's health. A steady diet better for one than none at all.

♪ ♫

"How is your father, Tomás?" Don Alphonse asked after our meal one evening, when we were in the gaming room. Don Alphonse took a splinter and lit it in the fireplace, then lit his cigar and some of the others' cigars.

"He is not well," Tomás said, shaking his handsome head. He leaned in to Don Alphonse to have his cigar lit. "My mother is very worried." Tomás rubbed his forehead. "We all are."

I saw deep concern in Don Alphonse's eyes.

"What of Christopher?" Carlos asked. "Has he come home?"

"He visits often but still lives at the monastery," Tomás answered sadly.

They referred to the handsome, gray-eyed young man with the wolf-pet, the one who had reminded me of the lovelorn Don Quixote.

"What are his plans?" Don Alphonse asked. He lit his own cigar.

"He is unsure," Tomás said. "He waits for Luscinda. He won't accept she must be dead."

Ruffling his scraggly beard with his hand, Ramón asked, "Has he taken vows?"

"He considers it," Tomás said. "He says it is the best way to keep his vow to Luscinda."

I nodded my head, thinking of Daria. Here was someone who would honor the vows of celibacy. I admired him and wished to know the full story of this noble young man.

Don Alphonse asked, "But will he not come forward and become duke . . . if needed?"

Tomás shook his head. "I do not know."

"Would you become duke, if he does not?" Ramón asked.

His brown eyes somber, Tomás shook his head. "I pray Christopher does. He is the better man."

$$\backsim\!\!\backsim$$

While fishing one lazy afternoon with Don Alphonse and Carlos, Don Alphonse asked Carlos about Matilde.

"She is quite cold to me, scarcely speaking," Carlos said. "I fear she loves another." He threaded a grasshopper on a hook and threw it in the water.

"Watch her carefully," Don Alphonse said. "Women cannot help themselves when they fall in love."

I frowned but did not comment on yet another misperception of his. Instead I spoke to Carlos's idea of Matilde's being in love, for I had seen her nearly daily for several weeks, and I did not see signs of love in her demeanor. "I do not agree," I said. "And who could it be? I can think of no one who might encourage her."

"Nor can I," Carlos said. "But we have many visitors, and various men are among them." It was true; Brados hosted many hunting parties for it had vast woodlands.

"But no one who is here regularly–" I began.

"Tomás," he said, "is here often. And Jovi."

I laughed. "Tomás is devoted to Sonora and his children. And Jovi is a child."

"He is Matilde's age," Carlos said, scowling at me.

"Jovi has not yet noticed women," Don Alphonse said. "He is enamored with sport." He cast his line into the stream. "I guess that leaves you, Guido."

"What!" I cried, remembering how Daria had become attracted to Aldo. "No!" Then I saw he was teasing and we all had a great laugh.

Yet his comment made me worry about Matilde for she *was* quite friendly to Guido. I thought of our practice times when her voice was more lovely than when others were around. One recent afternoon when I had chanced upon her in the garden, she took my hand and walked with me. She had commented on the wonderful smell of the roses and had blushed when she handed me one.

Too, she often spoke of when her son became duke—something that seemed a long way away. I did not mention this to Carlos. I could not believe she wished him dead. How I wished now the healer nun had concocted a love potion for her!

∽∾

Carlos and I ventured up into the hills to see if we could get a deer or two. We were gone for three days, and when we returned, we were surprised to see several carriages and horses at the front of the castle. Servants were carrying water and supplies into the house as if preparing for a grand festival.

Carlos joked, "Our paltry two deer are scarcely a cause for celebration."

I nodded, wondering what complications the guests would create for Guido. But my concerns were short-lived, for the cause of the preparations was this: Don Alphonse was dead. He had died in his sleep the second night we were gone.

I walked to Don Alphonse's room. I felt the tears want to come, but I decided, as Guido, I must be strong. Inside the duke's room, I picked up a shirt and held it to my face. At the bed, I touched the pillows. I took a sip of water from the pitcher, still there. I sat on the stool and listened for his voice, the beat of his heart beneath my ear. In a while, it came to me that I would not be hearing these again. I walked to the shelf to get the baskets of herbs, no longer needed.

No! I saw the small basket for the foxglove sitting on the lower shelf, empty. I called for Risio. When he saw me, he said, "Don Guido, my master is gone," and began to cry.

"I am so sorry." I patted his stooped shoulder. "Risio," I said, when he had stopped crying. "Do you know about this basket?"

"It has herbs for the master in it," he said. "His medicine. The nun left it."

"This smaller basket was only for emergencies," I remarked. "It is empty."

"That last day, I was sick and asked another servant to give him the medicine," the old man explained. "I don't know about it."

I stood there stunned. If they had given Don Alphonse this much foxglove, it could have killed him. I began shaking. Had I killed him with my herbs? Here was a death I could not recover from. I sat on the low chest below the shelves for a long time.

Carlos was busy for the next two days with guests and details for the burial, and I had no time alone with him. I felt out of place, but the pain of my loss kept me occupied, and I sought empty and quiet places in the castle. I climbed to the top of the corner tower and walked around it on a narrow balcony.

I could see all of Brados—the stream where we had fished, the fields we had fenced and practiced in, the gardens of roses and lilies we had walked in. I could see the tiny cabin at the edge of the woods where I had dried the hawthorn for Don Alphonse, where the sad young knight Christopher had stayed.

I thought of the best times I had had with Don Alphonse. I was happy he had begun speaking to his wife because of me. I closed my eyes and saw the pictures on my walls at Le Reino that he had painted of me, for me, for my rooms. My heart broke each time I remembered I would not see those smiling eyes surrounded by the lines of kindness again.

Had I been responsible for his death? It was unfair, I thought; he had only meant me well. I had been his mistress, and he would have called me that. I had tried to call it many other names, had tried to justify it many times, as if it were wrong. And maybe in the eyes of others it was, but when I thought of Don Alphonse and Dulcinea together, I could think of nothing sinful about it.

I remembered the afternoon Aldonza, Ana, and I had sat in Ana's yard after the sheriff's baby had died in my arms. They had talked of death—of losing someone they had cared for. *Oh, I cared for Don Alphonse in so many ways!* Yet I had learned the pain of death lessens through time—I had lived through losing Margret, Carlota, Aldonza, and Lorenzo. I missed them still, but this fresh pain, mingled with guilt, was for Don Alphonse.

Unnoticed, Matilde had joined me on the tower balcony. She took my hand and pulled it toward her. "I love you," she cried impetuously. It burst out of her mouth as if she could not stop it. She took my other hand, but I extricated myself from her and backed away. Fervently she said, "Everyone is sad. I want to be happy." I did not see love in her eyes, but desperation. "When you leave, take me with you." When she reached for me again, I realized the desperation was mine and that she did look at me with keen affection.

I put out my hands as if one could ward off a bad spirit, but she drew closer. "Teach me of love." She closed her eyes and leaned forward as if to kiss me.

I pushed her away. "This is unseemly behavior. Go comfort your husband."

"I cannot," she said.

"I do not love you," I said, firmly. "I am your husband's friend, not yours. Think of his honor; think of yours, your son's."

I walked away.

"Don't leave!" she called, her words partly taken away from the wind. ". . . sorry . . . son . . . duke."

I left her on the balcony. The phrase, "The game is over," pounded again and again in my head, one word per step, as I descended the tower.

When finally I saw Carlos alone, I told him of my fear of what had happened with the foxglove, but I mentioned nothing of Matilde. Perhaps she would heed my advice, and her foolishness would be over. Carlos was angry with Risio for entrusting the medicine to another, but in time, he saw that it did no good to blame him.

"I blame myself," I said.

He shook his head. "No, do not. You brought him more joy than anyone. He would have died of loneliness before, if it had not been for you."

In the morning I readied myself to leave. I would return alone to Le Reino. I dressed for the trip, rapier and dagger at my side. Marchioness was at the door, packed and ready. I ventured once more into Don Alphonse's room and saw a man sweeping the floor. "What are you doing?" I asked.

"Something was spilled here, behind this chest," he said.

I looked at what he had gathered up. The foxglove!

What immense relief! The heaviness of my heart lightened, as it became only sorrow, not guilt. I went to tell Carlos the news.

I found Carlos and Matilde in the library, a very large room with books from floor to ceiling and large windows in the corner.

Carlos was angry, his jaw tense, his brow furrowed. When he saw me, he said, "We were speaking of your treachery."

I thought he spoke of the foxglove. I said brightly, "I have been mistaken." I walked to clasp his hand in my relief, but he pulled away from me.

"Mistaken in your right to call me friend?" He raised his hand to hold me off.

I stopped, astonished by his words.

"Matilde says you forced yourself on her," he said. "While I was busy with arrangements for my father."

I stood speechless waiting for him to say the truth, but he said nothing. Matilde stood with her hand on his arm.

"You must kill him, Carlos," she said. "I will love you truly then." She smiled a lopsided smile. "Defend my Honor."

I stared at her in disbelief. "What game is this?" I asked.

"No game," she said. "You betrayed your friend. I have told him of it." She tossed her head and scowled at me. To Carlos, she said, "Defend your Honor."

Carlos looked tired. "If I kill you, then you will be a bad memory instead of a living reminder of betrayal."

"I have not betrayed you." I protested my innocence though I knew he knew I was innocent. *Why has Matilde started this?*

Matilde placed her hand upon his arm. "Do not believe him," Matilde cried.

"He has taken what you could not have." She pressed her hip against him.

Carlos's eyes widened; then his face tightened with pain and his eyes narrowed.

"Carlos, you know she speaks untruth," I said.

"I am honor bound to believe my wife," he said. "If adulterer with my wife you are not *in fact*, still you *are* to this marriage. I defend its Honor, my Honor, the Honor of my wife."

"If it is adultery you seek, seek a mirror." *What now? My friend is not himself.*

His mouth curled with disdain. "Not with a simple whore for even priests have such. This trifle cannot count. It simply satisfies the second mind of men, much like the words of books, the first."

"Do not equivocate with me," I said, my heart breaking, though I stood tall. *How could he wound me so?* "Your words do not satisfy, but grieve my heart, my very soul. I thought we were friends."

"No friendship born as ours can last." His golden eyes were clouded, dark, and sad. He did not want to choose Honor, but he, as any noble man would, did.

My hands were cold. I put one to my chest. "I truly love you, my friend. Do not seek duplicity. . . ." My arm fell to my side again. I was numb.

"Seek! Duplicity need not be sought, when *your very life* is that." He said this cruelly; his mouth contorted with anger. "Look where you live, your way of life. Why would you expect a better end?" His words came in volleys.

How could he attack me so?

He drew his rapier. Matilde stepped back, her hand before her mouth. "Yes, Carlos, my love. Dispatch him from our lives."

To Matilde he said, "I will defend your Honor, prove my love."

"Carlos," I said, as evenly as I could, though I was alarmed to see his rapier directed at my heart. "Does not your code of Honor demand reason?"

But he was out of reach. I had lost him.

He said, "I must fight you to your death as our friendship is now dead." With his weapon he drew measured circles in the air.

"Carlos, my blood in death will not restore your Honor. My leaving will." I backed toward the door.

"Kill him, your grace!" Matilde cried.

I saw her twisted motive. If I were dead, her indiscretion died with me; if Carlos were . . . "If you are dead, her son is duke."

He winced and drew his knife. He brandished it, and I knew I must defend my life. I drew my weapons. Our rapiers clashed in rapid discord. I thought the din would bring others. Surely Elena or Alejandro would listen to reason.

Breathlessly, I said, "I beg of you. Remember." I parried his thrust. "Let us set this right." I parried again. He beat me back to the wall.

He said with gritted teeth, his eyes narrowed to slits. "You, my dead friend, do not understand the meaning of Honor."

I recoiled from the words, "dead friend," and anger filled me to my eyes, and I saw I had no choice. "Then I will fight to prove your idea of Honor is wrong and will only bring your own demise." I forced his release of me and with strong resolve I met his every move.

Would this jolt him into reason? This talk of his death?

He laughed a cold and hollow laugh. "Were I to suffer death at your fair hands, I would truly die dishonored."

"Then leave off now, for I will not die by yours," I cried. "It is too unkind."

The opening came to knock his deceitful rapier from his hand, but with this stroke I lost my grip on mine, and there we stood with only knives, and soon I found his at my throat and mine at his, our empty hands holding each other's knife hands in deathlike grips.

My love of life found strength to match his. "I fear we are 'too close,'" I said. My hand began shaking from the effort of holding him off. "Don Carlos," I gasped. It was Aldonza of the gypsy fair who spoke.

Our eyes locked, and what did I see in his for one brief instant? Those golden orbs reflected my wish for life and the desire to recapture what we had been—friend to friend not foe to foe, and there in them, his precious soul I saw, and just as I had hope—Yes!—that this dishonorable fight would end—that he would see me for me and not his enemy—he was dead.

Picking up my rapier, Matilde had run her husband through the heart.

And there was one brief cry from him—his recognition of betrayal's rightful mother. Not I! No! It was Matilde!

His eyes went blank—that look that sparked my now dead hope was gone—as was Carlos, my treacherous friend.

Carlos! Treacherous! No! Only insane! for this brief time.

His body crumpled—oh so slowly. Was it an hour that I held my breath?

Honor's scapegoat!

Or was it only seconds till he fell *there* at my feet, the red hibiscus bloom upon his chest.

And that was all.

Who decreed that Honor defend itself with death and not with charity? Let me challenge them! I would fight with the strength of a hundred glorious knights to right this wrong.

Now my breath came rapidly. The knife was still poised in my hand.

Matilde, the color returning to her face as I looked at her, had shadows of a smile upon her lips and yes, it blossomed, full of life. Relief was there! Upon that face! The traitor!

"Guido, you can love me now," she said, her hand to her heart.

"He was my friend." The pain of loss was finding roots in my chest.

"But I thought . . . you and I might," she stopped.

"For you, *princesita,* I have only contempt," I declared. I looked at my knife thinking it should glisten with the blood of this deceitful woman, even as my rapier was warm with the blood of the man who loved her.

The anger rose again within me as if my own blood were warmed to boiling. I grabbed her and pushed her over Carlos's body so she would see her terrible deed. I held the knife at her neck. "Perhaps you would find the mingling of your blood more to your liking than the mingling of your bodies."

She gasped and her eyes widened. Her hands trembled as she tried to push at me. Weakly, she screamed for help. Then she stiffened, seemed to gain some inner strength, and said, "Another will avenge his death with yours."

My knife nicked her neck and droplets of blood fell on Carlos's chest, a trail of traitorous beads . . .

She pulled away from me.

How could I compound this tragedy with another death?

This strange meaning of Honor, an Honor that cries for death, now struck me full. I knew I had to leave, for she was right, and right or wrong, someone would avenge Carlos's death on me as if I had struck the mortal blow, not just my weapon.

I took my rapier and wiped it on her skirt. I had to see his blood on her, the rightful owner. Then I sheathed my guiltless weapon and ran from the castle. I mounted Marchioness and galloped toward La Reino.

I was numb, and then as I neared home, I began shaking so badly that I had to dismount. I remembered when I had appeared as the nun, that day at Brados, and Matilde had wanted a love potion. I had encouraged her to pray. I had meant for her to pray to fall in love but had she misunderstood me and instead found a way to secure her place but without Carlos? I sat on a rock and cried until the shaking stopped.

I knew where this had all gone wrong. I thought of Aldonza sliding beans out of the shells with her thumb and telling me to live my life with moderation. The thrill of the secrets, the thrill of being something other than I was, a manly man: I had loved all this too much. It was too prideful—I had thought I could do anything, have anything, and never pay. From my desire for excitement, I had lost too much.

Could I have killed Carlos? I do not believe I could have, yet I cannot swear that I would not have, for I honored my life, and my code of honor was to live.

A fortnight later the duchess and Matilde came to see me. I greeted them in La Corona's darkened room, where I now spent my mournful days. Rudolph and Blalock escorted them in and stayed near at hand.

After introducing themselves, the duchess said, "Señorita Dulcinea, we have come to tell you that we know quite well you have been the whore of our husbands." She paused. "They are dead." She said this flatly without expression. I remembered how her laughter with her grandchildren had sounded. "No more money will be coming from Brados to you."

I did not choose to cry in front of these two women, but I could not stop myself. "I am sorry for your husbands' deaths," I said quietly. "I would rather have them alive and safe with you, than all your money."

This seemed to anger them, for which I was glad. I cared for neither of them. And Matilde was a murderer, though I had not the energy to confront her.

Matilde said, "I will raise my son to leave these places to the sinners. He will not look for your kind."

"He will unless he finds a warmer and more constant wife than you." I said this bluntly, without regret.

Matilde rose and said, "You will not speak to me that way."

"Then you must leave," I said and stood also. "Rudolph, please." I waved my hand to dismiss them and watched my two great friends, towering over the women, escort them through the door. I went to the window. In a few minutes, they all appeared in the courtyard, Rudolph and Blalock each holding one woman firmly by the arm, the women struggling and uncomfortable to be treated so.

Rudolph and Blalock did not let go of them, however, until Matilde and the duchess were in their carriage. My friends stood there and watched the carriage pull away, as if seeing the carriage fade out of sight would be the end of this dark chapter of my life. But it was not.

I went to my room and as the last act of Guido Scherzaro, I wrote to Tomás Solidares, telling him of Matilde's treachery. Why would I hope they would believe a letter from a man who did not exist? I cannot tell you, but they did. To be a man held so much more sway than any woman, my letter was more powerful than a living, breathing Matilde.

And though I skip ahead in time, I will tell you that Tomás shared the story with King Philip, and he saw that the undeserving Matilde and her son did not inherit the title or Brados, but Elena did, for women could inherit in Castile to keep the family title and property in the family line. And that was the best ending that story could have.

As for me, my story took a strange detour. That night after I wrote the letter, I sat restlessly in my room, as if it did not fit me, as if my body did not fit me. Then, pulled by some unseen hand that held my soul within it, I dressed in the transparent bright green dress that had been Melisandra's, the one that had made me feel like a beautiful swan, that I had never worn, for I had thought it was too decadent for me. I added a corset and laced it tightly, pulling in my waist and pushing up my breasts.

Barelegged and barefooted I walked to Chalsea's room and found her makeup and painted my face white. I painted and waxed my lips. Leaving my hair down, I walked to the other side and played the hostess till the right thing hit my fancy.

It was a man and woman—I do not know if they were married—and they wanted to be with a woman together on the desire stage. I was ready. And so we played out their scene in front of many people. I, their visiting and innocent niece; they, her instructors in the art of secret pleasure.

I learned everything they taught and so much more. They did not know their *niece* was not the innocent. And when the uncle was satisfied, the niece found she wasn't, and the aunt and uncle watched as the niece welcomed lovers from the onlookers, crooking her finger at one here, then there, whispering, "Yes, come." "Come to me." "Let me please you," until it was time for the next desire troupe to take the stage.

I stayed on the stage, my corset and green dress abandoned, and even though I had not been orchestrated in this scene, I joined it, for I had learned well this night (and others) what to do. I fell to my knees before some swollen *cetro*. And it was there that Rudolph found me. Someone—that traitor!—told him where I was. Rudolph in all his manly wisdom thought I should not be. He pulled me from my knees to stand before him.

"This is my desire," I cried, putting my hand on my bare heart, feeling deeply that this flesh must be so misused. I needed this—my punishment, my lifeblood.

Ah, handsome man! My mind was sharp. I knew what I wanted. I had once lusted for him; now I would have him. I touched his hair, brushed his chest, took his hand, and placed it where my hand had been. I looked into his eyes and carefully licked my lips. I reached to pull his head to mine to kiss him.

He stopped me and took me in his arms, my naked body fighting to stay, but my struggle was nothing for this giant of a man, who saw the pain in me and knew this was no answer for it.

"Let me down," I said. "Do you not see that bulging cock?" I laughed a giddy laugh. "It needs me." He took me to my room and sobered me up, though I was not drunk on any wine or similar thing.

Rudolph held me gently and said, "Dulcinea, who have you become?" He

touched my hand. "I do not know you." Something in his eyes, a curtain of seriousness, made my laughter dissolve.

With fading bravado, I said, "That is hard to answer when I do not know." For
there *they* were in front of me, my alter selves: Aldonza, Donza, Aldo, Dulcinea,
Guido, even the healer nun, and before them? I did not know.

Tonight I had not been pulled by the Glamour of a frivolous and fancy life, but
by something else, something too deep to understand. Was it from that earlier life
sleeping somewhere deep inside me? That secret self of long ago: had it pulled me
to go seeking for ways to please?

Then I grew solemn, and I remembered what a comfort Rudolph had been the
first time we had met. I crawled into his lap and cried as if I were two. And this
man, my friend, said nothing but heard every tear and saw that my pain—even
more than I knew myself—was flowing out before him. His silence honored that.

Something shifted in my chest. It was as if I'd known Rudolph my entire life,
but no, it wasn't quite that. It was that I knew love like his. Someone had loved
me all my life, accepting me as I was, childish or silly, stern or fretful. This shadow
figure hovered near, over my shoulder. It felt a memory nearly ready to break into
the daylight of my mind.

By the time the sun was bright and clever in the sky, I saw, quite clearly, that
trafficking the other side was not the answer I was seeking. I would have to find
the answer in my life as it was, for it didn't matter where I went or what I did; this
question of who I was stayed with me.

CHAPTER 25

in which Christopher hears from Fernando why Cinda left

 IX YEARS HAD passed since Fernando and Patrecia married. While my one-time infatuation with her was gone, I still felt protective of her but it was not my place to interfere in her life. Yet recently word had too often come to me, as if I were the one who could solve it, that Fernando seduced the peasants not only on Solariego but also on our estate Gasparenza. After overhearing a laundress talking of her pregnant thirteen-year-old daughter who had given in to Fernando's flattery, I asked Fernando to meet me at the Archangels Cove.

He pranced around like the proverbial peacock and spouted a bit of nonsense.

"You are not lord of the manor." I answered his wicked reasoning for his right to do as he pleased. "That right is as outdated as slavery." I thought about how the Church inched along to protect God's children, finally decrying incest, slavery, and the wayward actions of its priests (at least it asked them to refrain from attending the weddings of their children). "Think of Patrecia, your children. Never has your father, or mine, acted in such a debased manner."

He stopped his pacing and looked at me. "My father is a not a good man."

"He is a nobleman and advisor to the king, admired by the court. He is well-known for his kindnesses to his farmers and their families." I ticked off his achievements.

"He kept his lecherous self within his family," Fernando said. "He did not go from house to house but from room to room."

"What say you?" A faint buzz caressed my ears. I sat on a nearby bench.

Fernando stood near me. "It is over now. He knows Catherine jumped from her window to avoid his attentions. He knows Cinda ran away because she had not protected any of us from him . . ."

My head snapped toward him.

". . . but I carry on."

I wanted to grab him and shake him, but I could not move. Catherine? . . . the mystery of her fall now answered. Cinda? . . . it would have taken something monumentally upsetting for her to run away.

It was as if great waves lapped at my ears. The world slanted for a moment before nearly coming aright again.

I remembered Cinda saying, "Do not think of me as innocent," the last night I saw her.

Fernando continued, "Patrecia keeps me away from our children, but I find other places. . . ."

"I do not follow." I shook my head trying to make sense of his words.

He laughed, a very ugly laugh. "Yes, you do." And he left.

Wanting to put the pieces together as best I could, I sat on the bench by the waterfall. Yes, it made sense what Fernando said. He was a man troubled beyond reason, and why not from a childhood that haunted him with memories or knowledge of things he did not want to know? My Sancha had been beaten by her father, and her answer to his actions was to go out and find ways to help the people who needed help, but she could have as easily beaten on her younger siblings.

I remembered a time when I had found six-year-old Cinda in the kitchens at Solariego. She was baking. She said, "My father wants me to be a good wife. I learn lots of things." Is that how he took advantage of her? By telling her she would be a good wife if she . . . I did not want to think of it.

I gasped for air, taking in heaving gulps, as if there were not enough air to satiate my need. I thought of my youngest sister Emilia—her delicate hands, her tiny bones. Easily crushed.

I thought of poor Sancha; of bright and gifted Catherine (who jumped! from the window), so young; of . . . of every girl, or woman, who was powerless, who had no choice but to obey, as if property—scarcely better than slaves.

Feeling again the rage of that night when I had killed three men and castrated them afterward, I rose from my bench and began running down the path. The running became easier and freer, and for the first time in a long time, I felt no remorse for revenge for Sancha. I had righted a wrong—just what she always tried to do. I had avenged a virginal girl. Perhaps in my most despicable act, I had been my most chivalrous.

I should have seen it. I should have stopped it. I failed Cinda, the person who loved me all of her life. Who believed in me.

It was now the monster father that I must punish for this crime.

———

I went to Don Marco after the midday meal when I knew he would be alone.

"Greetings, Christopher," he said. He stood and gave me a familial greeting, while my insides churned to have him touch me. "I have been hoping to speak to you of your father."

This derailed my plan to speak to him of Cinda but only for a moment.

"I have other business on my mind." I stood in front of him and told him I had learned of his unnatural attentions to Cinda. I paused in my speech for him to admit it.

His eyes widened and his mouth opened as if in surprise while I spoke. His hands fell at his side, palms open, toward me. "Christopher. No." He shook his head. "Cinda was my beloved daughter and only that."

I had not expected him to deny it. *Or had he? Beloved*, what did that entail? I had thought he would be truthful.

"Surely you know me to be an honorable man." His deep voice was steady. His eyes were wide and unblinking. His expression was grave, yet . . . can I say it? . . . noble.

I was bewildered and stammered, "F-Fernando says otherwise. He s-says . . ."

"Fernando is quite a troubled young man. Perhaps you could help him."

Stunned. Confused. I turned and left. When I heard his denial, I did believe it, but unsettling doubt quickly set in even before I reached my horse Beleza.

Could it be that he did not confess *even to himself* what he has done?

How could he erase these crimes from his mind? How could he live with the knowledge of what he's done?

Could he overwrite the church's rules? Could he believe himself innocent—and not be?

Were I the perpetrator of such heinousness by night and noble duke by day, perhaps I would *and could* forget too.

Oh, but there would be those who knew the truth. Servants, the priest, perhaps even my friend Brother Diego. . . .

Brother Diego was at the monastery in the workshop. The monks maintained a path called the Way of the Saints, and along it were dozens of figures of the saints. Brother Diego was handy with wood, and when I found him, he was working on a figure of about six feet tall. Only the lower portion of the body was visible. The figure appeared to be of a man who was dressed in clothing similar to what a nobleman would wear, clothing much more modern than most of the saintly figures along the Way.

"What are you working on?" It seemed better to begin the conversation normally rather than to start off by asking about Don Marco and his actions toward his children.

The gentle monk with the sad eyes paused in his efforts and ran his hand through his short brown curls, a gesture I was familiar with. He smiled. "I thought it was time we added Saint Christopher to our collection of saints."

I folded to the ground and cried. As he had years before when he first became my mentor, the kind monk allowed me my tears. Then, my tears had been for Sancha, for her death, for my vengeful actions. Today, I cried from frustration, from anger, from not knowing what to believe or do, from knowing I was an imperfect man, and I was far from being a saint.

Saint Christopher had helped a small child across a river, and the child was so heavy it was as if he were carrying the weight of the world. On the other side, the child revealed himself to be Christ, who, in truth, carries the weight of the world.

To Brother Diego, I said, "I hope Saint Christopher was with Cinda, whatever her journey was."

Brother Diego came to sit on a box near me. "I have never heard you speak of Cinda . . . in the past. As if she was dead."

I flinched at the word. I had not been conscious of any shift in the way I thought of her. I never intended to say she was dead, but in my distress, had I spoken what I truly believed? Or was it that I did not want to think of her as living with the memories of her past. *Was that why she stayed away?* Or was it that I could not accept her now if she were alive?

How would she have turned out? Like wicked Fernando or angelic Catherine or silent Alicia, who sat and sewed all day, never going out, never wanting to marry.

My tears now gone, I spoke with more certainty than I had felt for years. "I have learned from Fernando that Don Marco used his children in unnatural ways."

Brother Diego's face, if it were even possible, became sadder. He was silent, giving me full opportunity to talk.

"I don't want your silence!" I barked. "I want to know what you know." Immediately I was sorry for my burst of temper. It was not he for whom I felt anger.

Brother Diego shifted in his seat to fully face me. "I have heard nothing of this."

"But someone must know." I was insistent. "It could not have happened, and *no one* know it."

"I can only speak for myself. I know Don Marco as an honorable man."

I knew he was telling the truth, but I could see from his furrowed brow that my news troubled him.

"Will you help me find out?" I asked. He could approach anyone. Servants, Father Francisco, Doña Isabella . . .

The monk paused. "No. Why do you need to know?"

After years of searching conversations with him, I knew better than to answer too quickly. "Remember the first time we talked, when I was a slobbering puddle of wine over Sancha and the three men who raped her."

Brother Diego remained silent.

"Yes!" I said impatiently. "You are right. I want revenge. Revenge for my once-to-be wife. Revenge for small children everywhere. Revenge for virgins . . ." I sensed my rhetoric was out of control. I stood up, towering over the seated monk. "You will say God will forgive him. You will say I am a weak man and must admit it. That vengeance is best left to God." I ranted for a while longer and walked toward the door.

"I do not say anything," the monk said, almost so low I couldn't hear him. Louder he said, "You know everything you need to know."

The monk had foiled me, at least temporarily, in my search for truth. Don Marco had denied it and Brother Diego had heard nothing. Fernando was untrustworthy. I had assumed that if it were true, that whispers of it would be widespread to all but the nobility. I began to have doubts and so my thoughts on it again vacillated. I could reach no resolve. One hour, I *knew* it to be true; I *felt* it to be true. The next I doubted.

Father Francisco, the priest who had christened the children in Cinda's family and mine, could not tell me. And why didn't I go to Doña Isabella myself? I resolved to do this several times over the next few days but just as quickly lost the resolve.

She would not believe me. Or if she did, she *could* not believe me and continue with her life the way it was.

Given the choice of him or me, who would she believe? I was not a witness of these crimes. It was only hearsay that I knew of them. I understood the way these things worked.

I was strapped. There was nothing more I could do outwardly, but inside, I was unsettled, in turmoil.

And what if I had made a mistake? What if Fernando made up these accusations to justify his waywardness? What if Don Marco were innocent?

I was at a loss. Yet my anger did not evaporate.

June 1592

The summer progressed; the blossoms on the trees had dropped, and the fruits were beginning to show on leafy branches. I was overseeing the construction of a new winepress for the monastery.

Yet in each vacant moment questions about Don Marco, Fernando, Cinda fired my mind, and I felt myself sway from anger to apathy and back again. I wished I could forget all of it. I wanted to continue with our lives the way they were. Not knowing there was evil in my neighbor's house.

How could I feel two ways at once? Where was my resolve? I wanted to rip that man out of my life. Yet how my witless brain remembered all the wrong things. Not incest, no, but friendship. Laughter. And that time he carried me quite far, when in Cadiz I fell and sprained my foot. Like a father would, my own father absent.

And, too, I saw his smiling face, a white-toothed, wide-mouthed grin, and I remembered how amicable he was. What of his nobility! The king asked his opinion. Don Marco was respected for so many things. No one would say he was less than a righteous man. He was known to be honorable.

If they did but know what I know. My father cannot understand my rudeness to his friend.

My thoughts bombarded me. *Do we judge a man* (I should not judge, but still— how could I not!) *by his every action or by one? Do we weigh his actions? Put some value on his noble blood, tithing, kindness to his vassals, charity to frail old men, service to the king, comradery with friends, neighborliness, attendance in church, regular confession, rape of children.*

And how to value it? One point for rape and one for each of the others? Or one hundred for rape and one for all the others?

In the daylight all seemed normal and easy. Just smile. Just sit across the table from this man and smile. Ask *how is the grape crop to be this year? Has the new mill been completed? What of that blight in the olive trees? And has it affected you?*

Then what? If the news were bad, did I say, "Sorry." And give sympathy?

Or did I shun this evil man?

My father would not allow it!

Each night I prayed, *Oh Heavenly Mother, take me to your bosom. Leave me blind to next-door evil.*

That did not happen. Then I would pray, *Dear God. Let me see what I see, yet not feel it. Let me put it somewhere out there, where I do not have to think on it.*

I could not shake the pictures from my head. Of Cinda, Catherine. So small, so vulnerable.

And Fernando, Alicia. Yes, let's mount up his sins. There were more children. Estevan, Marta, Marco, Julia, Eugenio. What of them? Children deserved to be innocents.

Blessed Holy Mother save them!

This was the Devil Asmodaeus at work, the one that tempted and swayed mortal men. But, no, I held the duke responsible for his actions.

Did I judge him? Yes! Because I could not stop myself. And because he denied it. Surely God could not forgive this: God had not punished him. The duke's life continued as if he was innocent. (As it was with many sinners.)

July 2 1592

Avenging was better left to God. Why did I not remember this? Through my desire for punishment—to avenge Cinda—I've only brought shame to myself. Why did I not remember the pit of despair I fell in after taking revenge on Sancha's attackers?

It was a hunt. To Gasparenza's hinterland. I had not wanted to go, but my father insisted. Don Marco, in his everyday and jovial manner, challenged me to set chase with him against a certain eight-point buck and off we went.

Beleza had felt my anger then, for he raced the duke's Spartan pushing him to the limit and then—a fallen log, and Beleza and I sailed over, but not Don Marco.

He could not walk. What had I done! I was responsible for this. My anger out. Destructive this had been.

July 10, 1592

Where was my courage? I had faced worse than this. A cripple in a bed. I could not bring myself to go. Yet I had to. My father demanded it.

July 23, 1592

Don Marco said, "I do not blame you, Christopher."

He said, "It was an accident."

He said, "We take chances every day. Some are bound to go bad."

I cried. I am ashamed to say it. I cried and told him I was sorry.

July 24, 1592

Still no justice.

He did wrong. I merely wanted to see him punished. But the guilt is too great.

I needed to set my own house straight. Anger, revenge, judgment, and self-pity needed to no longer live with me because they could destroy me!

I noticed as I had many times before how Brother Diego's large brown eyes had a downward slant to them that made them look quite sad. Yet, today I thought he must actually be sad. Sad about my taking revenge into my own hands again. He talked to me: Yes, it is up to God to punish. Yes, it is up to God to forgive. "We are weak," he said: the same line he had told me before. "And it is a blessing. We only have to trust in God."

A blessing to be weak!

Somehow thinking I knew better than God how to mete out justice, I had not fully learned to set aside my pride. Did not Machiavelli say, "Men are always wicked at bottom"?

I did not *want* this to be true. Yet I could only avoid wickedness in myself. I had no control over others. I resolved that I would never again suffer the shame of revenge. Leave judgment and forgiveness to God!

The lesson here was: I am responsible for my own actions, not another's.

I could make no decision on how to think of Don Marco. He was a good father; he was a bad father. He was a good neighbor, a jovial and noble man; he was a wicked man.

I chose not to choose—it was impossible—how to think, to act, to feel about the duke.

He took a step. I felt relief.

I had let guilt replace my anger in what had transpired in his house. I was tired, so tired. I felt taut as a full sail, and I wanted relief.

I spent the night in the chapel in prayer, my knees boney against the cobbled floor, my head bowed, my hands irrevocably clasped until morning light. To God, to Jesus, to Holy Mary, to anyone who would listen to me, I prayed: "I humbly bring myself before thee to ask for help. As Jesus said, 'Let this cup pass from me,' let my anger pass from me. Let me be, not a seeker of revenge, not a man who judges others, but a man who accepts others as they are, leaving all judgment to God. Let me be kind to my fellows."

And over and over and over, until I noticed changes in my body. It was as if tiny knots of twine uncoiled in my neck and shoulders, making them fall and pull away from my body, making it easier for me to breathe, making my jaw slack and comfortable. The bundle of shame in the pit of my stomach that I always carried dissipated, and I saw it in my mind, like a bundle of fireflies expanding, expanding, and away. The burden gone.

When I took a breath, it was as if I could feel it down to my toes, as if nothing hindered it, no ire, no black thoughts, no guilt or regret. In my mind the breath was white, clouds of white, floating through my body, and when I exhaled, the clouds were gray from taking all hurt and bad thoughts away and up and up and up.

On my face I felt my brow rise and my forehead felt broader. My temples softened, and I felt my cheeks form a smile. I wondered how long it had been since there had been one on my face. By dawn, I felt waves of what I thought were laughter starting in my abdomen and rolling up. When I opened my mouth, no sound came out, but it did not have to for I understood what it was; it was not raucous laughter but a newfound freedom, even joy. Peace.

I knew that I was still sad. Sad for Cinda and Catherine and Sancha and Fernando, sad for everyone who was ever forced to do something unnatural, but the sadness was only a part of me. I knew it would live with this newfound me who was calm, who accepted man's frailty, who was willing to leave the hard decisions to God, so that I could live my life as best I could, helping anyone I could to have a happier life.

It was a miracle, of that I was certain. And I knew, for the rest of my life, I would never seek revenge again; it was debilitating to me, a man who sought to be good and honorable.

∾∝

My father's illness progressed. I left the monastery more often and helped Tomás with the estate and other businesses. My father's sharpness had faltered for longer than I realized. (Was that what Don Marco had wanted to tell me?) The affairs of the estate were in a muddle. The success of Gasparenza affected so many people, not only my family but hundreds of peasants, so I felt duty-bound to explain our situation to Don Marco. He was most open to helping me for my father's sake. They were lifelong friends.

He agreed to help us build our wine business. He had had much success copying the methods of the Italians and the French.

∾∝

The weather was cool even for late summer. Soon the leaves would be in full bloom of fiery colors, orange, yellow, red. The peasants were burning the winnowed fields, ridding them of weeds for the next year's harvest. The smoke stung my nose and choked my insides, as much as grief.

It was during this time that my father died and because death was in the air, it seemed clear to me that Cinda was dead too. From every side of me, the deep bells tolled. Yet I thought of Cinda's tinkling baby bells, and remembered the day I gave them to her and how we had spent our childhoods together, fast friends, in spite of my being older.

Now I had to decide: Would I honor the duty to my family and become duke? Or would I stay within the monastery walls?

If only the choice were as simple as it seemed on the surface. I could live in either life, if it were mine alone to live. I knew I was comfortable in the world of hunting and business as I was within walls of silence, study, and good deeds.

It was in me to do either.

But what I had learned of me, after years of struggle, was that constancy is my nature. And I was a better man to me, and thus to God, for that constancy.

If I left the monastery and took my position as duke, it would be my duty to marry. Yet even after all these years, I felt married to my vow to Luscinda.

CHAPTER 26

in which Dulcinea leaves Le Reino

Summer **1592**

A CORONA'S DETERIORATION continued and reached a sad, sad level. Her tinkling laughter had deserted her completely, and she was often cruel. I hoped daily she would change and become her old self, or, I scarcely let myself think it, I might have to consider leaving, as others had.

Le Reino was my home. It was not a matter of paying my rent for I had my own investments and plenty of income. I concentrated on my herbs and creams and again played the harpsichord. I found comfort in the items from my childhood and often felt the caressing shadow of some memory seeking to come forward.

I detached myself from others. Most of my friends had left and had been replaced with women, and men, I had no desire to get to know. The last of my friends to leave were Moravia and Blalock, but I was happy for them as they had found a small house in Alcala and were expecting their first child.

La Corona was being careless of her health, and I wanted to help, but she seldom came to me anymore. My future was uncertain.

Empty day turned into empty night turned into empty day, and though I missed Don Alphonse and Carlos and painfully regretted their deaths, I was young and soon I was wanting more to occupy my time. I began to think of Gabriel Santo, the mysterious, handsome man I had befriended early on, who had taught me the language of romance and the nature of men. His blue eyes had been startling in his dark skin—the blue eyes, deep as lapis lazuli, from his English father and the darkness from his Italian mother.

One evening as if my thoughts had called him in some invisible way, Gabriel appeared. I had ventured into the greeting room and was talking to the Baron of Sentara when Gabriel interrupted us. He was older now (as I was, too), still broad-shouldered and narrow-hipped, tall and handsome. He pulled me to his table, and though the Baron jumped to reclaim me, Gabriel's dark stare won and the baron left.

"Jealousy is unbecoming to you," I said to him (rather coquettishly, I am ashamed to say).

Grimly, he smiled and ran his finger along my collar bone and down between my breasts. I pulled back from him and frowned.

"Jealousy is but another passion I enjoy." He leaned toward me, his voice vibrating at my ear. "I hear you are free now, my fair Dulcinea."

"Where have you been, Gabriel?" I asked, drawing back again, determined not to be taken in by his smoldering charm.

"I have been here," he said, leaning back in his chair, placing his boot on the stool opposite us. "You have been distracted." He looked at me with sharp lapis eyes, and it seemed he knew everything about my story. But how could he? I had told few here, only my closest friends, who would not confide in this bold man. I knew what people thought of him: a bastard of a widowed Italian duchess, his English father twenty years her junior. "I've been waiting to have you as my own."

Gabriel offered me better terms than I had had with Don Alphonse. I told him, "No," that I was finished with trading my body for money.

He was not convinced and said he would shadow me until I changed my mind. I did not reject his friendship; in fact, I liked him. He was, as I too was often now, intense and brooding.

He came frequently and took me with him to this gambling place or that, and though I joined in the games and often easily profited, more than once he had been forced into, or would force it himself, a duel. He lived for challenge, and it was as if some strange substance coursed through his body—he even smelled different—making him stronger, more desperate, more willful, and the country he lived in then was called urgency.

I watched him always, not from fear—he never hurt me—but because his love of danger was much deeper than mine had ever been. My intrigue as Guido, skirting discovery then or as the healer nun, was a child's game compared to Gabriel's intrigues, dueling, and forays into the underworld of criminals.

Perhaps it was his name. I expected him to be an angel or a saint, but he seldom was, though when we were alone, I saw a different side of him. He often sat with me in my rooms. My mirror cats, Midnight and Misty, lay close at hand, curled beside us like parentheses. Gabriel personified my favorite question. *This one or that one? Is it this way or that way? Most often, it's both.*

∽∾

One very slow evening I was in the greeting room. No one was waiting, though most of the women were occupied. I was standing near the door when a man I had never seen there entered. He was alone, which was odd for these powerful noblemen, and he was one who usually traveled with several servants. The stranger was a small man, striking: dark and intense. I thought he might be charming if he smiled.

He showed me a note from Gabriel for La Corona. It said that Gabriel would consider it a personal favor if La Corona would see to it that his good friend Señor Estallar was accommodated. The man said, "I understand La Corona has a son. He will do."

I felt sick. "Luis is not available."

He scowled and yelled, "La Corona!"

La Corona quickly came to see what he wanted. "Señor, señor, is there trouble?"

The dark man snapped the note from my hand and gave it to her along with a pile of coins—more than twice the usual amount.

"*She* tells me what I want is not available." His voice was low and dangerous.

"I cannot imagine that we could not please you." She frowned at me. "What do you wish?"

"Your son," he said impatiently. "What do you say?"

"I say I will get him for you."

"No. Do not." I whispered in her ear, the orange blossom fragrance sickening me. "Not for this side."

"No longer shall we have sides." She shrugged. "The two shall become one. Both together." She snapped her fingers, breaking one of her long fingernails.

"But not Luis," I begged, still whispering.

Frowning, she said to me. "He will not object."

"But I do," I said. I held her arm. Even in my distress, I noticed how thin it was, boney and narrow.

"It does not matter." She pulled free, looked at the dark man, and affirmed, "Your wish, señor." She smiled at the stranger, and in a cheerful voice that hinted of her former tinkly laughter, she said, "I will send Luis to you." To me, she said, "Take our guest to your room, Dulcinea."

An order! And proof that my opinion no longer mattered to her. Ah, Luis! My young friend. I twisted my handkerchief in my hands.

The man turned his dark, insistent eyes on me. "Dulcinea?" he asked. "Dulcinea. Ah, Gabriel has sung your praises many times. Yet he has not possessed you." He eyed me carefully as if trying to see why Gabriel was drawn to me. He murmured, "Yes, you are exquisite."

I knew what I could do.

In my most flirtatious manner (testing Fredrica's theory of the power of beauty; why couldn't it be used for good, not only for evil?), I said, "Take me instead of Luis." In a step I was next to him—I was his height—and whispered in his ear a few delights that might entice him.

He pulled away from me, but I approached him again, my fingertips caressing his temple, his face, provocatively. He drew back and said, "What do charms such as yours cost?"

"Nothing." I was glad I had thought of a way to correct this night. "Only that you leave Luis alone."

Without hesitation, he said, "I shall look forward to our night together." He bowed, sweeping his black plumed hat before him.

I smiled and gave him my hand, which he brushed to his lips. He searched my eyes. "Yes, you will please me." He slowly licked his lips.

I took his arm and walked him to my room. He sat squarely in the middle of the bed, his legs extended, and rested against the pillows. He was silent for a moment, twisting his heavy gold ring on his finger. He put his hands behind his neck and looked at me.

"You will be pleased with your choice," I said, ducking my head and looking at him through my lashes.

Wickedly, he laughed. He stood up, a question on his face. "Why do you object so strongly?" He spoke of Luis.

I helped remove his cloak. "Luis is like my brother," I said. "He is too young."

He asked, almost jovially. "*Is* he your brother?"

"No, señor," I said. "We are . . . close."

"Do you have brothers, Dulcinea?" he asked, as he unbuckled his sword and placed it near the bed.

"No," I replied. "None that I know of."

"Ah," he said. "Your father was a rogue." He looked pleased to say it.

I frowned but could neither deny nor confirm his conclusion.

A tap at the door and in came Luis. He was smiling, eager.

The man went to him and touched his cheek. I held my breath.

Luis said, "My mother says I am to do as you say."

"We have reached another agreement," I said and tried to place myself between them.

The man held up his hand. "But wait." He smiled; it was an inviting smile. "Tell me, Luis, what is it like living here? Do you get to dally with the women?"

I bit my lips in frustration.

"Oh no, señor," Luis replied, his palms open before him, declaring his innocence. "I have never been with a woman." His green eyes were bright with hope.

"Never? Do you wish it?"

"Oh yes, señor, I yearn to be," Luis said with much energy, his sandy hair bobbing around his ears.

The dark man pulled me to him and said. "Would you like to kiss her, Luis?"

Looking at the floor, Luis nodded.

"What of this, Dulcinea?" the man asked. "This one you think of as a brother."

I was angry. I took Luis by the shoulders and pushed him from the room. When I turned around, the man was laughing.

He sobered. "I wish I had had such a champion."

"Do you not regret what you do?"

He sat on the bed and pulled me to sit next to him. "I always regret it."

He was silent for a while, and I did not fight my tears, for I was pleased to protect Luis, but I was sorry for the alternative. I had thought to be free of using my body so.

The man got up and lit the candles in the holder on my night stand. He took a handkerchief from his pocket and handed it to me. I was surprised by this kind gesture.

I wiped my face and said, "You have a heart?"

He looked at the door where Luis had been. "You said you loved him like a brother."

His voice was husky with emotion. I saw tears come into his black eyes. I could not believe this change of heart, but here it was before me. He sat next to me.

"I have sisters," he said. "They do not love me."

"How do you know?" I asked, for surely his sisters did not know of his strange predilections.

"I even drove one away from home," he reported without emotion.

I put my hand upon his arm. What a strange confession!

His face grew taut; he pressed his hand against his stomach. "She was my friend," he said. "She stood up to me. She met me one on one, with sword or knife or bow and arrow, and held her own."

"Quite brave."

He nodded. "I only do what was done to me."

I remembered Rudolph, too, had spoken of adult transgression against him. I thought of the fragility of children, their wide eyes, their trusting hearts. I shuddered.

"I am cursed." He was in much pain; I recognized it. He said, "I want to stop," with such passion that my heart hurt for him.

"Are you married?" I asked.

He nodded. "Patrecia is a good person." He tensed his jaw and looked down.

"She keeps our children safe. Two boys and little Luscy; she's six."

How could he be responsible for what he did when he only played out what was done to him? Is this what happened on the other side? Were what we called *desires* merely *memories* in disguise?

He looked at me, his eyes now free of tears, and with clarity, he said, "I am evil."

I had seen evil in Fredrica. She never would have felt remorse. I sensed sincerity in the regret of this ignoble, yet noble man. He was trapped and troubled by his way of life; he did not freely choose it, this I believed.

"I see you are truly repentant." I touched his hand for a moment. "I think that God will help you." Thinking of Daria and of the peace she had found, I said, "I have a friend who found a change in heart, through God, through prayer."

He rose from the bed and began to pace the room. He stopped at the fireplace, his hand on the mantel, and stood in silence, staring at the orange and blue flames. "It is too late for me." He turned around. "Even you hated me minutes ago."

I could not deny this. I watched him walk around my room. He stopped at my mirror. I could see him in it.

"No one is safe from me." He rearranged his hair in the mirror before turning back toward me.

I scarcely knew what to think. I thought of his children. Could I protect them by helping this wounded man? I said to him, "I understand the feeling that you cannot stop." He spoke of the feeling I had had the night I went to the desire stage and beckoned man after man to come to me.

He looked at me. Was that a bit of hope I saw in his black eyes?

"It is a devastating pit," I said.

He nodded. "One is too many, and yet all are not enough to satisfy my longing."

"But what is the longing?" I asked, wondering if he knew, for I was not sure. "To please others? Be obedient?"

He shook his head. "To have power."

And that was the difference between us. That night on the desire stage, I could not give enough. I sought out those who would take from me. And here was one of those men. He could not stop taking. And because our seeking did not satisfy, we wanted more. And more.

Was it always this way—that the man wanted the power, and the woman wanted to please. Was the pleasing a way to get . . . power? . . . or safety? . . . or love? I was uncertain.

Yet I had stopped; I had lost the desire. My friend Rudolph had been there to listen, guide me through. Could I do that for this empty man?

The dark man was pacing the room again. His hands wandered over the things on my dresser. In an instant he was by my side, and grabbing my arm, he pulled me over and pointed to my brush. "Where did you get this?" His voice was harsh, a bark, like a wolf.

"I-I've always h-had it." I stammered. He was frightening me.

"You stole it."

I tried to pull free from his vise-like grip. "No, señor, I had it with me when I was found."

"What do you mean, *found?*" he demanded, looking again at the dresser.

"I was found by a family in La Mancha."

He spied my locket on the dresser. "My god, her locket!" He grabbed at my gown and pulled, baring my upper arm. He found the scar.

I did not understand what was happening.

He said, "Luscinda," and let go of me, backing away. His hands were up as if to keep me away—keep the truth away.

The room reversed in color; what was light became dark and what was dark became light.

An icy chill swept down my arms to my hands and dripped out my fingers, yet my face was hot, hot, and I shook my head.

I grasped my heart and felt my breath coming in quick bursts.

I felt sucked away, invisible, a shade, some slight spirit only.

In my head, I heard him say, *Luscinda.*

Luscinda.

Luscinda.

I remembered. *Luscinda.* I felt as if I were made of glass, transparent and ephemeral. Carefully I put my hand to my chest and took a slow breath.

Luscinda Estallar.

My name.

I was his lost sister. He was Fernando, *my brother.*

I felt strong, no longer like glass, which had fallen away with the tinkling of tiny bells. My baby bells. Topher. The shadow, that feeling that had been warmly close for several days, that feeling that someone quietly accepted me, now stepped forward; it was Christopher.

I kneaded my temples, my fingers firm as if digging for more information. The room came back into perfect color.

I was Luscinda Isabella María Estallar, daughter of a noble Andalusian family—my father, Don Marco of Riego, the duke of Solariego. My mother, Doña Isabella, who brushed my hair every night with *that* brush and had said to me, "You are beautiful."

With each beat of my heart, memories pulsed into place.

Within minutes I remembered and understood. Christopher Solidares, my betrothed, was Tomás's brother and the valiant knight who Don Alphonse had painted and given refuge. Christopher, who had searched and searched for the lost girl—me. I was the one Ruy had loved.

Slowly, I took the locket and opened it. The pictures were painted by Tintoretto's daughter Marietta. In the opening corner of my mind, I saw the sheen of her yellow dress, heard her throaty laugh. She had talked about *chiaroscuro,* the art of light and shade. *Chiaro,* light or clear and *scuro,* dark or obscure.

I knew the faces in the locket. *Papa.* Friend of the king, a duke: tall black boots on long legs, a raptor-like nose, broad shoulders, hands wide as wings . . .

Topher, my childhood name for *Christopher.* In the picture, he was twelve.

Another scene of memory: a meal he and I shared, small roasted birds, which were delicate and delicious, though I was impatient with eating around the bones. He deliberately tore off the meat and fed me from his noble and generous fingers. I saw the shimmer of grease on his hand, fresh from the roasted bird, as he brought a waving string of meat to my mouth. And ever kind to me, he was, though I was six years younger.

When I last saw him, he was seventeen, the soft shadow of a beard on his face; now he was a man, a goodly knight. He would still have dark hair, gray eyes with long eyelashes, and clefted chin, but how had he changed?

My breath swelled out of me, a bubble of newfound knowledge. "Fernando!"

I went to the dresser. The ivory comb and brush: from my grandmother—she taught us chess. I touched the uncut jewels—from Christopher. I saw him—his wide grin, his white teeth—holding out his hands for me to guess which one the emerald was in.

"I remember. I remember." I was jubilant. I now paced the room. Bits of memories flitted through my mind. Little mysteries were solved, like why I knew about the saints, why I could read, why I could speak languages. Why I knew of weaponry—it was Fernando who had taught me.

I turned to him.

His expression did not match my jubilation.

He pointed to the bed. "You are honorable. You traded yourself to spare the boy."

How close we had come to being together! My brother!

He grabbed my wrist and pulled me toward him. "You are beautiful. Please," his voice became husky. "Please me."

"Fernando! Stop!" But I felt my strength fading. It was another memory, the juxtaposition of *please,* a request, with *please me,* an order. The same word—a world of difference in their meanings; opposites, like *chiaroscuro*: light, dark; good, evil.

"No!" My voice was stronger than my body which could not free itself from his grip. A scene of long ago appeared before me. *A bevy of people, my father standing in front of us. I heard him say, "A man who loses his Honor is better dead than alive."*

Fernando released me and I stepped back. "Father," he said flatly, though I sensed a wash of emotions behind the word. "My life has not been one of honor." He clutched his head.

Were we having the same memory? *It is night. Logs are blazing, golden and red flames rise and sparks fly into the sky. It is a solemn event, Father giving Fernando the trappings of a knight. Father hands Fernando a silver-handled knife sheathed in deerskin.*

"My life is every day torture," my brother murmured.

I heard my father saying, . . . *better dead than . . . dishonor.*

In Fernando's eyes I saw years of pain, years of great shame.

"I can help. . . ." I began.

And there was *the* knife—silently leaving the soft sheath—silver, glinting in the candlelight, in his hand . . .

I stepped toward him.

. . . and he connected it to his neck.

"No . . ." I said.

A slice, and his neck opened, like a ripped seam, spreading, scarlet.

I could not move.

Blood pulsed from the wound . . .

I could not breathe.

. . . and within seconds he was dead . . .

His body slowly folded to the floor.

. . . both of us showered with blood.

I followed him down, a whoosh of my skirt, and touched his brow, moving the now matted curls away so I could see his face.

Death.

His nose, hooked like our father's. Noble. Raptor-like.

Right *here*, death—*from his own hand.* And now, no salvation, no honor. And could that be worse than his life? Perhaps he was faultless. Who *was* to blame?

For myself, I saw the shame in my own past behavior as a mistress. Yet the night in the desire theater—that had been an act beyond myself, beyond my pride, beyond the intrigue and the riches.

Scenes of the past I had forgotten paraded before me. That night when Father had given my brother the knife, he'd talked of knights and Honor. But he was the night father, my betrayer—our betrayer, and to escape the night father, Catherine, my amber-eyed sister, had flown from her window to her death. That was what Fernando had told me the day I had walked from our Madrid house and thought to head toward Christopher to help me set things right—what a detour I had been on, and now, I must return. He had been my faithful knight. And as for lauded Honor, it was our father who dishonored us; the noble duke, the regal eagle, yet the raptor predator.

Oh, Fernando.

᠊᠊᠊ ᠊᠊᠊

With silent Braden's help, I moved Fernando to the bathing room and undressed him. She helped carry bucket after bucket of water to fill the tub, then even more to clean my room of the wasted blood.

I prepared the water to bathe him. Carefully, I added lavender, roses, thyme, and other precious herbs before placing my brother's body in the tub. With exhausting effort I washed Fernando. The wound had congealed; certainly there was nothing left to seep from it. When I finished, I removed my brittle clothes and washed the unbearable stickiness from my body.

As neatly as I could, I stitched the slice on his neck closed and dressed him in the best of Guido's clothes—not of the quality for a duke's son but at least the falling band covered the cause of death. We carefully wrapped Fernando in a silken sheet, blue it was, and placed him on my bed.

I was chilled and stiff, in body, mind, and spirit. I wanted to ask him questions. What had he told me? He was married to Patrecia. Yes, Ruy's sister. They had three children. Two boys and a girl, Luscy. "Six," he had said. The same age as Catherine, the nightingale-songbird of my La Mancha dreams.

Through the sheet, I touched Fernando's hand, lying beside his body. I wanted to believe Catherine's brave innocent soul and his tortured soul were in a place of comfort. I wept for the despair that had ended their lives. I prayed over his unbending body.

I had kept his ring, the one that I'd seen in the torchlight in the alley in Madrid: *Truth, Mercy, Honor.* Sad irony. His ruined clothing and mine, Braden and I burned along with the cloths used to clean the rooms. His other belongings—even the treacherous knife—we placed near him.

As soon as the remnants of that evening had been removed, like shards of a broken mirror, Braden brought La Corona to my room. I yearned for the woman of old who would have known what to do and how to accomplish it.

"We have his money," she said.

"We can send it with his body," I replied.

"No." Her lavender eyes, circled in unhealthy yellow, squinted in a frown. "Was there more?" She checked the pouch beside him and found more coins. She added them to the bag at her waist. She laughed her tinkling laugh of old that I had so loved. Now I knew it reminded me of the tiny silver bells Christopher had given me.

Without another word, she left.

Stunned, I stood in the middle of the room unable to think or cry or do anything of use.

"In the morning I will bring a cart for the body." I turned to see Rudolph.

"He is my brother, Rudolph," I said. "I remember my past," and I gave him a brief account of my story.

He guided me to a cushion in the sitting room. "You need to rest. You can decide what to do in the morning." He arranged other cushions to make a bed on the floor. I was very tired and did fall asleep but not before I saw him sit by the door, as if to protect me, my gallant friend.

When I awoke, Rudolph was gone, but I soon saw him out the window. He and a couple of fellows from the other side were depositing the body into a casket that they then placed in the back of a cart.

I covered myself with a woolen cloak and went outside just as Gabriel rode up. He was accompanied by three servants who I didn't recognize.

The servants were Fernando's, and after understanding their master was dead, they collected his belongings and began the drive back to Solariego, his home. Gabriel promised to come behind them. "I will speak to his parents."

A vision of my auburn-haired mother listening to Fernando read to her came to my mind. My heart ached for her. Even my return could not lessen the pain of her losses.

Braden served Rudolph, Gabriel, and me porridge and a fig mash in my sitting room.

I turned to Gabriel and said, "I am Luscinda Estallar, Fernando's sister."

The smooth Gabriel opened his mouth but nothing came out.

Rudolph said, "I always thought you were from a noble family."

Every truth came tumbling out of my distraught and unguarded mouth, and the two men, whom I had considered friends, had little to say, but I found no condemning words between them.

"Fernando often talked of ending it," Gabriel said.

"Have you other brothers and sisters?" Rudolph asked.

"She has several," Gabriel said, "I remember her when she was six."

"Fernando gave you a black eye," I said. The memory of a long-ago tournament popped out from among many others.

"He was defending you," Gabriel said. "I wish I had recognized you."

We were silent for a while. I handed Fernando's ring to Gabriel, and he put it in an inside pocket.

"What will you do now?" they each asked at different times, but I avoided the question and merely replied with another memory.

But the answer to this common question came easily. As the sun reached my sitting room window, La Corona entered and said, "I do not want this talked about. Gabriel, the nobles must not hear of it."

Gabriel said, "I will do my best."

"It would hurt my business." Her lavender eyes, so dull now, looked at me, and I divined she wanted me to leave. As numb as I was from what had transpired, I felt ripped apart. To her, I said, "Thank you for all you have done for me."

But she walked out as if I had nothing of interest to say. Again I was being forced to leave my home, my family, just as I had when Fredrica had had the power to make me guilty of Aldonza's and Lorenzo's deaths.

If my true family found out the truth of my missing years or that I was present when Fernando died, I did not know if they would accept me. Yet I longed once again, even as I had longed it two years ago when I came here, to be a part of a family who loved and accepted me, a family who laughed together and cared for each other.

I remembered warm evenings of my childhood when couched with family in the gathering room we roasted nuts or played chess, or sang or prayed. All was well, as it had been many evenings in La Mancha. I wanted safety; I wanted security of family. I wanted to be wanted.

Gabriel and Rudolph agreed that I should leave Le Reino, and with Braden's help, we packed a few of my things, and my cats Midnight and Misty, in a cart and the four of us went to Alcala to stay the night with Moravia and Blalock.

ON MARCO'S MESSENGER arrived at Gasparenza when the sun was highest in the sky to tell me that Fernando was dead, that his body had arrived home that morning. I changed from the postulant's robe that I had become accustomed to wearing the years I was at the monastery and went to Solariego without hesitation.

The duke and duchess were near the chapel with portly Father Francisco. The duchess embraced me and sobbed. I remembered a similar time of sorrow—a day in Madrid after Cinda's disappearance. The duchess was older now, more frail, her grief as heavy for her son as it had been for her daughter. Today she wore Cinda's silver bells, like pebbles, on a bracelet, pressed against my back as she clutched at me.

And what of my grief? It was fresh, but for Cinda because only yesterday I had agreed with mother and Tomás that I would do my duty as duke, that I would marry. The hope that I had once held onto, that I had fought to hold on to when everyone else encouraged me to forget Cinda, dissipated, like evening's fire's smoke.

"Your father wanted you to marry," my mother had said. Her rheumy eyes searched my face. "He wanted you to do your duty."

That had been a great difference between my father and me. I saw my duty as being true to Cinda, and he saw it as moving on, marrying someone else, securing the line of succession. Now my father was dead, two weeks past, and I saw that I had allowed our differences to keep us apart too often. I felt it was my duty to follow his wishes. I was duke; I would seek to marry another.

Today I felt true sorrow for Doña Isabella, and Don Marco, but my own pain, the pain of moving past Cinda to some other woman, hurt me much more than the loss of Fernando. He was a tortured soul who seemed only to hurt people. I felt shame for my thoughts, but I would not deny them as they surfaced throughout the day.

Don Marco touched Doña Isabella's shoulder and together they walked me to the cart that held the casket. It was a dastardly hot day in September, and the pile of fresh rushes and herbs on the cart were scarcely enough to mask the odor of the three-day-old dead body.

Don Marco explained the servant who had driven the cart had been abandoned in Madrid by Fernando's other servants and had had to bring the fetid cargo to Andalusia himself. He hadn't slept for three days and could scarcely talk.

"After he sleeps," Doña Isabella said, "he will tell us." She paused and said again, "After he sleeps," as if she'd forgotten she had already mentioned that.

"We should bury him," Father Francisco said. "Leaving him above ground helps neither him nor you, your grace."

Don Marco shook his head as if he couldn't bear the thought. "Christopher," he turned to me, "will you take care of him?"

I nodded because I knew I could do this for them; I scarcely felt for Fernando because of my own life's losses. The duke and duchess walked to the house, their arms around each other's waists, their shoulders stooped in sorrow.

"What happened?" I asked the priest.

"It's uncertain. The man was babbling, making no sense. He was gray from exhaustion, from the ordeal. Poor fellow." The priest motioned for us to enter the chapel. Inside the priest said, "It's no doubt a despicable story."

Did I need to know the story? Instead I would remember the dauntless Fernando as a child, the time we walked in the streets of Venice with Marietta and her pickpocket friend Arrigio. I would not, on any account, discuss Fernando's dark ways with the priest or anyone—at least I did not think so that day. "What is the best course of action?"

Father Francisco thought it best to bury the body quickly. He said he would do what he could to preserve Fernando's soul for company with God in heaven, but the rotting body was not helping anything.

I had two servants carry the casket to a stand of trees behind the chapel and open the box. Holding my handkerchief to my mouth, I looked. Yes, it was Fernando but not his clothing, I was fairly certain. I remembered having dug up the months-old corpse when I had been on my quest for Cinda, and there was quite a difference in their states but neither pleasant, of course.

I closely supervised the removal of the borrowed clothing and the washing of the body. I hoped that I was the only one who noticed the odd line at his neck, which seemed to be of stitches, in white, that masked a slash. But I could find nothing else that indicated a fight or other aberration in his body's covering of skin. So it was suicide or murder, though the odd angle and placement of the slash made murder seem unlikely. I decided not mention this to anyone. Let them all believe he had died of heart failure or something natural.

Patrecia, who, thankfully, did not ask to see the body, provided his wedding suit, which was a fine brocade threaded with gold and silver. Understandably, the servants acted quickly, and in a short time, the body was fully dressed even to his thigh-high boots and placed in a walnut casket.

With the approval of his parents and Father Francisco, the lid was nailed shut and the box deposited in the chapel until the next day, when it would be buried in the family cemetery, where the grave was being dug.

Later I heard that the servant who had brought Fernando home had run away, but this news was followed almost immediately by the arrival of Gabriel Santo, who claimed he knew the story, or part of it, of Fernando's death.

CHAPTER 28

in which Cinda returns to the village of Riego

RADEN STAYED IN Alcala. She would help Moravia with the soon-to-be-born baby. I left my cats with them because I could not take them on Marchioness, already burdened with other belongings.

Rudolph had resolved finally to return to the home of his birth in Austria. It turned out he had grown up in the Court of the Hapsburgs and was a distant relative of our king. He spoke of his mother and father, whom he had never mentioned, and hoped that they were still living.

As I rode Marchioness alongside Gabriel, he and I had discussed how I might make my return home, always coming to different conclusions and never making a decision. I believed I would never tell my family of my sojourn at Le Reino and the story of Fernando's death, his suicide.

Giving seed to Fernando's true story might cause its revealing tendrils to root out family secrets. I thought I would let this history lie dormant. I did not think telling my mother would make her life better. And I was unsure, for now, if speaking of it to my father would make my life better. Of course if he hadn't stopped, if he were still practicing his unsavory straying from my mother's bed, then I would reconsider my decision.

In the village of Riego, located between Solariego, the estate of my father, and Gasparenza, Christopher's estate, Gabriel found me a room at a *pension*. He would return to help me plan how best to make my appearance. I felt I would be in Riego for several days, as I was certain it honored Fernando best for me to not interrupt the funeral rituals that were sure to be executed. Let my parents fully mourn their son, be certain his soul had been sent properly on its way—though that seemed difficult given his unexpected death—before their lost daughter appeared.

Gabriel was no help in determining which was the best way to arrive home.

Should I see Christopher first, or should I see my mother and father first? I still had not made the decision as I watched Gabriel ride off, and I realized I was anxious for his return to let me know the situation. What would he say of Fernando's death? Would he tell anyone about me?

It was late afternoon when Gabriel left, and I did not expect him to return before morning. Exhausted from our relentless ride from Alcala, I went to bed, not knowing I would sleep the full cycle of the sun, only to awake at evening. Finding no Gabriel, I ordered some stew and sat in the shadow of a lime tree while I ate it. I was alone for the first time since my memory had returned, and my thoughts turned to the day I had left home.

Fernando and I were playing chess. It was a gloomy day, and he was grumpy. I had beaten him two games in a row, and when I said, "Check," the third time, he picked up a bishop and threw it at me. The piece stung my cheek, and I cried out. He reached over and brushed the rest of the pieces to the floor.

I jumped up and would have pushed him but for the look on his face. It was filled not with anger for me but with a desperation I had never seen before.

"What is it?" I cried.

He slumped in his chair, his hands covering his face. "Papa says I am to marry Patrecia now. Her father insists. He knows we have been together."

"What difference does it make when you marry Patrecia?"

"I'm not ready," he said. "I don't want it to be just one woman."

I was stunned, but I knew he had been with Patrecia and her sister Feliciana.

"You think I'm so bad?" he asked. "What about you?"

"What about me?" I said, not understanding what he meant.

"You're no virgin," he said. "What do you think Christopher will think of that?"

And here the secret was—wings widespread and circling above us. I sat speechless, staring at the chess board. Neat and even black and white squares before me. *Good secrets, bad secrets. Good wife, bad girl. Good daughter. Bad girl. Good sister.* I had saved my siblings from the swooping raptor night father. *Bad sister.* I had taken the love.

"You didn't think I knew, did you?" he asked.

I gasped and looked wide-eyed at him.

"He was generous with his attention." He placed the black queen and white queen in the middle of the board. Black on white, white on black. Mixed up. *Bad sister.* I did not protect my siblings. *Good sister.* I did not deprive them of love. I was mixed up.

He continued placing other pieces on the board, enough for each child in our family. Then the king. "It's not *his* fault," he said, sarcastically. "You bewitch him." He leaned toward me, waving his hands as if casting a spell. "We will all go to hell," he said quietly, resigned to this fate.

My stomach lurched. "I don't believe any of it," I said evenly.

I stood to get away from him, but he caught my arm. Pulling free from his grasp, I sat. My hands were shaking. "It is right to honor your father," I said slowly. I had not chosen to sin. I had not sought it out.

Fernando looked at me with pity. "That is not honor." He laughed, a caw like a hideous crow.

I ducked my head, recognizing that I had come to believe a lie. A lie that kept me from confessing, from seeking absolution. A lie that allowed me to live.

"Catherine?" I asked.

"Afterwards, she went to the window and jumped." Fernando's hands clenched and unclenched. "I heard him tell Father Francisco. He arranged for her to be buried in consecrated soil." His eyes were bright, not from tears, but from an inner fire that burned within.

I had run to my room. I wanted to get away. Away from Papa—even Mama. Did she know? Once I had known the proper name—incest—I should have called it such and told. Yet I had ignored that I was a part of it.

A part of it, yes, but a party *to* it? Where was the choice? Perhaps there could never be a choice. We, of the weaker sex, of the lesser sex, perhaps we never had a choice. We were treated like property. My thoughts had come so quickly, I could barely keep track of them.

I lived in a body that my soul inhabited. Was the body mine? Or was it his? And who was *he*? God? My father? Then Christopher? . . .

No one anywhere had told me that I would not always be the prey of the falcon. No one told me I could run at the swoop of the owl's wings. Could I contradict the voices I had heard and believe that I had choices—could I choose what happened to me?

The eleven-year-old Cinda knew what to do. Go to Christopher. I packed a bag and left the house. I walked to the end of the street and turned toward the center of town. In front of a store full of furniture, I saw a man with a cart. When he went into the shop, I climbed in the cart and covered myself and my bag with straw.

The man returned, and the cart bobbled as he climbed on the seat. He slapped the reins and said, "Home to Aldonza."

It was dark now; my half-eaten stew, stone cold. But I knew what I needed to do. Find Christopher.

CHAPTER 29

in which Christopher hears from Gabriel

HRISTOPHER," GABRIEL SAID. "You were his true friend today."

I was too tired to say anything, but I was not certain I had been a friend to Fernando. It occurred to me that Cinda might have been his only friend; if so, he had been friendless for many years.

Gabriel and I were riding to Gasparenza; the sun had long since sunk behind the hills, and the moon and stars lit our way. The day had seemed to flash by and drag on at the same time. It seemed only a moment ago that dawn had broken, and I had gone to our kitchens to be sure plenty of food would be taken to Solariego for the funeral feast. Yet the funeral mass felt measured in days, not hours.

Dozens of peasants, maybe even two hundred, crowded into the chapel and surrounding area for the mass. Throughout the day I had heard not one unkind word about Fernando, though God knows, many of them had reason to complain. But their words were of sadness for Doña Isabella and Don Marco, for Patrecia and the children, seven-year-old Felipe, Luscy, and one-year-old Fernando.

Through my head marched scenes of the day, yet between them the day was a blur or a blank. I saw Luscy, her small hand, grabbing a handful of dirt to throw in the grave and squealing at a worm, then throwing the dirt, missing the hole. Doña Isabella holding little Fernando on her lap, letting him eat from her trencher, red sauce spotting his robe. Scene after scene of Don Marco in tears, his shoulders heaving, a man in unbearable grief, yet he'd asked not one question of Gabriel about what had happened to Fernando.

Instead it was my brother Tomás and our sister Luisa and Fernando's sister Alicia, both girls eighteen, who surrounded Gabriel wanting to hear the story. The details were brief: Fernando went to Le Reino. When he had not returned by morning, Gabriel went looking for Fernando and found his body loaded in the casket on a cart.

"But who was he with?" Alicia asked.

"Boy or woman?" Luisa asked. Had she said that in public, I would have censored her, but we all knew the possibilities.

"What happened?" Tomás said. "Surely someone knows."

Gabriel patiently replied each time he was asked, "I don't know." He returned Fernando's ring, saying, "It was not robbery." As if that fact in itself meant there had been nothing out of the ordinary, the ordinary for Fernando, about it.

I remained mum about my suspicions that it was suicide. I might tell Tomás at some point but not with Alicia and Luisa present.

Summing it up nicely, Tomás was the most optimistic. "God is helping him now."

Gabriel and I left our horses with a stablehand who had waited up for us.

As Gabriel handed the man his reins, he said, "I will be leaving first thing in the morning. Please have my horse ready."

The man, who was missing one front tooth, said, "Certainly, sir."

We walked to the house in what seemed like complete darkness. The moon that had accompanied us from Solariego and had dimly lit our way was now behind clouds.

"Won't you stay awhile longer?" I asked. I was feeling lonely and realized that, perhaps, I was as friendless as Fernando. Gabriel had been a sound companion these past days.

"No," Gabriel said. "And after you hear what I have been keeping from you, you may not want me to." His voice was low and confidential, although there was no one to hear. We had not even reached the steps to take us inside and to our respective beds, for which I was yearning. I was ready for this day to be over.

Inside I groaned. He must know what happened to Fernando or something worse, if there were something worse.

"I know the fate of Luscinda," he said.

CHAPTER 30

in which Cinda finds her way back to Christopher

 ABRIEL HAD NOT returned by the second morning. It was too early to descend upon Christopher or my family. I was restless, so I dressed in breeches, shirt, and jerkin and pulled back my hair in a single braid, which I slipped down my shirt. I covered my head with a cap. I rode Marchioness to the Way of the Saints of my childhood, because there I was going to pray for patience and courage to face Christopher and my family.

∽ ∾

I walked slowly down the path, a path my siblings and I, and Christopher and his siblings, had walked with our mothers each Friday of our childhood. The path was familiar, though ten years of growth had occurred since I was here last. Near Archangels Cove I stopped and sat on a flat rock overhanging the pond at the foot of the waterfall, which reminded me of the waterfall on the hill behind Lorenzo's.

I bowed my head to pray, barely aware that someone walked behind me. When I finished praying, I looked up and saw a solitary figure, a cowled monk in a brown robe, kneeling and bowed in prayer near me at the foot of Saint Rafael.

I stood. My mind was idle and I watched the water splashing from the waterfall. When the praying monk rose and turned to leave, I turned at the motion. Our eyes met.

I knew it was Christopher. He knew I was Cinda. I felt, at once, the joy of seeing him, and I saw in him the pain I had caused.

For a moment, startled at our discovery, we stood, like silent gateposts. Then slowly we walked toward each other. He cupped my cheek in his hand. "You are here," he said. "Before he left, Gabriel told me. . . ." His voice, which was deeper, richer than I remembered, trailed off. His hand pushed the cap from my head and he touched my hair. He did not smile, or frown. His look was one of wonder, disbelief.

"I did not know if he would tell," I said. My voice was husky.

"He would not tell me your story. I came to pray until I thought I could come to see you." He looked at the sky, the hour too early for him to call, as it had been for me to seek him out.

I saw in his gray eyes the same clarity I had trusted as a child. No words came, my tongue listless in my mouth. No, not listless, anxious, not knowing which word to grab to say out loud. Where to begin? I chose silence. Without touching him, I traced the shape of his face, noble brow, fine-boned cheeks and broad chin, the cleft now hidden by a close-cut beard.

The years had passed well on him. From seventeen to twenty-seven, as I from eleven to twenty-one. From boy to man, from girl to woman. That was the path we traveled to here.

For a brief moment, his noble fingers rested lightly on my shoulder.

I am finally here. At home. With Christopher.

Around his neck hung a shell, like the pilgrims of Santiago de Compostela wear, shaped like the one in my keepsake bag. I brushed the cowl from his head to better see his face and hair. His dark hair was short, yet wavy. His eyes, now slate gray, had darkened with the years. *My secrets will come out.* My fingers brushed along his temple. His eyes shut and his breath came short, as did mine. *He is beautiful,* I thought. *He has confidence and gentleness.*

"I am sorry about your father," I whispered, my voice still unsure. Gabriel had told me of Don Hernando's death, but he had not known what Christopher's decision had been: monastery or duke.

He cleared his throat. "It has been difficult."

I felt tears come to my eyes.

Gently, with his thumb, he wiped away a tear.

I touched his robe, thinking he must have taken vows and let Gasparenza pass to Tomás.

He clasped my hand in both of his.

I felt sad to think I was too late, that now he was a monk.

He looked in my eyes and said, "I am duke now."

My heart quickened; perhaps it was not too late. *Could we . . . ?*

"I decided to do my duty," he said, letting go of my hand. "To marry."

I felt my eyes widen, but I refrained from making a sound, though the thought of his marrying someone else struck me hard.

He continued, "To finally give up on the future as I always thought it would be.

And now here you are." He struggled with emotion, taking out his handkerchief to wipe his eyes.

I knelt before him and took his hands in mine and held them to my face. "Forgive me, love." I felt the alchemy of love had taken the place of childhood admiration. "It was not on purpose that I let the years drag on." I took a breath.

He took his hands from mine and pulled me up. His eyes were curious and somber. He sat on a bench and motioned for me to sit near him. "It is good to see you, Cinda," he said. I noticed he used his name for me, Cinda, not Luscinda, as if he still saw me as a child. "To touch you and know you are alive and here." He picked up an elder leaf from the bench between us and twirled it between his fingers.

I caught a glimpse of the tortures his mind had put him through on my account. I touched his shoulder, then let my hand fall to my lap. "Poor Christopher," I murmured. "You did not deserve this."

"Nor you," he said fervently. He tossed the leaf away and turned toward me, as if to hear my tale was the most important thing, and I supposed it was. But what he said surprised me. "I know some of your story." And he told me that he knew I had run away because Fernando had told me how Catherine died.

"My intent was to come to you."

He smiled. "It was my thought, and hope, that you were coming to me."

My mouth was dry. "What did Gabriel tell of Fernando's death?"

"That he was at Le Reino—a place of too much pleasure—and died. Poor fellow."

I nodded.

He was silent for a moment. "How is it Gabriel found you?"

But I began at the beginning and told Christopher how I had climbed into the cart and how I had fallen asleep and woken with an empty head. I gave him a sketch of what my life had been like with my adopted family—of Lorenzo's wood carving and Aldonza's herbs. Carlota, Meta, Margret, and Fredrica. I was brief because if we stayed together, I would have years to tell him all, and if we didn't—I did not like that thought—well, it wouldn't matter if he knew the story.

"What a blessing they kept you well."

I told of the Madrid trip.

"Being too fearful to help Daria . . . and Pablo," he said. "It was self-defense, not murder as I . . ."

"But still I confessed and did my penance." I told him of helping Ana Alonso and learning of midwifery.

"That is wonderful, Cinda," he said smiling.

I felt hope.

Then he told me of his quest and his squire Sancha, of Sancha's demise and what he had done. What an irony of life that we had been faced with these parallel situations—though Daria lived—where one of us was guilty of inaction, and the other, guilty of extreme reaction.

I understood Christopher's rage at Sancha's senseless death—perhaps like what I had felt when Matilde had falsely killed Carlos, yet more, for Carlos had chosen his path of unchangeable Honor and had begun the fight with me, while Daria and Sancha fell victim to most inhuman actions.

"It is an unbalanced world," he said, "where men have unquestionable power over women. And children."

"It is a thought I have had too."

He continued, "And where nobles are deemed infinitely better than common-ers." His gray eyes darkened with the seriousness of his comments.

I nodded. "Being powerless is too despairing a way to live." I remembered my thoughts of the last evening at the inn when I had felt without choices in regards to my father. Wars, rape, murder, and even lesser immoral things were incited by the powerful—or those who wished to be. I wondered out loud, "How can it change to be more . . . ?" *Equitable* was the word that came to my mind, but it seemed so impossible I did not say it out loud.

We were silent for a moment, perhaps because we were void of solutions. Then I told of Señor Quesano and how he became in his squire Sancho's eyes a true chivalrous knight, and how I was his inspiration. To this, Christopher laughed and said, "You were mine also."

"Don Quixote had an internal vision of neverending hope for a better world."

"One must have hope that good will oust evil. At least in the end. Else why live?"

I then told how evil Fredrica had started a fire that killed her parents and I had run away.

"You were forced to leave your adopted family." His voice was tinged with out-rage.

"Yes."

"And then began another chapter of your life," he said. "You still had no mem-ory of us."

I felt unsure about how to proceed. "In that chapter I met Gabriel and even Tomás but did not know . . ."

"What say you!" Christopher cried. "My brother!"

I told him that I had met Carlos in La Mancha but also later and that he had told me of Christopher's quest and his belief that he would find his betrothed. "I saw paintings of you in Don Alphonse's house."

"You knew Don Alphonse and saw his paintings?"

I remembered the paintings I had left at Le Reino and blushed.

He put his arm along the top of the bench, perhaps a way of propping him up as I delivered the news.

"Gabriel found me at Le Reino. For years, he did not know who I was. We had become friends."

"Le Reino." He paused. "You lived there?"

"I was found along the road. I was sick nearly to death. The owner took me in . . ."

"La Corona."

I nodded. It wasn't surprising that Christopher knew of such a place (though I had never seen him there); all the nobles knew of it. "At first I provided medical herbs and unguents for the . . . people there."

"Everyone knew Don Alphonse and Carlos shared a woman from there named Dulcinea." Christopher said. "Did you know her?"

Were these affairs so open? Words stuck in my throat. He took a wooden cup from his nearby bag and brought me a drink from the waterfall. It was cool and refreshing.

"I was called Dulcinea."

He stared and I wished I could hear his thoughts to know how much he condemned me. Or, kind fellow that he was, might he accept me? Or could he even comprehend what I was saying, so much information had come his way.

As briefly as I could, I explained the arrangement with Don Alphonse that allowed me to stay in my newfound home. "In Le Reino I found a new family. La Corona was kind and the women were like sisters." I struggled to explain how I had felt. "I had lived with peasants, and I woke up in a place of luxury. I was taken in by wealth and ease. I wish that I had held more onto Virtue, but I was inexperienced," I said with regret.

Christopher did not smile, but his voice was not strained when he said, "I remember what it is like to be young and inexperienced. We think we know best, only to fall on our faces. Some humility is in order!"

I couldn't know what he was thinking, but I was glad he could understand that I had made poor choices.

"I was treated with kindness and Don Alphonse was good to me."

Christopher was silent for a moment, and I saw a question play across his face as if he did not know whether to let it come out his mouth. "Were there others?" he asked. "I want to know." His eyes sought information; his hands lay helplessly in his lap. "Gabriel?"

"I was faithful to Don Alphonse and Carlos—though that must sound strange." Of the night at Le Reino when I had visited the desire stage and there were many men, I would never speak . . . it would serve no purpose, and with Rudolph's help,

I had sought to exorcise the demons that drove me there. I said firmly, "I am here now and that is what matters."

He looked away when I said this. I feared it was because he could not love me. Of my indiscretions, he made no sign of condemnation, no sign of acceptance. He moved to the bench across from me. His eyes were somber and his arms, crossed.

CHAPTER 31

in which Christopher tells of Cinda's return

MOVED TO THE bench across from her. Her nearness quite took my thoughts away, and I wanted to give her words my full attention. My travails, my years of constancy, seemed to have been rewarded now that I saw her. She was beautiful even with her hair pulled back and hidden in her shirt and even though she was in breeches and not the usual dress of a woman. But all the better because I could focus on seeing her for her, the better to divine the truth of her being. There was more to her than her beauty.

She said, "I was there when Ruy Bonheur died. My hand was at his cheek." Tears welled up in her eyes.

"Tomás told me that Don Alphonse's mistress was at hand," I said, rather stiffly, stumbling over the word *mistress*. I would strive for the idea not to bother me, but it was too soon. How could I take in all the information she gave me and even begin to understand what I thought or felt? Instead I would try to focus on her; then, later, I would play the conversation over in my head and give it crucial thought.

Her hands shook, as she said, "Ruy recognized me, for he asked his old question, 'Toss the bones?' Then he was dead."

"He was never without his bag of knucklebones. Always ready to play this game or that." I smiled. Knucklebones were usually the knee bones of sheep, but Ruy always insisted his were human bones! They may have been—there was nothing our noble fathers could not procure.

"He had my handkerchief when he died." Her lips trembled.

I was silent for a moment. "It is strange to hear events I heard from Tomás coming from your mouth. To think that you were there and I was not."

It was as if we were dancers gliding around the floor of Spain, coming close but never meeting. She had traveled in a world in which so many people knew our families: Don Alphonse, Carlos, Tomás, Ruy, and Gabriel. Yet she had remained lost!

She told me of her time as Guido and that Tomás and Jovi were there also.

I laughed, but with some bitterness, at the irony of Tomás being so close to her so often and not knowing it was she. "Maybe we will tell him," I said. "Someday we may see humor in it."

"I am glad you see a glimmer of humor," she said. "But it is hard for me to think of telling anyone . . . save you."

I spoke softly. "In time it will come clear who we can tell, and what." In front of me, a swallow, its tail feathers twitching, worked at pulling a worm from the ground.

My mind was running through the things she'd told me, and I gasped as the pieces fell in place. "Then it was you who wrote Tomás, claiming Matilde had falsely played Carlos to his death." I paused, my mind running to a new discovery about the event that caused the letter to be written. "And then Carlos *knew* his wife was lying!"

She nodded. "It was for Honor that he challenged me."

I stood up. "Honor! Pride is the truth of it! It can get sorely out of hand." I paced between the benches.

She nodded.

"I, too, have struggled with the truth of Honor. It takes humility to find the right of it, I think." I thought Fernando might have acted more from desperation than Honor. His demons, scarcely of his own choosing, drove him.

Her thoughts followed mine because she asked, "What is the story Gabriel told about Fernando?"

"Story?" I said, puzzled. I saw no reason to think what Gabriel had said was false. "That Fernando died at Le Reino. Gabriel wasn't there so he doesn't know the details." I sighed. "We may never know."

"It is because of Fernando that I remembered who I am."

"He was . . . *with* you?" I said, trying not to think the worst.

Vigorously, she shook her head. "No, but for the grace of God." She explained how she had offered to exchange herself for the boy Luis, but instead Fernando had discovered who she was. She swallowed. "He . . ." She made the motion that she had watched her brother make—the knife to his throat. "Fernando knew he had disgraced his name, his family's name, our father's. He knew he wasn't going to change."

I sat near her on her bench. "One time he thought I might end it for him," I said. I thought of the day he told me the truth of Cinda's running way and remembered the whoosh of my rapier as I had whipped it from its sheath. "I never thought he'd end it himself."

"I know he has children."

"Two boys, Felipe and Fernando, and a girl." I paused and smiled. "The girl, Luscy, is very smart, like Catherine. Luscy looks much like you."

"How is Patrecia?" she asked. "I remember she was always kind to me, even keeping me company the time I disgraced my parents at Court."

"I remember. You led all the children in a mad tumble down a hill into a pond—without clothes!" I laughed. I had not been there, but I had heard about it. "Patrecia is as well as she can be." I clasped my hands and laid them in my lap. How I wanted to touch my Cinda! "Fernando was tormented. I prayed for him to find release from his beleaguered soul." I paused. "I did not mean in death, but that was what God chose." I then told her I knew of her father's actions toward his children. I tried to keep my expression neutral. It was a struggle not to hold her when I saw the pain across her face.

She looked away. "How can you forgive me?"

"It was not your fault," I said firmly. "I came to believe that with all my heart."

She gasped, as if she hadn't realized until that moment she was not to blame or as if she couldn't believe I believed it. "I don't know." She sighed. "But I failed to protect the people most dear to me. . . ."

My fingertips touched her shoulder for a moment. "Your desire was to protect. As far as your father, his actions are abominable, but I chose not to choose—it is impossible—how to think, to act, to feel about him." My hands accentuated my words. "Let him be both—good and evil—and let God decide." I bowed my head. "Cinda, I am a weak man. In this I am no better than he." The shadows of my revenge on Sancha were ever ready to haunt me.

She protested the comparison, but I had to tell her what I had done to her father. "I wanted to avenge you, too, but it went all wrong." I told her how I had pushed forward when riding till Don Marco's horse had fallen, and the duke was hurt. I explained how guilty I had felt and how, through ardent prayer, I learned again that I must leave judgment to God. I had found peace, an unassailable peace that comes from accepting life as it comes and leaving any idea of changing what is to God.

She whispered, "What of my virginity?"

I answered gently and touched her arm so she would look at me. "It is not a state that I think much on." And I told her of my brief affair and declared I would not judge her for an act that was not her choice and she must not judge me for my lapse of fidelity.

"But surely you came to believe I was dead."

"I don't think I ever gave up hope." I believed that statement true even though I had begun to think of her as dead after I knew of her father's actions. But perhaps my change of thought had been because I discovered she was no longer pure. Was

I fooling myself to believe I could not bear to think of her alive after enduring her childhood, a childhood that I did not protect her from?

We sat quietly. The sun was gentle in the sky, making the pillowy white clouds shine and shimmer and making the trees bright. I thought we needed to change the topic because, in my mind, we had said all that needed to be said. Our conclusions might change with time, but the facts remained the same.

I then told her how I had discovered Sancha's family so they would know of their daughter.

"You did not want them to live with the not knowing as you had, as my family had." She shifted on the bench toward me, and her hand softly touched my arm. "I'm glad you were able to settle their minds." She continued on a sad note, "But not your own."

I nodded.

"And look," she cried and reached into her pocket. "I have the little bag with your gifts." She pulled out the now worn and stained bag of her childhood and dumped the contents in her hand. "The shell, the stone, the jewels." The locket fell out too.

"I remember when you made the bag. The colors were much brighter then." We shared a little laugh at that window into our past. I took the pink stone from the pile in my hand. "From the day King Philip blessed us."

"I was six," she said. "I remember how I felt when you explained what 'being true' meant." She swallowed. She might have felt she'd failed in light of her life, of her decisions. "It was a rush of feeling as strong as the feeling of knowing Jesus is my savior, which I also felt back then. That was the strength of the feeling I had for you."

"You never knew your life without me." I put the stone back in her hand. "You knew no other to be your love but me." I loosened the cowl. The day was becoming warm.

"You make it sound as if I only loved you because I had to," she said.

"We were but children. This match was not our choice." I was uncertain as to our future; there was so much to consider. For her, as well as myself.

"It was for your actions that I loved you, not your name."

I shook my head. "Feelings change." I would not try to influence her.

She blurted, "I do not know if we are still to be married." She covered her mouth with her hand as if she thought that it was too soon to mention our future. But that was the question that we both would be thinking. It would be the intelligent Cinda who raised it.

It was as if the years filled the space between and held us apart, for though we had touched, we had not embraced. I was not ready, but I was unsure what held me back. I was swayed by her beauty and sincerity, but I felt we needed more time. She, as well as I, must be certain. All clouds needed to be dispelled.

The silence sat between us for a moment. She moved to replace the keepsakes in her bag. I took the uncut jewels. "I must have these back," I said softly. I had plans for them, but I did not tell her.

"Of course," she said lightly, but I wondered if this action bothered her. I did not want to spoil my surprise. She would have to wait.

We parted soon after, and as I walked away, my mind quivered with thoughts. *She has returned. I touched her hair, her face, and wiped tears from her cheek.*

My scheduled and passive monastic brain was in turmoil. I wanted her. Yes! I wanted her, yet I was afraid of her. She was full of passion. She was full of courage.

What was I to think?

I scarcely faulted her. Would I so easily overlook her actions if she did not stir me so? Yet it was not for me to forgive, only to accept her as she is, only to love her as if ignorant of her actions. And is forgiveness needed for merely living one's life in the best way one can?

It was not as if she chose to have her father visit her or run away, or forget me and her family, or have misadventures in Madrid, or as if she sought to become a mistress, those were but circumstances and lucky for her perhaps. She was alive.

Yes, lucky for her! For if she hadn't had the experiences that made her the person she was today, who might she have been? Would I have liked her? Would I have cared for her?

I thought about how my forays with Sancha helped me grow from a prideful, naive young man to a man who gave concerted thought to right and wrong action.

Would I have ever discovered that the old idea of Honor was unworthy of me? For I had had too much of pride and a view that I was perfect in my noble state. I was rooted in a belief that I knew what was best. I liked the man I had become, and I would not be he except for my experiences, the tragic, the bountiful, the mundane—all of them.

I would be grateful for her experiences too: good and bad, fortuitous and not. I could not find it in me to wish for her to be different; instead I was intrigued by and enamored with the woman she was.

Adversity, mistakes, helped color us into the intricate people we were. Perhaps sins were but teachers that spurred us on to be better and compassionate people. Who was I to pine for something different?

I was not in control. I trusted that our lives had God's hand in them. My peace came through wanting what I had before me, not what I believed I would prefer, which was sure to be of my selfish self, my judgmental self, and I had found that only brought me pain.

Still, I had to be certain my mind had let go thinking on her wayward and immoderate ways, her other lovers. There! I said it. And she must return my regard. It was time for her to have a choice. She must choose me even as I must choose her.

What I once felt for Patrecia or any woman paled by comparison to the longing I now felt for Cinda! What a fool I had been! I should have known that on this stage of life the second mind takes second place, settling for the nearest one, while Cinda was in the wings, waiting to become a player.

I had become accustomed to the gift of celibacy which allowed me to see all God's people in the same even way. I administered to the peasant the same as the noble. There was no hurried pace to finish this or that and then on to the next. Each deserved the same.

But if Cinda were waiting for me at the end of each day, I could see I would fly through my appointments, listen for her voice instead of theirs, my equilibrium broken.

Yet I desired this. In the end my mind, and second mind, agreed. I chose Cinda, the Cinda she had become.

CHAPTER 32

in which Cinda returns home

H MY MOUTH! Why had it blurted out that I didn't know if we would be married?

As I'd gathered the keepsakes into my bag, he'd taken the jewels. Why? Was it a sign he did not want me? I'd given them up as easily as I could, but it did not feel good—nor give me hope—to have the once mysterious stones taken from me after all these years.

He'd risen and stood above me. "Our future is uncertain." *Was he saying he cannot love me?*

I was afraid to ask. Better to give him time to sort this out.

He added, "It may not be up to us." Now he spoke of the king, who had so long ago blessed our betrothal.

Perhaps Christopher would find me unworthy. I bowed my head. I must wait, I saw, to discover if our lives would be linked.

"Now you know every mole and wart," I had said with a nervous laugh. "I would not want me if I were you." I glanced up at him.

He smiled the faintest smile and looked down the path. "I could say the same . . ." He turned and walked away. I could not help but admire his broad shoulders from which hung the brown robe.

He turned briefly and said, "When you return home, I will let your parents come to me as if I did not know of your return. That is only right by them. And then we shall see how time takes care of this."

I knew the answer I wanted. My childhood childish love had grown, and I hungered for time with him to watch his every move. Had he taken me in his arms and said, "I love you," I would have pulled him near and shown my love for him—but he had not.

I sat on the rock overlooking the pool at the foot of the waterfall watching the splashing water and hovering mist. It was odd—and somehow easier—that he had known some of my story already. I had Fernando to thank for that.

I was sure that while my sins might be many, my love for Christopher was great. How long would it take for a decision? And whose would it be? His. My father's. The king's. I would not wait forever. But he had waited for me for many years.

Yet in a different world were it my decision, could I freely take his hand? I was not the pure and virginal girl a knight, a knight true as Christopher, deserved. Were the truth of my past to come out broadly, I might sully his good name. Better a mistress, as I had been on the arm of Don Alphonse, than an unchaste wife.

I returned to the inn, where I was told that Gabriel had departed. I would miss him, but it was like him to flit away and return unexpectedly. On the morrow, I would see my parents. I did not plan to tell my family everything; they did not have my trust as Christopher did.

The next morning I dressed in my finest—my ivory baldekin, trimmed with many pearls, and gown with hanging sleeves. I wore a gauze partlet and a small ruff with matching cuffs. I missed Braden as I had to do the lacing myself. In my hair, I braided long strands of pebble pearls, then held the hair off my face with carved ivory combs.

I rented a carriage in which I placed my belongings, and, tying Marchioness behind, I drove to Solariego. I stepped from the carriage and stood looking at my childhood home. Oddly, no servants were in view, but playing at the bottom of the steps were two lads spinning tops.

"Good day," I greeted them. I knelt beside them, my skirt billowing around me, and asked, "May I try one?"

The elder lad was friendly and quickly passed his over. I wound the string and spun it. "Look," he cried, as it spun quickly. "And you are old."

I laughed. I could remember when I thought twenty-one was old.

"I did this often as a child and I have not forgotten how." I asked, "What is your name?"

"Marco Estallar," he said, and with a graceful arc of his hand pointed to the other boy. "And this is my brother Eugenio."

Two brothers I did not know I had. I looked at Eugenio and said, "Are you the youngest?"

He seemed shy and ducked his head. "Yes, señorita. I am eight."

Marco did not suffer from shyness of any sort. "What is your name?" he asked. "Do you know my mother and father?"

"My name is Luscinda Estallar."

"That is my cousin's name," he said, then asked, "Are you related to us?"

"I am your sister," I said. "I have been . . ."

"Our sister!" Marco said and took off running up the steps. "I must get Father. And Mother." He stopped and turned to me and said, "You will not leave again, will you?"

"No," I said. "I am here to stay." And that was my hope for that day.

My welcome was warm. I quickly remembered the charm of my father and beauty of my mother. Both were tall and held themselves nobly. Time had altered them but little—some graying of the hair, perhaps. My father, his regal nose—so familiar, his limp quite noticeable. Perhaps my return helped ease the pain of the loss of Fernando, for as the day went on, my mother brightened. Her gentle smile that I remembered, crossed her face more frequently, and the grief, at first so evident in her eyes, fell away.

The clamor of greetings from my parents and siblings, even some of the servants, was loud and joyful, and the questions were too numerous and came too fast to answer. I found myself laughing as I hugged each one of them to choruses of, "Where have you been?" "Is it really you?" "What is the horse's name?" "Can I ride it?" "What happened?" "Where did you get such a dress?" and more.

My father's voice boomed above the rest, and his comments accentuated the general rabble of questions and laughter. He alternated between asking, "Why have you stayed away?" and saying, "Thank God, you are safe and whole."

After her initial surprise and disbelief, my mother clung to my hand and sat next to me; even as we ate our midday meal she scarcely let go. Here we all were at one table. My father, mother, my three sisters and three brothers. Also Patrecia and her children.

My mother had asked the fewest questions, as if having me beside her were enough and all the years of not knowing had been swept away and were unimportant. Bright Marco, ten, and pretty Julia, thirteen, who did not remember me, talked the most, more often telling of their lives and the doings of the family than asking of my life. Their enthusiasm outstripped the need to know where I had been, and my parents finally allowed them the run of the conversation until they seemed out of words and slowed down much like gracious clocks needing to be wound.

"Now," my father said. "From the beginning to end, tell us your story."

I compressed ten years into as many sentences, leaping over scores of incidents and details to compress my time away—and lack of communication—as simply as possible. For today, that was all that was needed.

After the midday meal, I sat with my family in the gathering room where we had once spent our evenings, which ended with family prayers. Marco and Eugenio, bored by our talk, were at the chess set in the corner in what seemed like an equal match. Young Felipe stood by and watched.

I remembered my father buying that chess set in Seville in the little Frenchman's shop the day I met Cervantes, who would later become Don Quixote's chronicler, and I remembered playing many games with Fernando or my grandmother.

I was sitting with my fifteen-year-old sister Marta, who was telling me about her betrothal: she would marry the following summer.

Now that the shock of my return had come and gone and urgent news of life and death (Fernando, of course, and my dear grandmother Elizabeth had died; I was stricken) had been shared, more questions came to mind and my father asked, "How do you come to be so richly dressed?" With a gesture I remembered from my childhood, he rubbed his close-cut beard along his cheek, now more gray than dark. "Surely the farmer Lorenzo was not so wealthy."

"When I came to leave his family, I made good investments," I said. "I must have some of you in me, Papa." I laughed; it seemed a mirthless laugh.

"Well done," my father said. "But what of capital?"

"I sold the rosary the king gave me." I was discovering the way to lie was to tell a little of the truth.

Her eyes widening, my mother gasped. "How could you?"

"I did not remember how I came by it," I said. "You do not know what it is to have no food." I thought of the summer of the grasshoppers when sometimes roots were all there was to eat. Nothing had been left untouched or untainted.

Patrecia had been quiet for the most part. I smiled at her and said, "Your children are wonderful. They must be a comfort to you."

She nodded without smiling. I remembered the two small beauty marks near her mouth; she had olive skin, dark eyes, and glossy straight black hair.

I searched for something more to say to her, to see if I could draw her out. I remembered her as talkative. "How are your parents?"

"My mother is quite ill," she said. She looked down.

"I am sorry," I replied. "What nature is her illness?"

"Dropsy," Patrecia said. Luscy walked near her mother, and Patrecia pulled the child close. Nervously, it seemed, she played with the child's braids.

Perhaps it would take time to renew our friendship. Surely, she had no idea of my part in Fernando's death. "I might recommend some herbs for her," I said.

She nodded as if that would be all right.

My mother said, "Luscinda, you are home now; you do not have to trade in herbs, this wretched business of your peasant life." Her fingers played with her lace cuff. Her face was thinner than I remembered, making her auburn eyes appear larger.

I looked at her and said, "Mother, I have learned to be a healer and midwife and am likely to remain so."

My father cleared his throat and coughed.

Christopher was in the doorway. Here he was in all his manly glory! Not in a cowled monk's robe, but in a duke's regalia of gray velvet with long black leather boots turned back at the knees. His hat had plumes of gray and red. Over one shoulder, his cloak was thrown back, and through his paned sleeve, I saw a finely embroidered cambric shirt. He wore a falling band with small ruff and cuffs to match. At his side were rapier and dagger.

To say he took my breath away would be trite. Is that not said by all lovers? Or shall I say that time stood still? Is that common also? I do not know. I only know it was as if the room and all its occupants were motionless while I gathered the strength to rise and go to him. You see, he did not only take my breath away, but all my strength and will, and I felt melted in my seat, wanting him to come to me and mold me into his chosen love. But then I shook myself and thought it was not for him to mold me, but for him to accept me as I was.

I took a deep breath and in a moment, when I was able, I got up, and we walked to greet each other. It seemed as if our eyes were for ourselves. I drank him and all his splendor in, and he seemed as taken with me. But I was not sure. Was this an act?

But for me it was no act. I was seeing him for the first time in ten years. Not Christopher, my knight, at seventeen, but Christopher, the duke, at twenty-seven.

I curtseyed low. "Your grace," I said.

He bowed in return. "Doña Luscinda, for this very day I have prayed. To know your fate. For mine is linked to it."

His pewter eyes were veiled as they had been in the cove. I could not perceive what was in his heart. He did not move to take my hand or touch me. Instead he motioned that I should sit again. He drew a chair near, but still it seemed he drew a boundary, which I perceived as doubt, between us.

My parents told Christopher everything I had thus far told them, which was very little compared to the events of my missing years and to what he already knew.

"We are blessed that you were taken in by a loving family," he said. "It is a miracle that you have returned to us whole."

"I regret your distress, your grace," I said.

"You did not choose it, I am certain."

Don Marco said, "Luscinda, you must let Christopher know if your honor has been compromised." His voice had become deeper, even grating.

The room grew silent. My neck grew hot and then my cheeks. My father! I knew him to be both a good father, the day father, and an evil father: the night raptor. I noticed the noble lines of his cheek, his chin.

My mother said, "It is true. You have not mentioned suitors or a marriage. You are old to have not been married."

"I will speak for myself to Christopher," I said.

"It is not that we blame you," my mother said. "You had no memory."

My father looked to Christopher. "We will find the truth of any treachery, Don Christopher. I promise." He cleared his throat; his countenance remained stern. While up till now he had seemed happy to see me, I was hurt by his severity.

My choler rose. "I came home in good faith. It is not right to doubt me."

"But Luscinda, Christopher deserves the truth," my mother said. "His future lies in your chastity."

To my father, I said, "I am as much a virgin this day as the day I ran away." My boldness flooded away and humiliation leaked in. I knew I had to leave or I would cry . . . or say, if my courage returned, too much.

At the door, I paused, but did not turn. "Father. Mother. You must accept me, or I will leave." Outside the room, I leaned against the wall to still my shaking knees. Now tears came and I sobbed as quietly as I could.

I heard the murmur of my father's deep voice, then ". . . the king will decide. I don't know how I will recommend it."

Christopher replied, "Nothing has changed. She is my wife." He added, his voice firm, "You must treat her with kindness and compassion."

Yes! Forthright man! He came to my defense and gave an *order* to my father. A smile warmed my face, and while I had been moved by his grand appearance and good looks, I remembered his soul was just as grand, and good.

"Do you think to let the contract stand?" my father asked. "You must think twice about it." Again, my father seemed against me. Was there a place for me in this decision? Why would he not consult me first? How simple it had been yesterday when it was only Christopher and me.

My mother said, "You are an honorable man, but her story is odd."

Christopher replied, "We are strangers to her, as she is to us."

My father and mother agreed.

"We will continue this discussion," Christopher said, and I heard the rustling of clothing. "Good day."

I didn't want him to see me—it seemed I was skulking—so I moved into a shadow, but he found me.

He removed his glove and with his handkerchief wiped leftover tears from my cheeks. He grasped my arms. "Cinda, I am sorry for their rudeness. A bit of time is needed." His hands gave me a gentle squeeze and then dropped to his side. He smiled, a smile of wonder. "You were magnificent in there. I am so proud of you."

I remembered that I had thought him magnificent in looks. I scarcely understood he was complimenting me on my forthrightness to my father.

"I am happy you are returned. For your family it is a lot," he said. "Fernando's gone and you are here. Let's give them time to settle their thoughts. All will come right." He leaned in and kissed my cheek then turned and left.

My knees became weak again; even walking away from me he was a handsome man!

Where did we go from here? On the one hand we had my story and on the other hand, we had Christopher's. We were fallible humans, descended straight from Adam and Eve, as any priest would quickly point out.

Did our stories weigh the same? If so, couldn't our actions, the good and bad, the noble and ignoble, cancel each other out and leave us where we once were—betrothed and happy to be?

Yet I had demanded of my parents that they accept me, and here in the grandeur of their home and with the grandeur of nobility, in the home of my childhood, I began to wonder if I could accept who I was. For even had I been a virgin when I left my home, would I not still have found it easy to make an arrangement with Don Alphonse? I had lived with ease in a brothel, where I had enjoyed many pleasures with my lovers. Surely I had known all along that chastity was what was expected of a good woman.

Don Quixote had put Aldonza on the pedestal of courtly love, even giving her a lofty name. That knight, whom some called crazy, saw good everywhere and sought only to be hopeful and honorable. He fought to protect virgins and children. Surely, had he known my full story, the story of what I became, I would not have been the inspiration of his goodly actions.

I walked out the back of the house and found Patrecia in a small garden. The chrysanthemums had quite taken it over: orange, brown, rust, and yellow. I was glad to have a chance to speak with her. I had voiced my sorrow at Fernando's death to her earlier, so I could turn the conversation to other topics. Were my family to find out I was at hand when Fernando died, would they not blame me for his death?

I said, "Tell me of your sisters and brothers," knowing I was asking to hear of Ruy's death during the bullfight.

I knew of Sonora, of course; she was married to Tomás. Feliciana was now in a convent in Cadiz. ("Quite where she belongs"—Patrecia's judgment, and I, too, knew Feliciana to be unchaste.) Jovi, now in line to be duke, was with Christopher's youngest brother, Franco, in Italy. "Ruy is dead," she said at the end of her recitation about her siblings.

I swallowed. "I am so sorry."

She smiled. "He always believed you would be found, and he would be so happy to know you have been."

I nodded, not trusting my tongue to not say, "He knew." I remembered his husky voice when he had asked me for a token and his smoky eyes that pulled me to him, even though I had been at the side of Don Alphonse. Had Ruy not died when he did, perhaps I would have been home so much sooner.

After a mutual silence, she said, "I loved Fernando, even for his dark and uneasy ways."

How much did she know of his ways?

My cheeks began to burn. Her husband was gone, and I might not be guiltless in that. "Patrecia, I wish you well in life."

"That is generous of you," she said brightly. "What of you? When will you and Christopher be together?"

I liked that she assumed we would be together, unlike my parents who merely wanted a recitation of my possible trysts.

I smiled. "I am unsure."

"He has much on his mind," she said. "They say Don Hernando's investments had soured before he died."

Here was other news—surprising news—but, wait, I knew it. I had heard it from Don Alphonse some time ago. Would Christopher tell me?

CHAPTER 33

in which Cinda spends time with her father and her mother

ITHIN A FEW days of my return, my father invited me
to go for a carriage ride to the vineyards with him. In
spite of his limp, my father carried himself nobly: tall and
straight, his shoulders squared.

I sensed my father had something in particular he wanted say. I was determined to stay in good humor with him.

He cleared his throat then began in his deep voice,
"I want information to help clear up the question of your future." He snapped his
whip at the horse. From his side, I could see the outline of his raptor-nose.

"Christopher and I are betrothed," I answered, knowing that while it had been
decreed by the king, it could also be set aside by him.

"You know what I mean," he said glaring at me. "Swear by your grandmother's
grave, you are free to marry Christopher. That nothing has happened to you, in
your absence, to dishonor him."

"I will not deceive Christopher." I could not make square in my mind why this
question so plagued my father. It seemed that if Christopher accepted me; that
was all that mattered. I changed the subject to let my father know the question of
my position was answered as well as it was going to be. I said, "I am sorry about
Fernando."

My father opened his mouth: Was he going to try to hang onto the old topic?

Quickly, I said. "Who will be heir now?" A question that was no more my business than the one my father asked me.

After a hesitation, my father answered, "Marco's a fine lad. He is not troubled
as Fernando was." He pulled the horse away from a stand of chicory along the side
of the road. "But young Felipe seems fine too. I have not decided."

"It will be a difficult choice."

Gravely, my father said, "I have not asked—though Christopher may know—how
Fernando died."

My breath caught. "Knowing will not change anything," I said.

In a trembling voice he asked, "What if he were at a bawdy house; what if he were murdered? . . . What if he killed himself?" He swallowed and ducked his head.

I was stunned that my father would open the door to suicide, that he might know the nature of Fernando. "You think he may have killed himself," I said softly.

"No! Of course not," my father cried, angrily. "Someone may have killed him!"

If told the circumstances, my father might believe I was the murderer! My palms grew warm and moist. He could indict me; I remembered how a letter from phantom Guido had counted more than a live Matilde.

I swallowed and tried to pick up the string of the conversation. "I know suicide is against your code of Honor." I cleared my throat. "Though I remember your saying sometimes it was better to be dead than dishonored."

"What could have dishonored him so much?" my father said puzzled. But his face changed. He swallowed. "I had heard . . ." He shook his head. "But in the end it does not matter. He . . . my son is . . . dead."

"It could have been a natural death."

My father took out his handkerchief. Regardless of what I knew, I was moved by his genuine sadness. And losing a child was a sorrow I never wanted to bear.

That evening, my mother and I went to my room. I sat at the dresser, and she brushed my hair as if I were still three, or eight, or eleven.

"I have many years to make up for," she said with a catch in her throat. "I am glad you still have the comb and brush your grandmother gave you." Tears came to her eyes.

"Yes," I said softly, thinking I should take flowers to my grandmother's grave. "You must miss her."

"My mother combed my hair like this when I was little. She would tell me of her native England, their estate Whispering Leaves. How her father, the duke of Sorrels, had been angry when she had married a Spaniard." My mother cleared her throat. "I met her brother once. When I was five, he came to Spain to visit us." With each stroke of the brush, her bracelet jingled a tiny silver song.

"What was he like?" I asked.

My mother laughed at happy memories. "He was wonderful and brought me a doll and stayed some time with us. He read to me in the afternoon when I was supposed to be asleep. I remember the English tale was called *Beowulf*." She was silent for a moment. "The day he left he gave me a ring and said, 'Isabella, if Grendel, or his mother, ever comes after you, send this to me, and I will rescue you.'"

"You must have loved that."

"It made me feel as if I were fifteen, not five." My mother laughed. She bundled my hair in sections and began to braid it for the night.

"That is a nice memory," I said. "Grandmother loved her memories." I thought of how my grandmother taught me to see things with senses, to tell of my day as if I were painting a picture for her blind eyes to see.

After she tied my braid with a white ribbon, my mother showed me the ring, a braided gold and silver band.

"Do you write him?" I asked. I had never heard of my English uncle before—much like how Margret, Aldonza's sister, surprised us.

Her auburn eyes looked thoughtful in the lamplight. "I have never thought to try."

"Why not?" I asked. I touched her hand.

"Perhaps, I shall," she said slowly, then brightly added, "Yes, I would like to know I have family too."

I remembered a similar feeling from when I first came to Le Reino. I had been alone, and I had wanted to belong. I supposed for my mother it was that she missed her mother.

"His father is my grandfather. Perhaps he is still alive." She held the ring out to me and told me she wanted me to have it.

"Someday," I said and put it back on her finger. "I wonder if it is still worth a rescue."

She laughed. "From what do I need to be rescued? There are no threats here." She bedded my comb in the brush and set them aside for morning.

I patted her arm. I envied her this thought—that nothing in her world would go so wrong that she would need help.

She looked at me in the mirror.

I looked back. "You are beautiful." I said to her what she had said to me every evening of my childhood.

She blushed and said, "Not anymore."

I turned to her and said, "Yes! You are and you must see yourself that way." I sighed, thinking of all the evenings I had missed of our little talks, of her brushing my hair.

She smiled but tears teased her eyes.

To brighten the mood, I said, "I would rather have this bracelet." I pointed to the bracelet that had the little bells entwined on it.

"Yes," she said. She held out her wrist and I helped remove the bracelet.

"I remember the day Christopher gave the bells to you. He was so regal in his manner. A born nobleman." She held the bracelet by an end and shimmied it in the air, the little bells tinkling, like they must have the day Christopher gave them to me. "He was only six but he held you steadily and I trusted him." She handed me the bracelet.

I understood. I'd always known him to be kind and steady. Trustworthy. I cradled the bracelet in my hand, and then she tied it on my wrist. Having the bells back on my arm felt as if some circle had been completed. Yet I knew it was not certain. I was beginning to doubt.

My mother was silent, and with the hair-tending over, it seemed she might leave. I tried to think of a question that would keep her longer. "And on Fridays, do you still walk the Way?" I asked, thinking of how it had grown and how Christopher and I had sat by the waterfall the day we had chanced upon each other there. "How is Brother Diego?" He had always walked with her, and, more recently, he had been a good friend to Christopher.

My mother's gentle smile was enigmatic. "He is good," she said. "We are friends."

It was only then that I realized my mother loved him. I wondered if . . . but shook my head. Surely not. Though it was pleasurable to think my father might have been the cuckold.

ꙅꙅ

Because I had not seen her yet, I called on Doña Chirique, Christopher's mother. She seldom left Gasparenza. Her vision had become so poor, she could do little. Sonora, Tomás's wife, and daughters had stayed with us awhile but then left—the children seemed to make Doña Chirique nervous. When I left, I met Christopher. He grinned broadly and waved his hand in a friendly salute.

"Good day," he said pleasantly. "Are you leaving?"

"Yes. I'm afraid I've tired your mother."

"You must visit more often."

"Or . . ."

He pulled me to him and held me close. We were laughing. "Or . . . live here." He squeezed me. "Yes, of course! We will see the king soon."

He took my hand and touched my bracelet. "How did you . . . ?"

"My mother gave it to me."

He nodded. "As it should be."

Together we walked to get Marchioness. As we approached the stable, I saw Tomás talking to the tall and handsome Jovi Bonheur. Jovi, as was his habit, was gesticulating broadly. I could see Tomás grinning, his dark wavy hair blowing in the breeze.

"I didn't know Jovi was back," I said.

"Let me introduce you," Christopher said, reminding me that the last I should have seen Jovi was years ago—not at Brados.

When we reached Tomás and Jovi, Christopher said, "Jovi, surely you have heard of Luscinda's return."

He looked at me. "Yes."

"I doubt if you remember me," I said.

"I heard Ruy talk about you." His eyes were dark like Ruy's, though Jovi was fairer and tall, not as intense as the compact Ruy. We were silent for a moment.

Tomás said, "I was telling Jovi about Carlos Mentos's death."

Jovi shook his head. "I cannot believe his wife betrayed him so." Then he looked at me. "Did you know Carlos?"

My impulse was to deny, to shake my head, but I simply said, "I have heard the story."

Jovi said, "I would not have challenged Guido."

"Why not?" Christopher asked. His eyes glimmered with curiosity.

"He was good with a sword," Jovi said. "Better with a knife."

Tomás nodded. "He was an honorable man."

Christopher said, "I never met him." He glanced at me. "What happened to him?"

They both shook their heads: They did not know.

Wiping his forehead with his sleeve and squinting in the sun, Jovi said, "Maybe we will see him at a tournament."

To Christopher, Tomás said, "He'll hold his own against you." Tomás and Jovi walked away.

Christopher laughed and took my arm. We went in the stable.

He led Marchioness outside for me. "Do you think I might someday see the talents of Guido?"

"To make fun of me?"

He quickly turned to me, his gray eyes flashing. "I would never do that!"

I saw the truth of what he said. "Guido must stay in the past."

He gave me a leg up on Marchioness then mounted his own steed to ride alongside me to Solariego.

CHAPTER 34

in which Christopher escorts Cinda to Riego

INDA AND I found little time to be alone (perhaps a disadvantage of large families and myriad servants), and I thought to take her to Riego on market day so we could enjoy each other without interruptions from family and home. The very air was full of smells—meat pies, baked fruit, roasted turkey legs, warm pastries, leather goods. People—lots of people, talking, yelling, even singing.

I was comfortable walking along beside her. I was taller but not by much, and it was easy to look into her blue eyes, which were the very color of her dress, and watch her dimples play across her face as she was greeted by this person or that. Some she remembered, others she did not. Everyone in the village knew of her return for their fortunes were tied with Don Marco's, and mine.

As we walked by a game of knife toss, she told me of the day at the gypsy fair when she met Carlos and how they'd matched their throws, one by one. She laughed merrily to tell of it, showing me how such a flirtation of young love makes one feel. At twelve, I'd tried to declare my love to Marietta, but she had gently rebuffed me, and through the years when my second mind guided my first, I had pined for Patrecia or other pretty girls with slender ankles or rounded bosoms. My affair with Bella had skipped flirtation. I found I envied Cinda's afternoon of pure delight and enjoyment with Carlos.

Maybe envy was too strong a word. And anyway, I was here with her now, and we could collect flirtations with each other beginning today. Felling taller at the thought, I marveled how her presence made me aware of even tiny things. How I loved the smell of grapes, her scent. How her laugh made the sun seem brighter. How I could find ways to touch her, her shoulder when I wanted to show her something, her waist to guide her beside me, her hand . . . I needed no excuse. Being beside her filled me with more happiness and exquisite pleasure than I had ever imagined.

We stopped to watch a round of gameball. I knew some of the lads who were playing, some from Solariego and some from Gasparenza. The game had few rules, and its purpose was to train young men for battle—it did not matter if the white team had three more players than the blue: battles were often unequal. The object was to get the ball past your opponents to their "castle," a line in the dirt, really, to mark the end of the playing field.

After placing a small wager between us, Cinda cheered the white team (she was persuaded by their numbers) and I, the blue. She was nearly hoarse when the game ended. Perhaps it was not entirely fair because I knew two of the lads on the blue team were seldom defeated, but the wager was for a small amount, and she had chosen the team she was backing without asking about either.

We went to the tavern for dinner. Sitting next to each other on the bench seemed to affect both of us as if we had imbibed heavy mead for we were giddy and breathless, and I continued to press against her, her arm, her leg. The titillation of having her near me erased my years of longing and searching—at least for that moment.

Near evening, from the plaza, we could hear music and clapping. I knew there would be dancing, the excuse I needed to have her in my arms. The thought incited me, thrilled me, but I sought to maintain calm befitting a duke.

On our way to the plaza, people moved aside to let us through the crowd. We found a place near the musicians where we could watch the *flamenco* dancers, who were dressed in costumes of reds, yellows, greens, and blues with flowing sleeves. A couple of the women had on high headdresses.

First the couples danced slowly, carefully, following each other's moves, but not touching. Then they began dancing faster, moving their feet so fast, yet keeping them so close, that it seemed the feet did not move, that the dancers merely floated across the plaza. The women snapped their fingers. Their hands moved gracefully, like thoughtful birds, while their feet tapped and clicked. The crowd clapped in time with the music. Tambourines clinked and jangled.

One of the couples came for Cinda and me. The woman pulled at my wrist, and the man offered Cinda his arm. I was disappointed that we were so easily parted but glanced her way often, finding her movements with the man—a rival, who could not be my rival—were graceful and fetching. Our eyes met and it was as if we could touch without touching.

Then our partners returned us to each other, and I took her in my arms and the world shifted. Everything slowed down. I saw the people clapping and talking around the perimeter of the circle. I saw the musicians playing, but all I heard was a gentle soughing, a summer breeze through laden branches. The sound transformed into our breathing, our in and out breaths, hers and mine. We were in an empty and silent world full of Cinda and me.

Then, just as quickly, it was normal again, and the noises of the night and the music flowed through our bodies and unified us. The rhythm demanded that we move in just this way, which was, miracle of miracles, the exact movements of the dance. It felt so right, so exhilarating, dancing in the plaza surrounded by the people who again expected that one day we would be their lord and lady, and now they clapped their hands, yelling words of encouragement to us, as if their expectations had been restored now that Cinda was back again.

Once more, we were separated, and for the rest of the evening person after person asked each of us to dance. We could not find fault, for they only wished to see Cinda and tell us that they were happy for her return.

It was late when we left the town square. The dancing had fired my body and my imagination, maybe even more so because I was seeing Cinda across the way. She was delightful and gracious with each person. I knew I would never forget the moment in the plaza when the world fell silent except for Cinda's and my breathing. I now had my gypsy-fair memory, like Cinda's. It mattered not that I was twenty-seven and not sixteen.

In the carriage—we were not even out of sight of the village lanterns—Cinda and I agreed—it was a silent agreement, only looks passing between us—that we would go together to Gasparenza that night, and before morning the Knight of the Seeking Heart became the Knight of the Satisfied Heart.

♫ ∝

Don Marco summoned me with a cryptic note that only said to come, no other explanation. Though I was years younger than he, we were now equals, and I felt I had to struggle to ensure he treated me with the same respect he would any other duke, as he would have my father.

I would have written back that I was busy and needed the reason for the summons, but I was eager to see Cinda again and had planned to ride to Solariego anyway.

Very early that morning, when the top of the sun was level with the horizon, I had deposited her at the doors of her home. We wished to keep our tryst a secret because our being together was so precious to us, after waiting so long, that we agreed to jealously guard our privacy. We did not want to share our joy—not yet.

When I arrived at Solariego's entrance, for the second time that day, Cinda was there with Marco and Eugenio. They were tossing knives into a circle inscribed in the dirt. She greeted me with her sunny smile. My heart raced and a feeling of well-being surrounded me.

"Are you here on business?" she asked lightly. "Or to see me?" We stood close but did not touch. It was tantalizing, and I loved that each moment with her was a discovery of an aspect, or feeling, of life that I had not yet experienced.

"Your father sent for me." I bowed slightly. "But I hope to visit you also. Shall we walk after I am finished?"

She picked up one of the knives and holstered it in a carrier at her waist, nearly hidden by the folds of her skirt. To the boys, she said, "We'll continue another time." To me, she said, "I will ensure our visit by accompanying you." She took my arm and walked in with me.

"I have received a response from the king," Don Marco said. Cinda and I were standing before him. He had not offered us a seat, though he was seated at his desk. The desk was inlaid with gold scrolling. As a child, I had admired that desk and had wanted to acquire one as soon as I were old enough. As an adult, I knew I could never have one as gaudy as it. I was glad that I had not yet begun redecorating Gasparenza now that I was duke. I looked forward to that pleasure with Cinda at my side.

Don Marco continued, "The king summons you to Madrid. He wants to speak with you before he retracts the betrothal."

"What!" Cinda and I spoke in one breath. In the few days since her return, I had not once considered this possibility—that the king would void the agreement, even though Don Marco had hinted at it. I put my arm around her waist. Now that she was at my side, I felt nothing could get in the way of our life together. Yet, the king . . .

"We go to Madrid . . ." Don Marco began.

I interrupted. "It is unnecessary for you to make the trip. We can go . . ."

"Doña Isabella was already planning the trip. And a small party to welcome back Luscinda." He touched a letter on his desk and pulled it toward him. He dipped a feathered nib in ink. "Perhaps a match with a duke is too much and some other match will present itself." He signed the letter, as if in that motion he were striking down our contract.

My breath nearly left me. "You speak too boldly, sir." My voice was low; I felt the growl in my throat as anger beset me. I don't know how I kept my temper constrained. "Surely the choice is between Cinda and me."

"Highly unlikely," he said, as he sanded his signature.

I was not sure, but did he take pleasure in disconcerting me, and what about his daughter?

Cinda opened her mouth to speak, but Don Marco said, "We are all going. We may as well travel together." He waved his hand to dismiss us, but I was going to stake my place as his equal. I sat in a nearby chair and motioned to Cinda to sit also.

"Don Marco, I was hoping to discover the name of the person who supplies your wine casks."

The look of annoyance passed quickly from Don Marco's face. Or had I imagined it? I wanted to discover his true feelings. Did he think his daughter unworthy of me? Or did he merely wish to keep her under his roof? My stomach twisted at this thought, though I trusted Cinda to defend herself, if needed. I had not forgotten that she carried a knife and she knew how to use it.

After a few minutes of business discussion, I rose, and Cinda and I left Don Marco.

We walked in silence. It was not even a week since she had returned, and I had already decided that all our years ahead would be together. Yet at the same time, it felt as if our future were going to break apart.

"I've been wanting to go to the cemetery," Cinda said.

It felt as if that was the right place to be, given the heaviness in my chest, where a small fear had seeded itself. "Then we shall walk there."

We neither spoke of the news from her father, but I could not quell my thoughts. Had we acted too soon? Suppose the king should set aside the betrothal. Our being together may have compromised her. The thought of our joy causing her pain was too much for me to contemplate.

Along the way we kept up a stream of light conversation. Each sentence, it seemed, began with *Remember.*

When it was my turn for a memory, I said, "Remember the day you first went hunting with us."

"Yes! I threw up the minute I saw your father fell a doe."

We laughed. "Quite right," I said, throwing out a challenge to her. "Leave the hunting to the men."

She reached over and pushed me gently. "Only for that day!"

I laughed and said, "I know! You will do whatever you want!"

Her step hesitated for a moment. "I regret that I always did whatever I wanted. You deserve a better person for your wife."

I took her hand and turned her toward me. "The question is resolved for me. You must learn to accept yourself."

"What seemed acceptable in my former life, seems impossible here." A wisp of wind blew strands of hair across her face. "I should have had more pride for my chastity." She pulled back her hair and fastened it more securely with her amethyst-studded combs. I admired the expertness of her actions, the sureness of her fingers. In short, I was enamored with every movement she made.

She continued, "I should have looked to Mother Mary to guide me. Instead I looked only to myself." She told me how she did not go to church and, even in the little chapel where she sought to pray, she had only believed in her own thoughts and actions and had not considered how her actions might affect her future.

I felt the conversation had become too heavy for such a beautiful day, the day after our first lovemaking, and so I said, "It will all become clear in time." I was thinking about how my own prayers had helped me find peace, how I had stopped judging my actions and others', leaving forgiveness to God. I squeezed her hand.

The rest of our walk was a pleasant cacophony of more memories.

Outside the cemetery, we saw the swing of our childhood was still on the big tree outside the fence.

"A new seat," she cried. "It's big enough for the two of us!"

I was uncertain I was ready to swing with her. We were no longer children. So I said, "Shall we sit under the tree as we often did?"

She nodded and we sat on the incline under the big tree from which the swing hung. I noticed how the sun sent shadows of her long eyelashes down her cheeks, and they flickered there as she blinked her clear blue eyes.

"Remember how we looked at the stars." I was too keenly aware of her scent, grapes and primrose. It had lingered on my hands since early this morning but now it was fresh from her.

"And never the clouds?" She ruffled her fingers through her dark hair. The sun sparkled off her amethyst combs.

I laughed. "I suppose we did." I pointed to a poufy cloud and said, "There's an elephant's head complete with trunk."

"And a horse." She pointed up and to the left.

I felt the breeze shiver the plumes on my hat. I didn't see the horse and moved a little closer to stare up her pointing arm. "That's a puny horse."

Showing her perfect white teeth, she laughed. I caught my breath; very aware of her nearness. "What then? A house, a church, a lady bug?"

"It only takes a circle to be a bug," I said mirthfully.

"Then every cloud can have a name and none will go to waste." She looked at me.

How I wanted to hold her! I knew our banter cloaked our true desires, but broaching them would be for naught. We must await the king's decision. "Shall I push you in the swing?"

"What fun," she said. We raced to the swing. I was glad to take action. She sat in the giant seat and I put my hands on her waist.

Maybe this had been a mistake. How could I touch her and not want so much more? Within a half dozen firm and strong pushes she was flying high. An innocent thrill, for each of us.

As she slowed, I took the rope and pulled her to a stop. The ungainly swing flopped against me, setting us knee to leg, but I took the other rope and set her straight and still.

"Join me," she said and scooted over, making room.

I sat. "I hardly think this is befitting a duke," I said lightly.

"Enjoy this day," she said. "We do not know for how long . . ."

"Sshhh," I stopped her, but silently I agreed. We gently swung, and while we did, I told her of the problems of being duke. "My father had been ill for many months." Years, perhaps, I was not certain. "I had been at the monastery and did not realize the extent of his neglect to our business affairs."

"In what way?"

"Many things are in disrepair," I said. "We lost nearly an entire orchard of olive trees." I sighed, remembering the skeletons of the trees before they had been cut down. "Some of them were three hundred years old."

"I'm sorry."

"But most distressing is the state his investments are in," I said.

"How bad is it?" she asked bluntly. My Cinda had become a strong woman, yet I remembered this very directness as a child. She was always ready to ask questions.

I put my arm behind her and held the rope on her side of the swing. "You speak boldly still," I said.

"Like a child?" She smiled and then looked away.

"No." I tucked my finger under her chin and turned her face back to look at me. "Like my equal. Do not be embarrassed," I said. "You make it easier, in your way, for me to talk to you."

"Good."

"I must pay close attention for quite some time to put us back on the way to prosperity," I said easily. "Your father, who is gifted in business, as you know, has offered to help, quite graciously, but I would rather figure it out on my own." I began to swing us with my feet, my leather boots scuffling the ground. "Still I would be foolish to not listen to him."

"Let me help you," she said. "I can . . ."

But before she could make her offer, I put my mouth on hers and kissed her. Her lips were warm and soft. Her breath was sweet and our arms embraced each other like young lovers do, afraid to touch the wrong place. How soon would our future become clear?

CHAPTER 35

in which Cinda and Christopher see the king

ROM THE MOMENT I was born, it was intended that I be with Christopher. He had waited a long time, and it appeared he would continue to wait, though maybe not as patiently.

After the kiss in the swing, we broke apart and in the silence, my mind covered every possible scenario from us parting and never seeing each other again to falling on the grass and taking up where we'd left off that morning. And on his face I saw similar thoughts; still we neither moved toward the other or away.

My father's letter from the king, while not dampening our desires, gave us pause. I was baffled by my father's comments and wondered again at his intentions. I sensed all was not right.

I took a deep breath and led us through the wrought-iron gate of the cemetery. After all, that was the reason for our walk, though the other pleasantries were an added treasure. A spray of fresh yellow roses sat by my grandmother's grave. And the brightness of the flowers and the softness of Christopher nearby allowed me to put the kiss aside momentarily while I honored my lost family members. At Grandmother Elizabeth's grave, I knelt and prayed. My grandmother, who had become blind shortly after my birth, had had to learn to live her life a different way. She could remember the entire chess board, the entire game, every move, in her head.

At Catherine's grave, I also knelt. It gave me pleasure to think that Luscy might fulfill the lost promise of my sister. I thought of an evening in Catherine's room— she had been four. She went to her open window, and standing on her toes, she looked out.

"Careful!" I held her nightgown firmly. We watched as three storks flew across the moon, their long wings waving and changing shapes as they flew. Catherine waved her arms as if she were a bird. "Are you practicing?" I said, teasing her.

She sighed. "If I flew away, I would miss you, Cinda."

I hugged her. "You will not fly away; you will always be with me." I had been wrong.

Catherine's choice had freed her from the night vulture. Fernando had spread his pain to many. Some part of me had tossed my memory away for many years. And the part that was wrong, it seemed to me, was not that one of our choices was better or worse but that we had had to make the choice.

There, that day in the cemetery beside Catherine's tiny grave, I held onto my resolve to let our history be silent, even as I wanted some of mine to be, and I hoped that cauldron never broke to spill out those secrets.

I'd forgotten Christopher was there. He'd knelt by my side. Putting his arm around my shoulder, he pulled me to him. His tenderness allowed my overwhelming grief to come. I sobbed, and it seemed I would be unable to stop. He held me firmly, though he was silent.

When in time I quieted, I pulled back to look at him. Tears were on his face too. "Oh, do you cry for Catherine?" I asked, puzzled.

"For her." He smiled and said, "And you." He paused. "I am sorry for you." He took my hand but did not look at me. "I would have done anything for it not to have happened, but it did and now we are together."

I did not know to which of so many things he referred, but I accepted the spirit of his words—he accepted me, no matter what had happened to me. But how could he? And could I?

Holding hands, we walked back to the house. I wondered if he wanted to kiss me again as much as I wanted to kiss him.

Yet I knew he was thinking that if the king set aside the betrothal, Christopher did not want there to be even more reason another man would not have me. I suspected he might have regrets about our night together, for today he was treating me as if I were the most virginal of young women. How could I love him any more? I would never wonder about the nature of Honor again. It was Christopher.

That afternoon I sought out my sister Alicia. We had yet to talk one on one. She was in a sitting room, one with big windows and much light. She had her handiwork on her lap.

"How is it with you, Alicia?" I asked.

"I will not marry," she said. She was, as she had always been, unsmiling and solemn. "Do you think I must go to a convent?" She was plain-looking, though each of her features taken separately was fine enough. It was her eyes—they were lifeless, unhappy.

"I think you may do as you like."

"Mama and Papa do not." She sounded bitter and perhaps to hide her eyes, she picked up her handiwork.

"Can I help?"

"I often wished I'd run away with you." She was crocheting the edge on a handkerchief. It was fine work. "You left me here . . . alone."

In my mind I heard Fernando saying, "*None of us* escaped."

I said, "I was wild with anger. I was confused." I remembered how, that day after Fernando had revealed all the secrets, I had run to my room, wanting to get away. Away from him, and from Papa—even Mama—to somehow go to Christopher to ask if I could move to Gasparenza then and away from my family. I went to her and knelt in front of her. "I am sorry. I was only thinking of me when I left."

"Catherine was gone by then."

I flinched. Alicia had always been grouse-like and glum, and I had favored Catherine. I remembered a time when I had planned to stay the night with Catherine in her room. I had crawled into her nest of bed. She fit in the curve of my body as if she were the egg to keep warm, and I, the mother wren.

It was later when the night owl came. I heard him, a quiet whoosh of silk sleeves. Papa sat on the side of the bed. He touched Catherine's cheek. I had to keep my fragile egg safe. "No, Papa," I said. "We can go to my room." I pulled him from Catherine's bed; he followed me.

To Alicia, I said, "It was thoughtless and I am sorry."

"After you left, I said I would tell Mama and Father Francisco."

"Alicia, you are so brave!" I said to my sister whom I had never admired.

For an instant her eyes lit up. There! A strand of beauty on her face. "Papa injured himself in a fall from Spartan," she said. "Did you notice his limp?"

I nodded.

"At first he could not walk at all," she said. "But then he did." She smiled grimly. "I like to think his blemished soul took on an outward deformity."

I wondered at the glumness of a spirit who would think such a thing, but I found I was taken with the idea. We sat in silence for a moment.

"It may have damaged him in another way also." She allowed herself another smile.

"How?"

"There have been no more children." She wound her finger around the thread and picked up her tiny hook. "I take pleasure from thinking it so, a sort of divine justice."

"Are you saying . . .?" I was still unable to say exactly what I thought she meant.

She shrugged. "If so, the punishment complements the crime. Isn't that the best way?" And she started laughing. I couldn't remember ever hearing her laugh. It was a wonderful laugh. Her whole face lit up and I saw that she could be beautiful, but she didn't wish it. Unlike Fredrica, who only needed a little suggestion to bring out her beauty and to find its power, Alicia preferred to hang on to homeliness and remove herself from the world.

Yet I felt happy for her. Our laughter must have rung through the halls for soon Luscy and Felipe came running in to see what was happening.

"Are you tickling her?" Felipe asked me.

"You mean like this?" I tickled him under the arm, and the four of us fell in a heap of tickles and peals of laughter.

Later on our way to dinner, Alicia, who I thought looked younger, said to me, "Will you tell?"

"I am unsure," I said softly. "I prefer to leave it alone."

She nodded.

I could not settle in my mind the things that needed to be out and the things that needed to be in. My way of life, my presence at Fernando's death, the root cause of my running away were all incidents that I thought might be better left to languish. Could they die their own death?

In the evening, I retired to my room. I had been staying in my childhood bedroom since my return. The furnishings were different. Not the same mirror where my mother had brushed my hair. Now there was a chair instead of a stool. It was not the same bed.

I was both drawn to this room and repelled by it. From night to night I remembered more of my childhood. Scenes of easy childhood things were fun, but others brought sorrow into my heart, brought restless sleep and sometimes nightmares.

I had been a child, and fathers should protect their children. That I could stay in this room now, a grown woman, knowing that I could fully protect myself, seemed to strengthen my resolve that I could leave the past alone and move forward with Christopher. I had hope that I could find acceptance of my life, even as he had.

Some nights I lay awake, unable to even close my eyes, thinking I heard my father's step. I imagined his palm on the door, pushing it slowly. And maybe he did come and pause there. I did not, nor would I ever, know.

My father's professed concern for my marriage to Christopher was my chasteness, my virginity. Yet he knew me to not be a virgin. I remembered him telling me, "I teach you to be a good wife, and when the time comes, I will see that you know how to pose as a virgin."

I remembered when I first met Don Alphonse that as soon as he whispered in my ear, "Please me," I no longer acted of my own free will. I had been under the influence of unseen forces in the form of my unremembered father. The following morning Don Alphonse had recognized I had not been a virgin, but I had dismissed his conclusion.

When I was a child, our priest Father Francisco gave lessons from the catechism to Fernando and me. I thought of one in particular. We were in the chapel. Father Francisco's legs spread wide and his robe hanging like a big basket below his round belly, the priest sat on a stool near the Mary statue. Fernando and I sat on the floor in front of him.

The priest put his hand on his thigh and leaned forward to tell the story. "The angel Gabriel came to Mary and announced that she, of all women, was to be blessed with a son. The Son of God."

"Jesus," I had said, proud of my knowledge.

The priest nodded. "Now Mary questioned this news for she was a virgin."

"But," Fernando asked, "how could a virgin have a baby?" Because Fernando was older, he knew much more than I, for I had not understood this word.

Solemnly, Father Francisco replied, "Nothing is impossible with God." A whiff of garlic came our way as he continued, "What is out of the ordinary is that as soon as Mary agreed to the announcement, the sacred body of Christ was immediately formed." The priest clasped his hands in wonder. "And just as the rays of the sun penetrate glass without breaking it, so did Jesus emerge from His mother's womb without injury to her perpetual virginity."

In awe of this miracle of God, I cried, "I want to be a virgin too!"

The priest's eyes sparkled as they often did, for he, more than anyone I have known, believed in the total goodness of God. He said, "Guard yourself well, for once lost, it cannot be found."

But I had passionately felt that if all things were possible in God, I could surely find it as many times as I lost it.

Tonight I chuckled briefly at the naiveté of my five-year-old self.

Could I have stopped being with Don Alphonse and Carlos? I supposed I could have, but I was presented with no reason to stop. I enjoyed them and they enjoyed me, and it had seemed harmless enough, until Matilda had fallen in love with Guido.

Just as Rudolph had thought, there was a tie between what happens to us as children and how we act as adults. Could we put a stop to it?

I thought that we could and that I had thrown out my demons that night in the desire theater; but there was more to it, I decided. There was fear, like my thinking my father was at the door. Like the cold sweats I had woken up with, like my hands shaking as I tried to sleep.

I thought back to another fair in Riego that I had attended with my father, Fernando, and Christopher. That night I had also danced with Christopher, and the peasants had clapped, proclaiming us the future, knowing that we would be their noble duke and duchess in time. My father had come to me that night. I was sound asleep and his crying woke me up.

"What is it, Papa?" I asked.

"I couldn't stand seeing you dance with Christopher. Everyone cheered you." His breath caught in his throat. "You are *mine*!" he said vehemently.

Jealousy! that had to be his objection to the marriage. I remembered the day I had returned, how his voice had changed after Christopher—oh heart!—had appeared, the commanding Duke of Gasparenza! It was then he had questioned my chastity. I saw the pattern now.

∽∾

The following morning I sought out Brother Diego. I wanted the assurance and peace that Christopher had acquired over the years.

I found the monk in the vegetable garden of the monastery turning under a row of now-exhausted squash. Though it was a cool morning, his forehead glistened with sweat.

"May I speak privately with you?" I asked the tall man.

He nodded and led me to a large sycamore tree by a gushing stream that ran handily through the monastery grounds. A series of stumps sat around in a half circle and we each sat on one. I found mine was a little unsteady as it was no longer rooted but only used for sitting among this little chorus of stumps facing the water.

"How may I be of service to you, Doña Luscinda." I remembered his sad eyes from when I was a child, but I also remembered him to be of good humor.

"I want to find the peace that Christopher has," I said. "He says he found it through prayer." I looked away. "I . . . no longer pray." He did not speak immediately, so I sought to fill up the void of wordlessness. "I had a friend," I was thinking of Daria, "who also had such a miracle. Through prayer. That is, where all anger and hatred were lifted from her."

He continued his silence, and I found myself telling him everything about Daria and how I had come to meet her and how she was in a convent and how I'd come to enter the convent (though I left out the part of my lack of clothing).

Then one thing led to another and I told him about Carlos and Don Alphonse and the words now came tumbling, just as the water was rolling over the stones in the stream, and I thought my tongue would not stop.

When it did stop, more from a dry throat than wanting to stop, there was more that I could have said. I had told him the most important things that had to do with my feelings about my life now and how I fit into this world of nobility, of dukes and king's decrees.

He remained silent, though he got up and brought me a drink in a cup tied to his belt. Greedily, I drank the cool water but not all of it so I could offer him some. He smiled and finished the water. Then he sat down again, still silent, so what was there to do but for me to continue speaking?

"I think I know what I must do."

He nodded in encouragement.

"That first day when I came home—to my parents," I began. "I told them, rather sternly, that they must accept me as I am or I would leave." Brother Diego did not waver in his listening. He did not look away nor take up any other occupation. "And also I thought, that day, it was for Christopher to accept me."

A sunfish jumped from the stream and splashed nearby. I jumped and laughed a little. "But now I see."

He nodded, but I couldn't tell if it was in encouragement or because he saw my answer too.

"It is for *me* to accept me." The sentence nearly exploded out of me but the deflation followed immediately. "But how can I?"

"Why couldn't you?" The monk broke his silence.

"But you heard I am no virginal girl. I became enamored with an easy life and nice things. I took money for . . . my body." I was sorry he would not understand the word *princesita* because I could not say *whore* to a monk. But there it was. I owned it and was sorry for it.

"Tell me why you cannot accept this, why you cannot forgive yourself."

My mind turned over the reasons. I chose: "It is against God's design."

The monk looked surprised as if that were not what he expected me to say.

"What is God's design?"

"For me to be a good and honorable woman. For me to be chaste and . . . obedient." I hesitated at the word "obedient" because it was my obedience to my father that had sent me off the narrow path.

As if the monk read my mind, he said, "Your situation did not allow you to be both."

"I see." I had been in an impossible situation without help. I could not go back and change what had happened, but I could go forward knowing I could protect myself, that I could make my own choices for my well-being.

"I must move forward," I said. "I am punishing myself—perhaps keeping me from happiness—over things I cannot change."

"Yes." The monk smiled and his sad eyes brightened. He looked happy for me.

めα

Shortly after we arrived in Madrid, I was summoned by King Philip to an audience at midafternoon that very day. I assumed Christopher had received a similar letter, but he was staying at his family home in Madrid so I was uncertain. I would find out when I met with the king.

I had not much time before the appointed hour, so I dressed as quickly as I could in a pale green silk dress and gown; the under sleeves were white and embroidered with pearls. At my waist I wore a swagged pearl belt, the pearls as large as gooseberries. I sprayed on my special scented water, grapes and fresh flowers.

My father was silent, but my mother, who knew I wanted to marry Christopher, said, "Be honest. The king is a good man."

My father's brows knitted. "You must tell him everything."

"Then I will," I said, meeting his eyes.

"About your time away, of course." He coughed and looked away.

I turned toward the door. I would not let my father's jealousy derail me. He no longer had power over me because I chose to leave the past in the past, not to forget it, but to move forward knowing I could take care of myself.

When I arrived, I was taken to the king's private office. Christopher was not there. The king rose to greet me. I was shocked to see his state of health. He used a stick to stand upright, and it was evident he was in pain. I could see his main complaint was gout and wondered what they were giving him for it.

The king sat on a cushioned bench, I on a chair, a low table between us. "Your highness," I said. "I can see you are not feeling well. Let me not bore and tire you with the details of my absence, other than to say, I, in a fit of childish anger, ran away and through some injury, perhaps, lost my memory. I was found by a peasant family in La Mancha. They took me in and were kind to me for many years."

"You look well, Luscinda," he said. His breathing was labored. "We were worried."

I bowed my head, contrite. "I would not have caused such worry on purpose."

He smiled. "Of course not. For you are a good and religious girl." Gingerly he moved a swollen ankle. "Tell me," he said. "Do you still have the blue amber rosary?"

My heart stopped. How was I to tell the king I had sold a gift which was precious beyond words!

"Your majesty," I began, "as I said, I lost my memory and did not know how I came by the precious rosary. When my family lost their crops to pestilence and we had no food or money, I disguised myself as a lad, walked to Madrid, and sold the rosary." I paused a moment, caught my breath, and quickly said. "I am so sorry." I clasped my hands as if I were praying to him for forgiveness.

He raised a swollen hand in nonchalance. "It is too bad," he said. "However if it saved your saviors hardship, it was a just reward to them for taking you in."

"Thank you," I said fervently.

"Now tell me," he said. "Who would buy your rosary?"

"Sebastian Boscan, marquis of Dierba," I replied.

The king's eyebrows raised. "And how much would the marquis pay for such a piece?"

"One hundred *ducats*."

"A lot of money for a peasant family," he said. "This marquis is not known for being fair."

"He thought to get the money back." My hand flew to my mouth, for I wished I had not said it.

"How is that?" The king leaned forward in interest.

I took a breath and began, "He sent a servant after me."

"And what happened?" he asked. It was sad to see how much he had aged.

My cheeks grew warm. Finally, I said, "I escaped from him and returned home."

"Well done, Luscinda," the king said with a twinkle in his rheumy blue eyes.

A servant entered and announced Christopher Solidares, duke of Gasparenza.

The king remained seated, though I stood and curtseyed when Christopher entered. He looked handsome in dark green velvet trimmed in gold threads, his hat under his arm. Though a gentleman wore his hat indoors, he removed it in the presence of a superior. Christopher had few superiors now that he was duke, but the king, of course, was one.

Christopher greeted the king and then sat in the chair nearest me, across from the king.

The king whispered to a servant, who left the room. To us, the king said, "You are here to discuss your betrothal."

I glanced at Christopher.

"Your match was approved at Luscinda's birth," the king looked at me. "It was . . . a good match. Too often we get requests for unequal or ill-thought-out liaisons." He took out his handkerchief and wiped his brow. He was sweating, perhaps from pain.

"We do not wish to wear his majesty out," I said quickly.

He waved his hand. "No, no. Seeing you gives me much pleasure." He asked a servant to bring us iced strawberry water. He continued, "Your match brings the two great houses of Andalusia together, the Estallar and Solidares families. Here," his hand swept an arc taking in the two of us, "are a handsome man and woman who would have handsome children to carry on their families' traditions."

I blushed and glanced at Christopher. My heart quickened.

The king turned to Christopher. "It is soon after your father's death, and you have taken on great responsibilities."

Christopher nodded. Though his hands rested calmly on his lap, his jaw remained tense.

"What do the two of you . . ." but he did not finish. The servant he had first sent away returned with the marquis of Dierba!

I was startled. He had aged, not well, since I had seen him. I saw signs of syphilis in his nose and hands. He was doomed to die a madman.

Without exchanging pleasantries, the king said, "It has come to my attention that you have an exquisite rosary in your possession."

And to my surprise, the marquis pulled the rosary from his pocket and handed it to the king, who looked it over, touching the signature stones, and nodded. He handed it to me. He waved the marquis away. "You are excused."

"But it cost me a lot of money," he began, scratching the Z-shaped scar on his cheek. "I do not understand." He stood for a second and then said, "The lad who sold it to me must have stolen it. But that is not my fault." He was blathering and perspiring. "I should have something for seeing it returned to its rightful owner." A drop of sweat fell from the tip of his nose, which he wiped on his sleeve.

I nearly laughed. Christopher's expression was one of disgust.

"The *lad* who sold it to you did not steal it. A good source says you would have taken your money back, even seen the lad dead for it," the king said.

"I thought he had stolen it and I sent my servant after him. To ask him." The man was swaying from one foot to the other, dropping beads of sweat to his left, now his right. He continued swaying. Drip. Drip. "I'm out two hundred *ducats*, your majesty," he said. "Please . . ."

"You are relieved from your post," the king snapped. "Do not return to court." He clapped his hands, and two guards came forward to show the marquis out. They grabbed his arms, and beneath him a dark ring appeared on the silk rug. Here was a man whose body had no problem letting go of water. The marquis was quickly taken away. Two servants rolled up the rug and carried it off.

I sat there, my mouth open. I could see surprise on Christopher's face also.

"Luscinda," the king said. I did not look at him. "Luscinda."

I shook myself and turned toward him. "I am sorry." Clutching the rosary in my hand, I knelt before him. "I cannot thank you enough. When I recovered my memory, I keenly regretted losing this."

"Your kind nature is not forgotten," the king said. "It has remained with you."

"'When we do a good deed, we cannot know the value of it; only the receiver knows.'" I quoted what Christopher said the day the king gave me the rosary. "What you have done is invaluable to me."

"Your gratitude is worth a carpet then," the king said jovially, though he grimaced from pain. He motioned for me to sit. Christopher helped me into my chair. I was dizzy from his touch, his nearness tangy and sweet.

The king continued as if there were no interruption. "This match was perfect in every way. I am uncertain whether it should stand." After a brief pause, the king spoke again. "There are questions, considerations here. Luscinda has been out of society for ten years." He straightened his moustache with the same quick gesture I knew from Don Alphonse. "Her beauty has not suffered. We can see that." He smiled broadly and looked to see if Christopher agreed. I did not look to see his expression. "But perhaps in other ways she will not be acceptable to you, Don Christopher," the king said earnestly. "I may decide the match is unsuitable."

Christopher and I looked at each other, somehow hiding our disappointment at his announcement.

Christopher said, "We would like the betrothal to stand."

But the king did not respond. His face white, his hand on his stomach, he said, "Please. Leave me now." He bent over and I turned to find a servant but two were already running to help, and the Secretary was showing us out of the room.

Outside, I said, "I hope King Philip is all right."

The Secretary replied, "He sometimes has these spells. Nothing serious, only urgent . . . and private."

"Of course," Christopher said. "Shall we wait?"

The man, whose wig was slightly askew, said, "I believe you were nearly finished. He will contact you."

CHAPTER 36

in which Christopher and Cinda find a chest of Lorenzo's

DISMISSED CINDA'S DRIVER and she rode in my carriage to the center of the city.

"I thought we might do some shopping," I said. It pleased me that we were both dressed in green, she a pale green, and I, a darker one. It was as if we'd planned the congruency . . . or better yet that we were so attuned that our minds thought alike.

Cinda said, "We are both in green today."

"I was just thinking about that."

"We look as if we belong together." Her voice was a bit shaky.

"Are you worried?" I leaned forward and told the driver to stop the carriage near the fountain in a place where the street was dry. I helped Cinda down. We took a few steps before she answered.

"It sounds as if King Philip is going to set aside the contract."

"I will write the king and tell him I do not wish it." I wanted to focus on more positive thoughts. I explained that while we were in Madrid, we should choose new furnishings for our bedroom, for our home.

"When I was here some years ago—to sell the rosary," she patted her handbag at her waist, "I walked by shop after shop and wondered how it would feel to be able to buy whatever one wanted. I wondered if my family, the one I had been born in, was a rich family."

"Ah, and they are!" I laughed. "I, perhaps, not as much but enough for you to have new things in our home."

"Our home," she said. "I like the sound of that."

As if some grand idea had taken her, she grabbed my hand and began walking quickly, pulling me out in the street to the opposing corner. Without pausing, she walked directly into a bank.

To my astonishment, she was greeted by a man, a Señor Ricardo, who knew her well, though she interrupted him before he could call her by name. Explaining that she had recently discovered she was Luscinda Estallar and that I was her betrothed (she introduced me), she asked, "Please write the entire balance of my account on a piece of paper so Don Christopher can see it."

The man retreated and returned even before my surprise allowed me to muster up a question. He held out the sheet of paper so we could both see the figure.

I gasped, but before I could speak, she took the paper and pulled me out of the bank. She led me to a solitary bench near a fountain and said, "I served as book-keeper for La Corona and was paid well for it."

I nodded, still astonished at the amount she had shown me.

"Also from investments," she said.

"Who managed them?" I asked.

"Señor Ricardo."

"I must switch my investments to him."

She laughed. "I highly recommend him!" She sobered and said, "Consider it my dowry and if my father comes up with more, we'll take it too. And together we will restore Gasparenza."

I do not need to record my stuttering and stammering in response to this ex-traordinary news, but in the end, I determined that if the money came with Cinda, and I wanted Cinda, then I would accept it.

"There are some things we can change and some things we can't," she said. "I am glad to change your fortunes."

I squeezed her hand and we smiled big happy grins. Mine was probably a bit silly.

Shortly we continued on our shopping venture, and by late afternoon we had found a mahogany bed with four finely polished posters, matching chairs uphol-stered in green (our color for the day), new tapestries for our bedroom, and other household goods. Cinda was most happy with a chest that she recognized as one that her farmer Lorenzo had carved. She knelt beside it.

"I remember it well," she said. Her fingers traced a dolphin and wave, and on the bottom was a plate that said Lorenzo Corchuelo. "I sanded and smoothed this wood myself."

"It is still in wonderful condition," I said, pleased to see her so pleased. "There are few scratches."

"And I can fix them," she declared.

After leaving the store, the chest paid for and bound for Gasparenza, she said, "I feel as if it is a blessing from him, and Aldonza."

"A blessing?" I asked.

"A blessing for our home," she said. "Our life together. From the parents who loved and protected me best."

We both realized our future was still uncertain even though, from my point of view, I had determined to move forward as if we would be together.

CHAPTER 37

in which Cinda's return is celebrated

HE LARGE CELEBRATION my mother planned to welcome me home took place in the evening after Christopher and I had gone shopping.

As my mother combed my hair before the event, I gave her a rundown of the items already on their way to Andalusia, ". . . crystal goblets and silverware, enough for his family and ours."

My mother sighed.

"What?" I asked. "Are you not happy for us?"

"I am, but you know it is not certain you will . . . move to Gasparenza." Before I could respond, she said, "Let's hope that soon you'll be wearing your hair up as a married woman." She looked through the combs on my dresser and found pearl-studded ones.

I shook my head. "For the party, I will braid these in my hair," I said, showing her some new green ribbons that I had found in a small shop that afternoon. "You will see why after I am dressed."

She sat on my bed.

I turned to look at her. "Mama, did Papa write the king and ask him to set aside the betrothal?"

My mother's auburn eyes widened and her mouth opened but no words came out. Then she said, "Oh, Cinda. He wouldn't. He wants you to be happy. He is glad you are back."

"He keeps questioning . . . my chastity." I turned back to the mirror and began sectioning my hair for one of the narrow braids.

"Yes, but he wants you to be happy. He is caught."

"What do you mean?"

"One day he talks as if you and Christopher will be together, and the next, he talks about Honor and how it cannot be honorable for Christopher to take you."

"Why?" I asked.

"He is not satisfied with what you've told him about the years you were gone. He's made some inquiries, and he knows Lorenzo and Aldonza died several years ago. Where have you been since then?"

Her words stayed my hands and my heart raced. Could I trust my mother? Should I tell her the truth? Instead I turned back to her. "Were you a virgin when you married my father?"

She gaped at me, her mouth a circle of nothing. Her emotions changed from shock to anger to . . . she began laughing. "That was so many years ago."

"Christopher is willing to accept me, and I have told him of my past. Can't that be enough?"

"Why won't you tell us? Or tell me?"

"I am no longer a child. I am not obliged to tell you everything."

"I am aggrieved by your tone." She looked away from me.

I reached out and took her hand and pulled her back toward me. "Christopher wants me and does not question. Shouldn't his opinion matter the most?"

"I will speak to your father." My mother rose and smoothed her skirt. She was wearing a spring green chiffon. It was a color she had always favored because of her auburn hair, which now had streaks of gray.

"Let us speak for ourselves," I said, but I was uncertain whether she heard me.

I did not know if I had been successful in assuaging my mother for my bluntness. But she sent in her handmaiden (how I missed Braden!) to help me put together a costume of cobweb lawn, several layers, so its transparency did not in any way compromise my modesty. The bodice had an intricate pattern of small flat beads, which caught the light and sparkled at my every turn. The sleeves were seeded with diamonds. My fan was of peacock feathers, the blue matching my dress, the green matching the ribbons in my hair.

During the celebration, I was often interrupted by people, some of whom I remembered and some of whom I did not. I was not surprised that the king did not come. His ill health was common news, and we had seen it firsthand. Archduke Albert; Prince Philip, who had been about five the last time I saw him and was sixteen now; and the Princess Isabel came.

The archduke bowed to greet me and said he was glad for my safe return. Then he went on to talk with my father. I curtseyed to the young prince and could see immediately that he was very shy and ill at ease. I suggested that we sit for a moment. He seemed relieved. We walked side by side. I was a bit taller than he.

"You have grown into a man."

"Not man enough to help my father," he said, bitterly. He had the Hapsburg jaw, though his eyes were his mother's. Queen Anne had been a kind woman—once she had asked me to tell her a story.

"I am sorry your father is unwell," I said. We sat across from each other in a little alcove outside the ballroom. "He was very kind to me." Years ago, the king had discovered me in the chapel saying prayers for the little princess María after her death. He had been touched because he felt she had been forgotten by most—that was the time he gave me the rosary. He had had it commissioned for his queen, but before he could give it to her, she too had died.

Prince Philip looked at me as if he had never heard anyone say the king was kind. I sensed the prince's life was difficult.

He said, "I am glad you have returned. We were all sad when you were lost."

"How very nice of you to say!" I said, quite flattered. "Tell me about yourself?"

"I do not like to hunt," he said with distaste but went on to say, "I play the violin. And I am quite good at it."

"That's wonderful!" I said. "Would you play the violin this evening?"

"If you'll accompany me."

I knew my parents would be pleased for me to play with the prince.

"Let us see what we can do." I took his hand. It was a moment before I realized that this was not the boy Philip, and I dropped his hand and apologized. He laughed and took my hand and on we went.

He stood by the harpsichord, and we played. I was perspiring and not from heat by the time we finished. It was difficult to play knowing there were high expectations of me and knowing there were those who would, no doubt, for it is so with courtiers, find fault. It was not at all like playing at Le Reino, where people were scarcely listening and where they only wanted the music to ignite their inner desires.

When we finished, the prince was swept away by two noblemen from Valladolid. "Thank you," I called after him and he waved. I turned and there was Christopher, so handsome in white and silver samite. He bowed in greeting; oh, his broad shoulders, his long legs so fine in white hose . . .

"Now that you have played," he said, his eyes smiling, "perhaps you'd like to dance." As he led me to the floor, he said, "Your father asked about our audience with the king."

I could not look at him. "What did you say?"

"That he took ill but that it seemed positive."

"Ha!" I said. "You have twisted the truth." For my part, I felt more and more uncertain, with each passing hour, that the king would favor us.

He squeezed my hand and I felt my cheeks grow warm.

The musicians began a Spanish Pavan. I drank in our nearness—his male freshness and barberry. Years before at the gypsy fair, I had had this thought: *If this is only for now, if this is only for this minute, this feeling is what we are made for*—Oh! the excitement, the alchemical pull, such a distracting delirium. Breathless from emotion, I could not talk but followed his every move flawlessly, through all sixteen figures, ending with the Grand Reverence—the dance was ours, as if written for us, only us.

He said he was warm and took my hand. We walked to the rose garden. It was a pleasant summer night. "Do you remember a discussion we once had about roses?" he asked.

He spoke of a time in our rose garden at Solariego; I would have been ten, less than a year from my running away. I remembered how he carefully cut the thorns from a dozen stems before handing me the roses.

"You said a rose held a secret," he said. "And the secret was the answer."

"The whole idea—it was a childish thought," I said, lightly, though I thought it was not childish at all, but wise, for I still believed there was a secret to the universe—to life—that, if known, would take the pain of living away. Perhaps I had found it with Brother Diego's help. Hadn't understanding there are things we cannot change given me peace? And changing things I could, also given me peace? I thought of the visit to the bank and I also remembered how I had been firm with my mother. But for tonight, I didn't want to be philosophical; I wanted to have fun, not think too much. Why not be amorous here by the roses?

"But I loved your thoughts." His grin caught the lantern light. "What would you say now about the beauty of the rose?" He picked one and handed it to me. Careful not to prick my finger—he did not remove the thorns now as he did when we were children—I breathed deeply of its fragrance, the fragrance of a deep red rose, for I knew well each color held its own odor.

With humor I recited, "I would say that rose hips are good for colds, fevers, and to cleanse your blood and that rose oils can be used as a base for numerous ointments and salves."

His long eyelashes veiled his eyes and a look of sadness crossed his face, as if he were remembering something. He swallowed and solemnly he said, "You seem to have lost your childhood notions."

I traced the silver braid on his chest with my finger, felt his breathing beneath my hand—I stroked his cheek.

He leaned toward me. *A kiss*, I hoped. But no, he took the rose from me and held it while he said, "You were a rose to me, Luscinda, as a child. You had its beauty, and I loved you as the angel that I thought you were—charming, alive, inquisitive."

"But now?" I answered before he could, "I am a fallen angel."

He looked in my eyes, and in his I saw a twinkle. "That is not how I see you." He touched my cheek with the rose and then my mouth. He handed the rose back to me. "You are an intelligent, courageous woman, who is capable of dealing with the thorns of your life." He smiled, his teeth flashing in the moonlight.

I was so keenly aware of him my mind was blank of thought. He leaned nearer . . . an inch more . . . and *there*. A *kiss*. Warm lips, warm heart . . . Interrupted!

"Oh! excuse me."

Christopher turned and I stepped beside him.

It was Prince Philip. He cleared his throat, the half-light of dusk hiding his embarrassment. "Luscinda and Don Christopher. I . . . I came to say good-night."

"I enjoyed our visit," I said. "You play the violin well."

He brushed my comment aside. "I heard them speak of your betrothal."

Christopher and I remained silent. One didn't encourage a prince to gossip.

To me, he said, "Our fathers seem uncertain of it."

I nodded.

Christopher said, "We are not. We are anxious to have it settled."

"Yes." The prince sighed. "I fear my father will do the opposite of what you wish."

I remembered the prince desired a victory with his father. Would he speak for us? Could our matter, certainly small in the scheme of things, be that victory? No, I could not risk it—the answer could be another disappointment for the prince.

Calmly, Christopher said, "Wish us well. The decision is pending."

"Do not become too discouraged then," the prince said. I was sorry for him and hoped that his father would be just with the prince *and* with Christopher and me.

We accompanied Prince Philip to the house to bid goodnight to the Princess Isabel and the archduke. Isabel invited us to come to a hunt on the morrow and we agreed.

After the guests and Christopher left, I found my father at his desk.

"I heard you have caused the loss of position of the marquis of Dierba," he said, putting his feet on the desk. I noticed his indoor shoes were new—of soft eel skin.

"In an indirect way."

"No one will miss him," my father said. "You have done the government a service."

"Then I would like to take credit for it, but it was the king."

"Tell me about your audience," he asked, reaching for a cigar.

"The king wishes Christopher to make the best marriage match." I did not like it that in some people's mind I would not be the best match.

I watched as my father lit the cigar from a nearby candle and drew his breath in. He blew circles in the air. The fragrance was nutty and bitter.

"Your mother asked me to speak in your favor—to encourage the king to affirm the marriage."

"I would not want you to do anything against your conscience." I wondered if he noticed the twinge of sarcasm in my words. "Let Christopher speak for us."

"I have more history with the king." I remembered my father had been great friends with Don Carlos, the king's first son, who had died many years ago.

"I am not yours," I said. "I can speak up for myself."

He blinked. He cleared his throat. "But the king . . ." my father began.

"My future is not your affair." My voice was firm, steady.

My father stared at his cigar. The smoke curled lazily toward the ceiling.

I changed the subject. "I am grateful for your helping Christopher with his business." I slipped off my shoes.

My father cleared his throat. "I'm glad to do it," he said. "I had not realized Hernando became so careless in later years." My father sighed and smoothed his unruly hair with both hands. "He was my oldest friend." Slowly he puffed the cigar. "I miss him."

"I remember that you enjoyed each other's company." I scratched the bottom of my left foot with the toes of my right. "I am sorry for your loss." My condolences were sincere; my feelings toward my father were complicated.

"I am proud of you," he said with a catch in his voice. "I always knew you were uncommon."

I had no answer for this. I picked up my shoes and left the room.

CHAPTER 38

in which Christopher takes action

HE HUNTING PARTY that Isabel had invited Cinda and me to join consisted of the princess and about two dozen nobles. Often, when we were children, I had hunted with the princesses. I would miss Catalina today, now duchess of Savoy. Isabel was not nearly as focused as Catalina had been, but they had both hunted as long as I had, and it had pleased their father.

As we were waiting for the carriages to transport us to the forest, I overheard a conversation that I hoped Cinda did not hear. The two women were discussing the chance of our marriage.

One woman, the baroness de Glisa, said, "She has not lost her beauty."

The other, the countess del Maraza, said, "Ten years with peasants. I can't imagine that he would take her."

The other agreed but she, at least, thought Cinda might still win me over. "After all," she declared, "having spent so much time in a monastery, he is an innocent and might be swayed by her beauty."

My cheeks burned to know they spoke of me, but my heart ached for Cinda. I thought if I could keep her away from the women, that the men would not speak their thoughts out loud, but I was wrong because next I overheard the duke of Feria say, "What a shame Don Hernando (may he rest in peace) did not listen to Don Marco about the Indian venture." And the baron de Glisa replied, "A complete disaster. Mortgage is in Don Christopher's future."

I walked around the corner to confront them, and to the duke, I said, "I hope it does not disappoint you to know that the reports of my failures are greatly exaggerated."

The duke coughed and nodded. "My apologies, Don Christopher, I had let myself get too interested in the opinions of others. I am delighted to hear you will succeed."

The baron was not quite so easily cowed. "Doña Luscinda would bring a great deal of money with her. Will you choose to go that way?"

I shook my head. "This conversation is beneath all of you. My affairs are well in order, and the question of my marriage is with the king." I stalked away and vowed to stay at Cinda's side the entire day to save her from other such unpleasant comments.

I found Cinda with the Princess Isabel. To the princess I said, "I see you have not brought the beaters." These hunts of court were often more slaughters than sport since the hunters sometimes used beaters to drive the animals into a fenced arena. "You have provided a fair match. A hunt of skill."

"Yes," the princess said, "but Cinda declines to hunt."

"I will ride along," Cinda said. "To watch." She had brought Marchioness, and I was uncertain why she did not want to hunt. I had heard of her skills from Tomás and Jovi, and I knew she did not feel at a disadvantage. Perhaps it was the opposite; perhaps she did not want to best the princess and the others.

"Very well, watch and learn." The princess's smile for Cinda was open and friendly. I hoped the others saw that the princess (and Prince Philip last night) had accepted Cinda back into the noble fold. I was troubled by the unfair words I had heard, and I thought that Don Marco and Doña Isabella must be aware of the uncharitable opinions. I wondered if that had influenced Don Marco . . . and the king himself, against her.

The hunt went well. Three deer in all. Cinda had handily spotted a twelve-point buck, but it was the duke of Feria who brought him down. Marchioness was well-trained for hunting, I could tell, and I was sorry Cinda had not chosen to hunt, if only to show the others her bravery and skill.

On the way back we stopped to eat in a copse near a stream. It was sunny, though a bit chilly. The servants built two large fires to help warm us. Princess Isabel sat with Cinda and me and the others sat a bit apart. I felt a twinge of regret at this outward shunning of Cinda. Even the attention of the princess was not enough to overcome their misgivings.

We ate cold chicken, cheese, bread, and fruit—apples fresh from a nearby tree. I used my dagger to cut a chunk of bread and placed the knife between Cinda and me.

Isabella and Cinda were playing the "remember" game, the one she and I had played often since her return.

"Remember the day the elephant arrived?" Isabel said. The king had allowed the children to see the elephant first, and we were in on the joke he had planned. "Fernando was fearless." Her face fell. "I'm sorry . . ."

"I am glad you have good memories of him," Cinda said. "What I remember of that day is how half the monks fell to their knees and the other half ran away."

"Next was a rhinoceros!" the princess declared. "It had an evil temper!"

The three of us laughed. We had had good times as children at court. We had been unaware of gossip and intrigue—too much the usual, I had discovered as an adult.

"Do you think you know something that might help my father?" Isabel said. She had heard Cinda was knowledgeable in herbs and was hoping she could bring comfort to the king.

Isabel and Cinda discussed symptoms and cures. The heat of the day made me sleepy, and it seemed Sancha was there, too, with Cinda. They had their healing arts in common. In my fuzzy mind they melded together with these words: Courage. Wisdom. Passion. And that I had known two such women was, I had no doubt, truly remarkable.

"I'm happy to send some herbs," Cinda said.

"Bring them yourself. My brother would be pleased to see you again," Isabel said. "He was quite charmed by you."

"Not at all," Cinda said. "He was the charming one."

Isabel looked as if charming were not the word she would apply to her brother. "I must spend more time with him."

"He would like that, I think."

Shouts from nearby—"Look out." "Move." "Isabel!" "Christopher!"—flew around us and I roused myself to see what was the cause of their alarm, and there was a dog, a large white and brown dog. His mouth was frothy, a sign of a terrible disease. His eyes were bloodshot, and though he was heading directly toward us, he seemed to be walking crookedly, his back legs out of line with the front.

I reached for my dagger, but it was not at my waist, because it was beside me ready for the next slice of bread. Before I could reach for it, Cinda had thrown it at the dog or rather into the dog. It must have been fifteen feet away, yet the knife went straight to its chest and buried itself to the hilt. The dog fell to the ground. Dead.

Phhht. Phht. Two arrows hit the ground near it. I looked to see. Glisa and Feria had grabbed bow and arrow but were not only too late to stop the animal, they had missed. Blood oozed in an asymmetrical circle around the animal's chest where the fur, glistening, was now matted.

Everyone gathered round to congratulate me! I didn't understand at first; then I realized that everyone had been looking at the dog or the princess. No one had seen Cinda throw the dagger.

Isabel kissed me on the cheek. "Thank you, Don Christopher."

"What a heroic thing you have done!" a nearby grandee, Don Sergio, said.

Others congratulated me. I was flushed and turned to Cinda, who was standing silently nearby. She was smiling and seemed perfectly content to have her skill remain unsung. It would likely reinforce some people's thoughts that she had been taken in by coarse people and was not, and could not be, the lady she had once been destined to be. Unlike bow and arrow, knife throwing was not a skill a noblewoman would engage in.

Looking at Cinda then, I saw acceptance on her face—acceptance that she would be what I chose her to be, without quarrel. I could declare her the hero or keep the news to myself. I could expose her to their ridicule, or I could save her from it and take her rightful accolades as my own.

A dilemma, yet not, because that instant affirmed she was the woman I wanted in my life. Quick, resourceful, beautiful, kind—no one else would fill me with happiness as she did. And let them talk as they would. She and I would weather it together.

"It was not I who downed the animal, but Cinda." I saw heads swivel toward her. To Isabel, I said, "We must thank her for acting so quickly and surely."

Isabel's eyes widened. "And with a knife! Cinda, you are amazing!"

Cinda blushed and ducked her head. "Thank you!"

Everyone, the hunting party and the servants, began clapping and cheering, but I took no regard of them. I had something else on my mind.

I pulled her to me. "We must go now to settle the question of our future. I will not wait one more day."

I hooked my hand in her elbow and walked beside her to a carriage. "To the palace," I said to the driver.

Inside the carriage, I said, "I don't care what the king says, or what your father says. I want us together, you and me, for the rest of our lives." I kissed her. Then pulled back. "I choose you."

She smiled, a smile dazzling as the morning sun, and said, "You are my choice past, present, and future." Her arms flew around me and mine around her. I breathed her in—heat and ice—and felt how my body fit next to hers. Oh, glorious day!

CHAPTER 39

in which Cinda tells how Christopher secured their future

OMEDAY I WILL tell our children about the day their father told the king how our lives were going to be.

When we arrived at the palace, Christopher sought an audience with the king, and because the Secretary remembered us, he said, "Make it brief."

"I promise," Christopher said. The Secretary announced us, and King Philip, who was at his desk signing papers, looked up.

Christopher stood before him. "Your majesty, I have learned that dukes, as well as kings, can write their own rules. And this is the rule I write: Cinda is my wife." He stood straight, so tall, in his deerskin hunting vest and breeches.

We were totally in the wrong, acting outside the usual social way. We were in improper dress to see the king, and we had arrived without a summons or appointment. Christopher continued, "I want what I want, and I want her."

Yes! My heart sang. O magnificent man!

The king laughed. It was a good day for him. The swelling in his hands was noticeably less. "And you, Cinda. What rule would you write today?"

"That Christopher is my husband."

"Then it is so." The king smiled, but we could see he wanted to get on with other things. We bowed and removed our unexpected selves from his presence, scarcely believing our good luck.

Back at his Madrid house, Christopher took me in his arms and said, "You are my lady, and I want you by my side, neither ahead or behind me, above or below."

And I remembered the day, not so long ago, when I had wanted to imagine the world as equitable but could not even pronounce the possibility of it, and now, my husband was saying he wanted the world—our lives, at least—to be equal.

My flying heart had no doubt that all would come round in our favor. I was sure nothing would diminish the joy of this day. The fixed point of my universe was Christopher and our love. There was nothing we could not overcome! That is how it feels with love.

Christopher stood in front of me and holding out his closed hands, he said, "Choose."

As a child, I had missed my first guess. Now I pointed to a hand. He opened it, and there were a diamond ring and ruby earrings.

"The stones! You had them transformed!" I said. Central to the diamond ring was a large pear-shaped stone girdled by lesser stones—diamonds and sapphires—around the band. The earrings were perfectly matched ruby tear drops—tears of joy!

He opened his other hand—ah! there was no wrong guess—and showed an emerald bracelet.

The jewelry was the symbol of our journey to here—this time in our lives. The uncut stones were cloudy seeds that had been sheltered through the years in my keepsake bag, and they now bloomed into glorious bouquets.

The word of the fulfillment of our marriage contract spread, and members of the court and my family came to wish us well, and the gathering turned into an impromptu celebration. Tables were set up on a nearby green, and a large spread of food appeared. In the evening the boards were cleared, and musicians appeared, as if the event had all been planned! When the music started, Christopher swung me to a table top and joined me there to dance a *jondo*.

Having lived in La Mancha, having lived in Castile, I could truly say that no music was like that of the Andalusians. Our musicians knew the rhythms of the body and the rhythms of the heart. During every couples dance, I was by Christopher's side seeking his hand, as he sought mine. More than once everyone cleared a circle and watched us dance, the dances of our country, the dances of our souls that set our blood pulsing through us, warming us, exciting us, creating us. *Yes! I am alive! Feel the rhythm.* The rhythm of life itself. Our very existence could be translated into a dance.

At the end we danced a *malagueña*, where the couple entwines, crossing each other's path with certain and measured steps. Knowing the guests would move from our path, we looked steadily in each other's eyes. The guests quieted and watched as we executed the dance like two swans floating in unison on a lake.

And there was another dimension to this experience, for I knew what came after the dance, when everyone was gone. I would, from this night on, be with Christopher.

Do you know the pleasure of waiting? Perhaps you think waiting is painful. If I asked Christopher that night, he might say all of waiting was painful, for most of his ten years of waiting for me were. That is not the waiting I speak of.

But how we wait for our lovers till the end of the day. How we wait for this pleasure. A titillation of desire, the thrill of anticipating the satisfaction that awaits when you are together alone. And that is why each moment of this celebration was pleasant torture to me, for I anticipated my night, or should I say, I anticipated my knight.

Later in his, no, our rooms, I stood by a window in an alcove of the bedchamber and thought about how my life had changed that day because Christopher chose to address the king. He created, through his ardent desire, the beginning of our life as duke and duchess. And everyone had seemed eager to wish us happiness and blessings, even the Countess del Maraza, who had only that morning doubted my worthiness to be Christopher's wife.

"What are you about?" Christopher said, as he entered the alcove. He was wearing only his breeches. His chest caught the glimmer of the full moon, shining in the window. I clasped my hands together behind me, so I would not reach out and touch him. The promise of what this evening held was too great to rush to the end of it.

"I was thinking of the happy events of this happy day." I went to him. He touched my arm and brushed his fingers down the length of it, returning to my elbow to caress it.

"The dancing made me want you. All the more," he said. His eyes sparkled in the candlelight. "I imagined I could feel the heat of your wanting me."

"Yes," I said, gasping at the memory of those dances. It had been deliciously torturous to be so close to him and not be able to kiss him.

The haunting rhythms of the dances hammered away in my mind. Now I heard the gentler melodies of the evening and let them continue rolling through my head as we moved slowly closer together, eyes locked.

Christopher broke the gaze to sigh at the layers of my clothing. "I cannot take them off fast enough," he declared.

"Then take them off slow enough," I whispered.

And he did. As if in another kind of dance he moved with careful and measured slowness to undo each hook and lace. With the slightest brushing sound, the ribbons whispered through the eyelets. Oh, the pleasant agony of it. Then I stood there in front of him, the moon now shining on my chest.

He took my hand and placed it on his heart, and he put his hand on my heart, and there we stood feeling each other's rhythm, which was not together at first, but slowly came to be one and the same.

In the bed, carefully he picked up my hand and kissed each of my fingers, then my arm, following my body on the slow path to certain pleasure. It was excruciating! It was exciting! I saw his teeth flash in the dim light. He was smiling! Was he laughing at my desire? Ah, no, because he said, "I want you."

He entered me. *Yes.* But he stopped. *No!* He rolled over, leaving the action to me. Could I keep the turtle's pace he had set, putting off the finale as long as possible? I rose above him and imagined he could see the curve of my fullness just above his eyes. He touched me there once, and kissed me there, and soon after . . .

I did not want to move. *One,* I thought. *We are one.*

He held me; my head nestled under his chin.

"We are beautiful together," I murmured.

He whispered in my ear, "Ah, as my Mistress of Adventure," he kissed my palms, "each day will be a quest all its own." His eyes twinkled in the candlelight with cheer and hope for our years ahead. We circled each other with our arms and lay back on the bed in this fond embrace. We fell asleep just so, each to our own dreams.

THE END

ACKNOWLEDGMENTS

The idea for this book was suggested to me by my late friend Terry Lester. Without his encouragement, I would never have begun it. With suggestions, guidance, and support from other friends, I completed it. Many thanks to Beth Adler, Leigh Bond, Jenell Buckman, Sue Christenberry, R. Scott Colglazier, Penny Costilla, Kathleen Driskell, Susie Gandolf, Gayle Hanratty, Martha Johnson, Karen Kaye, Stacey Long, Carl Lutes, Peggy Lutes, Carey Mann, Maureen Morehead, Kim Reinhart, Mary Lou Schmitt, Sandy Sundheimer, Jan Weintraub, Thelma Wyland, and Katy Yocom.

Thank you to Ellyn Lichvar for her many services during the publication of this book, to Jonathan Weinert for the book and cover design, to AJ Reinhart for the cover art, and to Liz Dallmann and Katy Yocom for their proofreading skills.

I wish to thank the Kentucky Foundation for Women for a fellowship to the Mary Anderson Center that gave me time to write.

I am grateful to the many alumni, students, and faculty of the brief-residency MFA in Writing Program at Spalding University for their encouragement over the years. In particular, I want to thank Roy Hoffman, who never failed to ask me about Dulcinea, and Richard Goodman and Julie Brickman, who gave me wonderful feedback on my writing. Also many thanks to Kenny (K.L.) Cook and Eleanor Morse.

And most of all, thanks to Sena Jeter Naslund, my editor and friend, whose belief in me made it possible for me to believe in me. Without her, nothing; with her—all this.

ABOUT THE AUTHOR

Karen Mann grew up on a farm near Indianapolis. She attended Indiana University and the University of Louisville. Her essays and short stories have appeared in various anthologies and journals, including *Place Gives Rise to Spirit* and *Christmas Is a Season*.

Her many careers, including service representative, accountant, newsletter editor, office manager, proofreader, and instructor, prepared her for her current position as Administrative Director of the brief-residency Master of Fine Arts in Writing Program at Spalding University in Louisville (spalding.edu/mfa) of which she is the co-founder. She is managing editor of *The Louisville Review* and Fleur-de-Lis Press (louisvillereview.org).

Her second book, *The Saved Man: The First Century*, the first in a series of paranormal romances, is due out from Page Turners Publishing in 2014 and will be available as an ebook on amazon.com.

She lives in California, where she enjoys working, writing, and spending time with her two grandsons, Kaleb and Korben.

Fleur-de-Lis Press is named to celebrate the life

of Flora Lee Sims Jeter

(1901–1990)

❧